"[A] lyrical, almost mystical story that reflects life on a Kentucky farm, the wildness of the Red River Gorge, and the Genteel South of Charleston, South Carolina." —*Pittsburgh Post-Gazette*

"Hoffman is a master at crafting a gentle story fierce with emotion. . . . Her writing immers[es] the reader in detail that's as multidimensional as it is visceral. Exquisite care is lovingly bestowed upon each word, exposing, bit by bit, a story brimming with heart." —*Examiner.com*

"Hoffman's novel of a woman putting the pieces of her family's secrets together combines a deep dramatic impact with Southern charm." —*Publishers Weekly*

"Packs a hefty emotional punch . . . a completely original story line." —*The Free Lance-Star*

"Hoffman has a good ear for dialogue, and Teddie and her friends are realistic, appealing characters. Perfect for fans of family centered women's fiction, this book will have special appeal to readers interested in antiques and 'shabby chic' style." —*Booklist*

"If you want a charming look at Charleston, a do-it-yourself book on the intricacies and value of furniture restoration, or some evocative reminiscence about good Kentucky home cooking, then *Looking for Me* is the book for you. In fact, somewhere in the midst of Beth Hoffman's pages of this discovery-of-self novel about a young woman named Theodora Overman, you'll probably want to take a break, head to a nearby yard sale, and pick up a treasure or two of your own to refurbish." —*Bookreporter.com*

"With her eagerly anticipated second novel *Looking for Me*, Hoffman delves into some of the darker places in life, while still retaining that Southern charm her readers have come to know and love. . . . Sure to delight her legions of fans and those new to her work." —*SheKnows.com* (Red Hot Book of the Week)

"Hoffman invites the reader to look deeply in places from which we sometimes turn away to see their true value and worth. Through tender care of others, Hoffman's characters touch our hearts and invest us in their struggles and triumphs. After reading *Looking for Me*, there is a lot in the world that I will never look at in the same way." —Erika Robuck, author of *Hemingway's Girl* and *Call Me Zelda*

"After reading *Looking for Me*, you'll never think of Emily Dickinson's line 'Hope is the thing with feathers' in quite the same way again. Sure to be a big hit—and to spark fabulous conversations with friends and book clubs." —Claire Cook, *New York Times* bestselling author of *Time Flies*

"Once in a blue moon a book comes along which rocks your very soul with its honesty. *Looking for Me*, with its exquisite detail and memorable characters, is such a story. . . . A truly magical and transformative book!"
—Lorelle Marinello, author of *Salting Roses*

"[Hoffman's] prose is so visual, the book unfolds before your eyes. You don't read it, you SEE IT. *Looking for Me* is simply a tour de force."
—Molly Campbell, author of *Characters in Search of a Novel*

"Beth Hoffman has used her exquisite gift to write a tale that transports the reader to another time and place."
—Stuart Ross McCallum, author of *Beyond My Control*

Praise for *Saving CeeCee Honeycutt* by Beth Hoffman

"Anyone in need of a Southern-girl-power fix will find [*Saving CeeCee Honeycutt*] engaging. And it offers an invaluable reminder: Even when things look bleak, a few good friends can turn your life around."
—*People*

"A peach of a novel."
—*Ladies' Home Journal*

"CeeCee Honeycutt is a sweet, perceptive girl with a troubled family, and this story of the summer that transforms her life is rich with hard truths and charm. This book unfolds like a lush Southern garden, blooming with vivid characters, beauty, and surprises."
—Kim Edwards, bestselling author of *The Memory Keeper's Daughter*

"An absolutely delightful debut novel packed full of Southern charm, strong women, wacky humor, and good old-fashioned heart. From the moment you first step into young CeeCee's unique world, you'll never want to leave."
—Kristin Hannah, bestselling author of *Fly Away*

"Reading *Saving CeeCee Honeycutt*, I barely stopped laughing, even as my heart broke and broke again for CeeCee. She goes through the wringer with Southern grace, but you never forget all she's lost, and you never lose sight of her courage and deep resources. Beth Hoffman has written her heart out in this novel that will clearly be the first of many."
—Luanne Rice, bestselling author of *The Lemon Orchard*

"A tender and touching debut. Charming, disarming, sweet as the scent of magnolias on a Southern summer night, *Saving CeeCee Honeycutt* is a true delight."
—Mary Kay Andrews, bestselling author of *Ladies' Night* and *Christmas Bliss*

"A confection so delightful readers will not be able to put it down. Beautifully written, brimming with decency and humor, and sparkling with a cast of women who are by turns wise, generous, and deliciously eccentric, this book is a joy to read. Beth Hoffman has written a debut novel to be savored."
—Connie May Fowler, author of *How Clarissa Burden Learned to Fly*

"I'd save CeeCee if she asked me! I love this bright, funny, spunky girl, the zany women in her life, and the way they enclose CeeCee in a circle of warmth and friendship that heals all hurts. A joy to read."
—Sandra Dallas, bestselling author of *Fallen Women*

"From a talented artist with the written word, Beth Hoffman has given us a gift. *Saving CeeCee Honeycutt* is a gem. . . . A beautifully written novel to be savored." —Pamela King Cable, author of *Southern Fried Women*

"[A] charming debut. Readers who enjoy strong female characters will appreciate CeeCee, a survivor despite her heartbreaking childhood, and Aunt Tootie and her friends, all of them steel magnolias. Exemplifying Southern storytelling at its best, this coming-of-age novel is sure to be a hit with the book clubs that adopted Sue Monk Kidd's *The Secret Life of Bees*."
—*Library Journal* (starred review)

"'Welcome to my world, baby girl' (to paraphrase Fannie Flagg's title) is what came to my mind on meeting the narrator of Beth Hoffman's delightful debut. This lovely novel has earned the status of 'LizPick' even before it's published."
—*Publishers Weekly* "Galley Talk" by Liz Murphy, the Learned Owl Book Shop, Hudson, Ohio

"Charming . . . A gem of a story, lovingly told. The 1960s Southern setting and coming-of-age angle may remind readers of favorites like *The Secret Life of Bees* . . . [and] will also bring to mind classics like *Anne of Green Gables*. . . . A novel to treasure." —*BookPage*

"[A] Southern charmer." —*Publishers Weekly*

"A refreshing dose of hope. There are gems of wisdom sprinkled throughout. From the beautiful cover . . . through to the very satisfying ending, [*Saving CeeCee Honeycutt*] will chase your winter blahs."
—*Minneapolis Star Tribune*

"A debut of uncommon grace that beautifully illuminates the power of female friendships, it will have you laughing out loud . . . and leave a satisfying lump in your throat." —Book-of-the-Month Club

PENGUIN BOOKS

LOOKING FOR ME

Beth Hoffman is also the author of *Saving CeeCee Honeycutt*. She was the president and co-owner of an interior design studio in Cincinnati before becoming a full-time writer. *Looking for Me* is her second novel. She lives with her husband and two cats in northern Kentucky.

To access Penguin Readers Guides online,
visit our Web site at www.penguin.com.

LOOKING

for ME

BETH HOFFMAN

PENGUIN BOOKS

PENGUIN BOOKS
Published by the Penguin Group
Penguin Group (USA) LLC
375 Hudson Street
New York, New York 10014

USA | Canada | UK | Ireland | Australia | New Zealand | India | South Africa | China
penguin.com
A Penguin Random House Company

First published in the United States of America by Viking Penguin,
a member of Penguin Group (USA) Inc., 2013
Published in Penguin Books 2014

A Pamela Dorman / Penguin Book

ISBN 978-0-670-02583-1 (hc.)
ISBN 978-0-14-312543-3 (pbk.)

Printed in the United States of America
1   3   5   7   9   10   8   6   4   2

Book design by Nancy Resnick

This book is dedicated to:

My husband, Mark—a gentleman of enormous patience and good humor.
My gratefulness for your love and support is immeasurable.

My whip-smart literary agent, Catherine Drayton—for rearranging the constellations in my sky. I'm privileged to have your friendship and guidance.

My brothers Mark and Lee—for memories made in shadowed woodlands and secrets shared in Grandpa's barn.
How I wish we could do it all over again—and do it better.

and

To the memory of Eddie—the finest four-legged friend I've ever had.
I'll see you at the Rainbow Bridge.

ACKNOWLEDGMENTS

Just down the street there lives a man and woman who are family to me—not of blood but of heart. They have championed my work and put up with my writerly madness for years. A big, Southern-style thanks goes to Steve Knopf, aka Commander Click, a man of uncommon insight and courage, and, to his wife, the indomitable Marlane Vaicius, precious friend and confidante. How blessed I am to have both of you in my life.

For the luminaries of the publishing world, I begin with gratitude to my brilliant editor and publisher, Pamela Dorman, whose dedication and vision are without equal. And to the unflappable and gracious Kiki Koroshetz I give warm thanks. I am indebted to Susan Petersen Kennedy, Clare Ferraro, Leigh Butler, Hal Fessenden, Carolyn Coleburn, Nancy Sheppard, Shannon Twomey, Langan Kingsley, Veronica Windholz, Roseanne Serra, Nancy Resnick, Dennis Swaim, and Andrew Duncan. I'd also like to offer abundant thanks to Kathryn Court, Patrick Nolan, John Fagan, Maureen Donnelly, Dick Heffernan, and Norman Lidofsky and their terrific sales teams—it couldn't happen without you.

My journey through this chapter of life has been enriched by book lovers across the globe—readers, librarians, bookstore folks, book bloggers, and fellow authors have extended a hand of friendship and embraced my work. Y'all are dear to me.

ONE

Some people run toward life, arms flung wide in anticipation. Others crack open the door and take a one-eyed peek to see what's out there. Then there are those who give up on life long before their heart stops beating—all used up, worn out, and caved in, yet they wake each morning and shuffle their tired legs through another day. Maybe they're hoping for a change—a miracle, even—but runaway dreams and lost years hang heavily on their backs. It's the only coat they know how to wear.

They've become accustomed.

That's what I thought when Mama pushed open the screen door and stepped onto the back porch.

I was sitting on the steps folding pillowcases I'd just pulled from the line, fresh as the day and still warm from the sun. One by one I set them into the laundry basket and watched Mama from the corner of my eye, shoulders sagging, slippers scuffing as she moved toward her favorite chair.

It seemed to me that at the age of sixty-nine Mama was too young to walk the way she did, and I fought the urge to ask her to lift her chin so I could see her eyes—eyes the color of an Irish hillside and so arresting that I still caught myself staring at them. I wanted to tell her that if she'd greet the day with her head held high, she'd see the beauty surrounding her and just might feel better about the world and her place in it.

But I had no right to say such things. I hadn't lived her life or carried its weight, so who was I to judge?

Mama's blue housedress, sun-bleached and long overdue for the trash bin, ballooned in the breeze, then collapsed over her thin frame when she eased herself into the chair. A low groan escaped her lips as she bent over and plucked her knitting from the basket, and a moment later the clicking of the needles began, needles that I swear weren't all that much thinner than her arms.

When I was a little girl, Mama had been a head turner, slender and long-legged with thick red hair that played tricks with the sun. Though I never saw her respond to a whistle or a sideways glance from an admirer, I always suspected she secretly enjoyed the attention. Not having inspired many whistles myself, I didn't know how that felt, nor did I know the sadness that must have come when the whistles stopped.

I set the laundry aside and breathed in a long, slow breath. The air was perfumed with scents from the garden: basil, tomatoes, and chives. Ever since I'd left home after high-school graduation back in 1972, the aromas of harvesting season always drew me back to the farm. And of course there was the row of crepe myrtle that grew tall along the fence—all those pink blooms against the August sky.

Eddie was stretched out next to me, baking in a spot of sun. I reached over and gave his belly a rub. "What do you think of Kentucky?"

He yawned and slapped his tail on the floorboards.

Mama wound a strand of yarn around her finger and looked at me. "You know what, Teddi? He reminds me of that little black-and-white dog in those cartoons. What was his name—do you know who I'm talkin' about?"

"Snoopy."

"Yes, that's it. He looks like Snoopy."

"I think so, too. When he wakes up in the morning and realizes that being loved isn't just a dream, he grins. I swear he does."

"Where was it you found him?"

"Limping down the side of the road. It was during that awful rainstorm back in March. I wrote you a note about it, remember?"

"Maybe he got lost. Did you try to find his owner?"

I pulled a dish towel from the basket and smoothed it over my knees. "No, he wasn't lost. He was runnin' away from home. A bad home."

"Now, how in the world do you know that?"

I looked at Eddie and winked. "He told me."

"The *dog* told you?"

Mama shook her head, and we fell into a comfortable silence. I didn't know why, but everything about this visit seemed different. I had the feeling, or maybe it was just a hope, that in our uniquely inept ways we were trying to build a bridge toward each other. A fragile bridge, but a bridge just the same.

While folding an apron, I glanced toward the barn. Soaring above the silo was a red-tailed hawk. Round and round he went, the pale underside of his belly catching the light, his wings outstretched as he floated in the sky.

I couldn't see a hawk without thinking about my brother, Josh. When we were kids living here on the farm, raptors were frequent visitors—hawks, peregrine falcons, and even an occasional eagle. Early in the morning, Josh and I would often watch on the back porch, as they soared out from their homes in the woods that stood behind the barn. The birds spent their days gliding low over the fields as they hunted for unsuspecting rabbits and squirrels. Sometimes they'd ride an air thermal and just glide and glide. After supper, when the sun hung low and shadows stretched long across the grass, the raptors would return home to the mysteries that lay hidden within the pillars of the giant trees. All the raptors were beautiful, yet it was the red-tailed hawks that left my brother spellbound.

There were times when Josh would run through the hay field with his eyes set on a hawk soaring in the sky, and he'd end up tripping in a tractor rut and falling flat on his face. And once, when he was racing alongside the barn trying to keep a red-tail in view, he ran smack into a fence and got a bloody nose.

One summer's evening when he was no more than six, Josh trotted across the lawn, overalls rolled up to his knees, his bare feet caked in dirt. "Look, Teddi," he gasped, pointing toward the barn. "See up there? That's the big guy, the one I told you about yesterday. I know that's *him*."

I got up from the porch swing and joined him on the back steps. And sure enough, perched on the tip of the silo was a red-tailed hawk.

My brother looked at me. "What do you think he's doin' up there?"

I draped my arm around his shoulders. "I read a story about that hawk's great-great-granddaddy. He guarded an Indian who lived in a cave high above Red River Gorge. The hawk watched over him from the time he was just a little boy. They were best friends for all their lives. When the Indian grew old and died, do you know what happened?"

"What?"

"The hawk swooped down, spread his talons as wide as they'd go, and lifted the Indian's spirit right out of his body. And then he flew up through the clouds, past the moon and the stars, and straight into heaven. They're still together."

My little brother drew in a breath. "They are?"

I nodded. "And now this hawk is watching over you. He was

born way up in Clifty Wilderness. And from all the other red-tails in Kentucky, he was chosen to fly down here and be your guardian." I looked deep into my brother's eyes. "Now I'm going to tell you a secret. His name is Menewa. Do you know what that means?"

Josh shook his head.

I leaned close and whispered, "Great Warrior."

And what I would remember most about that moment was the way my little brother turned and looked at the hawk—lips parted, eyes fixed on the bird as if he'd suddenly stepped into a boyhood ritual so full of wonder that it changed his life.

Perhaps it had.

I sat quietly and watched the bird swirling off in the distance, its rusty-red tail feathers dipping into the blue of the sky. I wanted to believe he was a messenger sent from Josh, and I could almost hear my brother's voice ride in on the breeze: *Don't worry, Teddi.*

∞

The first feather appeared on the fifth of February in 1967, the morning of my thirteenth birthday. I woke to a chilling wind that rattled the window and rippled the hem of my bedroom curtains. I rolled over to look at the clock, and on my night table I saw a feather resting on a folded piece of paper. The air was so cold that a shiver ran through me when I pushed my arm beyond the thick layers of quilts and picked it up. The feather was about eight inches long, soft rusty-red with stripes of brownish black. I smiled and smoothed it over my cheek, then picked up the paper. In green crayon letters, my little brother had spelled out the words HAPPY BIRTHDAY TO THE BEST SISTER. Below, he'd printed the name MENEWA.

Often Josh would be gone for hours, scouring the floor of the woods in search of feathers, fossils, and the occasional arrowhead, none of them easy to come by. For my brother to give me a feather from his collection was one thing, but to part with one of his prized red-tailed hawk feathers? Well, that was special.

I still have that feather. I have the birthday note, too. They're tucked away in a shoe box at the back of my closet, but I can't bring myself to look at them. If I did, I might split wide open.

Mama's voice startled me. "Good heavens, Teddi, what's so interesting out there? You look like you're in some kind of trance."

I wanted to point out the hawk and tell her I was thinking about Josh, and I wanted to look directly into her eyes and say, *We need to talk about him, Mama. We need to remember him and say his name.*

But I knew she'd get upset, so I began folding another dish towel and said, "I'm enjoying the beautiful day, Mama, that's all. I forgot to tell you what I did last week. There was a flea market in Orangeburg, so I drove up there to see what they had. I bought the prettiest old lightning rod. It's solid copper with two cobalt-glass globes that don't have so much as a crack or a chip. Once it's polished, I'll put it in the front window of my shop. People love antique lightning rods. They put them in their gardens."

Mama frowned. "A lightning rod? I worry about you, Teddi. You're thirty-six years old and still a junk picker. I wish you'd find a job with a future. Something with benefits, like health insurance and a retirement plan. Remember that girl from your high-school class, Adele Stafford? She got herself a job as a secretary for a big funeral home up in Louisville."

I rolled my eyes. "Well, of *course* Adele works for a mortician. She had a subzero personality, just perfect for working with dead people. I can still see her sitting in the cafeteria, all that stringy black hair hanging in her eyes. She was creepy."

"I hear she makes real good money and has every benefit you could think of."

"I'm sure that's true. They probably give her a quart of embalming fluid for Christmas instead of a turkey."

The corners of Mama's mouth quivered as she fought against a smile. "I hear she has a cute little house."

I shook out a dish towel with a snap. "Well, *I* live in a carriage house that has original heart-pine floors *and* a walled garden."

"Adele Stafford owns her house. You just rent."

And there it was, Mama's coup de grâce, delivered with precision straight to my heart. I had driven all the way from Charleston, South Carolina, to try to have a nice weekend with my mother, and we just couldn't stop ourselves from poking each other.

So much for that bridge I thought we were building.

For most of my life, I had hoped my mother would see me. That one day she'd open her eyes and, as if a rush of sunlight had poured into a darkened room, she'd see who I was, not the shadow of what I wasn't. But if I were to be honest, I suspect she wished I'd do the same for her. So here we were, mother and daughter, sitting on opposite sides of the porch while holding tight to our opposite truths. Truths that always ended up canceling each other out until there wasn't much left but a big hole filled with years of disappointment.

After shaking off the sting from my mother's comments, I tried for the umpteenth time to explain myself. "I'm not a junk picker, Mama. I'm an antiques dealer and faux-finishing specialist. I see things differently than you do, that's all. If you went to an estate sale or an auction with me, you'd just see a bunch of trash. But you know what I see? Endless possibilities. And I see history, too. It's amazing how old furniture speaks to me. The older it is, the more it has to say."

"So, now you're tellin' me that your dog *and* old furniture speak to you? What's gonna talk to you next, Teddi, your car? How about that dish towel you're foldin'—what's *it* got to say?"

I couldn't stop from smiling at her sarcasm. "C'mon, Mama, I'm trying to tell you about my work. A few months ago, I found an old chest of drawers someone left in an alley. It was an unusual piece, shaped like a tall bombé with pineapple feet. I painted it with antique silver leaf and replaced the handles with crystal pulls. When I was done, I had a piece of black soapstone cut for the top. Then I upholstered the insides of the drawers with a deep pink satin moiré. I wish you could have seen it. That old chest looked like it came straight off the cover of *Architectural Digest*. And you know what else? I sold it within a week to a lady from Louisiana. She never even blinked when I told her the price—sixteen hundred fifty dollars, plus shipping costs."

"Theodora Grace Overman. I mighta been born at night, but it wasn't *last* night. Now, that's a tall tale if ever I've heard one."

"It's true, Mama. I swear."

"Well," she sniffed. "Some people have more money than sense."

I flashed her a look. "*Some* people appreciate art."

Neither one of us spoke for a long while, stubborn mules that we were. But the beauty of the day wouldn't allow me to stay mad, so I perked up and said, "I have a wish, Mama. Wanna know what it is?"

A good ten seconds passed before she replied, "What?"

"That you'd come for a visit. I bet you'd like Charleston. The houses alone are enough to make your heart ache. You could visit Grammy Belle, too. You haven't seen her in a long time."

"I don't like to travel," she said, starting another row on her knitting. "And your grandmother had a home here. It was her choice to go down there with you. Why don't you bring her the next time you come for a visit?"

I turned and looked at her. "I wish I *could* bring her here, but you don't have a bathroom on the first floor. And with her wheelchair it's—"

"If she hadn't got that wild hair and gone down there with you, she wouldn't have fallen and broken her hip." Mama let out a huff as she worked the knitting needles faster and faster. "Now look where she's ended up, in a nursing home."

"It was an accident, Mama. She missed a step and lost her balance. It could have happened here, too. C'mon, don't be sour. Please come for a visit. It'd make me so happy."

I waited for her to say something, but the clicking of her needles was her only reply. Picking up the laundry basket, I walked into the house and let the screen door slam behind me.

After putting the dish towels away, I closed the drawer and bleated, "I bet Adele Stafford's house is just as plain and cold as she is. She probably sleeps in a damn coffin."

A little laugh skipped in through the open window.

To Mama the words "carriage house" probably translated to "garage." Most likely she envisioned me sleeping on a cot next to a lawn mower, and unless she saw where I lived, nothing would convince her otherwise.

For nearly five years I'd been renting a nineteenth-century carriage house. Set behind an old mansion on Rutledge Avenue and constructed of brick and stone, it was as charming as it was private. A steep stairway led to the second-floor living quarters, where all the rooms had nine-foot ceilings framed by plaster moldings. There was even a little screened-in porch off the kitchen that cantilevered over the garden. When a breeze came along, the scent of jasmine whirled in through my open windows.

I walked down the hallway and stepped into my mother's bedroom. Everything was the same as always—*scrubbed, washed, and pressed to perfection*. Other than the matching brush and comb lined up neatly on top of her chest of drawers, the room lacked anything personal.

Years ago Daddy had kept the Bronze Star he was awarded after WWII displayed on his bedside table. When I was a little girl, I'd sometimes sneak into my parents' bedroom and lift his medal from its velvety case. I loved the feel of the grosgrain ribbon and how the five-pointed star sat cool and heavy in my hand. But after that terrible autumn night in 1977, Daddy put the Bronze Star in his drawer, and I never saw it again.

I set a stack of sheets and pillowcases on Mama's bed, grabbed the empty basket, and headed downstairs. From the kitchen window, I saw the familiar old green-and-white Rambler careen into the backyard and come to a stop beneath the oak tree.

Stella Rose was here.

She and Mama had been best friends since first grade, and while Mama had grown thin and brittle over the years, Stella Rose had grown soft and round. When she smiled, it looked as if two big thumbprints had been pressed into her cheeks. For as far back as I could remember, Stella had always worn full-skirted floral dresses, and today was no exception. A riotous print of poppies swirled around her thick calves as she climbed out of the car.

I dropped the laundry basket on the kitchen table and rushed out to greet her.

"Teddi!" she cried, opening her arms. We hugged and swayed as if we were about to set off in a waltz. As she held me, I became a child again when I closed my eyes and buried my head in her softness.

Stella stayed for the rest of the day. After the sun dipped behind the trees, the three of us had chicken and dumplings for supper, and then Mama pulled her playing cards from a kitchen drawer.

"Want the radio on, Mama?"

"Yes, but not the news. I can't stand hearing about the Gulf War. Makes me nervous."

I fiddled with the radio while Mama shuffled the cards. When I took my seat at the table, Stella said, "Teddi, how's your work?"

"It was rough after Hurricane Hugo. But once the insurance settlements started coming in, people flocked to my shop. You wouldn't believe how many antiques I've restored . . ."

We played three-handed euchre, talking and tossing our cards on the table while oldies from the forties played softly in the background. I could hear the *tap-tap-tap* of my mother's feet keeping rhythm to the Andrews Sisters and Glenn Miller. When Stella won yet another hand, Mama dropped her cards on the table and pushed back her chair. "Anybody interested in coffee and pie?"

Stella's face lit up. "Pie? Oh, count me in, honey. What kind did you make?"

"Rhubarb."

"Mama, you made my favorite?"

She didn't say anything, but as she measured coffee into the pot, her lips edged toward a smile.

While Stella headed up the stairs for the bathroom, I sat quietly and watched my mother pull plates from the cupboard. It occurred to me that maybe her way of trying to build that bridge between us was different from mine. Maybe we were working on the same bridge but approaching it from entirely different directions.

"Mama, I'm going to take Eddie for a walk. I'll be back in a few minutes." I pushed open the screen door and said, "Come on, little boy." His nails clicked across the linoleum floor as he scurried to join me.

The moon was round and fat, and a light breeze tickled my skin. Outlined against the sky was the barn, its white paint weathered away to reveal the original gray siding. For more than a hundred sixty years, it had clung to its stone foundation, sheltering animals from the elements, storing farm equipment in its belly, and supporting mountains of hay above its wide-beamed shoulders. It was the great-granddaddy of the Overman homestead, and for all my life I had admired its staunch beauty. I slowed my pace when I came to Daddy's old workshop. Though cancer of the liver had taken him from us four years ago, it felt like only yesterday. I stepped through a tangle of weeds and pressed my palm against the locked door. "I miss you, Daddy. I miss you every day."

Around the silo Eddie and I went, picking our way along an

overgrown path that edged the woods. The air was alive with the chirring and flutters of night.

When my brother and I were little children, Grammy Belle often walked us into the woods. Twigs crackled beneath our feet, and the trees would reach out their branches and give us a poke, as if to say hello and remind us to visit more often. As we worked our way deep into the shadows, my grandmother would point out the treasures—clusters of jack-in-the-pulpit, spotted green tree frogs, and wide fans of fungus. One evening when we were sitting on a rock, a cecropia moth landed on the toe of my shoe. Grammy winked and said it was giving me a blessing.

My grandmother taught us to honor the woods, to enter its wonders with respect. She told us to never intrude or cause any harm, saying we were Mother Nature's guests and to mind our manners. One afternoon the three of us were hiking and came to an ancient black walnut tree. My grandmother stopped and patted its rough bark. "A powerful healing force lives deep within these woods. Whenever you children are hurting or can't make sense of things, just come out here and spend some time with the trees. Give their trunks a good strong pat. When you go home, you'll feel better."

I pressed my small hand against the tree, looked up at the sunlight filtering through the leaves, and absolutely believed her.

I believe her still.

And tonight, as I gazed into the dense woods, I took in a slow breath and gratefully accepted whatever offering might come my way. I thought about that old saying, how we can never go home again. But I think it's more like a piece of us stays behind when we leave—a piece we can never reclaim, one that awaits our next visit and demands that we remember.

TWO

At the age of ten, I got a glimpse of my destiny. It happened on a steamy summer's day back in 1964.

What I remember most vividly was how the legs of that old chair poked up from the weed-choked ditch. And how, when I pulled it to the side of the road and stood it upright, its threadbare seat exhaled a tired puff of dust into the air. Even beneath the layers of dirt, I could see that the chair was beautiful. A dining chair, I guessed, the kind that once sat in a fine home and had seen lots of fancy dinner parties, birthday celebrations, and holiday feasts. The arms were curved and graceful, and the back was shaped like an urn. What that chair was doing in a rural Kentucky ditch is something I'll never know, but I wanted it something fierce, so I took it.

Finders keepers.

Though I was a good half mile from the farm, I hauled that chair all the way home. First I looped my arms through the chair's arms and carried it on my back like a wounded soldier. When it got too heavy, I dragged it behind me. The air was hot and thick with humidity, and when the wind kicked up, it was like walking toward a blowtorch. But that old chair was mine, and nothing was going to make me leave it behind.

When I finally arrived home, light-headed from the heat and parched with thirst, I lugged the chair up the dirt driveway and into the backyard. As I set it in the shade beneath the oak tree, Jigs, my dog, did a happy lope-hop off the back porch and greeted me. I loved him up for a minute, took a long drink from the garden hose, and then collapsed on the grass. Jigs sprawled out next to me, and we just lay in the shade enjoying each other's company. While scratching his ears and wondering how I'd fix the seat of the chair, I heard the squeak of the screen door.

I looked up to see my mother step onto the porch. Her sundress hung limp in the heat, and her sweat-dampened hair was pinned high off her neck. She shook out a rug, draped it over the porch rail, and looked at me. "Where in the world did *that* come from?"

"I found it in the ditch, down by Will Fowler's farm."

"Clear down there—how'd you get it here?"

"I carried it."

"In this heat?" Mama walked down the steps to have a better look. "Oh, Lord. It's junk, Teddi."

"No it's not. It's beautiful."

"I never know what you'll haul home next." She threw an unfavorable glance at Jigs and shook her head. I wrapped my arm around his neck, pulled him close, and met her eye to eye. Jigs licked my face.

My brother and I had found him at the edge of the cornfield the previous summer. He'd been shot in the rump and was whimpering and limping something awful. We lifted that poor dog into the wagon and carted him home, and when Mama saw us coming, she got upset. She said we couldn't afford a dog, much less a vet bill to fix one up. But Daddy had a soft spot for animals, so he paid the vet to make Jigs well again. Sometimes when Mama wasn't looking, he'd even slip Jigs a piece of meat from his supper plate.

Mama gave my chair a flat-eyed look, then reached down and lifted my hand. "I see you've been messin' with my nail polish again."

Right when I thought she would make me go inside and take it off, the deep *chug-chug* of Daddy's tractor sounded. Mama and I turned to see it appear from the side of the barn. Puffs of gray smoke lifted into the air from its tall exhaust stack, and Roxy was hunkered down for the ride.

Earlier that summer, Daddy had taught Roxy to do something amazing. After folding an old blanket and setting it on the front of the tractor, he tied it down with twine. When he had it just right, he whistled for Roxy. She was big and beautiful and loved my dad something awful. Roxy was a Brahma chicken—fluffy white with feather pantaloons that went all the way down to her toes.

Daddy lifted Roxy onto the blanket and taught her how to ride on the front of the tractor. She'd hook her long toenails into the wool, shake her tail, and then nestle down and get comfortable. When she was ready, he'd fire up the engine of his tractor and off they'd go, bouncing along the path that led to the cornfield. Roxy sat up there like a feathery pom-pom, all plump and proud. There was no mistaking how much she liked it.

I thought it was the cutest thing I'd ever seen, but whenever Mama saw Roxy and Daddy out in the field, her lips would thin or she'd roll her eyes. Sometimes both. Mama said Daddy spent more time talking to that chicken than he did talking with her. I never knew anybody could get jealous over a chicken, but there you have it.

While Daddy headed down the driveway toward us, Grammy Belle stepped out to the porch carrying a tray with a pitcher and glasses. "Got some nice fresh lemonade," she said, walking across the lawn and setting the tray on the picnic table. She waved her hand in the air to get Daddy's attention.

"What do you have there, honey?" Grammy asked me.

"I found it in the ditch. Isn't it pretty?"

She pushed her glasses up on her nose and leaned close. "Oh, it's a beauty."

"I'm gonna fix it up and put it in my bedroom. Will you help me, Grammy?"

"Why, sure I will."

Just then Josh, who was covered in mud and smelled like the pond, came running up with a bullfrog hugged to his chest. Mama stood, her face expressionless as her gaze traveled from Grammy and me to Daddy and Roxy and lastly to Josh and his frog. Then she looked down at Jigs. Mama shook her head and went back inside the house.

My grandmother and I worked on that old chair for hours, bleaching off the mold and scrubbing every inch. The more I cleaned, the more I loved what I saw. I pointed to a row of carved flowers at the top of the chair. "How'd they do this?"

"It takes a real old-time craftsman to do that kind of detail. They have lots of special tools. Some as tiny as the ones dentists use."

In my imagination I could see the steady hands of a man working a piece of wood, carving each flower patiently and smoothing his fingers over what he'd just done. It was while we oiled that old chair and buffed it to a satiny sheen that I began thinking about what it might be like to fix up old furniture and sell it in my very own shop.

ᴗ

On Saturdays after breakfast, Mama would shoo everyone out of the house so she could mop the kitchen floor. Josh would head for the woods, Grammy would put on her straw hat and wander to her flower garden, and I'd whistle for Jigs. We'd hop into the old green pickup and wait for Daddy to climb in and crank the engine. Then the three of us would set off for town, bouncing our way down the road with the windows opened wide.

Our first stop was the bank. Daddy worked real hard, most times putting in seven days a week. He had lots of land for crops of sweet corn and hay, hay so rich with alfalfa that fancy horse farms in Lexington sent trucks to take every bale he made. He also had a shop on the side of the barn where he repaired things—lawn mowers, vacuum cleaners, and even the occasional toaster. Just about everybody in our town had brought him something to fix at one time or another. Often he'd come in at the end of the day looking so tired I thought he'd collapse, yet I don't recall him complaining.

After stopping at the post office, we'd head for Gilson's Farm & Feed, where Jigs always got a rawhide chew bone, Daddy got a stick of jerky from the glass jar by the cash register, and I got a Coke from the soft-drink machine. Sometimes we'd take the long way home, and I'd push the floor mat aside with the toe of my shoe and watch the pavement zoom by through the hole in the floor. If I got lucky, we'd pass a yard sale. And Daddy, knowing how much I loved to fix up old furniture, would pull to the side of the road until the weeds brushed against the belly of the truck as he slowed to a stop.

We'd climb out, and he'd hand me a few dollars and say, "Okay, Peaches. Go find somethin' good. Take your time, I'm in no rush." Then he'd draw a cigarette from the pocket of his blue work shirt, light it, and lean against the chubby wheel well of his truck.

I'd trot off to see what I could find—a little telephone table, a rocker, or even an old spin-style piano stool. Then Daddy would load my treasure into the back of the truck and we'd head for home. We didn't talk much, sometimes not at all, but we always chewed whole sticks of Black Jack gum.

I spent my summers fixing up the things I'd found. When I'd collected a fair number of pieces, I'd set them by the side of the road along with a For Sale sign I made. Jigs and I would sit in the shade of the maple tree and wait, and sure enough, some of the tourists who came to hike through Daniel Boone National Forest or spend a weekend at Hemlock Lodge would stop and have a look. They seemed happy to part with their money, and some of them even gave me a tip. When I was fifteen years old, there was $482 in my cigar box, every penny of it from my furniture sales.

One day I was in the library and discovered a book where page after page showed how to hand-paint furniture. Techniques called *strié* and marbleizing filled my imagination, and there was a section about trompe l'oeil that made my head swim. When I came to the chapter about upholstering the insides of drawers . . . well, that did it. My destiny spread out in front of me as clear as a brand-new day.

It wasn't until I began teaching myself to paint furniture that I realized I had some semblance of talent. I'd practice the techniques described in the book, taking notes along the way. When I messed up and all but ruined a chair or a table, I'd strip off my mistakes and start over.

During nights when I couldn't sleep, I'd tune my transistor radio to a classical-music station, turn the volume down low, and fantasize about the shop I'd own one day. Year by year my fantasy grew, and by the time I was seventeen, I envisioned myself scouring the countryside for all sorts of chairs, chests, and tables. I'd be known for my artistry and keen eye, and I even went so far as to imagine that I'd be famous.

And now, thanks to a gentleman named Jackson T. Palmer, in a small way I guess I was.

THREE

It had taken me more than a week to faux-finish a small bedside table I'd bought at a garage sale for a dollar. I began by stripping off the original finish, and then I whacked the table with a bicycle chain to make it look distressed. After painting it a soft French blue, I dipped a toothbrush into dark brown paint and lightly spattered the surface. When it had dried, I glazed the entire thing to give it a warm patina. I loved the word "patina" and felt smart whenever I said it out loud.

With the last drawer knob screwed into place, I stepped back and studied my work. It was the best I'd ever done. I ran up the cellar stairs and into the kitchen. "Mama, come see the patina I created!"

She pulled a skillet from the dishwater and rinsed it off. "I should *patina* your behind for not washing these dishes." Though she gave me a weary look, she dried her hands on her apron and followed me to the cellar.

"What are all those marks?" she asked, squinting at the table.

"Distressed antiquing. I learned how to do it from a library book."

"It's real pretty." I waited for her to say more, to open one of the drawers or run her fingertips over the surface, but all she said was, "Now, don't forget to do your chores."

As she climbed the stairs, I called, "I'm gonna take this outside and see if I can sell it. But I'll vacuum and change the sheets when I come back."

Careful not to bump the table against the wall, I carried it up the steps and into the front yard. After leaning my For Sale sign against the mailbox, I sat beneath the tree and waited. It was a brisk and bright autumn morning that set the highest points of the mountain ablaze in colors that lured photographers, hikers, and sightseers from far and wide.

A few cars and a caravan of RVs went by, but no one stopped to have a look. When my butt grew numb, I figured I should go start the laundry before Mama got angry. As I stood and brushed off the seat of my jeans, a black panel-style truck slowed to a stop at the side of the road.

The driver's-side door opened with a rusty squeak, and a gray-haired man, tall and thin as a sapling, eased himself from the seat. His white shirt was dull and slightly frayed at the cuffs, and from a pair of leather suspenders hung a pair of baggy brown pants.

"What you got there, missy?"

I smiled and straightened my shoulders. "It's a French night table. I painted it myself."

"Is that so?" He stepped closer to have a better look. Reaching out, he smoothed his hand over the top. Surprise registered on his face when he opened the drawer and saw that it was lined with white brocade. I didn't tell him the fabric came from an old wedding dress I'd found at a rummage sale.

"You say it was you who did this? Did I hear that right?"

"Yessir. I've been refinishing furniture since I was ten years old. I taught myself from books."

He gave me a narrow-eyed look. "Well then, go ahead and explain it to me. How'd you do it?"

My face grew warm when I realized he didn't believe me, so I stood tall and recounted exactly what I'd done.

He listened, lips pursed and his gray eyes locked on me. When I finished telling him about the antique glaze I'd concocted, he nodded but didn't offer a word one way or the other. Reaching into his pocket, he pulled out a pouch of tobacco, took a pinch, and pressed it inside his cheek.

"So how much you want for it?"

"Fifty dollars." A bold price, but I held my ground.

He considered me for a long, agonizing moment. "You think it's worth *fifty* dollars?"

There was no turning back. I lifted my chin and said, "Yessir. It's a one-of-a-kind piece."

He scratched the stubble at the side of his jaw. "Fifty dollars . . . hmmm. Well then, I reckon you've made yourself a sale."

I'd never sold a piece of my work for that much money, and though I wanted to jump for joy, I checked my excitement and simply said, "All right."

I carried the table to his truck while he opened the back doors. There were so many chairs, chests, and headboards packed inside that there was hardly any room left. The old man pulled a roll of twine and a blanket from the cab of his truck and began wrapping my table.

"You still in school?"

"Yessir. I'm a senior."

"What're you gonna do when you graduate?"

I grinned. "Have my own furniture shop."

He offered no comment as he lifted the table into his truck and pushed it next to a chest of drawers.

"Well, I suppose you're itchin' to be paid," he said, closing the doors with a thud. He reached into the back pocket of his pants, removed a wafer-thin wallet that looked as old as he did, and pulled out a hundred-dollar bill. "All righty, here ya go."

I'd never seen a hundred-dollar bill, let alone touched one. "I keep my furniture-sales money in my bedroom. Wait here while I go get change."

I was about to turn and run for the house when the old man said, "What's your name?"

"Teddi. Teddi Overman."

He spit a thin stream of tobacco into the ditch. "Now, Teddi, I don't want any change, but I do want you to listen to me for a minute. You've got yourself some mighty fine talent. I'd even go so far as to say that what you do is art. But here's the thing: You sold your piece for a whole lot less than it's worth."

He leaned toward me and raised his eyebrows. "I'm gonna share a secret. You listening?"

"Yessir."

"Always start your price higher than what you're willin' to take. People like to haggle a bit, makes 'em feel like they got a bargain when you finally settle on a deal."

I looked at the crisp bill in my hand, not knowing what to say.

He dipped his bony fingers into his shirt pocket, pulled out a card, and handed it to me. "If you're ever down my way, look me up."

And with that he shook my hand and climbed into his truck. As he rattled away in a swirl of dust, I looked at the card he'd given me. It smelled of tobacco and was soft and lightly stained around the edges.

JACKSON T. PALMER ~ FINE ANTIQUES
WENTWORTH STREET
CHARLESTON, SOUTH CAROLINA

FOUR

School had let out for Easter vacation. When I arrived home and walked into the kitchen, the air was warm and spicy. An apple pie was cooling on a rack by the stove. I was about to break off a piece of crust when Mama walked in holding a manila envelope.

"Teddi, don't pick at the pie. Come sit for a minute. I want to talk with you."

"Okay." I pulled out a chair and sat across from her.

"I have some brochures here. Now, your father and I know you're smart as can be, but we can't afford to send you to a regular college. So I've done some checkin', and there are several schools within driving distance that offer courses—"

"I already know what I want to do. I'm gonna sell antiques and refinish furniture."

She leveled her green eyes at me and opened the envelope. "You need to get training so you can take care of yourself. Now, let's take a look at these."

I halfheartedly spread the brochures across the table. There was one on court reporting, another on medical transcription, and three from secretarial schools. I pushed them to the far end of the table. "I'm not interested in any of these. I'm good at refinishing and painting furniture. I want to work with my hands and—"

"You're a good typist, and that *is* working with your hands."

"No, Mama. It's not the same thing. I have so many ideas that my head's about to pop. I want to—"

"Let me show you something." She stood and motioned for me to follow. We walked into the living room, and Mama opened the door. The century-old floorboards creaked beneath our feet as we stepped onto the front porch.

She pointed toward the road and stabbed the air with her finger. "See that? Take a real good look and listen to me. That's not the Yellow Brick Road. Without training, you could end up stuck in a life you *never* wanted and no way to see yourself clear to change it. I realize you've had fun with all that old junk you've worked on over the years, but now you need to buckle down and make something of yourself."

Her words stung as if she'd hauled off and slapped me.

"Teddi, it's an ugly world out there, and—"

"You're wrong, Mama. The world's beautiful, but you're so busy being disappointed in everything that you don't see it!"

She glared at me, lips parted, eyes glistening with tears. "Take those brochures and go to your room. And don't come out until you've read each one." Her voice quivered when she said, "Give those schools a chance. Lord, don't you see I'm tryin' to help you?"

But I didn't.

Against my vehement protests, Mama made arrangements for the two of us to visit the Alice Brown Secretarial School in Richmond, Kentucky. Our appointment was set for a Friday, just a few weeks after my high-school graduation. Mama was so excited about it that she never shut up. The more she talked, the more furious I became.

One night we were in the kitchen, Mama washing dishes, me drying, and Grammy putting everything away. Mama gushed about how wonderful that school was until I got so mad that my hands shook.

"Just think," she said, rinsing a glass and placing it in the strainer, "after you graduate from secretarial school and get a job, you'll be able to afford nice clothes and a cute apartment. And I bet you'll even—"

"Stop it, Mama! Since you're so thrilled, why don't *you* go to that stupid school and leave me alone!"

She pointed a soapy spoon at my nose and gave it a shake. "Don't sass me!"

Grammy's eyes widened as she looked from me to Mama. Without making a sound, she took off her apron, hung it on the hook, and quickly left the kitchen.

"I *won't* go to that dumb school!" I tossed the dish towel across the counter and bolted from the house. I was down the road beyond the bend when I heard my mother calling my name. I never looked back.

I ran until I was so winded that my lungs burned and my chest heaved. Then I walked and cussed and cried until the sky turned deep purple, as if a giant bruise had formed above the trees. Though I was a good five miles from home, I kept right on walking straight into the dark of night. I wrapped my arms tighter around myself and tried to massage away the chill in the air. I didn't know what to do or where to turn. All I knew was that I wasn't going home and I sure as heck wasn't going to secretarial school.

From behind me I heard the rumble of an engine. A moment later I was bathed in a halo from a set of bright headlights. I stepped to the edge of the road, my ankles wobbling as I maneuvered over stones the size of red-skinned potatoes. My heart slammed against my ribs when the vehicle slowed to a stop, and all my senses snapped to high alert. I heard the truck's door creak open, and I set off running across the open field as fast as I could go.

"Hey, Teddi. Hold up, girl!"

I stopped and turned around. The headlights blurred his silhouette. A sharp *click* sounded, and a blue flame shot up as he lit a cigarette. A swirl of smoke rose into the night air.

"You all right, Peaches?"

I took in a gulp of air to calm my racing heart and then walked toward him. "No, Daddy. I'm not all right, and I'm *not* goin' to that dumb school. I want to be a secretary about as much as I want to shave my head! Mama won't listen to a thing I say. She's so stubborn."

"Well, that's what she says about you."

"Having a dream doesn't make me stubborn. Mama thinks *everyone* should do as she says, and if we don't, she gets mad. I'm sick of it, Daddy."

He dropped his cigarette, red sparks skittering across the road as he crushed it out with his boot. "We'll talk on the way home."

I looked into the night sky and shook my head. "I won't go to that school, no matter what she says."

"Being out here on a dark road won't solve anything. Now, c'mon and get in the truck."

For several minutes we drove in silence, and then Daddy glanced at me. "Come Monday, I'll go down to the bank and talk to Lloyd Turner about a loan. I've got plenty of good land as collateral. That way you can go to a regular college."

I leaned my head against the back of the seat and tried to smile. "Thanks for offering, Daddy. I wish there was a college that offered a degree in antiques and furniture painting, but my school counselor checked everywhere, and there isn't."

The lights from the dashboard seeped into the folds around my father's eyes, and I felt bad that I'd caused him to worry. He reached into the pocket of his shirt, pulled out a pack of Black Jack gum, and offered me a stick. The aroma of anise rose in the air as I pushed it into my mouth. Daddy did the same. We both knew there wasn't much else to say, so we drove home in the inky darkness, thinking our private thoughts.

❧

On the day I graduated from high school, Mama gave me a big box wrapped in silver paper. Thinking it was the oil-painting kit I'd been talking about, I could hardly rip off the paper fast enough. I was devastated to see a picture of a blue typewriter on the top of the box. Mama smiled and smoothed her hand over the name "Smith-Corona" as if it were scripture.

Grammy Belle gave me a handmade card she'd decorated with dried flower petals and scraps of lace. Folded inside was a fifty-dollar bill. Josh gave me a chickadee's feather and a pink quartz stone he'd made into a paperweight. But it was Daddy who surprised me most. He asked me to come out to the barn, his face revealing nothing as he slid open the door. Parked in front of the tractor was a white 1961 Ford Falcon sedan with a three-speed gearshift on the column, green plaid interior, and whitewall tires.

It was one ugly car.

Daddy's eyes twinkled. "I know you've been driving for two years—and you're good at it, Teddi, real good. But this has a lot more zip than my truck, and the clutch is touchy, so take it easy. Okay?"

We climbed in, me behind the wheel and Daddy in the passenger seat. He patted the dashboard and winked. "This buggy will take care of you just fine. I won't be worried about you breaking down on the highway."

"Thanks, Daddy. You know how much I love driving a stick shift."

After adjusting the seat, I pushed in the clutch and started the engine. I was so excited that I couldn't stop myself from stomping on the gas. Daddy laughed as we blasted out of the barn and set off for my inaugural drive.

"Runs like a top," Daddy said with satisfaction. "Nice suspension, too."

As I zoomed along, shifting gears and maneuvering around curves, I had to admit that, ugly or not, the car sure had some spunk. I looked at him and smiled. "This is a great little car. It's a lot different than driving your truck."

"You just be careful, you hear?"

"Yessir."

When we arrived home and I parked beneath the oak tree, Daddy reached under the seat and pulled out a large envelope. "This is between us, and we need to keep it that way."

I nodded and pushed it inside my handbag.

Daddy climbed out and closed the door, his face serious as he walked to my side of the car. "Teddi, I've got somethin' to say."

I curled my thumbs through the belt loops of my jeans. "Okay."

"I fought in the war so people could be free. Free from fear— free to raise a family and make an honest living." He looked into the sky, his head tilted back and his chin raised. It grew so quiet that I could hear the *tick-tick-tick* of the engine cooling.

"Freedom is the most precious thing you'll ever have, Teddi." He met my eyes and then patted the hood of the car with his hand. "Now, I know it might not look like much, but this little car is your red, white, and blue."

I thought he was going to say more, but all he did was give my arm a squeeze. Then he turned and ambled toward the barn, his arms swinging free from his wide shoulders.

When I went inside the house, Mama turned off the vacuum cleaner and said, "You like your car?"

"Yes, ma'am."

"Your brother wants to go to the ranger station, but I'm too busy to take him. Will you drive him over?"

"Sure."

I called for Josh, and he yelled from his bedroom, "Coming!"

He was nearing his thirteenth birthday, and a recent growth spurt had given him an awkward stride. I watched him bound down the stairs as if his legs were hinged with rubber bands.

While pulling out of the driveway, I asked, "So what's going on at the ranger station?"

"They had new brochures made up and asked me to help pass them out. Too many campers and hikers aren't following the rules. Ranger Jim says we have to stay on top of things. Lots of people are stupid with campfires, and last week three guys stole a baby fox cub—"

"Oh, no! What happened?"

"They bragged about it, and someone from the next campsite turned them in. Ranger Wiley went and got the cub and returned it to the nest, but those guys are in a mess of trouble. I've been keeping a close eye on the woods ever since."

I reached over and patted his knee. "You know what I heard Ranger Jim tell Daddy? He said you were the best woodsman he'd ever seen."

Though my brother didn't say anything, the pink in his cheeks revealed that he was pleased.

As I pulled in front of the ranger station, I turned to Josh and asked, "You need me to pick you up later?"

He closed the door and peered through the open window. "Nope. Ranger Jim will bring me home. See you, Teddi."

I watched him trot off, his worn-out sneakers slapping against the asphalt. Just before I pulled away, my brother turned and lifted his hand. Sunlight streamed through his open fingers, and he smiled.

Arriving home, I went upstairs to my bedroom and closed the door. From my handbag I removed the envelope Daddy had given me. When I ripped it open and shook out the contents, twenty brand-new fifty-dollar bills landed on my bedspread. Lightly I touched one and then another. I couldn't imagine how many lawn mowers he'd repaired to make all that money.

The thought of it made my throat tighten.

Something else fell out of the envelope, too. A map. Paper-clipped to the corner was a note that read:

> *This will help you find your way.*
> *Love, Dad*

I thought about how he'd spoken of freedom, how he'd said the car was my *red, white, and blue.* As I held the map in my hands, the full impact of my father's words hit me.

My head swam with possibilities when I unfolded the map and spread it out on my bed. This was my chance to have an adventure, and I didn't know where to go first. I'd always wanted to see the ocean and the Smithsonian museum. But above all else, I was curious about Mr. Palmer's antique shop in Charleston.

After folding the map and returning it to the envelope, I hid it, along with the money, beneath the liner paper in my bottom dresser drawer. Later that afternoon I walked out to the workshop and stood in the open doorway. Daddy was sitting on a wooden stool, dismantling the engine of a lawn mower. The old radio was tuned to a baseball game, the volume low. Sweat trickled down the side of his face, and his hands were blackened with motor oil.

I tapped my finger against the doorframe. He looked up, and our eyes locked in a way I'd never experienced. Deep in my chest, I could feel a tug of the thread that connected us. Would always connect us.

"Thank you for the money and the car, Daddy." I fought back tears as I leaned forward and whispered, "And the map . . . *red, white, and blue.*"

He winked but didn't say a word.

❧

Two days later I was sitting on the steps of the back porch, secretly planning my trip in a spiral notebook when Josh loped across the lawn. "Hi, buddy. How was your hike? Find anything interesting?"

He shook off his canvas knapsack and sat on the step in front of me. From a zippered pocket, he removed a book and opened it. Tucked between the pages was a small feather. It was slender and black, with four large white dots along each side.

"It's for you, Teddi."

I took the feather from his outstretched hand. "Wow, thanks. It's beautiful. Look at all the detail. What bird is it from?"

"Downy woodpecker. It's a secondary wing feather."

"You amaze me. I think you know more about birds than all the rangers put together." I pointed to the book in his hand. "What's that?"

He handed it to me—the title was *The Ultimate Wilderness Survival Guide.* Leafing through the pages, I noticed dozens of underlined passages and notes written in the margins. I looked at my brother and wrinkled my nose. "You can eat cattails?"

"Yep. Not the tops, but the roots. They're good."

I closed the book and set it down on the steps. "Why don't you just pack a bigger lunch?"

"Because that's not the point . . ."

For several minutes I listened to my brother describe what he'd learned about surviving off vegetation and making tools. When he finished explaining how he'd crafted a bowl from a small log of dead wood, he grew quiet and began fiddling with his shoelaces.

Glancing over his shoulder toward the kitchen window, Josh lowered his voice and asked, "Is Mama home?"

"No, she and Grammy went to the grocery."

My brother looked me square in the eyes. "You're leaving, aren't you?"

"What . . . ? Why would you say that?"

"You don't need to play dumb with me. I heard you sneak down the steps last night, so I got up and looked out the window. You loaded stuff into the trunk of your car."

My stomach sank. "You aren't gonna tell, are you?"

"No. I won't say anything."

I gave his arm a gentle pinch. "Thanks. I won't be gone long. I'll be back before you even miss me."

Josh looked away and picked mud spatters from his jeans. "But you won't come back."

"Sure I will. I just need to see what's out there."

My brother gazed across the hay field. "I could never leave the farm, but I sure wish things were like they used to be. Ever since they built that Sky Lift over by Natural Bridge, seems like all we get around here are tourists and city campers. A lot of them don't respect nature. Remember that giant rock we used to sit on, the one shaped like a turtle shell? Well, I was up there today, and you know what someone did?"

"What?"

"Carved a bunch of swear words in it. And when I was on my way home, I saw these two guys in a pickup. I watched 'em pull off the road and onto a hiking path. Both of 'em cussing and laughing. They were either drunk or high, maybe both. The ground was soggy from the all the rain we had last week, but the driver just kept on spinning the tires and laughing. He drove between two locust trees and busted the lower limbs real bad. Then he ran over a young red oak. Totally destroyed it."

I put down my notebook. "What a jackass. Too bad a ranger didn't see it—those guys would be in big trouble."

Josh unbuttoned his shirtsleeves and rolled them up. "Well, they won't be doin' that again."

"Why? What happened?"

"I hid behind some pines until they got their gear and went down the path. When I was sure they were gone, I snuck over to their truck and unscrewed the caps from the valve stems of the tires. I put a small pebble inside each stem and screwed down the caps till I heard a *pssssst* sound. When all four tires were leakin' air, I hightailed it outta there."

"Oh, my God! You really did that?"

He flashed me a grin, his eyes bright with triumph. "Those tires will flatten like pancakes, and the truck will sink real deep into the mud. It'll cost 'em a lot of money to have it towed out of there. Plus, they'll get fined."

"Good. Maybe those jerks will learn a lesson. But you have to be careful, Josh. What if they had seen you?"

"Not likely. Besides, they were idiots. The poachers are the real problem. They kill the deer and red fox. They even shoot hawks and eagles just so they can sell their talons and feathers on the black market."

Though I knew there'd been an ongoing battle against poachers, I'd never heard about the killing of raptors. "What does Ranger Jim say? Have they caught any of them?"

"They've arrested a few."

"You know what? You'd be a great ranger. Nobody knows the woods like you do."

"Well, *somebody's* got to do something. The wildlife needs protecting, Teddi." He looked away, his eyes fixed on the woods. "Yesterday Ranger Jim found the carcass of an eagle. I won't even tell you what somebody did to it. But I—"

"Hey, son?" Daddy called from the barn. "Come give me a hand."

When Josh stood, I reached out and took hold of his shirtsleeve. "Promise not to tell Mama I'm leaving?"

He leaned toward me, the blue of his eyes deepening. "Don't worry, Teddi. Everyone's got a secret." Then he took off toward the barn.

℗

That evening I sat on my bed and studied the map that Daddy had given me. After marking my route with red pencil, I put the map back in its hiding place and got ready for bed. When I opened the drawer to pull out my pajamas, I found a folded piece of paper. Inside was a feather—light honey in color with nine horizontal stripes of brownish black. In the note my brother had written:

> *From the highest branch he watches and waits.*
> *The horned owl keeps secrets.*

I didn't know where my brother came up with such things, but I smiled and tucked the feather and note into my handbag.

Late the next night, when everyone was asleep, I got dressed and made my bed. It was just after midnight when I closed my bedroom door. I left the typewriter my mother had given me sitting on the floor in my closet, still in its unopened box. Holding my breath, I tiptoed over the creaky floorboards and down the stairs. I opened my handbag and removed sealed letters addressed to Mama, Daddy, Grammy Belle, and Josh. After placing them on the kitchen table, I opened the back door and crept outside.

By the thin light of the moon, I put my suitcase into the trunk of my car, silently closing the lid with a gentle push. I gazed at the house, and then the fields, and finally the barn. My heart went wild with uncertainty, yet I couldn't ignore my longing for adventure. I climbed into the car and took one more look at the house. Silhouetted in his dimly lit bedroom window was Josh. The sight of him brought tears to my eyes. I pressed my palm against my window, and he did the same against his. We stayed like that for a long moment.

I started the ignition and rolled down the driveway. When I turned for one last look, my brother was still standing at the window, his palm still pressed against the glass.

FIVE

And now here I was all these years later, driving down the same road and feeling that familiar twinge of regret. Not for leaving home to go after my dream but for the thoughtless way I'd done it. Though Daddy claimed that Mama eventually got over it, I knew she'd never forgiven me. Most likely she never would.

Sometimes there's no way to fix things.

The drive to Charleston was plagued with heavy traffic, made worse by an accident and a detour along the way. It had taken me nearly eleven hours to get home. I woke the next morning feeling achy and disoriented. I had also overslept.

While hustling down the alley next to my shop, I glanced at my watch. It was ten minutes past opening time. I unlocked the side door and was greeted by the soft *shoo-shoo* sound of sandpaper being rubbed across wood. Peering into the workroom, I watched Albert smooth his aging hand over the top of a piecrust table.

"Hey, Albert. How're you doing?"

He looked up with a sly grin. "I'm doin' just fine, but your day ain't gonna start out too good."

"Why?"

"Your favorite person is waitin' on you. Been here since ten o'clock sharp. Got a bug up her butt 'cause I wouldn't let her in."

"Where's Inez?"

"Took the day off, remember? So it's all up to you." He laughed and went back to sanding.

I shoved my handbag into my desk drawer and turned on the showroom lights. My high heels made a sharp *clickety-click* across the wood floor as I walked down the hallway. I groaned when I saw Tula Jane Poteet standing on her tiptoes, hands cupped at the sides of her eyes as she peered into the window.

I unlocked the door and held it open. "Good morning, Miz Poteet."

She stepped inside and blotted her upper lip with a handkerchief. "Well, I was gettin' ready to leave. Your man wouldn't let me in. I know he saw me, but when I waved, he up and walked away. Left me standin' in this awful heat. Why would he do such a thing?"

"Albert is a repair specialist. He doesn't work in the front of the shop. It's my fault that nobody was here to greet you. So what can I do for you today?"

She fluffed her blue-gray hair. "Well, I just thought I'd browse and see what all's new."

"Nothing much new since your last visit. Maybe you should come back when—"

"You just go on about your business and don't mind me," she said, walking around an English armoire and disappearing behind a coromandel room divider.

As I set off to follow her, the front door opened and the UPS man walked in. He set a box on the floor and handed me a receipt to sign. "Hey, Teddi, how's it going?"

"Great, Tim. And you?" I said, scribbling my signature as fast as I could.

"Can't complain. Have a good day."

Before he was out the door, I slipped off my shoes and silently trotted past a china cabinet to find Miz Poteet, which I did, just as she was shoving a sterling candlestick into her handbag.

For three years I had put up with her frequent thefts, and I was sick to death of it. Whenever I called her son, a hotshot lawyer who lived with his mother on South Battery, he would tell me to send him a bill for whatever she'd "forgotten to pay for"—claiming she had a nervous condition. He would end our conversation by specifically requesting that I *never* embarrass his sweet little mama by confronting her.

Well, those days were over.

I approached Miz Poteet, my lips pressed into a thin smile. "Allow me to wrap that up for you. And please tell me how you'd like to pay for it. Cash or check?"

She didn't even have the decency to look embarrassed when she reached into her handbag. "Well, come to think of it, I believe it's a bit too short for where I had in mind."

Placing the candlestick on the Flemish refectory table from where she'd snatched it, Miz Poteet never missed a beat when she said, "I hear Trudy's makin' her Fredericksburg whole-wheat bread today, so I'd best be on my way and get a loaf before they sell out."

"Good idea," I agreed, folding my arms over my chest. "You'd *best* do that."

She turned and left, her pink shirtwaist dress flapping around her knees and her head held high as if she were the most upstanding citizen in all of Charleston. As she crossed the street, I shook my head and said, "Nervous condition my ass."

After slipping my feet back into my shoes, I headed for my office. But while walking by the mahogany display cabinet, I stopped. The glass door hung open, and a Limoges box was missing from the middle shelf. "Damn her!"

That little box was my favorite, a true collector's piece—painted with a frog on a lily pad, it was very old and in near-perfect condition. I marched into my office and opened my address book, muttering to myself as I dialed the number.

An efficient voice answered, "Green, Poteet, and Davis."

"Mr. Poteet, please. This is Teddi Overman." The receptionist put me on hold, and a moment later a voice I'd come to recognize all too well came on the line.

"Good morning, Miz Overman."

"No, Mr. Poteet. I'm sorry to say that it is not a good morning. Your mother visited my shop today and stole *another* Limoges box. I really wish you'd—"

"Miz Overman, my mother is forgetful, but I can assure you she's not a thief. I'm sorry for your frustration, but I believe you and I have an agreement. When she forgets to pay, you're to bill me and I'll take care of it. Now, that seems simple enough, doesn't it?"

"Simple for you. But, quite frankly, for me it's wearing thin. Every year when I do inventory, there are things missing that I just *know* have left my shop in your mother's handbag. And I really wish—"

"I'm happy to pay my mother's bills, Miz Overman. I'm comfortable with our arrangement. Now, you have a nice day."

And with that he ended the call.

"*Mama's boy,*" I snarled into the receiver.

I spent the rest of the morning at my desk catching up on the mail while Albert repaired a split in an oak library table. He hummed along with the radio, occasionally making a snide comment at an ad between songs. Every now and then, I'd lean back in my chair and peer into the workroom to watch him—how patient and exacting he was, how he mended each piece of furniture as if commissioned from above.

SIX

I met Albert James Pickens on the day I arrived in Charleston, back in the summer of '72. I wasn't prepared for Charleston, though no first-time visitor could be. Church steeples pierced a sky so blue it didn't seem real, and the streets were lined with trees that left me speechless. Some had branches so long and twisted they appeared to defy gravity, and others were tall palms that swayed in the breeze like giant green fans. While I was driving down a street that ran along the water, my mouth dropped when I saw the grand old houses that looked out across the bay. Many had porches on each of their three stories, and in the slant of sunlight I swear those homes shimmered with the soft pinks and yellows of fine mother-of-pearl.

Charleston was a unique place—one where it seemed as if two different worlds not so much collided but gracefully slid up beside each other and decided to just get along.

Realizing I was lost, I turned around and drove slowly until I found Wentworth Street. I parked at the curb, and with Mr. Palmer's business card tucked in my pocket I began walking. All the buildings were old and tall, and many had arched windows, keystones, and deep eaves accented by fancy cornices. Though I'd seen photographs of all these architectural details in the books I'd studied, seeing them in person was something else entirely.

I passed one shop after another, peering into windows that showcased everything from the latest fashions to fine bone china. After walking several blocks, I saw a small, weatherworn sign hanging cockeyed from a broken frame. The sign read: PALMER'S FINE ANTIQUES.

Wedged between a deli and a narrow, brick-paved alley, the shop didn't come close to the image I'd conjured in my mind. The window was so dirty it blurred the chest on display, the door was scarred with deep gouges, and when I pressed the old bronze latch and stepped inside, I was greeted by an aroma of mildew.

The entire place was crammed with furniture, paintings, lamps, and all sorts of knickknacks. Boxes filled with tarnished silver spoons and glass doorknobs sat atop a giant mahogany sideboard, and rugs rolled up like cigars and tied with twine were stacked in a corner. From a metal pole suspended across the ceiling hung two crystal chandeliers and a sock monkey. There was even an old one-eyed doll sitting in a porcelain soup tureen.

Mr. Palmer's shop was the messiest, dustiest, craziest place I'd ever seen.

I purely loved it.

The floorboards creaked, and I turned to see Mr. Palmer amble toward me. He pushed his way past a china cabinet, squinted, and pulled up right quick when he saw me. "Well, I'll be a three-legged jackrabbit! Am I seein' what I think I'm seein'? Could you be that farm girl from Kentucky?"

I smiled nervously and ran my fingertips over a stained-glass lamp shade. "Yessir. I like your shop. You sure have lots of stuff."

Mr. Palmer looked around, his eyebrows raised as if seeing his own shop for the first time. "Reckon I do. Want a nickel tour of the place?"

With an eager nod, I followed, listening to stories about where certain pieces came from and who had once owned them. He used words like "Rococo," "Biedermeier," "cyma reversa," and so many more that my brain hurt. The more he talked, the more I figured that Mr. Palmer was a human encyclopedia when it came to antiques.

When we reached the back of the shop, he led me down a hall and stepped through an open doorway. "This here's the workroom."

Shelves crammed with jars of stains and lacquers lined one wall. A pegboard held all kinds of clamps and tools, and the smell of turpentine hung in the humid air. Standing at a workbench was a man built like a cinder block. Beneath the bright lights, his bald head shone like polished mahogany. He was repairing a deep split in a chair leg, his face intense as he adjusted a clamp.

Mr. Palmer said, "Albert, remember that painted chest I brought back from Kentucky, the one I sold to Miz Fitch?"

Albert looked up, expressionless.

"Well, this here's the young lady who painted it."

I could tell that Mr. Palmer didn't remember my name, so I smiled and said, "My name's Teddi Overman."

Albert's eyes telegraphed his thoughts as clearly as if he'd spoken them: *So what?* Then he went back to working on the chair.

And that was that. I'd been dismissed.

I spent more than an hour with Mr. Palmer, listening to his furniture stories and asking questions. When I told him I'd driven to Charleston all by myself, he offered to buy me lunch. We went out his front door, walked a few steps, and entered the deli. Mr. Palmer waved to the cook, and then we sat on chairs with red vinyl seats and ordered from plastic-covered menus.

Mr. Palmer tucked a paper napkin into his shirt collar and commenced to eat a grilled-cheese sandwich that he dipped into a bowl of stewed tomatoes, while I enjoyed a tuna-salad sandwich.

I chattered away, describing things I'd recently learned about furniture-painting techniques. Mr. Palmer listened, but he didn't offer an opinion one way or the other. When he asked where I was staying, I took a sip of lemonade and answered, "I don't know. Guess I'll look for a cheap motel."

"You still have your mind set on workin' with furniture?"

"Yessir."

He took a bite of his sandwich and chewed real slow as he studied me, and then he turned his attention back to his meal. We finished our lunch in silence.

"So," he said, tugging the napkin from his collar and wiping it across his mouth, "you just visitin' Charleston or you plan to stay?"

"I'm not sure. But I like what I've seen so far."

"Do your folks know you're here?"

I said, "Yes." It wasn't a lie. Well, not exactly. I had left them a letter, so technically they *did* know.

"Let me ask you something, Teddi. You've got this dream of havin' your own shop, but my guess is you don't have any money. Am I right?"

I squirmed a little. "I have some."

"Well, whatever that *'some'* is, it most likely won't do you a lick of good. So if you're here," he said, taking a pepper shaker and plunking it directly in front of me, "and you wanna get to *here* and have your own shop," he added, pushing the salt shaker to the edge of the table, "then how you gonna do it?"

I glanced from the pepper to the salt and felt my cheeks color up. "I . . . well, I'll get a job, buy old furniture, and work nights and weekends painting and refinishing until I save up enough money."

"And where do you think you'll sell your furniture? You'll starve if you try and sell it at the side of the road."

I looked down and traced a crack in the tabletop with my fingernail.

"Now, here's another question. If you was to work, let's say, in my shop, for example, what would you see yourself doing?"

I met him eye to eye. "First thing I'd do is wash your window. Then I'd repair all the gouges in your front door and paint it. And then I'd take those two matching chairs you have shoved in the corner and paint them, too."

His woolly eyebrows shot up. "Paint the Gustavian chairs! Why, that'd be a . . . a sacrilege."

I shrugged. "They'd sell if they were painted."

He rubbed his hand across his stubbly chin and looked out the window. After a moment of silence, he mumbled, "What color?"

"Antique silver for the chairs and green for your front door."

"Green. Why green?"

"Well, it's a soothing color, *and* it's the color of money. Might put people in the mood to spend."

Mr. Palmer gave me the strangest look and then let out a hoot and slapped his hand on the table, sending the salt shaker flying into the air and crashing on the floor.

"So if you worked for me, what wage do you think you'd earn?"

While leaning over to retrieve the salt shaker, I thought of what Mr. Palmer had said the previous year, how I should start my price high and be willing to haggle. I placed the shaker on the table and lined it up with the pepper. "I'd say five dollars an hour."

"What! Nobody will pay that. I'll go two bucks, not a penny more."

I shook my head. "What I do is art—you said so yourself. Remember? But I suppose I'd take four."

He narrowed his eyes. "You're dreamin'. I'll give you two-fifty."

I held his gaze. "Three seventy-five."

Mr. Palmer tugged on his earlobe and looked at me for a long time. Right when I thought he was going to tell me to forget it, his lips twitched. "All right, goddamn it. You've got yourself a job."

When we returned to the shop, Mr. Palmer led me into his office. While I sat in a lumpy chair with springs poking through its

cushion, he made several phone calls. By four o'clock that afternoon, he'd found me a tiny furnished apartment to rent above a
bakery. Though it sure wasn't much to look at, it was clean and
smelled of warm bread.

That night while unpacking my belongings, I found an envelope
at the bottom of my suitcase. Inside was a note that read:

Three chirps into the sun brings good luck.

And out fell a bluebird's feather.

∾

The next morning I began my job. I spent the first three weeks
scrubbing the front window, painting the door a soft viridian green,
and working myself into a sweat as I cleaned and rearranged Mr.
Palmer's entire shop. After rubbing every stick of furniture with a
special beeswax paste I'd found in the storeroom, I took the
silverware from the shoe boxes and polished each piece. Once I was
done, the shop looked like something special.

Mr. Palmer grumbled when I begged him to buy a radio, but
one day he walked in and shoved a box into my hands. I set the
radio on top of a bookcase and tuned it to the best classical station
I could find. I knew this would be the final touch.

And I was right.

People walked into the shop with its glowing woods, sparkling
sterling, and classical music skimming through the air and they
couldn't help but relax and open their wallets.

With nothing left in the shop for me to polish or rearrange, Mr.
Palmer set me up with a small workbench and a stool in the far
corner of the workroom. When I began to paint the Gustavian
chairs, I had the sinking feeling I was headed for trouble.

Albert didn't like me.

He wouldn't say good morning or good night, and he wouldn't look at me when I asked a question, much less answer me. Sometimes I'd watch him from the corner of my eye, the way he'd smooth his dark hands over a break in a chair leg or a gouge in a table, assessing the problem with his touch, and how, when the damage was severe, he'd pull a penlight from his toolbox and shine it real slow over the areas that needed special attention. He'd select the tools, glue, and clamps required, lining them up neatly on a white towel like a surgeon in an operating room. The day he finished repairing a nineteenth-century armoire that movers had dropped off the back of their truck was the day I knew that Albert James Pickens was a wizard with wood.

The more I watched him, the more I came to understand that Albert had a rare kinship with furniture. I swear, the more damaged it was, the more he seemed to love it. Whenever he went out for lunch, I'd sneak to his side of the workroom and examine his craftsmanship. His finished work was so meticulous that it was impossible to find even the slightest indication that any damage had ever occurred.

I still don't know why I began talking to Albert—loneliness, I guess—but I'd babble on and on while I painted furniture or polished silver. I'd tell him things like how my mother baked the best pies in all of Powell County and how Grammy could close her eyes, run her hand over the bark of any tree, and know what species it was.

Albert said nothing.

"My brother has an amazing connection to wildlife. It's hard to explain, but things happen to him. Remarkable things. Once when we were running in the field and Josh was ahead of me, a woodchuck started running alongside of him. He was playing with my brother. I swear it's true. Our farm is surrounded by nature. Have you ever been to Kentucky?"

Silence.

"Well, it's really beautiful, and wait till I tell you about Red River Gorge . . ."

Albert never showed the least bit of interest, so I eventually shut up. Then one day when clouds blackened the sky and rain beat against the window, I felt lonely and started blabbing again.

"You know what, Albert? My daddy's good at fixing things. Not furniture, but anything that has an engine. He's real quiet, just like you. But when he says something, it matters. Now, I don't know if what *you* say matters or not, 'cause you haven't said anything. My grammy says the wisest people say the least, so the way I figure it, you must be some kinda genius."

When Albert didn't respond, I continued to talk. "Anyway, Daddy and I used to ride in his truck and go to town. Sometimes we talked and sometimes we didn't, but we always chewed Black Jack gum and enjoyed each other's company. There's nothing like that gum. Have you ever chewed it, Albert? It's got a real bite to it, and I love how it smells. It's amazing how much I miss it. I haven't had a single stick since I left home . . ."

Albert never once made a comment, ignoring me to the point that I was certain he'd completely tuned me out. But sometimes I just felt the need to talk, so I did. Those were the times when I was homesick, and I'd sit on my stool and recount my life in Kentucky so I'd remember that I had roots.

As the summer wore on, there were days when Albert would show up late for work, and sometimes he didn't show up at all. Mr. Palmer warned him, and then one afternoon he told Albert in no uncertain terms that the next time he didn't show up, he'd lose his job. That warning seemed to hit home, and for a while all was well. But then Albert went out for lunch one Wednesday and didn't come back. He had been working on the damaged leg of a Dutch walnut table, and the owner was expecting it to be ready the following day.

At three-thirty Mr. Palmer walked into the workroom. He looked at the unfinished repair and shook his head. "Miz Crenshaw's gonna tear into my hide. When Albert comes in tomorrow— well, *if* he comes in, I'll have to let him go." Mr. Palmer scowled at the table and then looked at me. "I'm going to the dentist and won't be back for the rest of the day, so keep your ears open and listen for the front door in case somebody comes in. Make sure you lock up when you leave."

"I will."

The remainder of the afternoon slid by, and when I finished screwing knobs onto a chest of drawers I'd painted, it was already past closing time. I was about to lock up for the night when I stopped at Albert's workbench and examined the unfinished repair. The table had intricate inlay down the front of its legs. I couldn't imagine what it was worth, but I figured it was plenty. Though I'd worked in the same room with Albert for more than three months and he'd never acknowledged my existence, I still felt real bad that he was going to lose his job.

৩৩

Early the next morning, I was the first to arrive at the shop. While I was sitting at my workbench polishing a silver tea service, the side door swung open. I could tell by the sound of the footsteps that Albert had arrived.

Not twenty seconds later, Mr. Palmer walked in and said, "Albert, I don't know where you were yesterday, and it's none of my business. What I *do* know is that you haven't been yourself since Reba left you. I can take your moodiness, and I don't care that you've darn near stopped talking, but Miz Crenshaw is expectin' her table this morning. When I tell her it's not ready, I can guaran- damn-tee ya she'll chew my ass from here to Sunday. Now, I'm sorry, but I'm gonna have to let you go."

Albert barely made a sound when he stepped into the workroom, his shoulders slumped and his denim overalls wrinkled as if he'd slept in them. He looked at the table he'd left half repaired, then pulled the chain to the light over his workbench. The bulb swung back and forth while Albert stared at Miz Crenshaw's table. I sat on my stool and wondered what was going through his mind. He reached out to touch the table but stopped and withdrew his hand.

As Albert's eyes shifted toward me, Mr. Palmer walked in with his checkbook. "It pains me to have to do this, but—"

When Mr. Palmer saw Miz Crenshaw's table, he leaned close and squinted his eyes. Then he turned to Albert and barked, "Well, why in Sam Hill didn't you speak up and tell me you came back yesterday and fixed it? It's not the best repair work you've ever done, but I think it'll pass."

Albert didn't answer, and I went back to polishing the silver.

"All right, you've still got your job. But, Albert, listen up. You're on probation." Mr. Palmer turned and left the workroom, grumbling to himself.

The morning passed, and Albert never so much as glanced my way. When lunchtime came, Mr. Palmer went to the deli while I unwrapped a peanut-butter sandwich. I thought for sure Albert would say something when we were alone in the shop, something like a simple *thank-you* or maybe even a halfhearted compliment on the repair I'd done. A repair that took me till ten-thirty at night to finish and had saved his sorry hide.

But he didn't.

When he turned off the light above his workbench and left for lunch, I was hurt and angry in equal measure. After finishing my sandwich, I went back to polishing the tea service. I kicked into high gear, wanting to get it done so I could begin painting a Prince of Wales chair. Mr. Palmer had given me free rein to do whatever I wanted, and I couldn't wait to get started.

While I was hunched over my workbench, the back door opened. I didn't bother to turn around, and I sure didn't say anything. For all I cared, Albert could take all his jars of glue, secret mixtures of oil resins, and countless special tools and drive his truck off the nearest bridge.

I dipped a toothbrush into a bowl of tarnish remover and worked it over the intricate handle of a sugar shell. My fingers had turned black, and my nose itched from the fumes.

A *click* sounded, and a breeze from Albert's fan began to whirl around the room. I heard the shuffling of his feet and the clang of tools. Then, from the corner of my eye, I saw a shadow moving toward me.

I sat stone still. The hairs on my arms prickled as Albert's hand came into view.

He moved closer.

I held my breath, my fingers poised motionless.

Slowly, Albert reached over my shoulder and placed a pack of Black Jack gum on my workbench.

SEVEN

Albert and I inched our way toward an amicable relationship. When he and his wife, Reba, patched things up and she moved back home, he was so happy that he started singing along with the radio. At least once a day, he'd initiate a conversation with me, and whenever I asked him a question, he always answered. Now and then when I babbled too much and got on his nerves, he'd tease me and say, "You flap them jaws much longer and I'm gonna get my special glue."

From his office I'd hear Mr. Palmer chuckle.

It wasn't long before Mr. Palmer and Albert became like two favorite uncles. In December of that year, I started going to auctions and estate sales with Mr. Palmer. He said I was born with *the nose*—a knack for sniffing out objects of value.

I had worked in Mr. Palmer's shop for nearly four years when Albert turned to me and said, "You ready to get serious about repairs?"

I stopped sanding a mirror frame and looked at him. "What do you mean? I *am* serious."

He pointed to a damaged mother-of-pearl inlay design on the leg of a Chinese table. "Pull up your stool and watch."

From that day forward, I sat at Albert's workbench one afternoon each week as he gave me lessons on everything from mixing the right consistency of filler paste to repairing marquetry. One day, while he showed me how to fix blistered veneer, I looked up at him in awe. "Where did you learn all this, Albert?"

"Watchin' my pap," he said, slicing into the veneer with a razor-sharp blade. "Never was a damaged piece of furniture he couldn't mend—had a steady hand like I never seen before or since."

"How old were you when you fixed your first piece?"

"Eleven."

"And you've been doing it ever since?"

Albert nodded, leaned closer to his work, and squinted his eyes while gently lifting the veneer with the point of his knife. "Now, hush and pay attention . . ."

ص

It wasn't quite a year after Albert began teaching me the finer points of repairs that Josh went missing. Though I saw concern in Albert's eyes, he always managed to say something positive—like how some people needed time to sort things out, how he believed that Josh would eventually come home. But when the weeks rolled in to months and Josh didn't come back, Albert said less and less.

One morning I got choked up when Albert rested his hand on my shoulder and told me that he and Reba had spoken to the members of their church. He said they were all praying for my brother's safe return. Though Mr. Palmer didn't say much about Josh, he always let me take extra time off whenever I wanted to go home to Kentucky, and he always paid me for the days I was gone.

During a visit back home, I took one of Josh's flannel shirts and stuffed it into my suitcase. When the pain of his disappearance left me cold and numb, I'd put on his shirt and roll up the sleeves. Those were the days when I'd sit at my workbench and clean old hardware with a wire brush while tears stung my eyes. I'd dip the brush into a jar of solvent and rub one area at a time, and with each circle I'd silently pray, *Please bring my brother home, please . . .*

I was scared and heartbroken and mad at the world. I had even stopped doing the one thing I loved most—taking repair lessons from Albert.

The months dragged on, the cuffs of my brother's shirt began to fray, and my body grew weak from lack of sleep. Everything felt delayed. My hands didn't work like they used to, and my mind drifted. I often didn't know what day it was, nor did I care. The sound of my own voice hurt my ears, so I'd even stopped talking.

One afternoon in the summer of 1978, while I sat quietly in my corner and filled a crack in a dictionary stand, Albert broke the silence of the workroom.

"When I was a boy, my grandpap took me fishin' every Saturday. He'd pack us a nice lunch—sometimes fried-catfish sandwiches, sometimes barbecued chicken and biscuits. One day we was sittin' on the riverbank havin' our lunch when Grandpap reached into his pocket. He pulled out two Chinese fortune cookies and gave me one. I tore off the wrapper, took a bite, and spit it out—tasted like old cardboard dipped in a little sugar. My grandpap didn't like his cookie neither, so we laughed and tossed 'em in the river.

"The next Saturday we went fishin' like always. Oh, that was some day. The redfish was tailin' in shallow water. Now, what that means," Albert said, raising his hand and weaving it through air, "is they come in so close to shore that you can see their tails flappin' above the waterline. That was the day I caught my first redfish. It was a nice one, too, about twenty-six inches.

"When we got back to my grandpap's house, he said he'd cook it up Cajun style. We sat on the porch talkin' while he spread newspapers and cleaned the fish, and when he opened it up, neither one of us could believe it. Right there in the belly of my redfish was one of them folded paper fortunes. Grandpap's eyes got real big, and he pulled it out and handed it to me. He said, 'Albert, this here's a message from the good Lord himself. Read me what those words say.' So I did. And you know what that fortune said? *'The waters of faith hold food for the soul.'*"

Albert chuckled and shook his head. "So I asked my grandpap if that meant we should go to church more often. Well, he thought for a good while, and then he said, 'No, what that means is we're supposta go fishin' on Sundays, too.'"

I felt a smile coming to my lips as I looked at Albert suspiciously. "Did you make that up?"

"You know I don't lie." But the way the corners of his eyes crinkled into tiny pleats led me to believe otherwise. He pointed his screwdriver toward the damaged antique jewelry box he was working on. "You about ready for more repair lessons?"

I nodded and pulled up my stool.

☙

On a chilly February morning in 1982, Mr. Palmer walked into the workroom. "Teddi, there's an estate sale over in Orangeburg on Sunday. Guess I'll go see what they have. You wanna tag along?"

"Sure."

"Be here at seven-thirty sharp or I'll leave without you."

When we arrived at the sale and climbed out of the truck, Mr. Palmer gave me a stern look. "Now, don't go gettin' excited if you see something you think is special, and for God's sake don't do that annoying little squeal, 'cause sure as blazes they'll jack up the price."

"I know."

"And don't smile and get all chatty."

"I *know*! You've told me all this a million times."

"Well, damn it. You sure as hell didn't listen a million times."

I gave Mr. Palmer a flat look and followed him to the front door. The house had the distinct smell of old age and dust, and though each room was packed with furniture and knickknacks, none of it was worth much. We climbed the stairs to the second floor, where the hallway walls were stained with oily fingerprints from the hands of children who were now probably older than I was. All the rugs were worn and dull.

"There's a lot of stuff in the attic," a man said from behind us. "My aunt was a bit of a pack rat." He pulled a rope in the ceiling, and rickety stairs unfolded. "Feel free to go on up. If you need me, I'll be in the kitchen."

As the man turned and left, Mr. Palmer looked at the stairs and shook his head. "No way I'm climbin' those. This is a waste of time. C'mon, let's go."

"I'll go up and see."

"Well, don't take all damn day. I'll wait here. If you see anything good, bring it down."

I climbed the stairs and pulled a string that illuminated a bare lightbulb. Cobwebs clung to the ceiling, and there was so much junk that I didn't know where to begin. I rooted through several boxes, but most were filled with old clothes, yellowing table linens, and Christmas ornaments. The ornaments made me sad. I wondered if they'd ever hang on a tree again. Probably not.

Wasp carcasses crunched beneath my feet as I pushed deeper into the dusty mess. I was about to leave when I noticed a cardboard box shoved behind a broken mirror. Reaching inside, I pulled out something heavy that was wrapped in a brown paper bag.

What I found inside was an intricately patterned sterling-silver box that had blackened with tarnish. On its bottom was a small turnkey. I wound it a few times and was startled when the top flipped open and a tiny mechanical bird popped up. He began fluttering his wings while a tinkly song played. I'd never seen anything like it. When the bird stopped singing, I closed the top and set the box on the floor. After digging through a few more boxes, I found a bronze door knocker and a solid brass match safe.

I went to the top of the stairs and whispered, "I found some things."

Mr. Palmer reached up, and I handed him the match safe and the door knocker, then finally the bird box.

He set the door knocker and the match safe on the floor, but before he could get a good look at the bird box, the man handling the house sale came down the hallway. "You folks find anything?"

"Only these," Mr. Palmer said. "But I can just as well take 'em as leave 'em."

The man took a quick look at the items. "How about fifty dollars for all three?"

"That price won't leave much meat on the bone."

I climbed down the ladder and wondered why Mr. Palmer was playing hardball. The door knocker alone was worth hundreds.

The man scratched his head and said, "Well, how about forty?"

"I reckon that's fair."

"What about this old vanity bench?" I said, walking into one of the bedrooms.

"Two dollars," the man said.

Mr. Palmer pulled out his wallet, counting his money like it'd be the death of him to part with it. "All right, here's forty-two bucks."

The man folded the bills and stuffed them into his pocket. "If you see anything else, let me know."

Mr. Palmer and I descended the stairs and walked out the front door. When we climbed into the truck, he turned the bird box upside down and squinted. Then he cranked the key, the music began, and the bird popped up. He let out a hoot, handed it to me, and started the engine.

"What's so funny?"

"Gee-howdy Christmas," he said, slapping the steering wheel as he roared down the road. "There's a maker's mark on the bottom of that box. It's a Griesbaum, for chrissakes. A *Griesbaum*!"

"What do you think it's worth?"

"Solid sterling Griesbaums are rare. That one's from the early 1900s. It'll sell for a grand. Maybe more."

I propped my feet on the dashboard to try to stop it from rattling. "Wow. We hit the jackpot."

"You earned your keep this month. Remind me to give you an extra fifty bucks in your pay."

"Don't you think anything less than two hundred is insulting?"

"Insulting!" He rolled down his window and spit a stream of tobacco. "I should *dock* your pay for all the lip you give me."

"And then there's that crystal sardine container I found in Georgetown. You made a ton of money on that, too. If it weren't for me, you wouldn't even have this bird box. You didn't go up in that attic—I did."

He pursed his lips and turned his attention to the road, but he knew I was staring at him. Finally he threw me a glance and said, "Oh, all right. I'll give you an extra two hundred. But don't go askin' for more."

I laughed. "Thanks. And thanks for buying me that old vanity bench. I can't wait to paint it."

"Ah, what the hell, it was only two bucks."

We rode in silence for several miles, and then I turned to Mr. Palmer. "The other day I was thinking about how long I've worked for you. It'll be ten years in June. Do you think maybe when you retire, you'd let me take over your shop?"

That question sent him careening toward the ditch. "Jumpin' Jesus! I give you two hundred bucks and now you want my whole damn shop? Well, don't go gettin' any big ideas. I'm not set to retire for a long while. Not even gonna think about it till I'm seventy-five."

I flashed him a look. "You said you were seventy-five three years ago."

His cheeks colored up. "Well damn it, I was wrong. But when I do retire, I suppose you could step in and run the place. Guess you wouldn't mess things up too bad."

I smiled and looked out the windshield. From Mr. Palmer those words were a big compliment.

Several months after we had that conversation, Mr. Palmer was in his office calculating prices for sterling flatware he'd bought at an auction. Albert was repairing the legs of an antique high chair that had seen one too many chubby babies, while I was creating a decoupage design on the top of a pine chest. It was my first commissioned piece for Miz Tedra Calhoun, a society lady who was a good customer. After cutting pictures of flowers from old issues of British gardening magazines, I glued them into position across the top of the chest, creating a collage of a lush summer garden. I knew that the decoupage had to be perfect or it would end up being my last.

A few minutes before noon, I heard Mr. Palmer's adding machine go into a rapid-fire frenzy. The *clickety-clickety* kept going, and I looked at Albert and said, "Those silver pieces sure must be expensive."

Albert chuckled and shook his head. "That old man comes up with some kinda crazy prices."

I was curious about what Mr. Palmer was calculating, so I put down my brush and headed for his office. I stepped into his doorway and found him hunched over his desk. His right hand was splayed out across the keys of his adding machine, sending a long ribbon of white paper curling down the side of his desk and across the floor.

Mr. Palmer was dead.

❧

At the memorial service, I sat with Albert and Reba, all of us stunned by grief. The preacher, a paunchy older gentleman, spoke endearingly of Mr. Palmer's curmudgeonly ways and long-standing reputation for driving a hard bargain and being a man of his word. When the preacher mentioned that Mr. Palmer was eighty-six years old, Albert and I looked at each other with surprise. And though I'd known he was a bachelor, I had no idea that Mr. Palmer had had a girlfriend for nearly fifty years. Her name was Bessie Wise. She wasn't at the memorial service because she was in a nursing home.

"Poor little thing," a woman behind me said. "Jackson went to see her every Sunday evening, bless his heart. But she didn't have any idea who he was."

Mr. Palmer had a nephew named Elgin who lived in Texas. Following the service he spoke to Albert, Reba, and me for a little while, ending the conversation by saying he'd be coming to the shop the next day to tell us his plans. Though I didn't much care for the emphasis he put on the word *plans*, I did my best not to overreact and jump into a pool of worry.

Elgin arrived at the shop early the next morning. He was nice enough, but when he told us that he was the beneficiary of Mr. Palmer's estate, which included the shop and everything in it, my stomach churned.

Is he going to run the shop, or will he hire someone? Should I step forward and tell him that I'm sure I can manage everything if he'd give me the chance?

I didn't know the etiquette of such things, and while I was try-ing to gather the courage to broach the subject as respectfully as I could, Elgin dropped the bomb: He was hiring an auction com-pany to sell the contents of Mr. Palmer's shop and would then put the building up for sale.

I rose from my work stool and said, "Excuse me, I don't mean to be forward, but what would it take to buy this business? Albert and I work well together, and I know we could—"

"I'm sorry," Elgin said, raising his hand. "I'll give you both a full month's wages and any vacation pay you have coming. If you need references, I'll give you those, too. After the repairs are done, you can go ahead and clear out your personal things."

And that was that. Not only had I lost a man I considered to be a wonderful, if cantankerous, friend and teacher, but his passing had obliterated my dream of taking over his shop.

When Albert and I left that night, I walked with him to his truck and posed a question. "I have an idea. What if you and I pooled our money? We could find a new location and open our own shop. We'd be fifty-fifty partners. Mr. Palmer's customers would come to us, I know they would."

Albert slowly shook his head. "You're young, Teddi. You got a whole lot of years ahead of you. I started workin' when I was four-teen. Come November, I'll be fifty-one. All I want is a decent job that pays my bills so I can go fishin' on weekends. Me and Reba got ourselves a nice life. I don't want to mess it up by takin' on a loan. The money I got saved is stayin' right where it is—in the bank. And I sure don't want any tension."

"What if I promised to take all the tension for both of us? You do your work like always and I deal with everything else."

Albert opened the truck door, climbed in, and rolled down the window. "That wouldn't be right. I know you got a big dream in your head, and stubborn as you are, you'll probably make it happen, one way or another. But, Teddi, you and I got different dreams."

I glanced down at my shoes. "I understand."

Albert closed the door and looked at me. For a moment I thought he'd changed his mind and was considering my idea, but he started the engine and said, "Now, don't go gettin' all hangdog. My grand-pap used to say, *'You can't see the whole sky from one window.'* You remember those words, all right? See you tomorrow, Teddi."

∽

Within ten days of that conversation, the last repair had been delivered. As Albert swept the workroom floor and I wiped down benches, Elgin walked in and handed us each an envelope. Then he asked us to return our keys before we left. Albert never said a word as he packed up his tools and hauled them out to his truck, but I let loose and cried while wrapping my sable paintbrushes in a towel.

At four o'clock that afternoon, we walked out of Mr. Palmer's shop. I blotted my tears on my shirtsleeve and sniffed, "I'm going to miss you so much, Albert."

His voice thickened when he said, "Won't be the same without you flappin' your jaws all day."

Three weeks later the entire contents of Mr. Palmer's shop were sold at auction. I couldn't bring myself to go and watch. Neither could Albert. Not long after, the building was sold to an investor from Raleigh.

It didn't get any more final than that.

EIGHT

Albert took a position at a furniture-repair shop on the out-
skirts of town. He said the owner ran it like a drive-through
and didn't give a spit about craftsmanship, but the wage was good.
Though I tried to find a job working with furniture, nobody had an
opening. Well, nobody except Miz Hightree, who owned an antique shop on King Street. She wanted someone to clean her store
and rewire lamps for minimum wage. I'd have gnawed on a rock
before accepting that job.

While I kept an eye on the help-wanted ads for something good
to come along, I began waitressing tables at the same diner where
Mr. Palmer and I had struck a deal ten years before. More than
once, while filling napkin dispensers and writing the daily specials
on the blackboard behind the counter, I thought about the typewriter that Mama had given me for graduation and how much
she'd wanted me to go to secretarial school. If she found out about
my current predicament, I knew she'd lambaste me with a big "I
told you so" lecture, so I didn't tell her—or anybody else, for that
matter.

A month after I began waitressing tables, I was walking to work
and saw a man put a For Rent sign in the window of Mr. Palmer's
old shop. That sign gnawed at me something awful, and I turned
around and knocked on the door.

When the man opened the door, I smiled and said, "Hello. My name's Teddi Overman. I used to work here when Mr. Palmer owned it. I'd like to talk to you about renting this building."

He eyed me up and down, taking in my baggy waitress uniform and scuffed-up shoes. I had barely begun explaining what I wanted to do when he interrupted me. "What kind of collateral do you have?"

That question brought me up short. "Well, I . . . I have a car, and I've saved up almost seven thousand dollars."

He shook his head and closed the door.

After working my shift, I ran home, changed into my best dress, and set off for the bank where I had my savings account. I pleaded my case to the manager, a bald little man who looked disarmingly like a mole. When I believed I had his interest, I told him I'd need about thirty thousand dollars. The moment that number left my lips, he avoided my eyes and began shuffling papers on his desk. "I'm sorry, Miss Overman. We couldn't possibly loan you that amount of money . . ."

I left the bank feeling emptied of hope.

෨෬

Months passed, and still the For Rent sign remained in the window of Mr. Palmer's old shop. The lettering had faded from the sun, and its edges were starting to curl.

Most days I felt lost, and sometimes I was scared, yet I believed I could run my own business if somebody would just give me a chance. But I didn't know who that somebody was. It wasn't until I was in the pharmacy and began talking with Miz Tedra Calhoun in the checkout line that I got an idea.

"You know, Teddi, I had a lovely fund-raising luncheon at my home a few weeks ago, and everyone raved about the decoupage you did on that chest."

"Thank you. I loved doing it."

"I'm so sorry Mr. Palmer passed away. This town won't be the same without him. So how are you doing, Teddi? Where are you working now?"

I felt ashamed when I answered, "Marty's Diner. But only until I find a job working with furniture."

Miz Calhoun reached out and patted my hand, "Well, with all your talent I'm sure someone will snap you up in no time. It was nice chatting with you, honey. You take good care." She gathered her purchase, and with a wave of her perfectly manicured hand she walked out the door.

Tedra Calhoun had something special that was hard to define. I guessed she was in her mid-fifties—one of those women who knew exactly how to apply makeup and dress to perfection. She wasn't a natural-born beauty, yet she exuded the illusion of beauty, which, as far as I was concerned, was a kind of beauty unto itself. As I watched her move down the sidewalk in a graceful stride, wearing her lime green suit and creamy pearls, I set off after her.

"Miz Calhoun," I said, running up to her side. "Do you have a few minutes? I'd like to tell you about an idea I have . . ."

We walked slowly as I told her how much I'd learned while working for Mr. Palmer and why I believed I could be a successful shop owner. "I'm a hard worker, Miz Calhoun. Mr. Palmer said I had a real eye for knowing what had value. And I'm patient, too. I never rush my work. I figure you know just about everyone in Charleston, so I was wondering if you might put in a good word for me at one of the banks. If somebody would only give me a chance . . ."

My words bumped into one another, and though I heard desperation in my voice, I couldn't control myself.

Miz Calhoun stopped walking and turned to face me. "Dreams are powerful, aren't they? When I was a girl, I dreamed of becoming a prima ballerina. I was a wonderful dancer, but I lacked the one crucial ingredient you need to have at the highest level of dance: courage. Right after I lost the lead role in the most important audition of my career, I met Preston. And when he asked me to marry him, I knew it was what I wanted. But I never danced again."

Her lips formed a sad smile. "Not that I have any regrets, but there are days when I wonder what might have been if I'd just reached a little deeper and believed in myself more."

Right when I had started to wonder where this conversation was going, she said, "So you have a dream, and it certainly seems like you have the courage to go after it. But what you don't have is the capital. Is that it?"

"Yes, ma'am."

She tilted her head, and what I saw in her eyes wasn't a wealthy woman taking pity on a farm girl. It was kindness. "Why don't you come to my home this evening? Preston is a very clever businessman. Maybe he'll have some ideas for you. He likes to relax with a drink before dinner. If you could come by around six o'clock, he'd talk with you then."

"Oh, thank you, Miz Calhoun."

She smiled and gave a slight shrug. "I can't presume to know what my darling Preston will say or do. But I know he'll listen to your ideas and give you sound advice. That much I can promise. Now, I've got to run. See you tonight."

༽✤༼

It took me more than an hour to get dressed and fix my hair. Wanting to look mature and professional, I chose a simple black skirt and a soft white sweater with tiny pearl buttons. After several failed attempts, I managed to get my thick hair up into a stylish knot with about a hundred bobby pins and so much hair spray that I nearly asphyxiated myself.

When I parked in front of the Calhouns' home, I closed my eyes and tried to calm the thunderous beating of my heart. As I stepped to the sidewalk and opened the wrought-iron gate, I wondered, *Is my outfit too simple? Does it look cheap? Oh, Lord, of course it looks cheap. I bought it at a thrift shop. I should have polished my shoes one more time . . .*

Just as I rang the doorbell, several bobby pins sprang from my hair and my knot began to loosen. I tried to quickly fix it, but the door swung open and I was facing a broad-shouldered gentleman with silver hair and wire-rimmed glasses perched on an unfortunate nose.

"Well, I'll bet you're Teddi," he said, offering me his hand. "I'm Preston Calhoun. Please, come in. Lets go into my office and have a chat, shall we?"

My stomach tightened and my hair inched down the back of my head as I followed him down the hallway and into a room lined with mahogany bookcases. The rug was Persian, and the furniture was well-worn brown leather. In the middle of the room sat a double-pedestal desk of solid burled walnut. It was nearly the size of my kitchen.

I smoothed my fingers along its edge and said, "This is English, from the Victorian era, right?"

"You know your antiques. This desk belonged to my great-grandfather. Please, have a seat. Would you like something to drink?"

"No thank you. I'm fine."

Mr. Calhoun sat down at his desk and poured himself a drink from a crystal decanter. "My lovely wife says you have an idea for a business. So why don't you tell me about it?"

I couldn't stop my knees from shaking as I explained what I wanted to do. Mr. Calhoun listened, taking notes on a yellow legal pad and asking all sorts of questions. If he noticed my hair migrating down my neck and bobby pins shooting across the room, he never revealed as much. But it was hard to ignore.

We talked for nearly an hour, and then he leaned back in his chair. "Your ideas sound good, Teddi. Real good. You'll have start-up costs, rent, utilities, inventory, and more. By my calculations, you'll need a minimum of eighty thousand dollars."

I gasped. "That's a *lot* of money!"

"Yes, it surely is. But if you're going to start this business and do it right, you'll need every penny of it. Though without collateral, I doubt you'll get a loan of this size without a cosigner."

Cosigner?

I sank deeper into the chair. "I don't have one. I could ask Daddy. He's the best farmer in Powell County. But last year's crops weren't very good . . ." My voice trailed off. I knew that this meeting had just taken a bad turn.

Mr. Calhoun had a sip of his drink and thought for a moment. "All right, young lady. I'll study these notes and formulate our strategy. We'll have to be ready for any questions a banker will throw across the table—and believe me, there'll be a lot of them. So while I'm thinking, what I need you to do is type out your business plan and drop it off to me when you're done."

Mama would just love this. I could see her shaking her head and pointing to the Smith-Corona I'd left behind.

I was too embarrassed to make eye contact with Mr. Calhoun when I said, "I don't have a typewriter."

Slowly he stood and looked out the window with his hands shoved deep into his pockets. I knew I'd made a perfect fool of myself, so I rose to my feet and gathered my handbag. I tried to discreetly pluck the bobby pins from the rug, but he turned and saw me. I straightened up, barely able to look at him. "Mr. Calhoun, I'm sorry for wasting your time. I guess I didn't think things through very well."

I felt the sting of tears in my eyes.

Don't cry. Shake his hand and walk out of here with some semblance of dignity.

With a slight lift to his chin, Mr. Calhoun squinted and studied me. "Teddi, there are two things I've learned in business that have served me well. One, we get what we negotiate. And two, never show weakness. Those two things will help you more than anything I know. Now, I can see that you believe in your talent, but you've got a whole lot to learn about negotiation. The minute you show a sign of weakness, you've taken the first step toward losing the game. And that's what negotiation is—*a game.*"

He tapped the legal pad with his finger and raised his eyebrows into high arches. "Tell you what. I'll have my secretary type up your business plan, and I'll meet you at Charleston First Bank & Trust on Monday morning. Nine o'clock sharp. We'll show them what you've got and see what they say."

I thought my legs might buckle for the gratitude I felt. "Mr. Calhoun, thank you. Thank you so much."

"Now, bear in mind, it's a long shot. But you'll never know unless you give it a try."

Right then another bobby pin sprang free and landed on the floor, and gentleman that he was, Mr. Calhoun pretended not to notice.

∞

As promised, Mr. Calhoun met me at the bank bright and early on Monday morning. In his hands was a perfectly typed business plan on the finest linen stationery I'd ever seen. We were led to a wood-paneled office where the bank manager was waiting—a tall, skinny man named John Hamilton.

Mr. Calhoun and I worked as a team, pointing out the highlights of my ideas and giving solid reasons that my business plan was sound. When the manager leaned back in his red leather chair and agreed to present my business plan to the loan committee, I swelled with so much happiness I thought I might pop. But that feeling of euphoria ended as fast as it had come when Mr. Hamilton said that he would do so *only* if I had a cosigner. Though Mr. Calhoun had warned me of this, I had honestly believed that if a banker heard my ideas, he'd jump at the opportunity to write me a big, fat check.

With my dream deflated and my ego in shreds, I rose from the chair. It was all I could do to shake Mr. Hamilton's hand. When Mr. Calhoun and I left the bank, I stopped outside the front door and looked at him. "Thank you for trying to help me, Mr. Calhoun. I was wondering—do you think if I asked Mr. Hamilton for less money, he'd give me a loan?"

"Less money would only ensure your failure. If you don't start a business out right, you're doomed, Teddi. Remember what I told you about negotiating?"

"You mean about how it's a game?"

"That's right. This is only the first quarter."

I fought back tears. "But if I can't start a business with less money and I can't get a loan for what I need, then how do I play this game?"

That question seemed to draw him up short. He studied me for the longest time. "I'll give it more thought and see what I come up with. And you keep thinking, too."

I shook his hand and walked across the parking lot. Plopping down inside my car, I let out a groan of frustration and pressed my forehead to the steering wheel.

∞

For the next two weeks, I trudged through my job at the diner. I forced a smile with each cup of coffee I poured, knowing that my survival depended on the tips my smile might bring. The way I calculated it, every smile was worth about seventy-eight cents, a little more on Sundays. At the rate I was going, it would take over ninety thousand smiles to earn enough money to open my own shop.

There weren't enough cups of coffee in my future to keep my dream alive.

Each day when my shift was through, I'd toss my apron into the hamper and head out the door with the newspaper tucked beneath my arm. I'd sit at the tiny kitchen table in my apartment and devour the employment ads, which were always filled with positions for bookkeepers, nurses, and of course secretaries, all of them offering Mama's most coveted prize—*fringe benefits*.

On a windy Tuesday morning, I was busy waiting tables when Mr. Calhoun walked in the door. I'd never seen him in the diner before, and as I watched him take a seat at a table against the wall, I prayed he'd come up with an idea of how I could get a loan.

Taking a deep breath and smoothing my apron, I approached his table. He smiled real friendly, but all he said was, "Good morning, Teddi. Two eggs over easy, wheat toast, and black coffee, please." Then he snapped open his newspaper.

I served his breakfast, hesitating for a moment after I set down his plate, but still he said nothing. When he paid his bill at the register and left without talking to me, I knew it was over—there was no plan, no game to be played.

From the front window, I watched Mr. Calhoun cross the street and get into his car, and when he pulled away from the curb, I felt sick to my stomach. Slowly, I began clearing his table. He hadn't left me a tip, not so much as a lousy dime. I piled his coffee cup and silverware onto the plate, and when I picked the plate up, an envelope with my name typed on the front was peeking out from beneath the paper place mat. I shoved it into my apron pocket, and when the breakfast rush wound down, I ran into the restroom, locked the door, and ripped open the envelope. Expecting to see a new business plan spelled out, one that would make my idea more appealing to a banker, I couldn't unfold the papers fast enough. But when I saw what those papers really were, stillness settled around me—the kind of stillness that comes when you're reminded of the powerful force that exists beyond your understanding.

I leaned against the wall and stared at the last page. On the bottom was a line with the name "Theodora Grace Overman" typed beneath it. To the right was another line. In a bold flourish above the word "Guarantor" was the signature of a man who would forever change my life: Preston J. Calhoun.

ဆာ

And now here I sat: Albert doing his repairs—slower than he used to but still with his trademark precision—and me in my small office that had once been Mr. Palmer's. The shop no longer had the wooden sign above the door that read: PALMER'S FINE ANTIQUES. Instead there were slender gold letters painted on the front window that simply read . . . TEDDI'S.

NINE

Though I had every intention of visiting my grandmother after work, I was still tired from my Kentucky trip. Deciding to take a quick nap on the sofa, I kicked off my shoes and closed my eyes. *Just a few minutes of rest,* I told myself. *Just a few . . .*

I woke with a start. My skirt was bunched around my waist, and threads of morning sun were weaving through my lace curtains. I sat up, feeling sweaty and disoriented when I looked at my watch. I'd slept for nearly ten hours. Eddie's bladder was surely about to explode. After taking him for a long walk, I showered and fussed with my hair before climbing into my car.

Traffic was light, and within fifteen minutes the entrance appeared on my left. A pair of old oaks stretched their twisted branches over the lawn, and the border gardens were well tended. The grounds were lovely and serene, but no amount of beauty could ease the sadness I felt each time I pulled in to the driveway. This was the Audrey Clayton Home—last stop for a handful of Charleston's most elderly citizens.

I never dreamed my grandmother would be one of them.

In the late summer of 1985, I had visited my family for a long weekend. On the morning of my departure, Daddy and Mama left the house for a Sunday breakfast meeting with neighboring farmers. When I lugged my suitcase out to the car, I saw Grammy sitting in the passenger seat. Attached to her glasses was a pair of oversize clip-on sunshades, and perched on her head was a red felt hat. I remembered the hat from an Easter when I was a child. It had been old then.

I leaned down and peered into the open window. "What are you doing, Grammy?"

"Well, not long ago I got to thinkin' that in all my years I'd never set foot outside Kentucky. Last night at supper, you said how much you wished we'd come for a visit. So here I am."

She was serious. In the backseat were a small suitcase and a tote bag filled with her favorite gardening tools.

My grandmother had loved Charleston so much that she stayed, claiming she didn't want to go home until Christmastime. But in November she fell, breaking her hip and femur, neither of which had properly healed. Grammy shocked everyone by deciding to live in Charleston.

That's when I found the Audrey Clayton Home. Italianate in style and built in the late 1880s, the house had been converted to an elder-care facility back in the 1960s. The main house offered the residents a feeling of home with its high ceilings, thick moldings, and arched doorways, but there was no mistaking the ever-present medicinal aroma.

I headed toward the yellow room, named for its sun-soaked walls and tall windows framed by floral chintz draperies. Miz Olson and Miz Fitzwater were sitting at a table having their morning tea. Though it was twenty past seven and both gals were still wearing robes, they were weighted down with multiple layers of jewelry: rhinestones, diamonds, and colorful gem treasures.

Miz Olson, who had been a Rockette back in the thirties, looked up. "G'mornin', Teddi."

Crystal-encrusted earrings, as big as walnuts, tugged at her thin lobes. One earring caught a ray of sun and threw a glint of light across the room.

"Well, look at you two, all glittery and glamorous this morning. Is there a special occasion?"

Miz Olson grinned. "It's Beauty Day. Those sweet girls from Lindy Lane's Beauty School are comin' to give us manicures."

"For free!" Miz Fitzwater added, resting her arm on her walker as if the weight of her bracelets were tiring her out.

I smiled. "Well, I hope y'all have fun."

"We always do." Miz Fitzwater waved, and the tinkling sound of her charm bracelet drifted through the air.

I passed the tiny library and turned down the hallway that led to the nonambulatory wing, a one-story brick addition at the back of the main house. While maneuvering around a cart piled high with freshly laundered linens, I saw a row of three brand-new wheelchairs lined up against the wall—the brightly polished chariots of the noble but failing aged. Dangling from the arms were large red tags printed with the words LIMITED LIFETIME GUARANTEE.

Yeah, I thought, *now, there's a safe guarantee. Limited lifetime. As if anyone living here needs reminding of how limited their lives have become.*

I ripped off every one of those tags and crammed them into my handbag. As I turned the corner, I could see her partially open door. On the wall next to the doorjamb was a green plastic nameplate that read: BELLE FORRESTER—ROOM 7.

I stepped to the doorway and peeked in.

And there she was, my Grammy Belle, sitting by the window in her rocking chair. Smack in the middle of the fault line of her final years, she was caving in on herself with each passing day. Arthritic, deformed knees peeked out from beneath the hem of her lavender robe, and wisps of white hair stood straight up from her scalp. On a small table next to her chair sat an open tin of cookies.

For a moment I stood and watched her, the way she examined a cookie before taking a bite. How she chewed with such simple joy that it made my heart ache. I waited until she swallowed, then lightly rapped on the door.

She looked up and smiled. Cream filling clung to the corners of her mouth, and her eyes grew huge behind the thick lenses of her glasses. "Teddi!" she said, brushing crumbs from her lap.

I wrapped her shrunken, brittle body in my arms and gave her a hug. "Good morning, Grammy."

"You smell so good. Just like bitin' into a fresh peach."

"Where'd you get the cookies?"

"Won 'em at bingo last night. Have one, honey. They're good."

"Maybe later. Would you like to go for a ride through the gardens?"

Her face lit up. "Oh, I would."

I helped her into the wheelchair, draped a sweater around her shoulders, and pushed her down the hallway. The electronic door opened with a *whoosh*, and fresh air rushed in, delighting my grandmother so much that she laughed. "What a *beautiful* day!"

As we approached the perennial garden, Grammy said, "You know what I just realized? I've only been on this earth for ninety-one planting seasons. Doesn't seem like much when you think of it that way."

I was caught so off guard by her statement that I didn't know what to say. All I could do was bend forward and kiss the top of her head. When we reached a shady spot, I parked the wheelchair and sat down on a bench next to my grandmother.

"Lately I've been missing my peonies. Remember how many I had? Lord, I loved 'em all."

Grammy slipped back in time and shared stories about her gardens, speaking of her flowers as if they were her children. Though she knew I had driven home to visit Mama over the weekend, she didn't ask about it. I couldn't tell if she was hoping to avoid the subject or perhaps had momentarily forgotten, so I decided not to say anything, at least not today.

While she told a story about planting tomatoes that segued into how, during a bitter-cold winter during the Great Depression, she'd stuffed newspapers between layers of her clothes to keep from freezing to death, I watched ribbons of light push through the trees and come to rest across her hands.

Grammy's hands: It broke my heart whenever I looked at them.

When I was a little girl, my grandmother had been a sorceress of all growing things—the high priestess of peonies and a heroine to any hollyhock that ever knew the pleasure of her touch. I swear her hydrangeas put out blooms the size of cantaloupes.

I could still recall a summer's day when I was no more than four years old. Grammy had taken me outside while she tended her garden. After spreading a blanket on the ground, she gave me a canning jar filled with pop beads so I'd have something to play with. Hanging her wicker basket over her arm, she disappeared into the riotous colors of her flowers. Then came the butterflies, and my grandmother told me all about them as she worked.

"See that one? That's a cookie-dittle. And see that one over there by the fence? That's a wise old bonnie-bow."

When the butterflies moved deeper into her garden, I emptied the pop beads onto the quilt while my grandmother began cutting flowers. "Smell this one, sugar," she said, pressing a bloom to my nose. "It's a peony. I suspect this is what heaven smells like."

Grammy encouraged me to sample the scent of every flower she placed in her basket. The more I smelled, the more I wanted to collect all that perfume. I took the empty canning jar and went from flower to flower, gathering each fragrance. I still remember the tenderness in my grandmother's eyes as she held the jar in her callused hands and tightened the lid.

But she was dealt a cruel card, and the hands that had once created magic with a little soil and a handful of seeds now lay gnarled with arthritis in her lap.

We talked and shared stories until nine o'clock, and after wheeling Grammy back to her room and kissing her good-bye, I set off for town. The minute I unlocked the side door of my shop, I heard the rapid-fire clicking of typewriter keys echoing down the hall.

Inez was a spitfire, at typing and just about everything else. I had hired her three years ago, and from the day she began her job, it felt like she'd always belonged. Last month she turned fifty and had ushered in that milestone birthday by treating herself to a complete makeover. Her once salt-and-pepper hair was now fiery red and supplemented by a pouffy wiglet she bobby-pinned to the crown of her head, and her formerly nondescript eyebrows were drawn on in a way that gave her a look of perpetual surprise.

Albert and I still weren't used to it.

"Good morning, Inez."

She continued typing and raised her voice. "Nothing *good* about it. The copy machine is on the fritz, and the repairman can't come till tomorrow. And you forgot to buy sugar and toilet paper *again*. We're almost out of both."

"Sorry. I'll run out at lunch and—"

"I already took care of it, gave Albert money from petty cash. He just left for the store."

"Thanks." I looked at the old IBM Selectric. "I wish you'd let me buy you a computer. It'd be easier, and you could use it to keep track of inventory."

"Forget it. They're nothing more than a crazy fad. Besides, they're ugly. I like my Selectric."

"All right, have it your way." Just as I turned to leave, I remembered. "Inez, when you've got a minute would you look up the price of the Limoges box that had the frog on the top? Then send a bill to—"

"Oh, let me guess." She stopped typing and swiveled in her chair to face me. "Miz Poteet's been at it again?"

"Ding-ding-ding, you win the prize. I caught her red-handed, right as she was shoving a sterling candlestick into her handbag. But she walked out with the Limoges box. I could wring her neck."

"Well, at least you're making an extra profit on her."

"Extra profit?"

Inez's eyes twinkled. "Last year I started adding ten percent to the bill for everything she steals."

"Are you serious?"

"Serious as a train wreck. Anyway, I think it's time to up the ante. Starting today I'm adding twenty percent."

I leaned against the doorframe and thought for a moment. "I like the idea, but it might be unfair—"

"Baloney. It's fair as hell." Inez crossed her legs and gave a tug to the hem of her skirt. "Think about it. When people get divorced, there's alimony. And what *is* alimony anyway? It's money owed for years of torment. Just ask me, I should know. That's exactly what Miz Poteet is giving you. She's been stealing from you ever since you gave her that quote to design her living room."

"I know, but I don't understand why."

"Because she wanted to tell her highfalutin friends that Teddi Overman redid her house, but she didn't want to pay for it. So anyway, from now on I'm adding twenty percent. If she keeps this up, I'll add thirty. Then we'll be able to retire in five years and I'll be driving a red convertible."

"Well, I—"

Inez peered over the top of her glasses and grinned. "Think of it as designamony."

"Designamony?" I laughed.

Looking enormously pleased with herself, Inez swiveled her short legs back beneath her desk and resumed typing.

After placing orders for gesso, oil paints, and sheets of silver leaf, I opened the shop for business. While straightening a painting that hung above a Savonarola chair, I heard the phone ring. A moment later Inez called out, "Teddi, it's for you."

I walked into my office and leaned across the desk to pick up the receiver. As I listened to every word being said, my mind chanted, *Are you serious? Do you mean it . . . do you really mean it . . . ?*

The call was brief, and the moment it ended, I dialed my best friend. Listening to the phone ring, I wound the cord around my fingers. I was about to hang up when she answered. Olivia had a late-night kind of voice that made it impossible to discern if she'd just woken up or had just gotten home from being out all night.

"Olivia, can you meet me at Pernelia's at one o'clock?"

"You *know* it's my day off. I was sleeping in. This better be important."

"It is," I promised, pushing my office door closed with the toe of my shoe. "You'll never guess who just called me . . ."

TEN

At twelve-forty I left the shop with a wicker lunch basket swinging from my hand. Turning on King Street, I walked several blocks, slowing to look at the window displays, especially those of my competitors. After crossing Clifford Street, I entered the rear entrance of the cemetery.

Set back from the sidewalk, the old iron gates stood open to a path so narrow it could be easily missed. Shaded by a canopy of ancient trees and fringed by overgrowth that tickled my ankles, I walked into the cool shade.

Though I didn't know many of the residents' names, I had the feeling they enjoyed my visits. Some might say the property was a tangled mess of plantings left to run wild, but I'd always thought that added to its charm. Olivia and I had been coming here for years and agreed it was the closest thing to a secret garden either one of us had ever seen.

Reaching my favorite spot, I brushed away a few fallen leaves and sat on the moss-stained marble bench. From my lunch basket, I removed a thermos of lemonade and gave it a few shakes. While unscrewing the cap, I spoke over my shoulder, "How are you today, Pernelia? I'm feeling wonderful. This is a big day. In fact, I circled it on my calendar in red."

Of course Pernelia never says anything, but I liked to think we'd become friends. I leaned over and blew a layer of dust from her stone. Sunlight settled across the carved words:

PERNELIA M. OWNBY
DIED ON MARCH 4TH 1889
IN THE 72ND YEAR OF HER AGE.
MAY HEAVEN'S ETERNAL JOY BE THINE

Other than its graceful arch, the stone was simple and devoid of decoration. I imagined that it suited Pernelia's personality.

While taking a sip of lemonade, I saw a flash of red on Archdale Street. I peered through the lacy vegetation and watched Olivia Dupree park her '64 Chevy pickup at the curb—a restored beauty, right down to the gleaming silver grille. A few moments later, she came around the side of the stone church, the oldest Unitarian church in the South.

Olivia maneuvered around the plots, her curly chestnut hair pulled in to a cockeyed ponytail; chances were good that she'd not even bothered to brush it first. The sleeves of her coral linen blouse were rolled up to reveal densely freckled arms, her jeans were worn to near disintegration, and peeking from above her brown leather ankle boots were ruffle-topped socks. Olivia possessed a chameleon kind of beauty. Though she was approaching forty, sometimes, in just the right light, she didn't look a minute over twenty-five. Some days she'd flounce around town in a Gypsy-style skirt and sandals, looking mysterious and as delicate as a cameo, while other days she'd dress in denim and black leather from head to toe. Those were the days when she looked as if she could easily, perhaps even gladly, kick someone to the curb. I could detect Olivia's mood by the clothes she wore more than by the words she said. Like me, she wasn't a native of this glowing city, but she'd succumbed to its lure back in the late seventies and had moved from Jacksonville, Florida, without looking back. Unlike me, Olivia had once been married. His name was Eric, and after five years into a marriage that Olivia claimed was blissful, he'd left her without warning. And he did so to pursue the love of his life—a young blond photographer from California, who oddly was also named Eric. Though Olivia's former husband apologized profusely and gave her everything, including the house they'd shared, the split-up had come close to destroying her.

Trotting at Olivia's side was her trusted guardian. Bear was a big brownish black mixed-breed dog that she adopted from a shelter on the day she got divorced. When he saw me, he looked at Olivia. She gave a nearly imperceptible command, and he joyfully loped forward, all but knocking me off the bench. "Hey, Bear," I said, regaining my balance. "Wow, you smell good."

"He had a bath yesterday," Olivia said as she plopped down next to me. "Rolled in something terrible. I don't even want to know what it was. He's the smartest dog I've ever had, but he loves to roll in the most disgusting things."

"Sorry about waking you," I said, unwrapping my sandwich.

Olivia peeled the top from a yogurt container. "Apology accepted. So now that I'm here, let's have it."

"Well, when I was up home, I all but begged Mama to come for a visit. But that's always our parting ritual. I beg, she says maybe, and that's the end of it. So when she called and said she wanted to spend a week with me, I about fainted."

Olivia licked her spoon and looked at me thoughtfully. "Any idea why she changed her mind?"

"I can't imagine. At first I wondered if she was thinking about selling the farm, but she's doing pretty well leasing the land to a neighboring farmer, so that's probably not it."

"You've lived here for . . . what, eighteen years? And all of a sudden she wants to come visit? Sounds serious to me. So will I get to meet her? I'm dying to, you know." Olivia turned on her hip and said, "Sorry, Pernelia—just a figure of speech."

"Of course you'll meet Mama. She's amazed that you make a living restoring and selling old books."

"Not old books, Teddi. *Rare* books. There's a huge difference."

"I know, I know. Sorry."

Olivia's lips curved into a wry smile. "I wonder what she'll think of my Pez collection."

I laughed and took a bite of my sandwich. "She'll be speechless. And she calls *me* a junk picker."

"Guaranteed that'll change when she sees your shop."

"I'm not so sure about that. Mama's not inclined to admit she's wrong."

Olivia tore open a bag of pretzels, crushed a few in her hands, and tossed the crumbs to a chickadee that was pecking around Emma Wilson's stone. On the opposite side of the cemetery, an elderly couple strolled arm in arm along a path. He was dapper in a beige seersucker suit and a blue bow tie, and she looked feminine in a flowery print skirt that moved gently in the breeze.

"Look how cute they are," I whispered, nodding toward the couple. "Do you think we're missing out?"

Olivia unscrewed the cap of her water bottle and took a long drink. "On what, getting old?"

"C'mon, you know what I mean. They just seem so . . . I dunno . . . so connected."

"Of course they're connected. They're holding each other up."

"I'm serious. Look how they walk in perfect unison. Maybe they used to be dancers. Do you think you'll ever get married again?"

Olivia unwrapped a cheese-and-tomato sandwich. "Well, if the past few years are any indication, then I'd say the chances are slim. That last one stripped me to the bone and left me for dead. I never want to go through anything like that again."

"Well, what did you expect? He was only twenty-three years old."

"Age doesn't matter," she said defensively. "I adored Louis. It was the most intoxicating two months of my life."

I laughed. "It was the most *lustful* two months."

Olivia gave me a narrow-eyed look. "What's with these questions? Have you met someone?"

"No," I said, grabbing my napkin as the wind tried to steal it away. "But some days I wonder if something's wrong with me. I mean, think about it. I'm in the prime of my life and I'm not even interested in going on a date. Why am I so happy being alone?"

Olivia nearly choked on her sandwich.

"What's so funny?"

"Teddi, you're the only person I've known who analyzes why she's happy. Does your mind ever rest?"

I gave her a nudge with my elbow. "No. It doesn't."

"Hey, on an entirely different subject, I forgot to tell you that I've got a new treasure. Do you have time to take a look after lunch?"

"Sure, as long as you'll drive me back to the shop."

While Bear lounged in a spot of sun near the stone of Jonas Buckley, Olivia and I discussed topics that ranged from how many more bookshelves I thought she could fit into her upstairs den to the nineteenth-century tulipwood desk I'd recently acquired for my shop.

When we stood to leave, I looked over my shoulder. "See you soon, Pernelia."

Olivia winked. "Take care, honey. Rest well."

Within a few minutes, Olivia turned her truck on Montagu Street and rolled to a stop in front of her house—a blue-painted Federal nearly hidden from view by a wall of dense hedges. When she unlocked the front door, a series of shrill beeps sounded before she punched in her code and the alarm fell silent.

Should anyone attempt to break into her home, he'd be in for a shock on three counts: Her security system was state-of-the-art, Bear was a highly trained guard dog, plus Olivia claimed to have a pump-action shotgun and swore she knew how to use it.

The reason for the heavy security was Olivia's work. As a well-regarded book conservator, she often had upwards of a million dollars' worth of rare books and manuscripts in her possession.

To enter Olivia's home was to experience a quirky smorgasbord for the eyes. In every corner, on every shelf, and behind every door, something offbeat was waiting to be discovered. A person could spend days wandering through the rooms and still not see everything. Her collections were eclectic and ranged from marionettes (Howdy Doody, Captain Hook, and Tinker Bell) to perfume bottles to her prized Pez collection. Her foyer walls were crammed with black-and-white photographs of old Hollywood stars—Jackie Gleason, the Lone Ranger, and her all-time favorite, Marlon Brando. The shelves above her kitchen cabinets were filled with at least fifty old soda-pop bottles, which wouldn't have been so strange had they not been topped by hand puppets.

Whenever I teased Olivia and called her a junkaholic, she'd lift her chin and fire back, "And *you* are a furniture slut. I swear, you just about drop your panties for any old walnut chest that comes your way."

Then we'd both laugh at the truth of it.

Today, as I did each time before entering Olivia's workroom, I joined her at the kitchen sink, where we washed our hands with a lemony astringent soap. The first time Olivia had invited me to handle a rare book she was restoring and had told me to wash my hands, I thought it was odd.

"Why don't you wear thin white gloves like they do in the movies?" I'd asked.

Olivia rolled her eyes. "That's a silly myth perpetuated by clueless Hollywood producers. She tapped her thumb and forefinger together. "A light touch and dexterity are most important. Only the pads of the fingers should be used."

With our hands clean and thoroughly dried, I followed her into her climate-controlled workroom, where overstuffed bookcases sagged beneath volumes of literary works—Tolstoy, Faulkner, and Elizabeth Barrett Browning.

Mirroring my passion for antiques was Olivia's strong relationship with books. She devoured them and often read as many as five a week. She hunted them down, mended their wounds, and brought them back to life.

Olivia walked past an oak worktable that sat in the middle of the room. To the left, a wheeled utility cart held jars of conservation glue, sheaves of acid-free paper, and glass tubes filled with bookbinding needles. On the far wall was a large framed photograph of the Little Rascals. Olivia slid her hand along the bottom edge of the frame and pushed a button. Hinged on the right, the photograph swung open to reveal a small vault recessed into the wall. She waited for me to look away so she could turn the dial. I knew the drill and didn't take it personally. When it came to the vault, she didn't trust anyone.

Reaching inside, she removed a small book and ceremoniously placed it in my hands. "You're holding a first edition, first impression of *The Tale of Peter Rabbit*. It's one of only two hundred fifty copies in the entire world—issued privately by Beatrix Potter—and it's signed. She was rejected by so many publishing houses that she self-published in 1901."

Carefully, I leafed through the pages. "The illustrations are fantastic. Josh loved this story. I read it to him so many times that both of us knew it by heart." I closed the book and handed it to Olivia. "Mama will be fascinated when she sees what you do."

"I can't wait to meet her. In fact, I'll cook a special dinner for the two of you. Something tells me it will be a *very* interesting evening."

From over my shoulder, I glanced into Olivia's foyer, where a soft-sculpture witch sat in a rusty Radio Flyer wagon. "I have no doubt."

Olivia set the book on her worktable and looked at her watch. "C'mon, I'll drive you back to the shop."

"You know what? I've changed my mind. It's a beautiful day for a walk."

After pulling my empty lunch basket from the seat of Olivia's truck, I strolled along the sidewalk and thought about my mother's upcoming visit.

Daddy had driven to Charleston once, about a year after I left home. He didn't tell me he was coming, and when I saw him walk into Mr. Palmer's shop, I was so surprised that I let out a whoop and nearly knocked him over when I catapulted myself into his arms.

His damp hair was lined with deep comb marks that reminded me of his freshly plowed fields. He wore a brand-new pair of brown twill pants that still had creases from being folded on a store shelf. Though he was wearing his old farm boots, I could tell that he'd slathered them with oil and cleaned them up as best as he could.

Daddy and Mr. Palmer hit it off, and after they talked for a while, I showed him around the workshop and introduced him to Albert. Mr. Palmer gave me the rest of the day off, which I spent showing Daddy my little apartment and giving him a walking tour of downtown Charleston. After dinner we strolled along the Battery, where the mansions were splashed with the last light of the day. We ended up at White Point Garden and sat on a bench that overlooked the water. As usual, neither of us said much, but we were glad to be together.

After watching a sailboat glide by, Daddy reached into his shirt pocket and pulled out a small envelope. "From your brother," he said, handing it to me.

Inside was a tiny gray feather tipped in bright yellow and a note that read:

> *It's good to fly in new skies.*
> *The goldfinch sends happiness.*

"He misses you, Teddi. We all do."

"I miss everyone, too. I'll try to come home more often."

Daddy patted my knee. "I'm not trying to make you feel guilty. I'm glad you're happy down here and doin' work that you enjoy. That's real important. I'm proud of you."

"Thanks, Daddy."

The evening light moved across his face, accentuating the deep lines of his hard-lived life. His callused hands were splayed across his knees.

"I want you to promise me something, Peaches."

"Sure. What is it?"

He glanced over his shoulder at the grand old homes, and his voice grew serious when he said, "Don't forget where you came from."

ॐ

While packing up Eddie's toys and food for my drive back home, I thought about my father's words. He needn't have worried. Charlestonians treated me kindly and trusted me to mend their precious antiques, but I wasn't one of them. And though I'd come to love Charleston, I did so with a detached admiration, much the same as one might feel while standing behind velvet ropes to admire a sculpture in a museum.

It was a privilege to live within the fragrant boundaries of this ornamental city. Shaped by a rich history and quiet formalities, Charleston was a genteel community of charm and propriety that gazed upon itself with restrained pride and satisfaction. Though a great many of its residents lived the gold-dipped life of the high-born, rarely was that fact flaunted.

I couldn't wait to introduce Mama to Charleston, and as I aimed my car north, I envisioned the two of us sitting on my tiny porch wrapped in our robes as we talked over breakfast. I wanted to walk her down the alleyways where, if you knew exactly the right place to peek, you'd get a glimpse of a garden that would surely take your breath away. I even went so far as to imagine us laughing together as we strolled along King Street and window-shopped. Maybe I'd slide my arm around hers and she'd give me a squeeze. Maybe . . .

&

When I reached Slade, my head was crammed with scenarios that traversed an emotional landscape from the most childlike (the two of us staying up late at night and sharing our secrets) to the most implausible (Mama would walk into my shop and gasp with pride).

I pulled in to the driveway, gathered my overnight bag, and went inside, but Mama wasn't there. I called out several times and climbed the stairs to see if she was in the bathroom, but she wasn't. When I stepped to her bedroom doorway and saw a partially packed suit-case sitting open on the bed, I smiled. It wasn't until I returned to the kitchen that I saw the note she'd left on the counter.

> *Teddi,*
>   *Stella and I are going to the beauty parlor and to run a few errands. We'll be back before 5. I hope you'll take a nap.*
>
> *Mom*

More hungry than tired, I rooted through the pantry and gathered a box of crackers, then filled a teacup with Mama's homemade applesauce. Grabbing the newest edition of *Woman's Day* magazine from the basket on the kitchen table, I walked outside. While Eddie chewed a handful of treats, I sat on the porch swing and dug into the applesauce. With the magazine spread across my lap, I began leafing through the pages filled with recipes and helpful hints that were as foreign to me as my choice of career was to my mother. I smiled when I saw the dog-eared page about the many uses of baking soda, but my smile faded when I came to an article in the center of the magazine.

Printed in bold letters at the top of the page were the words "Choosing the Right Name for Your Baby."

ELEVEN

SUMMER 1959

I was sitting on the steps of the back porch listening to the buzzing and humming that skipped across the fields. All sorts of bugs lived out there—crickets, katydids, and big green grasshoppers—busy doing whatever bugs did to create all that noise.

The grass beneath the clothesline was burned to wisps of gold, and the tiger lilies along the side of the house had fainted from sunstroke. I watched a chubby Baltimore oriole swoop from the sky and take a long drink from the chipped birdbath. Off in the distance, I could see Daddy cutting hay.

Balanced on my lap was a clear plastic bowl filled with water. Perry, my painted turtle, floated in the water while I sang him a song: *"Smile and swim and be happy. The sun is our best friend. It's summertime, and you and me . . ."*

Behind me, the screen door opened and Mama stepped onto the porch. She looked all puffy and was shiny with sweat. For a long time, she stood with her hands on her hips, her eyes fixed on something off in the distance. A low groan left her lips as she lowered herself down next to me. She lifted her hair off her neck and groaned again, her sleeveless blouse stained with sweat and frayed at the armholes.

"You think life's all happy-dappy, don't you? Sitting out here with that turtle, singin' your little songs. Well, go ahead and sing, Teddi. Get it out of your system now. When you grow up, all that singin' will stop."

She yanked her blouse over her stomach and looked down. "Lord, I don't want to go through this. I'm too old. Too tired."

My heart sped up. The look on Mama's face was scaring me.

Tilting her head, she studied me with red-rimmed eyes. Then she leaned forward and ran her hands through her hair, sending droplets of sweat splashing onto the step below us. "It's so hot. I can't take it anymore. Maybe I'll put my head in the oven and just go ahead and finish myself off. At least I'd be out of my misery. Then you could sing at my funeral. How about *that*?"

Her words set my ears on fire. The sun's reflection in the bowl of water grew bright, so bright that my eyes hurt. I didn't know what I done to make Mama so mad.

She grabbed hold of the porch rail and hoisted herself up. The screen door made a slap when she went back inside the house.

After that day I spent as much time outside as I could. But when I had to do house chores or stay inside because it was raining, sometimes I'd peek into the kitchen to see if Mama had her head in the oven.

When harvest season arrived and bushels of fresh-picked vegetables lined the porch in bright reds, greens, and yellows, Daddy drove Mama to the hospital. While she was gone, summer scorched the farm. It was so hot that Grammy and I wore thin cotton nightgowns from morning till night. We listened to the radio and canned tomatoes and butter beans as a fan hummed from the kitchen counter. After supper we'd walk through the fields and pick wildflowers while Grammy told stories.

About a week after Mama went away, a cool breeze blew in, and that was the day Daddy brought her home. I watched from the kitchen window as they came across the lawn. When Daddy opened the screen door, Mama stepped inside and handed me a yellow bundle.

Inside was a baby brother.

I thought he was mine, a gift from Mama as a way of saying she was sorry for setting my ears on fire.

After Daddy helped Mama ease into a chair, he turned to me. "We couldn't decide on a name. So we agreed that you should pick."

I looked at the bundle and chewed my lip. I was good at picking names for animals, but this? This was different.

Why are they leaving this up to me? What if I make a mistake?

I was so overwhelmed that I didn't know what to think. While peering at his little pink face, I murmured, "Gosh."

"Hey," Daddy said, "I like that name. Josh . . . Josh Overman. Has a real nice sound."

I snapped my head up. "But I—"

"I like it, too," Mama said. Though her voice was weary, she smiled when she added, "But, Teddi, try not to mumble when you speak."

Grammy handed Mama a cup of tea. "Josh is a fine name."

And that was it.

But naming something or someone brings on a natural sense of responsibility, or at least that's how it felt to me. So I took to caring for my little brother, bathing him in a rubber dishpan out on the back porch and pushing him all over the farm in a rickety buggy.

"My name is Teddi," I said while guiding the buggy down a slope. "Can you say Teddi?" I stopped at the edge of the vegetable patch and lifted a chubby toad from beneath one of Grammy's hosta plants. I placed him in the buggy with my brother and grinned. "This is my favorite garden friend."

I steered the buggy along a bumpy path and into the shifting shadows of the woods. "This is where animals and birds live." I pointed to the top of a craggy tree. "Mr. Owl lives right up there. Do you know what he says? He says *hoo-hoo, hoo-hoo.* Can you say that? And look, these are walnuts." I collected a handful and put them in the buggy along with my brother and the toad. When I returned to the house, Josh was all but buried beneath the treasures I'd gathered.

My little brother was so wonder-struck by the world around him that never once did I hear him cry. He'd sit in that old buggy with his eyes wide and his ears pricked sharp as a deer's. It seemed to me that nature spoke to him more plainly than any human voice. I'd watch how he turned his head, how his eyes would focus. He was aware in ways that I clearly saw but didn't understand—as if the wind moving through the trees and the subtle change in a blackbird's song told him the truth of things.

One day I was bouncing Josh on my knees and accidentally banged his head on the kitchen table. I hugged him real tight and told him I was sorry. His eyes filled with tears, and I thought for sure he'd wail, but he blinked them away and smiled at me. I could hardly believe it.

Mama said she'd never heard of a baby that didn't cry. She was worried that something was wrong with him. But Grammy said no, that she should thank her lucky stars. Mama looked away and said she didn't have any of those.

The first clearly spoken words to leave my little brother's lips came during the summer he was two years old. He was in a playpen under the maple tree, chewing on a soggy cracker. When he saw me walking across the lawn with a basket of tomatoes, he stood on his tiptoes and squealed, "Teddi!" Then he pointed to the woods and called out, "Mr. Owl—*hoo-hoo, hoo-hoo!*"

☙❧

With each passing year, my brother was drawn deeper into nature's wonders. By the time he was ten, he worshipped the woods and their creatures with a reverence few could grasp. He saw holiness where others saw only the ordinary. Trees formed the spires of the cathedral where his prayers were gentle footsteps over sacred terrain. He knelt on the rocks of the Red River and drank in the company of rainbow trout, and he whistled in harmony with the birds.

It was during his early teenage years that Josh became a solitary, singular boy—courageous, silent, and often unreadable. He was also observant. No bird sailed over our farm that my brother couldn't identify. Never was there an animal track he didn't recognize, no species of tree he couldn't name.

He was a boy who on a frigid winter's day stood in the middle of the barren cornfield and pulled an apple from his jacket pocket. Under the gaze of a young six-point buck, my brother slowly moved forward until he was within seven yards or so of the deer. He stopped and placed the apple on the ground. Taking two slow steps backward, Josh lowered himself until he was sitting.

The buck stood motionless, his eyes fixed on my brother, his tail flicking. Plumes of white left his nostrils as he took a series of tentative steps forward. When he was within reach of the apple, he stopped. Then, with one more flick of his tail, the deer lowered his head and began eating.

What had the deer seen in my brother's eyes, eyes that so rarely looked into those of his family?

But I never grasped how fully my brother's soul was bound to nature until I drove home during the summer of his seventeenth birthday.

TWELVE

It was a warm afternoon in September of 1976, and the air carried the first dry scents of autumn. I had driven home from Charleston, and when I parked my car and climbed out, Grammy Belle waved from the back porch.

"Honey! I'm so glad you're here." She made her way down the steps one at a time, and after I gave her a hug, she pointed toward the barn. "Go up and see your brother. But make sure you walk in real slow, and don't say anything unless it's a whisper."

"Why, what's going on?"

"It's a surprise. Go on, now. He's been waitin' for you."

When I reached the barn, the sliding door was open just enough for me to squeeze through. At first I didn't see anything, but as my eyes adjusted to the dim light, a flash of movement from the open doorway at the back of the barn caught my attention. After maneuvering around a stack of lumber, I saw a sleeping bag spread out on bales of hay. Off to the side sat a lawn chair and an old floor lamp.

Beyond the back door, I could see the outline of my brother. He was standing inside the old cowshed—a weatherworn structure with a rusted tin roof. Across the front of the shed was a newly built half wall, and the opening at the top had been fully enclosed with chicken wire.

"Josh?" I whispered.

He turned, smiling shyly as I stepped forward. Inside the shed were several tree limbs, each one propped into place between the ceiling and the dirt floor. Startled by a flash of white, my lips parted as a large bird came to rest on one of the limbs. A bird the likes of which I'd never seen.

"Isn't he great? I named him Ghost."

The bird's body was solid and compact; his curved beak looked razor sharp. The size of his talons was shocking. Other than the thin stripe of rusty-colored feathers that marked one of his shoulders, the bird was as white as fresh milk. Turning his head, he looked at me with intense, deep amber eyes.

I leaned closer. "What kind of bird is he?"

"Red-tailed hawk. But he's partial albino. I've seen pictures of them in books, but I'd never seen one in real life until Ghost. There's no way to know for sure, but since females are bigger than males, I'm pretty sure Ghost is a male."

"How'd he get here?"

"I found him over by Gray's Arch. Somebody shot him—probably a poacher. The bullet grazed his chest and passed clean through his left wing. I got him into my knapsack and brought him home. I held him while Grammy cleaned his wounds with tea tree oil, and then I made him a wing splint out of cardboard, Popsicle sticks, and thread."

"You *did?*"

Josh nodded. "Then we wrapped him in gauze so he couldn't move his wing. Dad helped me build the wall and put up the wire so we could keep him safe." Josh turned toward the hawk and smiled. "You've healed up real good, haven't you, Ghost?"

The bird's beauty was both delicate and powerful. In one graceful swoop, he landed on the limb closest to my brother.

"Menewa," Josh whispered, not taking his eyes off the bird. "Remember when I was a little kid and you told me the story of how the hawk was my guardian?"

I curled my fingers through the holes in the wire enclosure and smiled. "Yes . . . Menewa. Great Warrior."

Josh and I stood, he inside the flight cage with his back pressed against the half wall, and me leaning so far forward that my nose touched the wire, wire as necessary as it was symbolic. For I knew it was impossible to enter my brother's world. The most I could do was observe.

"So now what?" I asked.

"I'm gonna set him free."

"When?"

"As soon as you go down to the house and tell everyone so they can watch. He's been ready for over a week, but I waited for you to get here."

I pushed my finger through a hole in the wire mesh and touched my brother's arm. "Thanks."

Backing away, I turned and walked through the darkened barn. When I reached the door, I ran full throttle toward the house and burst through the kitchen door. "Hurry! Josh is getting ready to set Ghost free!"

Daddy set down his weather diary and pushed himself up from the recliner, Mama stopped peeling potatoes, and Grammy closed her recipe box and rose from the table.

When we arrived at the shed, Josh was wearing a pair of heavy suede gloves. He already had hold of the hawk, the fingers of his right hand threaded firmly around the bird's ankles. Ghost flapped his wings a few times when he saw us, but when Josh whispered something, he quieted.

Daddy opened the metal clip on the flight cage. "You ready, son?"

Josh nodded and pressed his left hand over the hawk's breast. "Okay, Ghost. This is your big day."

My father opened the door, and with Ghost held snugly against his chest, Josh stepped out. No one said a word as we followed him down the tractor path and into the center of the field. Stepping to the side, a good six yards away from Josh, we waited.

And waited.

My brother stood as if in prayer, his head tipped forward, his lips nearly touching the top of Ghost's head. He spoke low, his words rolling into an incantation I couldn't hear.

The landscape hushed, and even the wind stilled when Josh raised his head toward the sky. Again he said something I couldn't hear. Slowly, he lowered Ghost to his hip. Then, in a single fluid movement, he swept his arms high and released the hawk.

In a powerful rush and flash of feathers, Ghost lifted into the air, building speed as he flew over the field. He flew cockeyed at first and then straightened out, gaining altitude until he became a perfect silhouette in the sky.

I cheered, Grammy and Mama clapped, and Daddy stood with his hands shading his eyes and a smile on his face. Josh stood with his thumbs tucked in his pockets, a breeze blowing his dark curls away from his face, his eyes fixed on the hawk.

Just before reaching the woods, Ghost took a sudden hard turn to his left. I gasped and covered my mouth with my hands. His injured wing was giving out. I watched, horrified, as he began a heartbreaking descent.

But Ghost wasn't tumbling. He was turning. Turning back toward the field.

Toward my brother.

He swept higher and higher, and with his wings spread wide and held in perfect stillness, Ghost soared above Josh and then headed toward the woods.

It was then that I knew.

My brother belonged to the forest, its creatures, and all its mysteries. And they belonged to him.

৩৩

Sometimes I'd think of my brother and be overcome by paralyzing grief, while other times I felt a blistering anger. Anger so raw that if he showed his face, I'd slap him senseless. And then there were days when the emptiness he'd left behind was unbearable.

This was one of those days.

The year after he disappeared, Mama pulled me aside and took firm hold of my shoulders. With tear-filled eyes, she told me to stop going into the woods to look for him. She said it was time that I let him go so his soul could rest in peace—she said that he was dead.

But I had reason to believe otherwise.

After Josh disappeared, I made the long drive home every few weeks to scour the hidden places we'd loved since childhood. I'd hike deep into the woods, cup my hands around my mouth, and call his name. Then I'd listen, hopeful that the mountains would send the echo of his voice back to me. I wrote him letters that I folded inside waterproof plastic containers, leaving them tucked in secret places that we'd often visited. I even left one between two giant boulders we had played on as children.

Three weeks later and in freezing temperatures, I made the long trek again. All the containers were just as I'd left them, and when I reached the boulders, exhausted and numb from the cold, the plastic container was still there but it was in a different position.

And it was empty.

I wept and rejoiced and called out my brother's name, and then I sat on the boulder with the empty container in my hands and wondered what it meant.

Had Josh really found my letter, or had a hiker discovered my neatly folded pages and taken them? If it really had been Josh, wouldn't he have placed a message inside—a pebble or a leaf or maybe even a feather? And why was the plastic container resealed and put back where I'd left it?

But then again, that would be just like him.

THIRTEEN

Reliving that day was too painful, and I rose from the porch swing so fast it flew forward and smacked the back of my thighs. I yelped and tried to rub away the sting. With Eddie trotting at my heels, I walked inside the house and turned on the radio. While I was washing my cup at the sink and listening to a local news channel, the phone rang.

Grabbing a dish towel, I trotted around the table toward the wall phone while drying my hands. "Hello."

"Teddi! Thank goodness you're there. I called earlier, and when you didn't answer, I got worried."

"Hi, Stella. I just got in a little bit ago, and—"

"Honey, stay real calm. Everything will be all right."

I stretched the cord across the kitchen and turned off the radio. "What happened?"

"Your mother and I went to the beauty parlor, and then she wanted to stop at the dry cleaners. When she got out of the car, she wasn't moving right, seemed clumsy, and said she felt tingly. I got her back in the car and drove her straight to Clark Regional."

Slam went my heart into my ribs. "Is that where she is now?"

"Yes. But don't panic. She seems fine. Even argued with the nurses when they took her to have some tests done."

"I'll be right there!"

After gathering my handbag and reassuring Eddie that I'd be back, I set off for the hospital, which was a good forty minutes away. I drove fast, hands clamped on the steering wheel as my mind raced in every direction. I was knotted with worry, and yet the timing of Mama's sudden ailment seemed suspect. Was this some prank she'd conjured up to get out of coming to Charleston, or had something really happened? While passing a string of cars, I raised my voice and said aloud, "This better not be some stunt you're pulling, Mama. 'Cause if it is, I swear I'll never forgive you."

When I reached the hospital, a woman at the information desk directed me to Mama's room. As I hurried down the hallway, I glanced into a small waiting area and saw Stella sitting in a chair by the window. Though she smiled when she saw me, she couldn't mask the worry in her eyes.

"I just went down to her room, but she's not back from having her tests yet."

I sat in a chair next to Stella. "What kind of tests?"

"Well, they gave her medicine to lower her blood pressure, and then they hooked her up to some kind of machine that made a graph of her heartbeats. Not long after that, a neurologist came in. He asked her a lot of questions and had her touch her nose with her fingertips. Then he held up a pencil and had her follow it with her eyes while he moved it around her head. He spent quite a bit of time checking her reflexes and asking questions."

"How high was her blood pressure, did he say?"

Stella wrung her hands. "If he mentioned a number, I didn't hear it. Nurses and lab people were in and out—there was so much commotion. But he said he was ordering a CT scan. Lord, I feel so stupid. Is that where they take pictures of your brain?"

"Yes. Did she say anything about having a headache or falling?"

"No. And as far as I could tell, she was just fine up until we got to the dry cleaners. But—"

"Excuse me," a young nurse said from the doorway. "Mrs. Over-man's back in her room."

We hustled down the hall and into Mama's room, where she lay propped up by two pillows. Other than her hair going every which way and the annoyed expression on her face, I thought she looked fine.

Before I could speak, she shook her head. "There's nothing wrong with me, and I *don't* want to be here."

I leaned over the bed rail and gave her a kiss on the cheek. "What did the doctor say?"

"Haven't seen him since I went for the scan. But all these tests are a waste of time. I think that prickly numbness came from my neck. I slept wrong last night, woke up all stiff and sore. Even my left arm hurt."

Stella flashed me a look of concern as she pulled up a chair and sat close to the bed.

"Well, Mama, I'm sure you're right. But it'll be good to hear what the doctor has to say."

"I don't know why they have this IV in my arm," my mother said with a scowl. "I'm not dehydrated, and there's *nothing* wrong with me."

Stella reached out and patted Mama's hand. "Try not to get yourself all worked up, Franny. I'll bet you'll be out of here in no time."

Just then a doctor walked into the room, his crepe-soled shoes squeaking on the shiny linoleum floor. He had a no-nonsense, grandfatherly look about him, and I liked the way he made direct contact with everyone in the room when he introduced himself as Dr. Ashford.

I stepped forward. "I'm Teddi, Mrs. Overman's daughter."

After we shook hands, he turned his attention to Mama. "Mrs. Overman, from the things you've told me and the tests we've done,

I believe you've had a transient ischemic attack. TIA for short." He peered over the top of his glasses and looked from me to Stella and then to Mama. "I assume you've all heard the term 'mini-stroke.'"

I started chewing the inside of my lip.

"Like many TIAs," he said, looking at Mama, "yours appears to have resolved itself in relatively short order. But that doesn't mean you're out of the woods."

"What exactly do you mean?" I asked, crossing my arms over my chest.

"The CT scan is a test to rule out bleeding and other factors, but a TIA is often an indication that a stroke can occur. It's a warning, if you will. Now, let me share what we know thus far . . ."

I listened to him talk about high cholesterol, medications, and tests he'd ordered. When the doctor spoke of Mama's dangerously high blood pressure, I was stunned. And when Mama reluctantly admitted that she hadn't been to her doctor in more than nine years, I looked at her in disbelief. I kept my voice level as I said, "Mama, a few months ago I asked if you'd seen your doctor, and you said *yes*."

"Well, I did see him. We passed each other in the grocery aisle."

I stared at her, incredulous.

Though Dr. Ashford didn't scold or embarrass her, he was firm when he said, "Mrs. Overman, your body's in a tailspin. It's going to take concentrated efforts on *both* our parts to try to get you regulated. Once I have the results of all your tests, we'll talk about risk factors—those we can change and those we can't. Some of the medicines I've ordered will make you feel quite tired. Take advantage of it and get some rest. I'll see you tomorrow morning."

He tucked the clipboard under his arm and left.

Mama tried to put on a face that said none of this was a big deal. "Teddi, I'm so sorry we can't leave for Charleston tomorrow, but I'll bet we can go in a few days if you don't mind waiting."

"All that matters is that you get healthy. This is serious, Mama."

"It's nothing," she said with a wave of dismissal. "Remember Leroy and Cora Fuller who lived over on Piney Run? Leroy had mini-strokes all the time. Cora said it was like watching a string of Christmas lights flicker on and off. Not one of those strokes did him a bit of harm. He lived to be into his eighties and died from a heart attack when he was shoveling snow."

I groaned and covered my face with my hand.

Stella pushed herself up from the chair and smoothed her palm over Mama's head. "Franny, I'm not gonna get after you for not going to the doctor for all these years—what's done is done. But I want you to promise that you'll do everything the doctor says from now on."

Mama nodded and closed her eyes.

A nurse's aide brought in a dinner tray. "I'm not hungry," my mother said. "But you two should go on home and have some dinner."

I moved the tray to the table by the wall. "I'm not hungry either."

Stella lifted the stainless-steel dome and wrinkled her nose. "Well, I'm starved. I hope the cafeteria has something better than *this*."

I put my arm around her shoulders. "You've had a long, stressful day. Why don't you go home?"

Mama agreed. "Go home and rest, Stella."

"I'm not leavin', and that's all there is to it." Stella gave my mother a big smile and headed for the door. "I'll go have a bite to eat and be right back. You sure you don't want anything, Teddi?"

"I'm sure."

I took the chair and angled it so I could see Mama's face. I wasn't about to get her riled up by asking why she'd lied to me about seeing the doctor. I'd save that conversation for another day. She asked me how the drive from Charleston had been, and we talked about the change in plans and how long I could stay in Kentucky.

Mama rested her head against the pillow and said, "Do you have a mirror?"

I reached into my handbag and pulled out a compact. When I pressed it into her palm, the skin on her hand felt papery.

Opening the compact, she studied her reflection for a moment, then dropped her hand to her chest. "I wish you could have seen my hair before it got ruined. And what happened to my skin? I look awful."

I dug through my handbag and pulled out a pot of tinted lip gloss. "Here, Mama. You need a little color, is all. Nobody looks good under fluorescent lights." I put down the bed rail, sat close to her hip, and dabbed the gloss onto her lips.

She closed her eyes and whispered, "Thank you, Teddi."

Sliding the compact from her fingers, I swirled the brush into the peachy pink powder. "This blush will look perfect on you, Mama. It's called Joyous Spring."

An almost imperceptible smile curved at the corners of her mouth when I smoothed the blush over her cheeks. "So this is what you do with your furniture," she said, her eyes still closed. "Take something old and worthless and make it look pretty again."

"As far as furniture goes, I suppose that's right. But *you* aren't old and worthless, Mama."

"Oh, I know I'm lookin' worn these days. It's funny how age comes. Some people say it creeps up, but it hit me all at once."

"What do you mean?"

My mother's eyes became watery and sad. "Not all that long ago, I went to bed thinking I looked pretty good for my age. I swear, when I woke up the next morning, a haggard old woman was staring back at me in the mirror. When I decided to come visit you, I figured I'd better do something to fix myself up. I didn't want to look like a country bumpkin and embarrass you in front of your fancy friends."

"You've always been pretty. You have the most beautiful eyes and hands I've ever seen. And just so you know, I don't have fancy friends. I have some fancy clients, but—"

"Well, *you're* fancy. Always dressed crisp and nice with your face on and your nails done. You're real stylish now, Teddi."

I smoothed a little more blush onto her cheeks, holding tight to the closeness we were sharing. "I'm still me, Mama. I'm a farm girl in high heels, that's all."

Mama reached out and fingered my hair. Her touch was gentle, and it felt so good that a shiver tickled my neck. I held still, hoping she wouldn't stop.

"I'm real glad you kept your hair long and straight," she said, twirling a length around her finger. "Remember a few years back how girls wore their hair all ratted up? That was awful."

I leaned closer, wanting her to keep touching me, but her face saddened and she pulled her hand away. "I wish you could have seen how nice my hair looked this afternoon."

"I'll bet it did." I pushed a few unruly locks from her forehead. "Tell you what. When you get out of here, I'll treat you to a trip to the beauty salon. We'll have manicures and pedicures and get our hair done. We'll make a mother-daughter day of it."

My mother looked at me, her eyes slowly scanning my face and a small smile on her lips, as if she were seeing me as an adult woman for the first time.

Just then Stella walked back in and the tender moment I was sharing with my mother faded away. Stella gave me a wink and headed straight for Mama. I pulled my legs against the bed and made room for her to get by.

"What did you have for dinner?" I asked.

"Well, the buffet didn't look all that good so I just had a slice of cherry pie." She laughed and patted her belly before easing into the chair. "Looks like you two have been havin' fun."

"Teddi did some of that faux finishing on my face like she does on old furniture."

"That blush looks real good on you, Franny. I stopped by the drugstore yesterday, and I swear they have the nicest cosmetics aisle. Bought myself the prettiest new lipstick. When you get out of here, I'll drive you over and we'll pick out a new one for you, too. Then I'll take you to lunch . . ."

The three of us talked until the sky darkened and my mother's eyelids grew heavy. At eight o'clock Stella pushed herself up from the chair. Leaning over the bed, she rested her palm against Mama's cheek. "I'm goin' home now, but I'll be back early tomorrow."

Mama and Stella looked into each other's eyes. The unspoken language of their friendship was so intimate that I pretended to pick lint off my pants.

Stella patted Mama's thigh. "Tomorrow I'll bring you a surprise. Don't know what it is just yet, but it'll be something good."

As Stella disappeared, I reached out and untangled a curl in my mother's hair. "Would you like me to brush your hair, Mama?"

Her voice was flat with fatigue when she said, "How about you fix it up tomorrow. All those pills are making me tired. And you should go on home and get some rest."

"You go ahead and sleep, Mama. I'll stay right here."

"I won't be able to rest with you staring at me. I'm sure your little dog would like to see you. He's probably scared bein' in a strange house all alone."

I tucked the blanket over her bony shoulders. "All right. I'll be back in the morning. Do you need anything from the house?"

She thought for a moment. "Yes. I'd like my own nightgowns. Bring me the blue one with the lace collar, and I'd like the yellow flannel one, too, in case I get cold."

"If you think of anything else, just call. I hope you get some good rest." I gave her a kiss on the forehead and hoisted my handbag over my shoulder.

"Teddi, you'd better take my purse home with you. I don't want to worry about someone snatching my wallet."

I took her handbag and slung it over my other shoulder.

"On your way out, turn off the overhead lights, will you?"

While heading for the door I had the sudden urge to tell her that I loved her. It was so strong that I could feel it mushroom across my chest. But I was afraid. What if I said those words and they fell flat on the floor between us? What if she didn't say them back?

The words continued to rise in my throat. Instead of pushing them out, I did what I'd always done—swallowed them whole. For a moment I hesitated at the door, and then I flicked off the lights and stepped through the open doorway.

Why, I don't know, but I stopped and took a step back. Mama was watching me. I smiled, pressed my fingers to my lips, and sent her a big, lip-smacking kiss across the room.

An unexpected light, both fierce and tender, shone in her eyes. To my surprise, she blew a kiss back to me. For a brief moment, she held her hand suspended, her slender fingers opening like a pale flower.

FOURTEEN

Eddie squealed with delight when I opened the back door. After taking him for a walk and feeding him dinner, I locked up the house and went to bed. I was so wrung out that the muscles in my legs twitched, and yet I lay awake as a galaxy of thoughts swirled in my mind.

Mama shouldn't live alone anymore. Maybe I could talk her into coming to live with me. But she'd fight me on that, and what if it made her blood pressure go up? Maybe she and Stella could live together. How long can I afford to stay in Kentucky? How long can I expect Inez to handle the customers on top of her regular work? Will Albert be able to keep up with the extra workload? What about all the custom work that only I can do? And what if . . . ?

I woke to a shimmer of sunlight glazing the windowpane. My head felt heavy and my body stiff. Throwing back the covers, I wrapped up in my robe and padded to the kitchen. While Eddie ran around in the yard, I picked up the phone and called Olivia. The moment she answered, I blurted, "Mama's in the hospital."

A long pause was followed by the words "You're kidding."

"Unfortunately, I'm not. She had a mini-stroke. But she seems fine, fussin' like always. I'm worried about her, but I'm a little angry with her, too. She hasn't had a medical checkup in a million years."

"What did the doctor say?"

"Well, she has high blood pressure, high cholesterol, and Lord only knows what all else is high, low, or out of whack."

"I'm really sorry, Teddi. I know how much you were looking forward to having her visit. I was, too. Shoot, last night I even dusted my entire Pez collection."

I couldn't help but smile. "Well, maybe she'll still be able to come, and if not now, another time. Anyway, I'll talk to you tomorrow."

"Call me anytime, even if it's the middle of the night. I mean it."

After we said good-bye, I took a few moments to collect my thoughts and then called my grandmother. I all but chirped while making light of Mama's condition, softening the truth until I outright lied by claiming she'd suffered little more than a migraine. "Don't worry, Grammy, the doctor says she's doing great. She'll be released in a few days, and then I'll bring her to Charleston . . ."

I ended the call as fast as I could, and after a quick breakfast and a shower I slid Mama's nightgowns into a bag and left the house.

The morning air rolled in through my open window as I wound along the country roads. I passed cornfields left barren by the final harvest, some already plowed under in preparation for winter, others filled with geese pecking for stray kernels. As I neared the hospital, I noticed lights go on inside a small floral shop, and when I slowed to turn in, a woman placed an Open sign in the window.

From a stainless-steel cooler, I selected creamy white roses and Stargazer lilies, two of my mother's favorites. I paced at the counter while the shop owner took her good old time snipping the stems and arranging the flowers in a glass vase. When she was done, I grabbed the vase and nearly ran to my car. I didn't want to miss the doctor's morning visit.

I pulled in to the hospital parking lot thinking maybe, just maybe, Mama's mini-stroke was one of those upside-down blessings that would bring us closer together. If the way we'd talked last night was any indication, I had the feeling we might be in for a long-awaited mother-daughter treat.

With my handbag slung over my shoulder, the paper bag filled with Mama's nightgowns in my hands, and the vase of flowers cradled in my arms, I pushed through the door with a smile on my face. I inhaled the sweet scent of the flowers and knew she'd be surprised by the bouquet.

When the elevator door opened, I turned toward the corridor and found myself in the middle of a commotion. A young man in blue scrubs ran by, nearly mowing me down with the metal cart he was pushing. Two nurses scurried behind him, followed by a man in a white coat. I watched them bolt up the hallway and into a room.

Mama's room.

I sped up, my purse bouncing on my shoulder, the bag with Mama's nightgowns slapping at my side while water from the vase of flowers sloshed onto my sweater.

A gray-haired nurse ushered Stella Rose from my mother's room. Even from a distance, I could see that she was crying.

I broke into a run—flowers flying and water splashing everywhere.

Stella turned and spotted me coming.

Our eyes locked.

When I saw the way her lips quivered and the flush on her cheeks, I stopped running. Just stopped. I stood in the middle of the corridor as water spilled down my hands and onto the shiny linoleum floor.

Drip . . . drip . . . drip.

There was no need to rush.

I knew.

When the commotion ended, the nurses filed out of Mama's

room while the doctor led Stella and me to a small alcove at the end of the corridor. I stood with my back against the wall and watched his lips move, but his words seemed far away, as if whispered from behind a thick curtain. I didn't care what he said about high risk, the final stroke, or how sorry he was . . . *blah-blah-blah* . . . His words meant nothing to me. Still grasping the vase of flowers and the bag of my mother's nightgowns, I turned and walked away.

My legs felt unsteady. Nothing seemed quite real. A nurse approached me holding a towel. She tried to take the flowers, to dry my hands and blot my soggy sweater. Her face was kind, her words kinder. But I moved away and stepped into Mama's room. With my foot I closed the door behind me.

The lights had been turned off. The room was so still that I could hear a faint hiss of air streaming through the ceiling vent. "Your favorites," I whispered, stepping across the room. I set the vase on her bedside table. The bouquet was a mess—two rosebuds were broken off and several lilies were crushed. I took a moment and tried to make them pretty again.

How long I stood and looked at my mother, I don't know. But it felt like an eternity. Reaching beneath the blanket, I took hold of her hand. A smudge of the blush I'd applied the previous evening remained on her left cheek. The sight of it nearly brought me to my knees. Turning toward the window, I looked into the morning sky, so blue and bright with the promise of a new day. I wanted to rip it down and throw it away. I wanted black clouds, thunder, and unforgiving winds.

I wanted the world to hurt like I did.

Leaning against the wall, I closed my eyes and said, "Well, Mama, I guess this means you won't be comin' to Charleston anytime soon."

FIFTEEN

It's sad that so much is discovered about a person only after her death. From Stella I learned that Mama didn't want to be buried. She wanted to be cremated, her ashes set free into the wind. Where that wind was didn't matter—she just wanted to go wherever she pleased. This was confirmed when I opened the fireproof box that held the deed to the farm and the simple last will and testament that Mama had made following Daddy's passing.

She left everything to me. My brother was never mentioned.

I honored her wishes, cremation and a small memorial service, nothing more. The plot next to Daddy's would remain unused. Where I'd scatter her ashes I didn't know, was too raw and confused to know. But I'd figure it out.

Mama's sudden death had left me in a stupor of disbelief, and though I was devastated to dysfunction when Daddy had died, his passing was almost a blessing. For two weeks I'd sat in a helpless vigil and watched cancer shrink my once-powerful father to a skeleton, his skin waxed yellow as he writhed in pain. By the grace of God, he passed away the day he looked at me with sunken eyes and asked me to get him his gun.

But where was the grace of God now? Both my parents were gone, and my brother was still missing. I sat at the kitchen table, buried my head in my hands, and let out a groan that turned in to a sob. I didn't know how to begin to deal with everything—the paperwork, the farm, the furniture and household items.

A gentle knock sounded at the back door. I wiped my eyes on my sweater sleeve and looked up to see Stella walk in holding a foil-covered plate.

"Hey, honey. I brought you some supper. How're you holding up?"

"Not so hot."

She pulled out a chair, sat down next to me, and smoothed her hand down my back. "Me neither."

We leaned toward each other, and I rested my head on her shoulder.

"What can I do to help you, Teddi?"

"At this point I can't think of anything."

"Well, just remember—I'm only a few miles down the road, and Lord knows I have plenty of spare time on my hands. Why don't I come by a few days a week to check on the house?"

"That would be great if it wouldn't be a bother."

Stella stayed and talked while I picked at her supper. Wrung out as I was, I was glad for the company. I pushed a pea across the plate with my fork. "I'm going back to Charleston tomorrow. Grammy Belle needs to know what's happened, and I can't tell her over the phone."

"Bless her sweet soul. Give her a hug from me." Stella glanced into the living room, to the urn holding Mama's remains that sat on the fireplace mantel. Her voice broke with emotion when she asked, "Any idea where you'll scatter her ashes?"

I shook my head.

The next morning I woke to a dreary, flannel-gray sky that darkened the mountains. It was a good time to head south. From room to room I went, latching the windows and closing the blinds. Already the house felt cold and emptied of energy. I walked into

Mama's bedroom and looked at her half-packed suitcase. Reaching out, I ran my fingertips over her folded clothes. Next thing I knew, I zipped her suitcase closed and was carrying it down the steps.

After tucking it into the trunk, I went back inside the house and marched into the living room. "C'mon, Mama," I said, lifting her urn from the mantel. "A promise is a promise. You're comin' to Charleston." With her urn cradled in my arms, I walked out of the house and locked the door behind me.

And so it was on a foggy autumn morning that my mother and I embarked on what would become our first and last road trip. Surely not the way either of us had planned, but a road trip just the same.

"We were going to stop here," I said while passing the exit to Asheville. "The Biltmore Estate. I thought you'd like to see it, Mama." Later in the day, I zoomed by the town of Newberry and said, "Right off this exit is the sweetest little restaurant. I was planning to take you there for dinner . . ."

When I reached Charleston, I lugged everything up the stairs. After setting her urn on the night table in the guest room where she should have been sleeping, I put her suitcase into the closet. "Here you are, Mama. I hope you like your room." My voice broke when I added, "I even ironed your sheets."

Fatigue was folding me in half as I walked down the hall and collapsed on my bed.

Tomorrow I would have to tell Grammy.

∾

I woke before dawn, puffy-eyed and cotton-mouthed. After dragging myself into the shower, I dressed and was back in my car as the day opened above the trees. I drove aimlessly, turning from one street to the next while trying to gather my thoughts.

Once I'd parked my car at the nursing home, I took a deep

breath and slowly walked toward my grandmother's room. Grammy grinned like an elf when I stepped through her open door, her eyes bright with anticipation. When she realized that Mama wasn't behind me, her smile faltered, yet her recovery was remarkable. She straightened her shoulders and said, "What day is it, honey?"

Forcing a smile, I pulled up a chair and sat. "Tuesday."

"I lose track," she said, resting back in her chair. "I'm never sure anymore. That's just another part of getting old that drives me buttons . . ."

She rocked back and forth, jabbering away. I suspected it was her way of dealing with such deep disappointment. The minutes ticked on, and when she wound down on sharing what she'd done in my absence, she let out a sigh. "Anyway, that's about all I know, or at least all I remember." She looked down and smoothed her fingers along the arms of the chair. "So . . . Frances decided not to come."

It was not a question.

Please help me. How do I tell her?

I scooted the chair closer and covered her hands with mine. "Her bags were all packed. She wanted to be here, she really did. But she . . . she took a bad turn. There was nothing the doctors could do."

Grammy's face blanched, and I felt a tremor move through her fingers. "Oh, no. Oh, dear Lord. She's gone?"

I nodded.

The focus of her eyes drifted past me to the window, to a secret place known only to her. She resumed rocking. The slow, rhythmic creaking of her chair was the only sound in the room. A tear escaped my grandmother's eye, caught itself in a wrinkle, and slid into the corner of her mouth. She did not look at me when she asked, "Was it her heart?"

"A stroke."

"Were you with her when she passed?"

"No. But Stella was, and I'm grateful for that. Grammy, I hope you'll forgive me, but I couldn't tell you over the phone. I just couldn't. And then I thought—"

"Nothing to forgive, honey."

"I'm still so confused. Mama seemed fine the night before she passed away. I sat on the edge of her bed, and we talked for quite a while. I fluffed up her hair and even put some blush on her cheeks."

A sad smile crept to my grandmother's lips when she looked at me. "That was a sweet thing you did, Teddi. Got her dolled up for the big trip."

I traced my finger along a thick blue vein in her hand and lowered my head.

Grammy's bottom lip trembled when she said, "It's no secret we had our differences, but I loved Frances. Loved her very much." Her voice broke apart when she added, "We're not supposed to outlive our children. It goes against nature's plan of things."

I watched my grandmother's inner light fade as she lowered her eyes and began smoothing a wrinkle in her yellow duster.

"Right before I left her room, I hugged Mama and said good-bye. I don't know why, but when I reached the doorway, I stopped and turned around. And you know what, Grammy? She was looking at me. I mean more than looking at me. It was like she was studying me. So I blew her a kiss across the room." I swallowed against the thickness in my throat when I added, "And she blew one back to me."

"My Aunt Lil used to say that right before passing, a person sees with clear eyes. You're a good girl. I hope Frances finally saw that."

Another tear slid down my grandmother's cheek, and I reached over and wiped it away. Then, in perfectly choreographed unison, we turned and looked out the window at the garden. But my eyes lost focus, and soon the flowers became nothing but a watercolor blur.

When I looked at my grandmother, she had either fallen asleep or was so deep in thought that I wondered if maybe she wanted a little time alone. I closed the window blinds against the morning sun and went in search of a strong cup of coffee.

SIXTEEN

For the next few weeks, I trudged through each day at work. The teasing and laughter between Albert and Inez had diminished. I'm sure they didn't know what to say or do. And what *was* there to do? Nothing. That's the thing with death: There's no making it better, and that's what we did at my shop. We were the fixers and the healers—the go-to people who could take even the most damaged piece of furniture and find a way to bring it back to life.

So, piece by damaged piece, that's what we did. As we went about our work, I took to my restoration and custom-painting projects with a sense of purpose I hadn't experienced in years. I welcomed the smell of oil paints, stains, and turpentine, and I was grateful for the concentration my work demanded. I painted details on a shield-back chair with a brush so tiny its bristles were all but invisible, and I plotted a fleur-de-lis pattern along the edge of a tabletop with a surgeon's precision. When it came to my work, grief had not pulled me into its wreckage. Oddly, it had enhanced it.

Then one morning as I was dusting a lamp shade, the bell above the door rang and Miz Poteet walked in. I had thought that after being caught red-handed with the candlestick in her handbag she'd decided to do her sticky-fingered shopping elsewhere. But there she was, as if nothing had ever happened. I was in no mood to deal with her, so I quickly walked away and asked Inez to keep an eye on things until she left.

While Inez scurried out of her office, I went to see Albert. We talked quietly as I waited for Miz Poteet to leave. Thankfully, it was only a few minutes before Inez walked into the workroom with a satisfied smile. "Mission accomplished. I made damn sure she didn't steal anything. But she asked me to give you these." Inez handed me an envelope and a small gift-wrapped box.

I opened the envelope and was momentarily speechless. It was a Christmas card with an angel on the cover. Printed inside were the words JOYOUS GREETINGS. When I read what Miz Poteet had written at the bottom, I shook my head. "What on earth?"

Inez lifted her glasses from the chain around her neck and perched them on her nose. "Let me see." Her eyes grew wide as she read the card aloud. "*I'm so sorry about the passing of your mother. Now she's an angel watching over you. Was she baptized? Sincerely, Tula Jane Poteet.*'"

Albert looked over Inez's shoulder and scrunched up his face. "Baptized? That's a whole lotta strange, right there."

I peeled the wrapping from the box and lifted the lid. When I saw what was inside, I couldn't believe it. It was the Limoges box that Miz Poteet had stolen from me earlier in the year. The absurdity of it caught me off guard, and I burst into laughter and looked at Inez. "Guess you'd better credit her son's account."

"Not on your life! This proves it—she's a nutcase."

Inez and Albert began to laugh, and in that lovely, unexpected moment, my grief gave way and the three of us howled, just like old times. We were still laughing when the bell above the door sounded.

"I'll get it," I said, taking a moment to pull myself together before walking down the hallway. I was surprised to see Olivia.

"Teddi, there's a big yard sale over on Church Street. The sign says it opens at eleven o'clock. *No early birds.* It looked like they had a ton of books and glassware. Plus, there was quite a bit of furniture. So can you go with me?"

"I'd love to, but I'd better check the finances. C'mon back."

As we walked through the shop, Olivia came to a halt when she saw my newest acquisition. Crafted of satinwood, the Edwardian wardrobe was a behemoth that stood nine feet tall. Olivia opened the carved double doors and peered inside. "Whoa, are we going to Narnia?"

"Maybe later," I said, grabbing the sleeve of her blouse and tugging her along. I stopped at the doorway to Inez's office. "How are accounts receivable?"

"This is a good month, but we've got rent coming up, and that shipment of sterling from England will be here any day. If I remember right, it's COD." Rising from the chair, Inez gave Olivia a friendly swat on her rump as she walked to the file cabinet. "I'll make a photocopy of the financial sheet."

As Olivia and I headed down the hall, she whispered, "You sure lucked out when you found Inez. I love that woman."

Inez called out, "I love you, too, Olivia."

"I swear, Inez has eyes in the back of her head and hears better than an owl."

"I had to," Inez called out again. "I raised four children."

Olivia followed me into the workroom, where Albert was mixing a jar of custom-tinted stain.

"Hey, Albert. How about taking a break?"

He eyed us suspiciously. "What kind of break you talkin' about?"

"A yard sale over on Church Street. Olivia says they have a ton of stuff. Maybe we'll find a few treasures. Want to go?"

"Well, I guess so. But I'm tellin' you right now, I ain't lifting anything heavy. About broke my back with that bookcase you two fools brought back from Atlanta."

Inez came up behind us and handed me the financial sheet, then turned and left. I scanned the columns. "I'm in good shape, but I can't go overboard. Let's see what we can find."

Albert pulled off his apron, and the three of us climbed into Olivia's truck while Inez minded the shop.

And what a sale it was. Every inch of the front yard was packed with furniture, paintings, and housewares. Row after row of long folding tables awaited our inspection, each one smothered with everything from fine crystal bowls to sterling flatware to goofy tchotchkes. Olivia made a beeline for the book table, while Albert and I headed in the opposite direction.

"Hard to see what all's here," he said, squeezing behind a sofa and nearly knocking over a lamp.

Within minutes Albert found a fishing creel and I found a pair of opera glasses and a large, filigreed serving spoon that was as gorgeous as its intended use was puzzling. As I marveled at how unusual it was, a well-dressed elderly woman walked by and said, "Goodness, you don't see those very often."

"Do you know what it was originally used for?" I asked.

"It's a bonbon server." Then she smiled and moved toward a table filled with crystal stemware.

"There's more around back," a young woman called from the porch.

Albert and I walked along the side of the house and entered the backyard. I pointed to a table loaded with kitchenware and whispered, "So now I finally know. *This* is where old Tupperware comes to die."

Albert laughed and stepped over a garden hose.

Lined up along a border garden were boxes that overflowed with everything from leather belts to sweaters. I reached into a shoe box filled with old costume jewelry and picked up a strand of royal blue glass beads. Several were cracked, and three were broken. While rolling a bead between my thumb and forefinger, I wondered where all the damage came from. *Had the necklace been thrown against a wall in a heated lovers' quarrel or perhaps given to a child to play with and run over by a bicycle in the driveway?*

Old things held so many untold stories.

As much as I loved these kinds of sales, beneath the surface they were somber affairs—people picking through the belongings of the dead, or those soon to be. Rarely did I feel indifference when I touched the private items of perfect strangers.

On the back porch was a coatrack crammed with party dresses, overcoats, and jackets with poker-chip buttons. When it came to house sales, the old clothes were always the saddest—how limply they hung, moving in the breeze like tired ghosts.

Removing a red-and-white-checked dress from its hanger, I held it up to my shoulders. "This must be from the early forties. What do you think, Albert?"

He shook his head. "I know better'n to comment on a woman's clothes, except to say it's real pretty and, no, it don't make your butt look too big."

I laughed. "C'mon, tell me the truth. What do you honestly think?"

"Well, it kinda looks like it was made from a tablecloth."

I stared down at the dress and frowned. "I think you're right." I returned it to the rack and stepped off the porch.

That's when I saw it.

Before it had fallen into the wrong hands, before countless assaults had left it scraped and gouged, and long before forgotten cigarettes had burned its edges until they'd blackened like an overdone piecrust, it had once been beautiful. Even now the old chest sat in a sunny spot of lawn with a pride that was unmistakable.

"Oh, my gosh. This is mid-eighteenth-century Dutch," I whispered to Albert while kneeling to examine the drawer pulls. With my thumbnail I scratched away at the grimy film until I could see what lay beneath. I smiled up at Albert. "Ormolu."

"Now, Teddi, whatchu thinkin'? You know that chest is all whompyjawed. It's too far gone, and it's—"

"Walnut," I said, smoothing my fingertips over the top.

"Yeah. It's walnut all right, but that chest might as well be plywood 'cause it ain't worth much. See how all that marquetry's poppin' off? Now, you know that's a bad sign. And look how warped this side is."

I tried to open the top drawer, but it was stuck. The same was true of the next drawer, and the next.

"Them drawers won't open neither."

"Yes, I see that," I said with a chuckle. "I know this chest needs a ton of work, but—"

"That chest don't need work, it needs a *miracle*. And Albert James Pickens ain't the one to do it. Jesus hisself couldn't fix that old chest."

We stood in a slant of sun and stared at each other.

"I can rework the cigarette burns and do all the refinishing, but I don't have the skill to bring this old chest back to life. You do marquetry replacement better than anyone on the planet. And I've seen you do steam bends that defy explanation. Please say yes, Albert. I love this chest. It's like an old friend."

He rolled his eyes. "Then you'd best be findin' a different friend. What about that piece over there?" he said, pointing to a mahogany bench. "Now, *that* I can fix."

I dismissed the bench with a wave of my hand. "I don't want this chest to sell in the shop. I want it for me. Please help me with it, Albert. I'm in love with it, and I can't even tell you why. I just am."

"I got no time for this chest. All them extra hours I ordered ain't arrived yet."

I smiled. "I don't care if you can't get to it for a year."

He let out a grunt. "I'm tellin' you, this chest is in sad, sorry shape. But you got that look in your eyes, so I guess there's no sense in arguin'. Let's haul it on back to the shop."

While Albert and I hoisted the chest into the bed of the truck, Olivia showed up with a box of books in her arms. Behind her, one of the yard sale helpers was holding an old croquet mallet and a cuckoo clock. Olivia's face was flushed.

"What's wrong?" I asked.

She flashed me a look that telegraphed, *Don't ask*, and I clamped my mouth shut.

We climbed into the truck, and when Olivia pulled away from the curb, she nearly jumped out of her skin. "Holy shit on a stick of dynamite! Whoever priced the books didn't have a clue. I bought Winston Churchill's *Arms and the Covenant*. It's a first edition. And it's in pristine condition. My head's going to pop off!"

"What'd you pay for it?" I asked.

"Two lousy dollars!"

Albert rested his arm on the open window and chuckled. "Well, Teddi bought a chest that ain't even worth two dollars, but she up and paid twenty."

I lifted my chin. "Just wait. You'll see."

Olivia whipped the truck around a corner. "Maybe I'll go buy a yacht and we'll all go fishing. What do you think, Albert?"

"A yacht?" he said with a laugh. "How much you think that book's worth?"

"I'd say easily five grand."

Albert's voice shot up several octaves. "For a bunch of paper with words printed on 'em! Now, that right there is crazy. I bought my whole house for nine thousand, and it's got a kitchen and a bathroom."

"Yeah, but how long ago was that?" Olivia said.

"Don't make no difference when it was. All you got is a dusty old book, and I got a whole house!"

Olivia and I laughed. Albert sure knew how to boil things down to the bone truth.

After we'd unloaded my yard sale finds and hauled the chest into the workroom, Olivia all but danced out of the shop and headed home to start calling book collectors.

It was just before closing time when I checked to see how Albert was progressing with a difficult repair he'd been working on. "Miz Osgood's chair is done," he said, wiping his hands on a rag.

"Thanks, Albert."

He hung up his apron and grabbed his cap. "See you tomorrow."

I ended the day sitting at my desk and signing checks for Inez. On my way out the door, I walked into the workroom and turned on the lights. From my workbench I lifted a magnifying glass and examined the old walnut chest I'd bought at the yard sale. The marquetry, or at least what was left of it, was stunning.

Now and then it would happen, I'd touch an antique and feel a strange connection with the person who made it. My fingers would grasp the knobs as theirs once did, and a kind of alchemy occurred. Though nearly impossible to explain, it was as real as my own breathing.

"Somebody loved you, didn't they? Well, don't worry. I know you're in trouble, but we'll get you fixed up. I already know where you'll go. Right next to my bed."

SEVENTEEN

Though I wanted to dive right in and begin working on that old chest, I couldn't. I had a job to do in Kentucky before winter set in. After speaking with Inez and Albert about running the shop in my absence, I blocked out ten days on my calendar. It wasn't but a few hours after I'd finalized the plans for my trip up north that Olivia phoned all excited. "There's an estate sale in Atlanta on Sunday," she said. "It's slated to be a big one. I'm talking the *entire* contents of a thirty-room mansion. Want to go?"

"I wish I could, but I've rented a van and I'm leaving for Kentucky on Thursday morning."

She didn't skip a beat when she said, "Road trip? Count me in."

"This isn't for a long weekend, Olivia. I'll probably be there for nine or ten days. Maybe you can come another time. There's so much to do, and—"

"Hey, I've got an idea. Why don't I take a few days off and follow you up there? I can stay till Tuesday and help you pack up the things you want to bring back."

"Really? I'd love the help. But I've got to warn you, it's a long haul."

I felt her smile come through the phone when she said, "It'll be fun. What time do you want to leave?"

"Is five-thirty too early?"

"In the *morning!*" she yelped. "Hell yeah, it's too early, but I'll be ready anyway."

೧೦

It was midafternoon when I rounded the bend and the farm came into view. Olivia's truck was behind me, its usual gleaming finish dulled by a layer of road dust.

Fallen leaves crackled beneath the tires as I rolled to a stop at the back of the house. The landscape was ignited with the fiery colors of autumn.

Olivia pulled up next to me and climbed out of her truck while Bear and Eddie took off running across the yard. "Whoa," she said, stretching her back as she surveyed what lay before her. "That big barn and *all* this beautiful land are yours? How many acres are there?"

"Just over three hundred," I said, fishing the house key from my handbag. "My great-grandfather left it to Daddy. He took it over when he was only seventeen years old."

While the dogs raced to the barn, I climbed the porch steps and unlocked the back door. After we unloaded groceries and piled the bags on the kitchen table, we corralled the dogs and brought them inside the house. Olivia began putting the groceries away while I went from room to room, throwing open the windows to let life blow in.

"Hey, Teddi," she called out. "There's a pie in the refrigerator."

I walked into the kitchen. "What?"

"Look."

I pulled the pie from the shelf. A note was taped to the foil wrapping, and I smiled as I read it aloud. "'I thought you girls might like something sweet. Love, Stella.'"

"That's your mother's friend?"

"Way more than a friend. She's family. I really wanted you to meet her, and she wanted to meet you, too, but she left yesterday to visit her son and his wife in Pennsylvania."

Olivia lifted an edge of the foil and sniffed. "Ummm . . . lemon meringue. So what do you want for dinner?"

"How about spaghetti?"

"I'll get right on it."

While she banged around in the kitchen, I went upstairs and put fresh sheets on the beds. I laughed when she called out, "Wow. A *rotary* wall phone!"

A few minutes later, I heard a steady *chop-chop-chop*, and then I smelled onions. As I passed through the kitchen on my way out to the van, Olivia had the radio on and was busy making sauce.

After unloading boxes, packing tape, and rolls of trash bags from the van and piling them on the porch, I decided to tackle the easiest rooms first. In the alcove at the far end of the hallway sat Daddy's desk, a cumbersome rolltop that blocked half the window. I sat in his swivel chair and smoothed my hands over arms so worn that the varnish was long gone.

His wristwatch, silver Zippo lighter, and weather diary were in the top drawer. I held each one reverently before setting them inside a box. From the right-hand drawer, I removed an old *Farmers' Almanac* and dropped it into a trash bag. Next I tossed out a folder stuffed with receipts. At the bottom of the drawer was an oil-stained owner's manual for a lawn mower.

I was about to drop it into the trash bag when I noticed the yellowing edge of a newspaper clipping sticking out from between the pages. Pulling it free, I held it to the light. I hadn't read but a few sentences before the hairs on my arms prickled.

The date at the top of the clipping was July 17, 1979. Twenty-one months after Josh had disappeared.

My fingers trembled as I leaned forward, elbows on knees, and read the article one more time. Slowly, I folded the clipping and tucked it into the back pocket of my jeans.

Good God Almighty.

✂

After dinner Olivia and I took our pie and coffee into the living room and settled in for a quiet evening. I sat in Daddy's recliner while Olivia curled up on the sofa and opened a book. Bear and Eddie lay side by side on the braided rug, content with their rawhide chew bones. I gazed out the window, unable to pull my thoughts away from the newspaper clipping that was burning a hole in my pocket. So many questions flashed through my mind, and the biggest one was this: *Why didn't Daddy tell me about it?*

Olivia's voice startled me. "I've struggled through four chapters, and I can't get into this book. So I'm calling it—time of death, nine twenty-five." She dropped the book on the floor, then sat up and looked at me. "Hey, are you okay? You look so sad."

"It's just hard being here. My stomach gets churned up when I think about selling the farm. But no matter how I crunch the numbers, there's no way I can hang on to it. Every day I pray Josh will come home. Then he could take over and keep it going."

Olivia sat quietly, her face contemplative. When she finally spoke, her voice was a whisper. "Teddi, he's been gone for a long time."

I looked away.

"You talk about his sensitivity and the connection he had with nature. And once you even said he was 'otherworldly.' I'm not trying to pry, but you've never told me exactly why he left."

She was right, of course. Though I spoke of my brother in ways that depicted him as a deity of the woods, I'd never shared the details of what had sent him into flight.

The room grew so quiet I could hear the ticking of the rooster clock above the stove. Olivia didn't say a word, but I could feel her questioning eyes.

The clock ticked on and on.

Still she said nothing.

I rose from the chair. "I'd better make more coffee. This might take a while."

EIGHTEEN

NOVEMBER 1977

Albert and I had just finished restoring a mahogany break-front, a dining table, and twelve Chippendale chairs that had been smoke-damaged by a fire. It was a filthy job. The smell of soot was so overpowering that we opened the windows and turned on the fan even though it was cold outside. Piles of soot-stained rags littered the floor like drifts of dirty snow. My hands ached, and my nose burned. Albert's eyes were puffy and bloodshot. When the truck came to pick up the furniture and return it to its owners, we sat in the workshop and took a much-needed break. We were beyond tired.

Just before closing time, Mr. Palmer walked in and handed us both an envelope. While heading for the door, he said over his shoulder, "Go on. Get outta here. Don't come back till December."

Albert and I looked at each other and then tore open our envelopes. In a gesture of surprising generosity, Mr. Palmer had given us two full weeks off—with pay. In all the years we'd worked together, I'd never seen Albert smile wider or move faster. He pulled on his jacket and was out the door before I'd finished scrubbing my hands. After gathering my coat and handbag, I thanked Mr. Palmer and walked home. I was so dirty I looked like a chimney sweep.

Early the next morning, I packed my suitcase and set off for Kentucky.

I arrived to a kitchen warm from the oven and scented by yeast and spices. Mama had just finished canning applesauce, and two loaves of Grammy's whole-wheat bread were cooling on the rack. While the three of us talked, I opened a jar of homemade strawberry jam and slathered it on a thick slice of bread.

I moaned with the first bite. Nobody could put summer in a jar like Grammy.

With sugar surging through my veins, I dashed out the door to find Daddy. He was in his workshop sharpening the blades of his sickle bar. I gave him a big hug, and after we talked for a few minutes, I trotted toward the field.

Josh was on the tractor, disking the last of the empty cornstalks into the ground in preparation for winter. When the tractor came chugging over the knoll, sending puffs of exhaust into the crisp air, I climbed the fence and waved my arms to get my brother's attention. He lifted his baseball cap and waved back. After disking the last row, he drove toward the barn. I jumped from the fence and ran to catch up with him.

On the edge of the tractor path, I noticed the sun glint off something in the grass. I stopped and picked it up. At first I thought it was a coin, but when I rubbed it clean on the leg of my jeans and angled it to the sun, I saw it was a token, probably from a penny arcade. How it had gotten here was anyone's guess, but that's what happened on the farm—the earth released long-lost treasures when least expected. After giving the token one more rub on my jeans, I jogged to meet Josh.

"Hey, I said breathlessly, "I have a surprise for you. Hold out your hand."

Josh gave me a curious look as he opened his hand. I pressed the token into his strong, work-hardened palm and said, "It's got secret power."

He squinted to read the worn letters that spelled out ONE LUCKY WINNER, then smiled and tucked the token into his pocket. "Thanks, Teddi."

As he unhitched the disk from the tractor, I gave his sleeve a tug. "Take me for a ride?"

He was tall now, nearly as tall as Daddy. Over the past year, he'd lost the softness of youth, his jaw angular, his deep blue eyes intense. The energy he exuded was powerful but quiet, his movements quieter still. With uncommon grace he climbed onto the idling tractor and offered me his hand. I positioned my feet on the hitch bar and wrapped my arms around his shoulders.

Along the edge of the field we went, the afternoon sun warm on our faces, and then my brother drove over a hill that ran beside the fringe of the woods. The growl of the tractor flushed a pair of rabbits from beneath a shrub, and Josh cut the engine so we could watch them bound ahead of us, their white tails bouncing as they disappeared into the thicket. Overhead a formation of geese flew by, honking their good-byes as they headed south.

Tightening my arms around my brother, I held him close—so close I could feel the beating of his heart beneath his denim jacket. I leaned forward and spoke in his ear: "I love you, Josh Overman."

He lifted his hand from the steering wheel, reached back, and patted my head.

ᙣᙚ

Before going to bed that night, I rapped lightly on my brother's bedroom door.

"C'mon in, Teddi."

I stepped inside and closed the door behind me. "How'd you know it was me?"

"I know the sounds you make. If a hundred people walked by my door, I'd know which one was you."

He was sitting on his bed with a notebook in his lap. Lined up on his pillow were three black feathers. I sat at the foot of his bed and folded my legs Indian style. "What're you doing?"

"Updating my notes." He grasped one of the feathers by its quill and passed it to me. "Any idea what bird this is from?"

Solid black and shiny, the feather was about twelve inches long. "Well, it must be from a fairly big bird. I'd say a crow."

Josh shook his head, his eyes brightening as they always did whenever he had a secret.

"Are you going to tell me?"

"Only on one condition," he said, lowering his voice. "You have to give me your word of honor that you'll never tell a single soul for as long as you live."

"Okay," I said, handing him the feather. "I promise on my life."

He held the feather at eye level, slowly spinning the quill between his thumb and forefinger. "There's more folklore about this bird than any other. It's the largest in the family of Corvidae and has a complex vocabulary of sounds. It's the most intelligent of all birds."

"I'm stumped. So tell me."

My brother leaned close. "This feather is from a raven."

"Huh? We don't have ravens around here."

Josh met my gaze and slowly nodded.

"Where?"

"Clifty Wilderness. Back in the nineteenth century, ravens were all but destroyed in these parts. They were persecuted, Teddi. People killed them left and right. So far I've seen two nesting pairs. I've been watching them since last October."

"Wow, are you going to tell Ranger Jim?"

"Did you already forget what I said? *Nobody* but you and I can know about them. This is serious, Teddi. Ravens are endangered throughout Appalachia. If word gets out that they've made their way back, ornithologists and weekend bird-watchers will descend on the Gorge like vultures. It'll ruin everything."

Reaching beneath his pillow, Josh pulled out a book and leafed through the pages. "Ravens are mysterious-looking. See how thick their bills are?" he said, pointing to a profile photograph. "They're a lot bigger than crows. And they do these death-defying maneuvers— diving, rolling, and tumbling through the air."

"Will you take me to see them?"

He closed the book with a thump and shoved it back beneath his pillow. "I can't. It's a rugged climb, and you'd never make it. I haven't seen evidence that anyone other than me has been there, and I hope it stays that way."

"I'll keep my promise, but why is this a secret?"

My brother's voice dropped when he leaned close. "Something's going on with the ravens. And whatever it is, it's sacred. That's all I can say for now. But one day I'll tell you, Teddi. I'll tell you everything."

◈

The day before Thanksgiving, I woke to a clatter and clang from the kitchen. I showered and dressed quickly, eager to get downstairs and help with the preparations. As I peeled apples and Mama made pastry dough, Grammy began to gather the other ingredients for the pies we'd make, one apple and one pumpkin. While rooting through the spice cupboard she called over her shoulder, "I can't find the cinnamon."

Mama stopped rolling the dough and thought for a moment. "Oh, shoot. I forgot to get some at the grocery. I forgot waxed paper, too."

"I'll run to the store," I said, plunking the last apple core into a bowl. After washing my hands, I pulled on my jacket and set off for town.

The grocery was packed with last-minute shoppers, and I waited in line for nearly fifteen minutes before someone was nice enough to let me cut in front with my measly few items. Knowing that Mama was waiting to make the pies, I gathered the bag and ran to my car.

Less than a half mile from the farm, I happened to glance toward the old Hickson place. Sitting alone in the middle of dozens of acres, it was a small clapboard house with a dilapidated front porch. After Mr. Hickson passed away, the house suffered a series of negligent renters, and his son never bothered to keep the place up.

Off to the side of the house, a man was bent over by the rusted carcass of an old truck. He was pounding something into the ground. As I drove closer, I gasped. His flailing fists were beating a dog that was chained to the truck's bumper. From my open window, I heard the dog's panicked yelps, and before I knew it, I had turned in to the gravel driveway and was barreling toward him.

Throwing the car into park, I opened the door and jumped out. Adrenaline surged through my veins, and I screamed, "STOP THAT! What's wrong with you?"

The man glared at me from sunken eyes. His skin was the texture of oatmeal, and strands of greasy black hair hung to his shoulders.

The dog was on his belly, a pit bull—rusty-colored with dirty white paws. He looked at me with the saddest brown eyes I'd ever seen, his entire body quivering as he inched himself beneath the truck. Reaching down, the man wrenched a wooden driveway marker from the ground and pointed it at me. "Get outta here, you *bitch*!"

"Not until you stop abusing that dog! If you don't want him, I'll take him."

The man's lips torqued into a hateful sneer, and his words left his mouth in a spray of saliva. "I'll gut ya like a pig."

His chin jutted out as he took two steps toward me, the stench of him so vile that my arms went limp in their sockets. I was horrified when he let out an inhuman growl and charged toward me.

Jumping inside my car, I slammed the door just as he raised the stick over his head and smashed it onto the hood—once, twice, and then a third time. Though half of me wanted to gun the engine and run him down, I jammed the gearshift into reverse and hit the gas. In a tornado of flying gravel, I blasted out of there.

He hurled the stick at my car as I roared down the road.

I was so angry and scared that I pulled in to our driveway too fast and fishtailed over Mama's forsythia. I drove straight for the barn, cut the engine, and raced to find Daddy. He wasn't in the workshop, so I ran inside the barn and found him working on the tractor.

"Daddy! There's a guy beating a dog, and he smashed my car. He's crazy!"

He put down a wrench and took hold of my shoulders. "Whoa. Slow down. Now, what happened?"

Gulping air, I told him exactly what had occurred, my words tumbling out in angry sobs. "He's beating a dog that's *chained* to a truck!"

Daddy pulled a handkerchief from his pocket and handed it to me. "Now, Teddi, I know that what you saw set you off something awful. It would have set me off, too. But you can't go pullin' in to a stranger's driveway and start yelling. You don't know what'll happen or what they'll do."

"But I *had* to. He was—"

"*Shhh.* Now listen to me. He could've hurt you. C'mon, let's go down to the house."

With his arm around my shoulders, we left the barn, but when he saw the dents in the hood of my car, he stopped. "That son of a bitch could have laid your skull wide open. He could've *killed* you, Teddi."

I choked down a sob and grabbed the bag of groceries from the backseat.

Daddy went straight to the phone and called his longtime friend Deputy Sheriff Jeb Davis. While Daddy talked with Jeb, I told Mama and Grammy what had happened. Mama was so upset that when Daddy got off the phone, he had to take her out onto the porch and calm her down.

Jeb came right quick, and with him was another officer named Walt. They asked me questions and took notes, reiterating what Daddy had said about never doing anything like that again. When Daddy took Jeb and Walt to see my damaged car, Mama grabbed a mop. I couldn't believe she'd wash a floor in the middle of a crisis—as if she could bring things back to normal with hot water and suds.

After she'd finished, she looked at me, her face reddened. "All right, now let's finish up those pies."

Side by side we worked, but the air in the kitchen was tense. When Mama slid the pies into the oven, I stepped to the window. "I want that dog, Mama. If you'd seen his eyes—"

She grabbed my arm and spun me around. "You put yourself in danger! What in God's creation were you thinkin'?"

"I had to—"

Just then Daddy came in and hung his jacket on the coat tree. He sat at the table and let out a low groan. "We got any coffee, Franny?"

Mama pulled a mug from the cupboard.

"What did Jeb say?" I asked.

Before he could answer, the back door swung open and Josh walked in. When he saw my face, he set down his schoolbooks. "What's going on?"

Daddy raked his fingers through his hair. "Sit down, son. Everybody, sit down."

Mama handed Daddy his coffee, and all of us took our places at the table. Daddy wrapped his thick fingers around the mug and calmly told Josh what had gone on. But the more he talked, the more my brother's eyes darkened.

Josh's voice dropped low as he looked around the table. "Why are we sitting here? We've got to get the dog."

"Hold on, son. Jeb and Walt went down there to talk with him, and—"

"Talk with him? *Talk?*"

"Josh, simmer down. This has got to be handled by the law."

"The law?" my brother scoffed. "*What* law?"

Mama reached over and pressed her hand on my brother's arm. "Hush. Listen to your father."

Daddy's tone left no room for argument, his words measured. "Josh, I've already told you, this is in Jeb's hands. Now, you let it be. I told him we'd be happy to give the dog a nice home, and—"

"You did?" Mama said, sounding none too pleased.

I flashed her a look. "Don't worry. If we get that poor dog, I'll take him back to Charleston with me."

Daddy took a slow sip of his coffee, stood, and pushed his chair toward the table. "Last thing I knew, *I* was head of this family. I want you kids to promise me that you'll stay away from that man and not go anywhere near the property. I don't know who he is or what he might do. And just so I make myself clear, let me say this one last time: Jeb will handle things. All right?"

I picked at my thumbnail and said, "Yessir." From the corner of my eye, I saw Josh nod.

But barely.

NINETEEN

On Thanksgiving morning, while Mama worked at the stove and Grammy set the table, I went outside to gather branches, leaves, and mums from the garden. Josh was down by the pond, standing close to the water's edge with his hands shoved into the pockets of his denim jacket. After filling the basket with everything I needed to make a centerpiece, I walked down the slope and joined him.

"Hey," I said, giving him a gentle nudge with my elbow.

He kept his eyes fixed on the water and didn't respond. I looked to see what it was that had his attention, but all I saw was a brother and sister standing side by side, our reflections broken by the skittering of a lone water bug darting across the pond's glassy surface.

Josh removed a handkerchief from his pocket and unfolded the edges. "I found this caught in a thistle. It's for you, Teddi."

I pinched the quill of a small gray feather tipped in vibrant blue. It was downy soft and less than an inch long. "It's beautiful, and so tiny. I can't believe you even saw it."

His eyes met mine. "I saw it because I'm awake."

"What do you mean?"

He just kept looking at me, his face void of expression.

"Tell me, Josh. What does that mean?"

"A while ago I was hiking and stopped to take a rest at Angel Windows. I took you there several years ago, remember?"

"The place where we found the fern fossil?"

"Yeah. I was standing in the opening of a stone arch with my arms above my head. While I looked out over the valley and stretched my back, this strange current started traveling up my legs and went straight up my spine. It was like my whole body was getting rewired. Anyway, it's hard to explain, but I've been awake ever since."

While I tried to absorb my brother's words, he looked down at my hand. "Today I was walking through the upper field and thinking about you. That's when I saw the feather."

"What were you thinking about me?"

"How brave you are."

"Brave?"

"When you tried to stop that son of a bitch from beating the dog. That was brave, Teddi. Not smart. But brave." He turned and began walking up the knoll. I fell in line with his stride, the basket of flowers hanging from the crook of my arm.

"That feather is from an indigo bunting. He left it for you."

I stepped over a tractor rut and took hold of my brother's arm. "Why do you say that?"

"Do you know what it means?"

I shook my head.

"Love travels long miles."

My brother picked up his pace and headed toward the barn, leaving me standing on the hillside with a feather in my hand and my mind spinning with questions.

❧

At two o'clock Mama set out a Thanksgiving feast. We all held hands around the linen-covered table while Grammy said grace.

Following a simultaneous "Amen," we began passing dishes and talking. Josh was quieter than usual, and several times I noticed his gaze drift toward the window. Beneath the table I tapped my foot on the toe of his boot and was glad when he finally gave me a tap in return. It was something we'd done since we were kids, one of those little things that probably meant more than either of us understood.

Grammy and I took care of clearing the table and doing dishes while Mama and Daddy relaxed in the living room, he watching football on TV and she with her knitting. Josh put on his jacket and went for a walk, saying he'd be back within an hour.

But he didn't come back.

After setting the table for dessert, I pulled on a heavy sweater and set out to find him. I walked through the barn and out into the field, calling his name again and again. When there was no answer, I gave up and went back inside the house. My brother loved dessert, so I knew he'd be home before long.

As I stood at the counter and whipped a bowlful of cream for the pumpkin pie, I glanced out the window and saw Josh. All but hidden behind the tall weeds, he was walking along the far edge of the field. I switched off the mixer, rinsed the beaters, and dried my hands. When I looked out the window again, an ice pick of panic pierced my chest. I turned toward the door so fast that I knocked the bowl of whipped cream to the floor.

"*Daddy . . . Daddy . . . DADDY!*" I flung open the back door with so much force that it slammed into the wall.

Daddy's voice boomed from behind me as I ran toward the field. "Teddi! What's all the—"

I skidded to a stop and turned to face him, but he was already looking beyond me. "Franny, get a blanket!"

My brother had crossed the edge of the tractor path and walked into the backyard. The front of his yellow flannel shirt was covered in blood, his face gripped by a look of shock, his eyes bright with fury.

Daddy came up by my side and grabbed hold of my shoulders. "Teddi, go in the house."

I buckled over at the waist and took in big gulps of air, and when I straightened up, Mama was spreading a blanket on the grass while Grammy scurried from the house with an armful of towels.

Reverently, my brother went down on his knees and placed the bloody bundle on the blanket. Daddy leaned over and lifted my brother's jacket from the dog's body. Ignoring my father's command, I stepped forward and knelt by his side.

The dog never took his eyes off my brother as Josh gently smoothed his hand over his flank. I leaned close and rested my hand on the dog's shoulder while Grammy covered him with towels.

Daddy looked at Mama. "Franny, hurry and call Doc Evans."

She took off for the house while I spoke to the battered dog. "Hang on, old boy. Hang on. We'll take good care of you. Nothing bad will ever happen to you again."

Bubbles of blood formed on the dog's nostrils.

"We'll call you Buddy," I said through trembling lips. "And when you get all better, you can run through the fields and sleep in the sun." I draped more towels over his body and leaned close to what was left of his ear. "Stay with us, Buddy. This is your last fight. Fight for your life . . ."

The dog and my brother kept looking at each other. Josh took in a breath and slowly let it out. The dog did the same, and then his body stopped quivering. As one more bubble of blood formed on his nostrils, I watched the light go out of his eyes.

Daddy hung his head and patted my brother's shoulder. "He's gone, son."

I couldn't see anything for the flood of tears. Mama came up beside me and tried to get me to go inside the house, but I pushed her hand away. "I'm staying with Buddy. I don't want him to be alone. And I can't stand seeing him this way. We need to clean him up and get all this blood off."

Daddy's voice spilled over my shoulders. "Teddi, we can't clean him up till I call Jeb—"

"No need, Henry," Mama said softly. "I already did. He'll be here directly."

Mama and Daddy set off for the house, their voices low. Grammy wiped her eyes with the hem of her apron and rested her hand on my head for a moment, then turned and followed them.

"Josh," I whispered, "is it okay with you that we name him Buddy?"

He nodded, then rose to his feet and walked away.

For several minutes I sat alone on the grass, quietly weeping as I smoothed my fingers across the top of the dog's snout. "I'm so sorry they did this to you. Go to heaven, Buddy. You'll have friends there waiting." I closed my eyes and remembered the photo I'd once seen in the newspaper of dog ripped to pieces in a dogfight, but that paled in comparison to what had been done to Buddy.

When I heard tires on gravel, I turned to see that Jeb had arrived. Before he could climb out of the patrol car, Doc Evans roared up in his veterinary truck. Moments later Daddy leaned down behind me and said, "Teddi, go in the house."

I shook my head. "I'm staying with Buddy."

Sliding his hands beneath my armpits, he pulled me to my feet. "Go on, now."

My eyes swept from Jeb to Doc Evans. Then Grammy took hold of my arm and led me away.

While I stood at the kitchen sink and scrubbed blood from my hands, I watched Daddy, Jeb, and Doc Evans lean over Buddy's body. Josh was nowhere in sight.

I was so upset that I paced from the kitchen to the living room and back again. From the window I saw Doc Evans on his knees examining Buddy while Jeb flipped open a notepad and began writing. A few minutes later, Jeb got a camera from his car and started taking pictures. I squeezed my eyes closed for the pain of it.

When I dared to look again, Daddy was coming across the lawn with Josh at his side. Jeb spoke to my brother for a long time, taking more notes and occasionally nodding.

After Jeb and Doc Evans pulled out of the driveway, Daddy and Josh walked into the kitchen. My brother looked at me, his face flushed. "I dug a grave behind the barn."

"I'll be ready in a minute," I said, pulling a bucket from the broom closet.

Mama planted her hands on her hips. "Teddi, what are you doing?"

"We're going to wash Buddy."

"Now, just let your brother wrap him up and—"

"No! He can't be buried covered in blood. He's going to heaven clean." I looked away and began filling the bucket with warm, soapy water while Josh went to collect an old bedspread. Then we went outside and began the unspeakable task of preparing Buddy for burial.

Once we had him wrapped in the bedspread, Josh lifted him into his arms. Together we walked behind the barn. With Josh on one end and me on the other, we lowered the bundle into the grave. Just as Josh took a shovel and began covering Buddy's body, Daddy appeared from the side of the barn with a shovel in his hands.

None of us spoke.

When Buddy had been buried and the mound of dirt tamped smooth, Daddy and Josh walked away while I stayed behind and said a prayer of good-bye before heading to the house. As I passed the barn, I heard Josh and Daddy talking. Stopping to listen, I stepped to the open doorway. Daddy was sitting on a wooden stool, scraping mud from the treads of his boots with a pocketknife. Josh was standing by the tractor.

"Then you went down there after I *told* you to stay away. And you—"

"I didn't set foot on that bastard's property until I saw the dog layin' there all chewed up and bloody."

"What if he'd been home? Then what? Jeb says the guy's flat-out crazy."

My brother's voice shot up. "Then why didn't he arrest the son of a bitch when he went there yesterday?"

"Because he didn't have grounds. Jeb thought he and Walt had scared the guy."

"*Scared* him? Yeah, they sure scared him all right. Scared him into using his dog for fighting bait!"

Daddy closed his pocketknife and pushed it into his back pocket. "Jeb's all torn up. He feels terrible, and—"

"Not as terrible as that poor dead dog."

I stepped forward and cleared my throat. "It's my fault. If I had—"

"No, Teddi. You're the only one who tried to *do* something!" Josh marched around the tractor, grabbed a logging chain from a hook on the wall, and headed toward the door.

Daddy jumped to his feet. "Hold it right there. What the hell do you think you're doing?"

My brother turned, his eyes cold slits of blue. "Things like this have got to stop. Well, today's the day, and I'm the person."

Daddy put a firm hand on Josh's shoulder. "Now, son, you listen to me and listen good. You think I don't have the same feelings as you? You think I don't want to kick that man from here to kingdom come? I *do*! But I know better. Mad as I am, this has to be handled by the law."

Josh's face went white as he shook the chain, the heavy clang of metal echoing through the barn. "See what leavin' everything to the *law* did? Well, this time—"

"Simmer down," Daddy warned, grabbing hold of the loose end of chain.

I stood, frozen, and watched the two most important men in my life holding firm to the chain between them, each clinging to his integrity and his own truth.

Josh looked my father square in the eyes. "You've got that medal upstairs. A Bronze Star. You ran through enemy fire to save one of your buddies, you fought in the Battle of the Bulge. You're an honest-to-God war hero. I admire you more than anyone I've ever known. But now you won't even stand up and fight for what's right in your own backyard, and I—"

"ENOUGH!" Daddy roared, tightening the chain. "You know nothing of war. I saw things I can't stand to think about. Boys your age with eyes sunk deep into their skulls, shoulders sticking up as sharp as the blades of my plow. All of 'em half dead. And let me tell you, son, those were the lucky ones."

The veins in Daddy's neck throbbed as he pointed to his face. "I saw evil with my own eyes, and I smelled it with my own nose. I promised the Lord Almighty that if I was lucky enough to make it through the war and have kids, I'd do everything in my power to keep 'em safe."

Daddy gave the chain a firm tug, pulling Josh off balance. "So I give you all the freedom I've got to give, the chance to spend time in the woods studyin' nature and animals, to have a real childhood. And *this* is what you want to do with it? Kill somebody and spend the rest of your life in jail? Now, go in the house and get hold of yourself. What happened to that dog is bad, real bad. I'm all ripped up about it, too. But this isn't war, son."

"You talk about the evils and slaughters of war, but what about the dog? What about what was done to him? How many dead dogs, decapitated birds, slaughtered foxes, and mutilated deer will it take for you and everybody else in this town to *do* something about it?" Josh's chest heaved when he pointed toward the back of the barn. "That grave out there? *That's* the result of evil, too!"

My father opened his mouth, but no words came. Blotches of purple flared above his collar, and his voice dropped low when he said, "You need to get hold of yourself, Josh. And until you do, you're grounded."

"You can't ground me. I'm eighteen."

"As long as you live under my roof, you'll abide by my rules."

For a long moment, Josh stared at my dad. Slowly he opened his fingers and let go of the chain, then he turned and walked toward the house.

Daddy stood motionless as the chain dangled from his hand—*clink, clink, clink*—his eyes fixed on watching his son's silent retreat. Though the light was dim, I could see exhaustion spread across his face. I turned on unsteady legs and left the barn, my stomach burning when I entered the house. Josh had already gone to his room and closed the door. After changing out of my bloodstained clothes and washing up, I flopped onto my bed and buried my face in the pillow.

I woke hours later with a parched throat and a headache. The clock on my night table read 10:40. The house was dark and quiet, the unsettling kind of quiet that takes over after a damaging storm. I climbed out of bed and stepped into the hall. The door to my parents' bedroom was halfway open. In the lamplight I could see Daddy sitting on the edge of the bed. He was in his pajamas, hunched over with his elbows resting on his knees. In his hands he held his Bronze Star. Over and over he rubbed his thumb across its surface, his face so sad I couldn't bear it. I was going to say something but changed my mind and quietly tiptoed to the bathroom to take some aspirin.

On my way back to bed, I noticed a faint glow from beneath my brother's closed door. "Josh," I whispered, tapping my fingernail on his door. When he didn't answer, I turned the knob and stepped inside, closing the door silently behind me.

He was sitting in a chair facing the window, his feet propped on the sill. On his desk a candle flickered from inside a jelly jar. Two feathers, one white and one black, lay crossed over each other to form an X. Arranged in a half circle below the feathers were three stones, a dried thistle, and a disintegrating monarch butterfly. It was a shrine of sorts, the place where my brother ceremoniously placed nature's gifts.

Though his eyes were set on the window, they were focused inward. He was still wearing the bloodied flannel shirt, and the soles of his boots were caked in dirt from Buddy's grave.

I knelt at his side and lightly touched his shoulder. "Josh?"

Though I'd seen him like this a few times before, disappearing into a dark spiral set off by an atrocity he'd heard about on the news or seen in the woods, I had the feeling this time was the worst.

Leaning forward, I rested my head on his arm. "Josh, please don't shut me out. It scares me when you go so deep that I can't reach you."

I remained in that position and waited for my brother to acknowledge me. I waited until my knees ached, but still my brother never moved, nor did he speak. Reaching out, I slid my hand beneath his fingers. I felt a wave of relief when he gave me a gentle squeeze. But still he said nothing.

"All right," I said, rocking back on my heels. "We'll talk tomorrow, okay?"

Stepping to his desk, I ran my fingers over the butterfly's wings, then cupped my hand around the candle and blew out the flame.

The following morning I woke feeling sweaty and raw. When I flipped back the covers and sat up, I saw a folded piece of paper shoved beneath my door.

I rose from the bed, the wooden floor cool against my feet as I stepped across the room. Reaching down, I picked up the paper and opened it. Taped by its quill to the center of the page was a slender feather, shiny and pitch black. Beneath it my brother had written the words:

> *When shadows take flight*
> *and the moon turns away from the stars,*
> *the raven delivers divine law*

Every nerve in my body snapped when I read the five words my brother had written at the bottom right-hand corner:

> *Don't come looking for me.*

I raced to Josh's bedroom and exploded through the door. His bed hadn't been slept in, and the closet door hung open. More than half the hangers were empty.

Barefoot and still in my pajamas, I thundered down the stairs and through the kitchen, where Mama and Grammy were preparing breakfast.

"Teddi! What in the world?" Mama said as I flung open the back door.

I flew down the porch steps and raced toward the barn. From behind me I heard Daddy call my name, but I just kept running as fast as I could go. Into the barn and past the tractor I went, screaming, "Josh. Josh!"

I darted toward the storage room, gasping for air. The padlock hung open. Reaching out, I gave the door a push.

My brother's camping gear was gone.

Daddy was coming across the yard when I ran back toward the house. "Teddi, what's wrong?"

"Josh is gone!"

For the first time in my life, I saw fear spark in my father's eyes. He turned and bolted into the house. As I climbed the porch steps, my bare feet freezing and so winded I couldn't catch my breath, I heard Daddy yell, "Franny, call the sheriff's office, tell 'em to get over to the Hickson place! *Now!*" He pushed through the door with his shotgun in his hands. "Teddi, go in the house and stay there."

As Daddy's truck roared down the driveway in a flurry of dust and flying gravel, I stood on the porch and prayed, *Please, keep my brother safe. Please, please . . .*

TWENTY

When I finished telling Olivia what had happened, her face was pale and expressionless. She tightened the afghan around her shoulders and shuddered. "My stomach is tied in knots. Your brother went after that bastard, didn't he?"

"I suspect he did. But what he didn't know was that Jeb had already arrested Sheedy."

"Sheedy?"

"That was the guy's name, Creighton Sheedy. He wasn't home when Jeb and Walt first went to his house on Thanksgiving night, but a few hours later they went back and he was there. He got belligerent when they tried to talk to him. Jeb said he gave them plenty of cause to haul him to jail, so they did. By eight-thirty that night, Sheedy was sitting behind bars. So that eliminated him as a suspect in any foul play."

This was the first time I'd ever told anyone the whole story, and the same burning sensation I'd experienced the day my brother disappeared now spread across my chest. I unbuttoned the top of my blouse and ran my fingertips along my collarbone.

"We all thought Josh was just so angry that he needed time alone to cool off. But when he'd been gone for two days, Daddy talked with Jeb and the park rangers. He was worried that Josh had gone deep into the woods, slipped, and was lying out there with a shattered leg. Or worse. Even though Josh was eighteen and had clearly left of his own volition, Jeb and the rangers organized a search. They even brought in dogs that tracked his scent all the way to Clifty Wilderness, but they lost it when they came to a cliff. The following morning a group of experienced climbers rappelled down the cliff, but they didn't find a thing. That's when I got busy and made up flyers with a picture of Josh. They were handed out to visitors at Daniel Boone National Forest and Red River Gorge, and all the fishing and hiking shops posted them, too. But days turned into weeks, and nobody came up with a single lead. It was as if the wind came and blew my brother clean off the map."

Olivia's forehead was creased with tension. "Oh, my God. This is more awful than anything I imagined. They found *nothing?* Did they comb the entire area?"

"Daniel Boone National Forest has more than seven hundred forty *thousand* acres."

When the magnitude of that number sank in, Olivia's lips parted.

"And let me tell you, a lot of the terrain is impassable. All sorts of theories floated around. Most people thought Josh was climbing and fell to his death into a crevice, and a few people said a bear got him. A group of campers swore they'd seen the shadowy figure of a teenage boy walking high on a ridge with a bird flying over his head. They claimed they called to him and he looked in their direction, but then he and the bird vanished into a blue mist. We all knew it was just campfire talk fueled by too much beer, but it wasn't long before my brother had become something of a legend. Some of the locals referred to him as the 'Invisible Boy.'"

Olivia shook her head. "Oh, Teddi. I can't imagine how distraught your family must have been . . ."

I squeezed my hands between my knees and thought, *No, there is no way anyone could imagine.*

The long days of unbearable tension followed by sleepless nights filled with the whys and what-ifs. And then came the arguments. Who to blame? Who to crucify?

Mama blamed me.

"This is *your* fault!" she cried. "Look what you've done. If you'd minded your own business and not driven to the Hickson place, this never would have happened!"

The fury of her words scorched my cheeks, and when I couldn't take it anymore, I turned and walked outside. Standing in the frigid night air, I watched my breath leave my body in small puffs of white. As much as they hurt, my mother's words were no surprise. I blamed me, too.

From inside the house, I heard Mama yelling at my grandmother. When I turned and looked in the window, she was shaking her finger in Grammy's face. "This all began with YOU! Taking my children into the woods and feeding them wild stories!"

One morning while Mama stood at the stove stirring oatmeal and laying into me about Josh's disappearance, Daddy brought down his hand on the kitchen table so hard that the breakfast dishes jumped. "Franny June! That's *enough*. If there's any blame to be had, it's mine and mine alone. You understand?"

Mama clamped her mouth shut and never uttered a word of blame again. In fact, she stopped talking altogether.

But the abrupt end to the blaming and yelling ushered in something far darker—a silence so thick that we began to suffocate. Words clotted in our throats. We kept our eyes cast downward at the supper table. The sound of forks scraping across plates was unbearable, as was the thunder created when Daddy stomped snow off his boots on the back porch. A sheet of paper towel being torn from the roll was startling.

These things became the language of a family ripped apart.

The calendar on the kitchen wall hung unnoticed. When December came, no one turned the page. Time at the Overman farm had come to a halt. One day we were a family holding hands around the Thanksgiving table, next thing we knew, my brother's picture had been stapled to telephone poles.

As the wordless months of winter gave way to spring, life slowly seeped back in, revealing itself with a simple gesture of kindness or an unexpected smile. One evening during my visit home in April, Daddy glanced up from his supper plate and said, "Franny, these scalloped potatoes are mighty fine."

Mama's face flushed, and she looked down at her hands and whispered, "Thank you, Henry."

That was when I knew my family, as broken and battered as we were, would try to mend the ragged hole my brother's departure had left behind.

"It's heartbreaking," Olivia said, her voice piercing my private thoughts. "Did *everyone* just presume Josh was either a runaway or dead?"

I had been squeezing my hands so hard between my knees they'd gone numb. I pulled them free and looked at Olivia. "No. Not everyone. After Christmas nearly a hundred climbers and hikers volunteered to do another search. Three of them came all the way from Colorado. They gathered with the rangers for a meeting over at Hemlock Lodge. The local TV station even filmed the meeting for the evening news. Mama couldn't take it anymore, so she didn't go. But Daddy, Grammy, and I went.

"Ranger Jim taped two giant maps on the windows in the dining room, one of Daniel Boone Forest and another of the heart of the Gorge. When I saw all those determined faces studying the maps, I broke down and cried. Daddy was so choked up he couldn't talk, and Grammy hung her head. You should have seen it, Olivia. Church ladies brought in all sorts of food. Farmers set up extra beds to house the searchers when they came off the mountain. It was a huge event, especially for these parts."

My chest heaved when I looked at Olivia. "But even while everyone was searching, deep down I knew they wouldn't find Josh."

She tilted her head. "Why?"

"Because he didn't *want* to be found. I think my brother set off to do what he believed was his destiny."

"Which was?"

Shifting on my hip, I slid the newspaper clipping from my back pocket. Without saying a word, I unfolded the paper and offered it to Olivia. She held it to the lamplight, her face draining of color as she read:

Naked Man Found Bound to Tree in Clifty Wilderness

Yesterday afternoon three hikers made a startling discovery on the south side of Clifty Wilderness. Alex Bell, Doug York, and Byron Jennings, all from Tennessee, were heading back to their campsite when they heard muffled moans and detected a stench. What they came upon was shocking. A man, naked and in great distress, was taped to a tree. A red fox, still snared in the illegal trap that had killed him, was tied around the man's neck.

During questioning, the man, identified as Arnold G. Paddick, 43, admitted he had been unlawfully trapping animals. After setting several traps on Tuesday, he returned on Wednesday to check them. Paddick claims that as he reached the trap with the fox, a roll of duct tape flew through the air and hit him in the shoulder.

He turned to see a man wearing dark clothing and a mask made of mud and leaves appear from behind a stand of trees.

Paddick alleges that the man aimed an arrow at his face and demanded he remove all his clothing. Paddick stripped and was then ordered to tape his feet together. The masked man bound Paddick to the tree and gagged him. He then tied the trap holding the dead fox around Paddick's neck.

According to Paddick, the masked man pointed the arrow at his nose and said, "You're going to remember what you did to this fox for the rest of your worthless life. Don't come back here again. If you do, I'll hunt you down."

For nearly two days, Paddick tried to free himself while the stench of the rotting fox carcass grew so unbearable that he claims to have lost consciousness.

Paddick was cited with five counts of poaching. Following treatment for exposure and dehydration, he was released from Clark Regional Medical Center.

Olivia looked at me, stunned. "*No!* You think the masked guy in this article is your *brother?*"

"I don't know what to think. But Daddy must have thought it was Josh. Otherwise there wouldn't have been any reason for him to have cut out the article."

"Teddi, why didn't you ever tell me about this?"

"I didn't know about it until today. I found the clipping hidden in Daddy's desk. I can understand why Mama didn't mention it. Over the years there have been plenty of strange occurrences in the mountains—murder victims dumped in the wilderness, campers robbed, poachers beaten up. If Mama saw the article or heard about it, she wouldn't have thought it had anything to do with Josh. By that time she was positive he was dead. But I don't know why Daddy didn't tell me."

Olivia glanced out the window. "Maybe he wanted to protect you, Teddi. Maybe he was worried it would reopen old wounds." She moved closer to the lamp, read the article again, and then handed it to me. "So was Josh a marksman with a bow and arrow?"

I folded the article and pushed it into my pocket. "Not that I ever knew. But I've come to accept there's a whole lot about Josh I didn't know."

Olivia took a sip of coffee, which had long since gone cold. The smudges of blue beneath her eyes were deepening with the late hour. "And what about that son of a bitch Sheedy? What happened to him?"

"Turns out he was part of a dogfighting ring. In exchange for a reduced sentence, he exposed the other members of the ring and pled guilty to lesser charges. He was sentenced to fifteen days in jail and had to do some community service. Hardly a punishment for what he did to Buddy. Even after Sheedy served his time, Jeb and his men rode him real hard. Jeb said Sheedy wouldn't be able to take a leak for the rest of his life without them knowing about it. It must have been true, because Sheedy moved away."

Olivia tilted her head and studied me. "What is it, Teddi? What makes you believe that your brother is alive? Other than the possibility that he was the guy in the article, has there ever been any trace of him?"

"No. Nothing." I closed my eyes and rubbed the headache that was forming at my temples. "I just have this feeling."

∞

For the next several days, Olivia and I worked from morning till night, our hands reddened and chapped as we sorted and cleaned.

Hour after hour the sharp squeal of packing tape being run across the tops of boxes echoed through the house. Soon the dining room was jammed with items to be given to charities or sold. Everything else we tossed out. By Monday afternoon we'd gone through all the rooms on the first floor.

We were exhausted.

"C'mon, let's get out of here for a while," I said, looking up at Olivia. She was standing on a ladder in the pantry, wiping down shelves with vinegar water.

"Where do you want to go?"

"I'm not telling, but I need you to drive, since we haven't tied down the things in the van yet."

She threw me a quizzical look, grabbed her truck keys, and off we went. Within a few minutes, we'd turned on a road nearly hidden by trees. Olivia grinned when she pulled in to the parking lot and cut the engine. "I was wondering if I'd get to see the Gorge."

We walked to the ticket house, and when I opened the door, I saw that Norma Higgins was working behind the counter. The gray hair I remembered was now pure white, but her smile was the same as always when she tottered around the counter to give me a hug.

"Teddi!"

I introduced her to Olivia, and she reached up and gave her a hug, too. That was Norma, ninety pounds of kindness. We talked for a few minutes, and then she pointed to the corkboard mounted on the wall. A glove here, a pair of sunglasses there, a pink flip-flop, a baseball cap—dozens of items lost by tourists and hikers. But when I saw what she was *really* pointing toward, words dissolved in my mouth and blood roared in my ears. Thumbtacked to the upper right corner was a faded flyer inside a clear plastic sleeve.

"I'll never take it down," Norma said, patting my hand and turning to look at my brother's face. "There's always hope, honey."

I could do nothing but nod.

Olivia paled when she looked at the flyer, but she rallied quickly and changed the subject. "You sure work in a beautiful area, Norma," she said, gazing out the window at the mountain.

"Oh, yes. I've worked here since the Sky Lift opened back in '67. Never tire of the scenery. You girls goin' up?"

"Yes. Two tickets, please."

I pulled money from my pocket, but Norma waved it away. "On the house," she said with a wink. "You came on a good day. The weather's nice and cool, and we haven't had but a handful of visitors. I imagine you'll be alone on the mountain."

While Olivia and I walked to the Sky Lift platform, she took hold of my arm. "Wow, talk about being blindsided. Are you all right, Teddi?"

"I'm fine. Norma didn't mean any harm. She's a good soul."

The cable pulley hummed overhead as a red chairlift scooped us from the platform. The attendant locked the safety bar with a sturdy *click*, and Olivia's eyes widened when she saw how far the cable stretched up the mountain. "Um, how far are we going?"

"A little over a half mile. So don't flip out on me, because there's no way to get off until we're at the top."

The higher we moved up the mountain, the quieter it became, until the only sound was the sharp *teacher-teacher-teacher* call of an ovenbird far below our dangling feet.

When we reached the top of the mountain and stepped off the platform, I led Olivia along a rugged path where nature offered gift upon gift: bulging tree roots with giant knuckles that formed steps over hazardous terrain, the echo of a pileated woodpecker hammering out its home, the fecund perfume of damp earth and moss.

As we came upon a crest, I turned and whispered, "Look." In the sun-checkered shade stood a white-tailed deer. We watched the young doe pick her way around a cluster of ferns, and then she disappeared beneath a dark scaffolding of leaning trees. The wind picked up, and with it came a hymn of the forest—the steady rush of a waterfall, the whistle of an eastern meadowlark, the rustle of dry leaves. To my ears no choir on earth could send a more glorious song through the air.

A surge of blue filled the sky when we finally reached our destination. Olivia's lips parted in awe.

We stood side by side on the highest point of Kentucky's famed Natural Bridge. As if by magic, more than nine hundred tons of ancient sandstone had been suspended across the mountain face. Sculpted into a soaring arch by 70 million years of weather, it was spectacular and eerie at once.

To stand here was to experience the magnitude of Mother Nature, to witness her artistry and ruthless power. I closed my eyes and felt the winds of her sympathy move through my hair, and I listened to her tender mercies echo across craggy cliffs.

To stand here was to feel inadequate and grand and connected to something far beyond comprehension. But most of all, to stand here was to feel forgiven.

TWENTY-ONE

"Thanks for all the kitchen gadgets," Olivia said, sliding a cardboard box across the bed of her truck. "I love that old grinding mill."

"You're welcome." Together we closed the tailgate, then covered the back with a tarp and tied down the corners. "Be careful going home. I feel guilty for working you half to death." I looked up and watched dark clouds plow through the sky. "I know you hate driving in the rain. The weatherman said it would hold off, but it sure doesn't look like it."

Olivia dug her keys from her handbag. "He'd better be right, or I'll hunt him down and stick a barometer up his ass."

I burst out laughing.

"Teddi," she said, opening the driver's-side door, "I don't like leaving you all alone. Are you sure you'll be okay?"

I gave her a fierce hug. "Don't worry, I'll be fine."

Though her eyes conveyed that she thought otherwise, Olivia let it go. She started the engine and rolled down the driveway while Bear stuck his head out the passenger window. I waved good-bye until she vanished around the bend, and then I knelt and rubbed Eddie's ears. "Well, it's just you and me." As much as he loved playing with Bear, he gave me a lick as if he liked that idea.

After gathering a few empty boxes and another roll of tape, I headed upstairs to Mama's bedroom. Stacked inside the old pie safe she'd used for storage were magazines, folders filled with recipes, and canceled checks bound together with dried-out rubber bands.

I sifted through each shelf: *keep, toss, save for auction.* The feelings and memories that surfaced from touching my mother's personal things twisted my insides, and twice I had to swallow back my tears. Much of what I found made no sense—an old green woolen scarf that moths had turned to lace, a bag of bobby pins, a chipped glass candleholder. Mama had saved those things, yet I found nothing that held memories of her family.

I stepped over to Daddy's night table and pulled open the drawer. It was empty. My eyes darted from the pie safe to her chest of drawers. "Where is it, Mama? Where'd you put Daddy's Bronze Star? I *know* it was here after he died."

Memories, Mama had once said. *Who needs them? The past is the past and best forgotten.*

She'd said those words when I helped her clean Josh's bedroom four years after he disappeared. In between his mattress and box springs, I'd discovered a manila envelope filled with handmade maps, each with detailed drawings and notes. When I set them aside to take home with me, Mama had turned toward the window and said, "He's gone, Teddi. Saving those maps will only break your heart."

And now, as I lifted her handbag from the desk chair, I spoke into the stillness of the room. "Memories matter to *me*, Mama."

I sat on the edge of the bed with her handbag on my lap and pulled open the zipper. Item by item I removed the contents: a wrinkled linen handkerchief with blue embroidered edges, her green vinyl checkbook stuffed with coupons for chicken soup and a two-for-one Glad Wrap special. Before Mama's death these things would have meant nothing, but now they had become so precious I could hardly bear to look at them.

Inside her brown coin purse were two quarters and a tube of lipstick in a shade named Pink Paradise. It was Mama's favorite color. That half-used tube of lipstick represented the end of my mother's life more profoundly than her death certificate. I held the lipstick in my hand until the metal tube grew warm, until the first drops of rain spattered against the window.

SPRING 1969

Mama was in the kitchen preparing supper. I watched her stand at the counter and roll out baking-powder biscuits, her mouth set in a thin ribbon. Though I didn't know why, she'd been in a foul mood for days, and by the looks of things she wasn't going to get happy anytime soon.

Using a jelly jar turned upside down, she cut the dough into circles and placed them on a baking sheet. Josh and I were sitting at the kitchen table playing a game of checkers. The rules of a quiet house were in force, and we were careful not to giggle or click the checkers together.

It had been raining for nearly a week, and the ground had swelled beyond capacity. Just that morning Mama had stood at the window and watched a torrent of water lift her marigolds from the ground and carry them down the driveway, the yellow blossoms spinning in circles before they drowned at the side of the road.

Black clouds rolled low over the house, and flashes of lightning sliced through the sky. Water had trickled into the cellar, and a musty odor rose through the iron grate on the floor by the kitchen table. Mama hated the smell of it and lit a vanilla-scented candle to freshen the air.

She put the biscuits into the oven and never so much as glanced at Josh and me when she walked to the closet. With an umbrella in hand, she opened the back door and stepped out onto the porch. I pushed back my chair and followed.

"Where are you going, Mama?"

"Out to the workshop, to get your father for dinner."

A gust of wind blew rain into my face as I pointed to the sky. "No, Mama. Not in this storm. You could get hit by lightning!"

She turned, her dress getting soaked as the wind ripped through her hair. The look on her face startled me, eyes empty of light, skin as white as paraffin. "Don't worry," she said, opening the umbrella. "I couldn't possibly be that lucky."

⁓

The memory of that day played over and over in my mind. With her tube of lipstick still clutched in my hand, I turned away from the window and looked around her bedroom. "Why, Mama? Why were you so unhappy? Just look where it got you."

From the top drawer of her pine bureau, I removed bras, panties, and slips, all of which I packed into a box. The next drawer held a few skeins of ivory wool and a photo album, its leather cover nearly mummified from age.

I sat on the floor with the album on my lap. Dried-out sheets of protective film crackled and threatened to fall apart in my hands. On the third page was a black-and-white picture of Josh. Sliding it from beneath the film, I angled it to the light. He was about nine or ten and was sitting at the edge of the pond. His smile was wide with innocence, his eyes crinkled into half-moons. I studied that picture for a long time, trying to reconcile the photograph of the child in my hand to the description of the mud-masked man in the newspaper article.

In the middle of the album was a photograph taken when Daddy had been in the army. He was standing on a Sherman tank with his arm around the shoulders of a man named Max Walker.

Max was Daddy's best war buddy, and the events of one single moment had left the two of them forever bound together.

It was December of 1944. The Sixth Armored Division was charging through Belgium. Inside the cramped quarters of the tank was a crew of four soldiers, two of whom were Private First Class Max Walker and my dad, Private Henry Overman, who was the bow gunner and assistant driver. The weather was brutal. Subzero temperatures froze the tank turret, and ice had to be chipped away to free the action of the gun. If ice or snow covered the periscope, the driver was rendered blind. That's when someone with nerves of steel had to climb into the open to clear it off, frequently under enemy fire.

It was under these conditions that Max Walker exploded from the hatch. While clearing ice from the periscope, he was felled by a bullet that tore into his hip. As he lay writhing in pain, someone jumped from the tank. Under a hailstorm of enemy fire, it was the Kentucky farm boy with the lopsided gait who carried Max Walker back inside the tank. That farm boy was my dad.

When I reached the last page, it occurred to me that the album in my lap was as fragile as my family's singular and collective lives, and I held it against my chest for a moment before setting it aside.

I opened the bottom drawer of Mama's bureau and removed packages of hosiery and cotton pajamas. Beneath a blue seersucker robe was a shiny white box. Even before removing the lid and unfolding the tissue, I knew what I'd found.

I had first discovered it when I was five, maybe six years old, and I still remembered every soft tuck and hand-sewn seam. I had touched it dozens of times in my youth, and more than once I'd pretended it was mine.

Layer by layer I unfolded the tissue.

Crafted of fine silk and clearly handmade, the nightgown was the color of pink face powder and had a cool, liquid feel, as if you could pour it into a teacup. It was obvious that Mama had never worn it.

When I was a little girl, I would sometimes tiptoe into my mother's bedroom when she was down the hall taking her evening bath. I'd wait until I heard her splash, and then would soundlessly pull open the drawer so I could feast my eyes on the incredible gown. Carefully, I'd run my fingers over the slender ribbon straps and marvel at the three perfect silk rosebuds sewn at the center of the gathered bodice. Some nights I would fantasize about the gown until I heard the bathtub drain, belch, and gurgle, and in a mad rush I'd fold the tissue over the gown, push the drawer closed, and hightail it to my bedroom before Mama came padding down the hall.

The gown looked just as beautiful to me now as it did then. I tucked it back inside the box and set it aside to take home, which I did just two days later, but not because I was done cleaning out the house.

While carrying an armful of boxes into the dining room and adding them to the dozens already filled with items I planned to tag for a spring yard sale, I stopped and looked around the room. Envisioning my family's history spread out on tables—the pink melamine dishes Mama had collected with S&H Green Stamps, Daddy's thermal vests, Grammy's chipped Mr. and Mrs. Piggy salt and pepper shakers, and my brother's collection of Lincoln Logs—all of it being picked over and, yes, some of it even chuckled over, was more than I could bear.

It was time to go back to Charleston.

↝

The overhead light felt harsh against my tired eyes as I climbed the stairs of my carriage house. I stood in the doorway of the guest bedroom and looked at Mama's urn. "I cleaned out the house, Mama. Well, most of it anyway. I have a van parked on the street that's crammed full of boxes. You know what's in all those boxes, Mama? *Memories*."

I turned and went into the kitchen to feed Eddie. From the cupboard I removed a tin of chamomile tea, and I set the kettle on the stove. While waiting for the water to boil, I marched back to the guest room and plunked down on the edge of the bed.

"And guess what else, Mama? I brought back so many boxes full of memories that I don't know where the heck to store them. If I had a house, it'd be different. But I don't. Wanna know *why* I don't have a house? I'm finally going to tell you.

"Remember how you poked me for not owning my own home? Well, I'd have one by now if Grammy hadn't broken her hip. But her medical insurance doesn't cover all the nursing-home costs, so I've had to bridge the gap. I'm glad I can do it, but damn it, Mama, I don't make enough money to pay my rent, take care of Grammy, and keep the farm, too. I love that farm, and it'll rip me apart to sell it.

"So while you're up there knitting white socks for angels or bitching about the food being too salty, just take a look down here and see for yourself—I have the prettiest little shop you could imagine, and if you hadn't up and died before you got here, you'd know exactly what I'm talkin' about. I miss you so much, Mama. And I'm mad at you, too."

Rising from the bed, I gave her urn a little *ping* with my finger and left the room.

TWENTY-TWO

There were several antique shops in Charleston, and though we owners had a healthy respect for one another's quirks and individual areas of expertise, there was no mistaking the undercurrent of rivalry. I was just about to head out the door to see what my competitors were showcasing when a man walked in. He was short and paunchy, with a baseball cap pulled low on his head. A plastic pocket protector with the words RODNEY'S WRECKING & TOWING printed on its front glared from his navy blue polo shirt. He was one of those people who filled up a room upon entering, and not in a good way. He spoke before I even had the chance to extend a greeting.

"My wife was in here on Saturday. She talked to a short woman with red hair about that chest." He pointed a beefy finger toward the eighteenth-century Renaissance chest that I'd recently acquired. "When she asked about negotiating the price, the redhead said all prices were decided by the owner. So that's why I'm here. Is the owner around?"

"My name is Teddi Overman. I'm the owner."

His eyes swept over me. "My wife says the price of that chest is three thousand dollars. I told her that was ridiculous. She must have misunderstood."

"Your wife is correct. This chest was crafted in Italy in the mid-

1700s. The Italians are known for selecting specimen woods. As you can see, it's in remarkable condition." I pulled open the top drawer and showed him how beautifully it was constructed. "This is Brazilian rosewood. Pieces like this don't come along very often. All things considered, it's a steal."

He narrowed his eyes. "A *steal?* Are you one of those Charleston trust-fund kids who don't know how hard it is to earn a dollar?"

Slowly, I pushed the drawer closed and looked him in the eyes. "No, I'm originally from Kentucky. And from where do you hail, Mr. . . . ?

"Barnes. Rodney Barnes. Came up from Miami to visit my wife's nephew. He's a cadet at The Citadel. Now, *there's* a place packed with trust-fund kids. Anyway, as for this here chest, I've gotta be honest with you—"

Oh, here it comes, the baloney that precedes the dickering.

"There's a shop a few blocks away that has a chest a lot like it for a whole lot less money."

"Well," I said, making a sweeping gesture toward the door, "then I suggest you go buy it."

As this clearly wasn't the response he was expecting, Mr. Barnes took a small step back. "I would, but see, my wife wants *this* one. It's her birthday, and I promised her she could pick out whatever she wanted."

"Oh, with your charming ways, I'm sure you can reason with her, Mr. Barnes. And who knows? Maybe you can get the other chest for even less than you think."

He glanced out the front window and sucked his teeth. I could almost see his mind churning to come up with his next strategy. But I had my own strategy, too. Though Mr. Palmer had taught me the art of haggling, there were rare events when holding firm rendered the best results.

"Look, here's the deal," he said, turning toward me. "I'll give you fifteen hundred dollars *cash* for this chest as long as you throw in the shipping."

"I'm sorry, but I don't have any wiggle room."

"Aw, c'mon," he scoffed. "When cash is on the table, there's *always* wiggle room. I thought you said you were the owner."

I flashed him an icy look. "I am. But I wouldn't be for long if I gave away my precious antiques. It's been nice speaking with you, Mr. Barnes. I hope you and wife enjoy your visit in Charleston."

Just as he opened his mouth, the bell above the door chimed and a woman walked in. From the look on Rodney's face, I knew that the chubby blonde was his wife. Her red skirt was as tight as a second skin, and she hurried forward with quick little steps that sent her hoop earrings swaying.

Rodney looked both surprised and annoyed to see her. "Chrissie, I told you I'd meet you when I was done. We're just now finishing up, so why don't you run along and—"

"I couldn't wait," she bubbled. "Isn't that chest the most beautiful thing you've ever seen?" Sliding her arm around his thick waist, she looked in his eyes. "Did you get it for me?"

His lips formed a stiff smile. "Yes, honey. I got you your chest for a real nice price."

She rose on her tiptoes and kissed his cheek. "Oh, Rodney," she cooed, "you're the *smartest* man in the world."

He patted her back. "Go on and let me finish up here. I'll meet you at that coffee shop around the corner."

Rodney watched his wife exit the door, then pulled out his thick wallet. His face reddened, and he avoided my eyes as he counted out the money and dropped it on top of the chest. He still didn't look at me when he slipped a pen from his pocket protector and wrote down an address on the back of his business card. Tossing the card on top of the money, he clicked his pen closed and grumbled, "Have it delivered to that address. What's the shipping cost?"

I smiled and threw him a bone. "Shipping is on the house, Mr. Barnes."

After writing out his receipt, I tucked it inside a white linen envelope and handed it to him. Our eyes never met when he all but ripped the envelope from my fingers and walked away. I pushed his money and business card deep into my pocket, and when the door closed behind him, I raised my voice and chortled, "Oh, Rodney, you're the *smartest* man in the world!"

While heading toward my office, I saw Albert and Inez standing in the hallway. Albert laughed and mimicked the voice of a radio sports announcer. "Teddi Overman takes the snap from Big Rodney and fakes a handoff. Then she goes straight up the gut for the *touchdown!*"

While I laughed along with him, Inez held out her hand, palm up. "I told you she'd get full price."

Albert slapped a five-dollar bill into her waiting hand. "Yeah, when that man said 'trust fund,' I knew I was cooked."

My mouth dropped open. "You two were *betting* on me?"

Inez pushed her hand down the front of her dress and tucked the bill into her bra. "Of course. We do it all the time."

Just then the bell over the door chimed. Inez pressed her hand to her bosom and whispered, "Oh, shoot. I hope he hasn't changed his mind."

Ready for battle, I turned and walked to the front of the shop. But it wasn't the return of blustery Rodney. Standing just inside the door was a short wisp of a man. His shirt hung limp from a hanger of bones, and his pants were so baggy they pooled at his ankles. He removed a straw hat from his head, and when he spoke, his voice was soft, almost apologetic. "Good morning, ma'am. I was wondering if your buyer might be handy."

"I'm Teddi Overman, the owner. How may I help you, sir?"

"My name's Willard Otis. Guess you'd say I'm a collector," he said while eyeing my shop. "I'm in need of . . . Well, it's time I cleared out some things. So I packed up my truck and drove down from Lee County. Thought I'd see if any of you city dealers might like to have a look."

This kind of thing wasn't uncommon, junk pickers and scavengers hoping to make a few dollars. In the past I'd always declined, but Lee County was poverty-stricken, and this man, who was eighty years old if he was a day, was clearly not doing well.

"I'd be pleased, Mr. Otis. Why don't you show me what you have to offer? Is your truck close by?"

"Yes, ma'am. Got it parked right down the street."

After asking Inez to mind the shop for a few minutes, I walked a half block with the old gentleman until we came to a rusty gray pickup with tall, makeshift sides built from weathered lumber.

His knobby fingers moved slowly as he unlatched the tailgate. Pulling a set of handmade steps from the back of the truck, he set them on the street and said, "Go on up and have a look."

The truck was crammed to capacity, and the only place to maneuver was in a narrow aisle hollowed out in the center. I inched my way into the mess and began to hunt.

Shoved next to a 1920s icebox was a hideous green velvet chair, and sitting on top of a TV was a western saddle, its leather stiff and cracked. Boxes filled with toasters, hand mixers, and all sorts of clocks were jammed beneath a wooden bench. A hairless doll stared up at me from inside a galvanized washtub.

While I rummaged around, I caught a glimpse of the old man standing by the tailgate, his watery eyes bright with hope, his lips twitching as if in silent prayer. The desperation on his face got to me. I mean, it really got to me.

Beneath a rather nice old quilt, I found a small teddy bear sitting inside a pressure cooker. The bear was only about ten inches tall, and a good bit of his golden mohair was worn off—or "loved off," as I preferred to say. He was an old bear with wide-set ears and boot-button eyes. I picked him up and gave his belly the squeeze test. He was stuffed with excelsior.

Clutching the teddy to my chest, I moved toward the tailgate. I was about to end my search when I noticed a small cedar case with double latches. Taking hold of the handle, I pulled it free, then gingerly climbed down the rickety steps.

"Will you hold him for a minute?" I asked, handing over the teddy.

The old gentleman took the bear and set his gaze on the wooden case. "You have any idea what's in there?"

"Art supplies?" I guessed, setting it on the tailgate.

His eyes sparkled as he shook his head. "I s'pect you'll be surprised."

I flipped the latches and opened the lid. Nestled inside was a tarnished brass telescope accompanied by a screw-threaded eyepiece and a short tripod base. It was a tabletop model. Though only about eighteen inches long and three inches in diameter, the telescope lay heavily in my hands. The circular backplate was inscribed with the name J. VAN DER BILDT, FRANEKER.

I ran my fingertips over a small dent along its side. "Does it work?"

No doubt fearing he might lose a sale, Mr. Otis began to fidget. "Well, I *think* it does."

Whether the telescope worked or not really didn't matter. It was a beautiful old instrument, and I loved it. That was the thing about my business: When I least expected it, a certain piece I had no knowledge about would grab me, and against all logic I simply had to have it.

"Mr. Otis, I'd like to buy the telescope and the teddy bear. So what's your price for both?"

"I'd sure like to get a hundred and a half for the spyglass." He glanced at the teddy in his hand. "How about a dollar for the stuffed toy?"

On an ordinary day, I would have jumped on it with both feet. I would have paid the asking price and waited until he drove away before I squealed. But this wasn't an ordinary day, and the man before me was no ordinary man. As I reached into my pants pocket, I wondered when he'd had his last meal. I removed the cash that Mr. Barnes had given me for the Italian chest, and counted out five one-hundred-dollar bills. Then I took the teddy from the old man's hand, and replaced it with the money.

I snapped the latches closed on the case and turned to face him. "Mr. Otis, I have no idea what this telescope is worth, but I believe it's more than you're asking. So if you're happy with the sale, I'm happy."

He looked up at me, confused. "You sayin' you're giving me five hundred dollars?"

"That's correct."

A wide smile spread across his face, exposing several blank spaces between his stubby yellow teeth. "Well, I . . . Thank you, ma'am. God bless you!"

After shaking my hand, he lifted the steps into the truck and closed the tailgate. I stood on the sidewalk while he started the engine. The muffler sent a puff of exhaust into the air as the truck lurched from the curb. I watched him drive away and said, "God bless you, too, Mr. Otis."

Later that afternoon I wiped down the telescope and screwed the eyepiece into position. Walking out the side door and down the alley, I looked for an open area where there were no trees. Holding the telescope to my eye, I gently maneuvered the setscrew attached to the cylinder. I saw nothing but a blur of dim light. With my thumb and forefinger, I kept moving the screw, my arm beginning to ache from the weight of the telescope. And then, with one last adjustment, a far-off chimney came into clear focus—so clear that I could see broken mortar between the bricks. I let out a hoot, took the telescope into my office, and attached it to the tripod base.

Pulling a stack of antiques-dealer reference books from the shelf behind my desk, I began to hunt. I went through book after book, and though I found several telescopes, none were like the one on my desk. I pulled down more books and continued my research, and an hour later, I found what I was looking for.

Jan van der Bildt (1709–91). Born in the Netherlands, he began his career making clocks and watches and then turned to making telescopes. He was revered for the masterful craftsmanship of his instruments, and his mirrors were of such a finely balanced alloy that the majority of them have maintained their reflectivity after more than two centuries.

According to my reference book, the retail value of the telescope was, depending on condition, between six and twelve hundred dollars. I priced it at $995, tied a tag to the tripod, and then spent a good deal of time cleaning and polishing the cedar box. Before leaving the shop for the evening, I placed the telescope next to its box on top of a masculine oak chest.

Though the bedraggled teddy was most likely worthless, I had fallen in love with his sweet old face. Placing him on the corner of my desk, I gave him a pat and turned out the lights.

TWENTY-THREE

It wasn't long after that day when I sensed the first winds of a retail slowdown. Prior to Christmas I'd sold several pieces of sterling and landed a home for a Norwegian polychromed console table I'd had for nearly two years, but sales of the big-ticket furniture items had plummeted, and I didn't know why. Whenever my shop had hit a slow period in the past, I'd wheel and deal and do whatever it took to push through the lean times, and I always managed to survive while many other shops closed their doors.

But something about this felt different.

By the end of January, I was deeply concerned; even the repair and restoration business had dropped by over 25 percent. When February came to a close, I was scared, so scared that I woke each morning with a tightening in my throat. Every Monday when Inez gave me a copy of the financial sheet, my stomach sank. She never said a word, but it was impossible to ignore the worry in her eyes.

Though I had no control over who walked through my door or what they might be looking for, I had no one to blame but myself. During the summer of the previous year, my contact in London had sent me photographs of two exceptionally rare antiques he'd found in North Yorkshire. I became greedy and purchased them both—a colossal Louis XV armoire with beautifully carved leaves and scrolls along its curved canopy and the pièce de résistance—an exquisite sterling-silver George III monteith bowl with an impressive domed lid. Crafted during the Regency period with elaborate Rococo-inspired repoussé designs, the bowl was hallmarked 1818— THOMAS GAIRDNER—a silversmith of renowned talent.

Both the armoire and the bowl were once-in-a-lifetime pieces with prices to match, but I felt it was time to raise the bar and align myself with the dealers in Atlanta and New York. It was a daring move, but one I felt ready to take.

While I suspected that the monteith bowl might take a while to sell, I was certain the armoire would all but fly out the door, and though it drew a great deal of attention, no one had made an offer. Every morning I'd unlock the front door for business, turn to face the four-hundred-pound beauty that had become an albatross, and wonder why it hadn't sold. As for the bowl, it sat behind the locked glass doors in the illuminated display case, a glaring reminder of my lust. I could hardly look at it without feeling sick to my stomach. It had taken over a third of my yearly purchasing budget to acquire the two pieces, and each week that they didn't sell, my funds were further depleted. In retrospect, my daring move had proved to be foolish.

My first priority was to pay Albert and Inez, and I managed to scratch up enough to make the shop's monthly rent, but there was no money left for me to take a salary. I struggled to meet my personal financial obligations—especially Grammy's nursing-home care. No matter how many sales I advertised or how many discounts I was willing to give, the bell above my door remained virtually silent. Each month I dipped deeper into my savings, and by mid-March my dream of buying a home slid further from reach.

∽

I was particularly depressed about my current state of affairs when, on the first Monday in April, the bell above the door rang. A distinguished-looking gentleman stepped into my shop, and he appeared to do so from an entirely different era. Dressed in a cream linen suit with a pocketwatch chain draped across his silk plaid vest, the man walked with the aid of a stylish pewter-tipped cane.

"Good morning, sir. Welcome. I'm Teddi Overman."

"Pleased to meet you, Miz Overman. I'm John Jacob Lee from Shelbyville, Tennessee," he said, seeming pleased that his name and home state rhymed.

"How may I help you today, Mr. Lee?"

"My granddaughter's getting married. If my wife were still alive, she'd know exactly what kind of gift to choose, but I've been on my own for quite some time. The groom comes from a fine Charleston family, and they just presented my granddaughter with a sterling tableware set that's been in their family since the Civil War. Now, here's the thing—I don't want to be outdone, so I'm lookin' for something mighty special."

"What would you say her style is?"

He leaned against his cane and raised his eyebrows. "Well, I'm sad to say she doesn't have any. My granddaughter is a wonderful girl, but unfortunately she has the taste of an onion. I'd like to give her something she can be proud of, something she'll pass down to her children. So what would you suggest?"

"Right this way," I said, stepping to the glass case where I displayed my finest pieces of sterling.

Before I even got the key into the lock, Mr. Lee pointed toward the monteith bowl. "Well, that makes a statement, doesn't it? I'd like to have a look."

Reverently, I lifted the bowl from the case and set it on the table in front of him, the sterling glowing softly beneath the overhead lights. "This piece is exceptionally rare."

"It sure is pretty, but what's it used for? Fancy casseroles?" he asked, rubbing his fingertips over the laurel-leaf handles.

"It was designed to cool wine goblets. After the bowl was filled with ice water, goblets were placed facedown with their stems resting in the decorative depressions along the rim. I've also seen these bowls used as centerpieces on dining-room tables, and they make gorgeous containers for floral arrangements . . ."

As I told the old gentleman the history of monteith bowls, he picked up the lid and seemed to enjoy feeling its substantial weight in his hand. He smiled with approval. "It's got some heft to it."

"Yes. Due to its rarity and exceptional condition, the price of forty thou—"

"My dear girl, please don't spoil my enjoyment," he said with a wry smile. "If I had to ask the price, then I most likely couldn't afford it. What matters is the pleasure I'll get from presenting this gift to my granddaughter."

The lid made a gorgeous *ting* when he set it back on the bowl. "Over the years money and I have come to be quite good friends. When it lands in my hands, I never squeeze my fingers. I just enjoy it and let it go. Seems the more I let it go, the more it keeps coming back," he said with a wise chuckle. He reached into his breast pocket and removed his wallet. "I assume you take American Express?"

I thought my head might explode. *Oh, sweet merciful God in heaven, he's buying it?* Somehow I managed to keep a placid look on my face and simply say, "Certainly."

"Will you gift-wrap it for me?"

"I'd be happy to, Mr. Lee. Please take a seat and make yourself comfortable," I said, gesturing to a Victorian chair. "Would you like something to drink?"

"No thank you," he said while easing himself into the chair. "I'll just sit here and watch people go by. As you can see," he said, tapping his cane against his shoe, "I've got a bum leg. I wonder if you might be kind enough to carry the bowl out to my car."

"Of course."

Little did he know that I'd have walked barefoot all the way to Tennessee to sell that bowl.

I picked it up and carried it into the back. As I ran his credit card through, I begged, *Please, please, oh please . . .* I nearly yelped when the approval number appeared on the screen. After gathering a large box and copious amounts of tissue, I wrapped the gift with white-on-white-striped paper and a wide silk ribbon that I tied in an extravagant bow.

I was careful not to make finger marks on the wrapping paper as I carried the box out to the showroom. Mr. Lee rose to his feet when he saw me coming and opened the front door. "My car's right there," he said, pointing three spaces down from my shop.

He walked by my side, his limp pronounced as he maneuvered along the uneven sidewalk. When we arrived at his car, an older-model Chrysler in pristine condition, Mr. Lee unlocked the trunk. Leaning his cane against the bumper, he helped me place the box inside. He did so with great effort.

"It's a terrible thing, this aging business. I've never gotten used to it. Every day I'm shocked by how much my bones betray me." He closed the trunk and looked at me thoughtfully. "You're a pretty woman, Miz Overman. But pretty only goes so far. What really matters is how nice people are. I'd like to thank you for your lovely smile and kindness."

"Thank you, Mr. Lee. I believe you've made my day."

"There's a young man imprisoned in this body," he said, pointing toward his chest. "And that young man is quite taken with you, my dear."

I didn't know what to say. What *could* I say?

"But . . ." He raised his woolly eyebrows in resignation as his voice trailed off.

Caught in a wave of grateful relief from the combination of selling the monteith bowl and Mr. Lee's gentlemanly ways, I stepped forward, took hold of his hand, and gave him a light yet lingering kiss on the cheek. He didn't look so much surprised as pleased.

I smiled and squeezed his fingers. "I hope you'll come back and see me again, Mr. Lee."

He leaned against his cane and bowed. "God willing, Miz Overman. God willing."

When I walked back into the shop, Inez was waiting with the credit-card slip in her hand, her eyes wide. "I don't know what surprised me more—that you sold the bowl or *who* you sold it to!"

"What do you mean? Has Mr. Lee been in the shop when I wasn't here?"

"No. But when I saw his name and the Shelbyville, Tennessee, address on the receipt, I about fainted. Not long ago *Time* magazine had a big write-up about him. He's famous—came up from nothing, and I'm talking the kind of dirt poor where none of the children had shoes. He's made a fortune in the preserves business. His elderberry jams have won all sorts of awards."

I glanced out the window. "Well, famous or not, I'll remember him for as long as I live."

∾

The sale of the monteith bowl had saved me from having to take out a loan, but it would be a year or more before I could rebuild my personal savings. Which is why, when a phone call came three weeks later, I was both relieved and heartbroken. The call lasted just a few minutes, but the result would be forever.

When I hung up, I grabbed my sweater and stepped into Inez's doorway. "I'm going for a walk."

She stopped typing and peered over the top of her glasses. "What happened? You look like hell. Are you sick?"

I shook my head. "I just need some fresh air."

The past few days had been unusually cold, and I pulled up my collar against the chill. I walked with my eyes cast downward until I turned off the sidewalk and stepped onto the narrow path that led into the cemetery. I sat down on the bench and folded my hands in my lap. "This is a bad day, Pernelia."

The wind increased, and bloated clouds lumbered through the sky. Elbows to knees, I rested my head in my hands and thought about my family, my life, and how much I wished I could do it all over again. Do it better. I could feel myself sinking into a dark place when I noticed a little woman come around the side of the church. She was lugging a heavy tote bag that gave a wobble to her stride. Sprigs of gray hair poked through the holes of her green crocheted hat, and her coat hung open and flapped in the wind.

Though there were plenty of places to sit, she eased herself down on the opposite end of *my* bench. She smiled, dug through her tote, and removed a thick wool sock. Pushing her hand inside, she drew out a tiny porcelain shoe and gave it a quick polishing with the end of her scarf. I knew right away the shoe was an antique from the Edwardian era. Had I not been so depressed, I would have asked her about it.

The old lady looked at me. "Your heart is heavy and your pain is deep, yes?"

For a moment I just stared at her. "Those sound like the words to a really bad country-western song."

She placed the shoe on the bench between us. "Twenty dollars to ease your pain."

"No thanks."

She shrugged, pulled a half-eaten sandwich from her tote, peeled back the waxed-paper wrapping, and took a bite.

From the corner of my eye, I watched her, my insides softening when I took in her threadbare coat and scarf—and Lord, those broken-down shoes were a sorry sight. I dug through my pockets and removed a crinkled five-dollar bill. "This is all I have."

"What day is this?" she asked, dabbing her lips with the edge of her scarf.

"Wednesday."

She pointed to the shoe. "Lucky for you, Wednesday is discount day. Put your money in there."

I took the bill and tucked it inside the shoe, feeling both sorry for the old woman and silly for taking part in whatever the heck this was.

"What's your name?" she asked.

I glanced at the headstone directly across the path. Chiseled into the granite was the name Suzanne Reynolds.

"My name's Suzanne," I said, avoiding the old woman's eyes.

"Hmm, interesting. Your name doesn't match your energy, but that's okay, I have your energy anyway." She folded her small, wrinkled hands on her lap and looked into the sky.

"So what are we doing?"

"I'm a sky reader."

I silently laughed at myself for sitting there with an old woman who had a goofy expression on her face and a five-dollar bill sticking out of a porcelain shoe. I wondered what had happened to bring her to this sad state of affairs. No sooner did I have that thought than I felt ashamed. After all, there I was, sitting in a cemetery talking to a headstone, so who was worse off?

She sniffed the air and exhaled. "They say it's a big dilemma, yes?"

"Who? Who says that?"

"My people," the old woman said while scanning the clouds. "Guides. Everybody has them, but most people don't listen. They say it's time to begin the journey. What does that mean?"

"I don't know. You're the one with mystery guides and five dollars sticking out of a shoe."

The old lady ignored my comment and continued. "Nothing

works until we find a place of peace. It's the way things work—here and over there, too."

"Over where?"

"On the other side. The other life."

None of this was making any sense, though I shouldn't have expected it would.

Her face grew serious. "They say it's time to put down the stone and begin your journey."

Stone? What stone?

She fell quiet and scanned the sky as if searching for something. Without looking at me, she said, "That is what I get for you. There's nothing more. Oh, wait. I see the sun coming up over a . . . What is it I'm seeing? Ah, there it is. A cornfield. Yes, it's corn."

"What?" I tried to rub away the chill racing up my arms. "You couldn't possibly have made that up."

She tilted her head. "No. Zelda makes nothing up. That is what I get for you. The energy's gone now."

"No! Call it back," I cried, waving my arms toward the darkening sky. "Can you tell me about my brother? He's—"

"I'm sorry, Suzanne. When the energy goes, it goes."

I fished a crumpled tissue from my pocket and blotted my runny nose. "Suzanne isn't my real name. I lied to you about that. Sorry."

"That's okay," she said, sliding the porcelain shoe back inside the sock. "My real name's not Zelda."

I pushed myself up from the bench and said good-bye to the old woman. Stepping onto the path, I wondered what on earth had just taken place. A few moments later, I stopped and looked back. Zelda was already tottering around the corner of the church.

When I left the cemetery, a fierce wind cut around the buildings. Ahead of me, two paper cups raced across the sidewalk, tumbling end over end. As I crossed Fulton Street, someone shouted my name. I turned to see Olivia trotting a half block behind me. The wind had whipped her hair into a froth of curls. I pulled my sweater tighter across my chest and waited.

"Hey, Olivia. What are you doing?"

"Trying to find you," she said, catching her breath. "But I wouldn't make a very good detective. I was positive you'd be with Pernelia."

"Actually, I just came from there. Why, what's up?"

"Inez called me. She was really worried, Teddi. She said you took a phone call and the minute you hung up, you left the shop all pale and out of sorts."

"She overreacted. I'm fine."

"No you're not. You should see your face. Come on, what happened?"

"It's nothing, really. I need to get back to the shop and put a coat of gesso on a table."

"The hell with the gesso." She took hold of my arm and didn't let go until we arrived at Marty's Café.

We slid into a lumpy green vinyl booth by the front window. A tired-eyed waitress pushed through the swinging door from the kitchen. The spicy aroma of warm apple pie followed her down the aisle. After she took our order and shuffled off, I blew into my hands and tried to rub away the cold.

"So tell me what happened," Olivia said, removing her gloves and unbuttoning her jacket.

"Joe Springer called. He's the farmer who's been leasing Daddy's crop fields for the past few years. He made an offer to buy the land. And not a 'let's dicker about price' offer—an honest, respectable offer."

Olivia looked puzzled. "But that's good, right? Especially since you've been worried about finances and all."

The waitress brought our order—onion rings and lemonade for Olivia and hot chocolate for me. I picked up a misshapen spoon and stirred the dollop of whipped cream until it disappeared. "But that means I'll have to split everything up. Joe doesn't want the house or the barn, only the fields. I can understand that, but the land has been in my family for so long. Anyway, his call took me off guard. That's all."

Olivia took a bite of an onion ring. "I know it's hard, but let's talk about the positives. You won't have to work so many long hours, and you'll finally be able to buy a house."

"Sad price to pay for owning a home."

Olivia's eyes narrowed as she learned forward. "What about the price *you've* paid? Working your ass off for six, sometimes seven days a week so you can support your grandmother. And then there's all that driving to Kentucky and back again. I honestly don't know how you've managed. The driving alone would have done me in long ago. It's your turn now, Teddi. Grab it with both hands."

I looked out the window. The wind was fierce, and I watched a woman chase her runaway scarf across the street. Wanting to move off the subject of the farm, I told Olivia about meeting Zelda.

She laughed so hard she nearly choked on another onion ring. "Ha! You fell for Zelda's spiel? Which one did she use? 'Your heart is heavy' or her old standby, 'Your pain is deep'?"

I draped a paper napkin over my head. "Both."

"You're such a banana. So what did she soak you for?"

"Five dollars," I said as the napkin slid over my face and onto the table. "It's all I had on me, so I hope you're picking up the tab."

"Don't worry, I've got it covered."

"When she asked me what my name was, I told her it was Suzanne."

Olivia scrunched up her face. "Suzanne?"

"Yeah. I don't know why, but I just didn't want her to know my real name. And then, when I apologized for lying, she told me her real name wasn't Zelda."

"Her real name is Ethel Townley, but that probably didn't sound exotic enough for a *sky reader*, so she started calling herself Zelda. She's been wandering the streets for as long as I can remember. I'm surprised you've never run into her before. She's part of Charleston's soft underbelly. Years ago—I'm talking the late sixties—she got hit by lightning and flew through the air like Mary Poppins, or so the story goes. Some people swear she's had 'the gift' ever since, but I think the poor old thing is off her rocker."

"Who knows? Maybe it's both." I swirled one of Olivia's onion rings through a river of ketchup. "I feel sorry for her."

"She lives with her brother and his wife in a nice house over on Lamboll, so don't feel too sorry for her. She's a lot better off than most people think. Tourists love her." Olivia paused for a moment and then laughed. "All right, here's a confession. I'm a banana, too. Several years ago I put ten bucks in that goofy shoe, but nothing she said made any sense."

"Well, that was pretty much my experience, except that she did mention a cornfield."

Olivia's eyes widened. "Really? That's just plain spooky, especially coming right after that phone call. What did she say about it?"

"Nothing. Only that she saw it."

Olivia leaned back and looked at me thoughtfully. "Teddi, I didn't come from a family who had land, but if I did, I'd probably feel exactly like you. The thought of selling it must be incredibly hard. But you're going to accept the offer, aren't you?"

I shrugged sadly. "I don't think I have much choice . . ."

Olivia and I talked for an hour, and when I got back to the shop, I felt a lot better. After applying a coat of gesso to the tabletop that I would soon marbleize, I locked the doors and set off to see Grammy.

TWENTY-FOUR

On my way down the corridor, I glanced into Mr. Lamb's room and saw him reading a book with a magnifying glass. I stopped at the doorway. "Hi, Mr. Lamb. How are you this evening?"

He looked up and smiled, his old dentures appearing a bit loose. "Hey there, Miz Teddi," he said with a click of his teeth. "Guess I'm doin' all right. Devil ain't found me yet," he said with a laugh. "You on your way to see Belle or you leavin'?"

"Just heading there now. And guess what? I'm bringing something special on Sunday, and I'll make extra for you."

His eyes widened with hope. "Macaroni and cheese?"

"Yep."

"Oh, boy. I'll be waitin'."

I waved good-bye and continued down the corridor. When I turned in to my grandmother's room, she was sitting in her wheelchair. The TV was tuned to her favorite nature show, but she wasn't watching. Her head was tipped forward, and a dinner tray was pushed to the side of her table. Her meal was cold and untouched.

When I knelt so I could see her face, her eyes were teary. "Oh, Grammy, what's wrong?"

"I don't like how they do their chicken casserole. So I opened the box of doughnuts you brought me. I was havin' one and enjoying my show when that new nurse came in." My grandmother pointed to the top shelf of her closet. "She put them up there where I can't reach."

"She took them *away* from you?"

"Yes, scolded me like I was a child. Said all that sugar would kill me. Well, I told her we all gotta die of *something*, and I couldn't think of a better way to go. So I asked her to give me my doughnuts. I asked her nice. But she just walked out the door."

"Is that right?" I stepped to the closet, pulled the box from the shelf, and set it on the table. I smiled at my grandmother as I opened the lid. "You go right ahead and have as many as you'd like."

She blinked away a tear, picked one out, and took a bite.

"Grammy, I think I forgot to lock my car. I'll be back in just a minute."

I could feel my cheeks begin to flush as I marched down the hall toward the nursing station. When I rounded the corner, I saw a tall, middle-aged nurse writing in a chart. I walked to the counter and waited. When she didn't acknowledge my presence, I said, "Excuse me. I'm Teddi Overman, Belle Forrester's granddaughter. I don't believe we've met."

She glanced up. "What can I do for you?"

I leaned over the counter so I could read her name tag. "Well, it's a pleasure to meet you, too, Rochelle. Are you new here?"

"Yes," she said, flipping a page in the chart.

"Did you take my grandmother's box of doughnuts away from her and put them in the closet?"

"Of course I did," she said, meeting my eye with a challenging look. "Doughnuts aren't to be eaten for dinner. She needs—"

"Let me tell you something, *Miz Rochelle*. My grandmother had to stuff newspapers in her clothes to keep from freezing to death during the Depression. She's almost ninety-three years old and has gone through more in her life than you could even begin to imagine."

"Well, I—"

"For the love of God, if my grandmother wants a doughnut, then she's to have one, or two, or a whole dozen! And if you ever take anything away from her again or speak to her in a way that's belittling or unkind, I guarantee I'll report you to the board of directors. And I demand—that's right, Miz Rochelle, I *demand* that you treat that wonderful little woman with respect."

From his room Mr. Lamb yelled in his gravelly voice, "Yeah . . . let Belle have her GODDAMN doughnuts!"

I nearly burst out laughing. With my shoulders thrown back and my chin held high, I turned and walked away. There was no mistaking the heat of Rochelle's angry glare on my back. As I passed Mr. Lamb's room, he gave me a thumbs-up. I smiled and gave him a thumbs-up in return.

When I turned right, I nearly plowed into my grandmother's wheelchair. She had rolled down the hall and was sitting just beyond view of the nursing station. She looked up at me and grinned. A few doughnut crumbs clung to her chin. "Get your car all locked up, honey?"

I winked, took hold of the chair's handles, and spun her around. On the way past her room, I stopped, grabbed two doughnuts, and wrapped them in a paper towel. "Wait here," I said, trotting down the hall and into Mr. Lamb's room. When I gave him the doughnuts, he smiled, and then we both laughed as I waved good-bye.

"It's too cold to sit in the garden, Grammy. Would you like to go for a ride to the parlor and sit by the window?"

"That would be nice."

As we passed a large window, my grandmother said, "Oh, no. Digger's here."

"Digger?"

"That's what we call the undertaker."

I had to stifle my laugh.

"Looks like somebody left us. Wonder who it was? Bless their soul. I know Mildred Coleman hasn't been feeling well. I hope it's not her. We have a date to go to craft class tomorrow."

I thought about how difficult all this was for my grandmother—making new friends only to have them pass away. I wondered how many times she'd seen Digger pull to the back door, how many beds stripped down and rooms sanitized in preparation for the next short-term resident.

"Here we are," I said, rolling her up to a window that overlooked a small terraced garden. I dragged an upholstered chair from the side of the fireplace and angled it next to my grandmother.

"Grammy, other than the nurse who took away your doughnuts, has anyone here ever treated you poorly or hurt your feelings?"

She shook her head. "All the other nurses are real nice. I don't know what got into *that* one." My grandmother's face saddened as she looked out the window. "It's a shame I couldn't send your mother to school—she wanted to be a nurse so much."

"Mama did?" I said, settling into the chair. "I never heard her mention anything about that."

Grammy fiddled with a loose thread on her sweater. "Oh, she wouldn't. It was a sore subject. She never really got over it. S'pose I can't blame her."

"What do you mean?"

"Her father promised he'd save money for her schooling. He saved some, not much, but he tried. When he got pneumonia and slipped away, I had to use every dime to keep a roof over our heads. I took in ironing and sold my bread and jams. Whenever Franny brought up nursing school, I told her I was savin' the money. I knew it was wrong to lie, but I thought if I gave her something to look forward to, it'd help her through the hard times. When she turned sixteen, I had to sit her down and tell her the truth. There wasn't any money for her schooling. Oh, if you could have seen her face. I broke my child's heart."

I reached over and took hold of my grandmother's hand. "You did the best for her you could. She must have known that."

"Well, I tried. But it's a shame she was never able to go to school. When your father came back from the war, I realized she had a knack for nursing. She took real good care of him."

"Daddy? But he wasn't injured."

"Not in body, but his mind was a frightful mess. Frances said he had terrible nightmares—up all hours of the night, pacing from room to room. He was always so jittery and short-tempered."

I rested my hand on her arm. "I think maybe you're confusing Daddy with someone else. He was never short-tempered."

"Oh, yes, long before you were born he was, especially with loud noises. A lot of the boys who fought in the war had a hard time. Back then they called it shell shock."

She looked out the window, and her eyes seemed to focus on a distant memory. "One Sunday I was up at the farm for a visit and Franny asked me to stay for supper. She accidentally dropped a saucepan on the floor. Oh, my word, your father about lost his mind—jumped from the table and started cussing. His eyes were as wild as a scared dog's. It took Franny a long while to calm him down."

"What do you mean *visiting* the farm? I thought you moved in with Mama and Daddy before the war."

She shook her head. "No. I lived in my little cottage until 1948. I'll never forget it. One day I was standing in the kitchen kneading bread when Henry came in the back door. He sat down at the table and said, 'Belle, there's a nice room waitin' for you up at the farm. We'd be pleased if you'd come live with us.'"

"Sweet Daddy."

"He surely was. I didn't know what to say, because as much as I liked the idea, I didn't want to interfere with their lives. So I gave it some thought and then called Frances a few days later to feel her out. We'd had our problems over the years, and I was worried it was mostly Henry's idea. I could hardly believe it when she said it made sense." Grammy chuckled and added, "Which for Frances was the same as sayin' she'd like to have me. So Henry packed me up and moved me to the farm. I surely loved that old place."

"Me, too." I closed my eyes for a moment and then turned to my grandmother. "Joe Springer called me today. He made an offer to buy Daddy's crop fields, and I accepted."

She reached out and patted my knee. "Joe's a good man. He and your Daddy go way back."

"But I love that land so much. I can't imagine giving it up."

My grandmother tilted her head, her face softening in the dimming light. "Honey, I've lived more years than I care to count. When I look back and think about all I've learned, there's one thing that always stands out."

She fell quiet for a moment, as if sifting through her thoughts. Right when I wondered if she'd forgotten what we were talking about, she said, "Sometimes it's not what we hold on to that shapes our lives—it's what we're willing to let go of."

I fingered the hem of my skirt and thought about her words.

"What really matters are the things we carry in here," Grammy said, tapping her gnarled fingers to her chest. "Your daddy's land lives inside you, Teddi. It always will."

I rested my head against the back of the chair, suddenly feeling very tired. "I'm driving to Kentucky to get things finalized. Before I go, I'll call a few liquidation companies and see what they say. There's so much stuff in the barn and Daddy's workshop that I think I should just sell it all for a single lot price. I'll probably lose quite a bit doing it that way, but I don't want people tramping all over the farm for an estate sale. I can't stand the thought of it."

"You're a smart girl."

"Well, I'm not so sure about that. Anyway, I won't be gone for more than four or five days."

"Will you see Stella when you go back home?"

"No. I forgot to tell you," I said with a laugh. "She and some friends from her church are going on a Caribbean cruise. She was so excited that she could hardly stand it."

"Good for Stella. I imagine it's been hard for her since your mother passed away. They were so close. I'm glad she's gettin' out and having some fun."

I pushed an unruly hair away from my grandmother's glasses and tucked it behind her ear. "I'm sorry I've been gone so much these past few months."

"Don't worry about me, honey. I'll be fine. What day you plannin' to go?"

"Friday after work. But I'll come see you before I leave."

She leaned her head back and smiled. "When you do, would you mind bringin' me another box of doughnuts?"

Oh, how I laughed.

❧

Eddie was so happy to see me when I arrived home that he ran in circles like his tail was on fire. After a quick game of fetch in the garden, I fed him dinner and then pulled off my clothes and wrapped up in a robe. On my way to the kitchen, I stopped and leaned against the doorway to the guest bedroom. Mama's urn was still sitting on the night table where I'd placed it the previous autumn.

"I don't know what to do with you, Mama. But I don't imagine spending eternity in my guest bedroom is what you had in mind."

I flicked the light switch and walked across the room. From the closet I removed my mother's suitcase and the box containing her silk nightgown and set them on the bed. I opened the box and traced my fingers over the lace. Why I don't know, but I took off my robe and slipped the gown over my head. The silk was as weightless and cool as winter's first breath when it skimmed along my bare skin. Other than being a bit snug in the hips, the gown fit perfectly.

Glancing over my shoulder, I spoke to my mother's urn. "This is the most beautiful thing I've ever seen. Why didn't you ever wear it, Mama?"

From the finely made lace stitched on the bodice to the ribbon straps to the silk rosebuds with seed pearls sewn into their centers, the gown was exquisite. I lifted my hair, wound it into a knot, and held it on top of my head. From side to side I swayed, the silk gliding across my legs.

But when I saw my reflection in the mirror, I stopped. Opening my fingers, I released my hair, feeling its weight fall down my back like a theater curtain. I slid the straps off my shoulders, wiggled the gown over my hips, and watched it puddle at my feet.

I pulled on my robe and gave the belt a tug, and while folding the gown into its box, I whispered, "This was private, wasn't it, Mama? I'm sorry, I had no right to put it on."

Though I had no idea why I felt as I did, it was as real as anything I'd ever experienced. Yet when I sat on the bed and opened my mother's suitcase, my reaction was entirely different. One by one I removed each item—a yellow linen blouse, a blue cotton dress, lavender slacks—each one resembling a carefully wrapped gift. As I spread them out on the bed, a rainbow of folded clothes revealed the message my mother had left behind: *Yes, Teddi. I really was planning to come to Charleston.*

TWENTY-FIVE

A low-slung fog played hide-and-seek with the headlights. Every so often a barn or a silo would appear on the horizon, but little else. Eddie was asleep on a blanket in the passenger seat, his paws occasionally twitching. Driving to Kentucky in the dark of night was something I'd never done before, and I'd enjoyed it. The roads had been virtually empty and I'd made record time.

It was 6:05 on Saturday morning when I arrived at the farm. The house had taken on the look and smell of abandonment. The air was damp and musty, and a thin layer of dust had dulled the linoleum floor. Even the curtains looked bewildered.

After opening all the windows, washing the kitchen floor, and making a big pitcher of iced tea, I grabbed a broom and walked outside. While Eddie explored the backyard, I swept the porch and thought about my life, my family, and the farm. Now that Joe was buying the crop fields, I'd been toying with the idea of hanging on to the rest of the property, but no matter how I looked at it, it didn't make much sense. The house was in need of renovation, especially the kitchen and bathroom, and though the barn was in good shape for its age, it needed work, too.

I had always taken for granted that Josh would run the farm after he graduated from high school. Often I'd watched him work Daddy's fields, smiling to myself at how naturally he performed even the most difficult tasks and how much he enjoyed the physical demands of harvesting season. I imagined him marrying a spunky, bright-eyed girl and having a passel of giggling children and a yard filled with all sorts of pets.

Not a day passed that I didn't think of my brother, but being at the farm spun me back in time until I felt his presence everywhere. Memories of him were both fierce and fragile. It was impossible to look beyond the barn and not hope to see him step out from the woods.

The human mind holds tightly to those things it can't reconcile.

Off in the distance, a red-winged blackbird sent his full-throated song into the air, the sun peeked above the trees, and the grass glistened with dew.

JULY 1975

It was the year I turned twenty-one, and I had come home to spend a long weekend with my family. A cold front had begun passing through and was blessedly taking the oppressive heat with it. The evening was lovely and cool, and I decided to sleep on the back porch. From the linen closet, I pulled a stack of quilts, made myself a reasonably comfortable mattress, and settled in. While I enjoyed the fresh air and listened to the sounds of night, Josh stepped onto the porch wearing plaid pajama bottoms and a white T-shirt.

"Hey," he said softly. "You awake?"

I patted the blanket, and he lowered himself next to me. His voice bubbled with amusement when he said, "So I guess this is your version of camping out?"

"Yeah. I wanted to soak up as much country as I could before going back to Charleston."

"You really like it there, don't you?"

"Yes, but not the way I love it here."

My brother smiled, as if glad to hear my allegiance to the farm. While we listened to the soft twitters and trills of night, Josh shook my leg. "Look, you've got a friend."

He pointed to a luna moth resting on the porch rail. I rose to my knees and leaned forward, moving so close I could see the fuzz of its antennae. "Lunas are so gorgeous," I whispered. "I swear they don't seem real."

"Did you know they only live about seven days?"

"Really? That doesn't seem fair. All that beauty gone in such a short period of time."

As if hearing our words and deciding to get on with what little life was left, the moth flapped its wings and lifted into the air, evaporating into the moonlight like a shimmering green soul.

Josh rose to his feet. "Don't be sad. Maybe one day to a luna is like ten years to us. G'night, Teddi."

I reached out and gave the hem of his pajama bottoms a tug. "Good night, brother."

It was just before dawn when I awoke to the sound of a dog barking off in the distance. A blue haze hung over the farm, blurring the woods into a dreamlike sculpture. As I lay waiting for the sun to rise, a light flashed across the kitchen window. I sat up and peered inside.

Josh was standing in front of the open refrigerator, his face awash in silvery white light and his hair a mess of curls. I watched him make two peanut-butter sandwiches slathered with a thick layer of jam. He folded them into a bandanna that he tucked into his knapsack along with an apple. After pouring lemonade into a metal canteen and sliding it into a loop on his utility belt, he flipped the strap of his knapsack over his shoulder.

Wanting to observe the rest of my brother's early-morning ritual, I lay down and pretended to be asleep.

The screen door barely squeaked when he opened it. From one eye I watched Josh creep across the porch and down the steps with the stealth of a cat. He made his way across the lawn and headed toward the hay field. Then *poof*—he was gone.

Pushing back the blanket, I rose to my feet so I could watch him, but he wasn't there. I scanned the field for his red shirt, yet he was simply gone. For a brief moment it felt as if I'd imagined it all, but proof of my brother's passage was there before me in the line of footprints he'd left in the dewy grass.

ʘ

Blocking that memory as best as I could, I finished sweeping the porch, and set the broom aside.

I whistled for Eddie and we set off for the barn. Turning the dial, I snapped open the combination lock and hooked it through a belt loop of my jeans. After flipping the door latch, I wrapped both hands around the handle and gave the door a yank. The steel rollers let out a rusty squeal as the door reluctantly slid open.

Entering the barn was like stepping into a sepia-tint photograph of the past. Daddy's old tractor was parked off to the side, its front tires gone flat. Draped over the steering wheel was a raggedy blue bath towel, and on the seat lay an old pair of his leather work gloves. I wandered deeper into the barn and stopped by the ladder to the hayloft. I hadn't been up there in years. The ladder groaned beneath my weight as if awakened from a deep sleep. Startled by my noisemaking, a pair of swallows swirled high into the rafters and vanished through a hole in the roof.

After opening both the front and back loading doors to let in some light, I walked around the loft. It was a beautifully built, cavernous space with hand-hewn beams that towered over my head. Everything about the barn was thick and sturdy and spoke of a time when craftsmen skimped on nothing.

Had it not been for the stream of sunlight pushing through that hole in the roof, I never would have noticed. But there was a faint outline of something on one of the lowest cross timbers. Thinking it might be a raised split in the wood, I stood back and tried to make out if that's what it was. But I couldn't. I dragged three moldy bales of hay across the floor, stacked one on top of the other two, and climbed up.

Still I couldn't see it.

Rising onto my toes, I stretched my arm as far as I could and ran my fingertips along the edge of the timber. Just as I touched something that felt like a stick or perhaps an old dowel, the hay bales wobbled and began breaking apart. I jumped up and grabbed the object, then fell to the floor as it dropped from my hand.

I sat in a swirl of hay dust, stunned at what lay in front of me. Pushing myself up onto my knees, I grabbed it from the floor, my heart beating a series of wild thumps as I descended the ladder. The moment my feet touched the lowest rung, Eddie barked and I heard someone call my name.

From the open barn door, I saw a white pickup parked in the driveway with the words WOODARD TUCKER LIQUIDATIONS painted on the driver's-side door. Standing on the porch was a stoop-shouldered older gentleman wearing a Stetson-style hat. Next to him was a young man.

My words sounded more like a scream when I called out, "I'll be right there!"

I was so panicked that I couldn't think straight. *What should I do with this?* My hands trembled as I yanked the old towel from the tractor. After taking a moment to collect myself, I stepped from the shadows of the barn and walked across the lawn with Eddie trotting at my heels. I tried to appear calm with the towel held firmly in my left hand. I imagined it looked odd, like a flag made of terry cloth. But what was I to do?

"Thank you for coming, Mr. Tucker. I'm Teddi Overman."

He tipped the brim of his hat. "Pleased to meet you. This is my grandson, Gabe."

Tall and lean, with sandy brown hair and clear blue eyes. I guessed him to be in his mid-twenties.

"Where would you like to start?" I asked as the edges of the towel began to unwrap.

"Well, I'd like to take a look in the barn. You said everything goes, is that right?"

"Everything but the tractor and lawn mower. And there's a workshop on the side of the barn. It's filled with lots of tools. The barn's open. I'll get the key and unlock the workshop in a minute."

When they turned toward the barn, I all but raced up the porch steps and into the house. After gulping a glass of water, I took the towel and went upstairs.

Josh's bedroom door was closed. It was always closed. I rested my hand on the knob for a moment and thought about how many times I'd walked into this room to see my brother sitting on his bed reading a wilderness book or sorting through his rock collection, how many times he'd looked up and smiled at me.

For the first time in nearly ten years, I gave the doorknob a turn. The latch released, and the door slowly swung open. My brother's bedroom looked surreal—a filmy, shapeless memory tinted with hues of blue. Grainy threads of light seeped around the edges of the closed window shade.

Even after so many years, his absence was incomprehensible.

The room was cool, the atmosphere unreadable—as if I were gazing through an eggshell. His bed and dresser were draped in white sheets that had grayed over the years. The closet door stood open. On the rod hung a lone wire hanger.

I moved to the window, feeling so frail I thought I might shatter. Reaching out, I grasped the cord of the roller shade and gave it a pull. Strands of cobwebs flew into the air, and sunlight pushed through the dingy window, filling the room with a peculiar yellow haze. I released the latch, and it took all my strength to push open the window. A white moth with brown-speckled wings was splayed out across the screen. I reached out and touched him, expecting him to fly, but he fell to the sill, stiff and dead.

In his early teens, my brother began to study Native American culture. He was particularly drawn to a Dakota Sioux proverb, liking it so much that he wrote it on the wall above his bed. Two years after he disappeared, Mama tried to scrub it away with steel wool, and even now I could see the scour marks she'd left on the pale blue paint. But Josh had used a green permanent marker, and the words, though drastically lightened by my mother's attempts to erase them, still remained:

We will be known forever by the tracks we leave

Not long after Josh disappeared, Jeb and two other officers came to the farm, their faces somber and their eyes downcast and apologetic. They were looking for possible clues as part of their ongoing investigation, and Daddy readily gave them access to the property. Though they went through the barn and the house, they concentrated their search in my brother's bedroom. It was something they had to do, we all understood that, but it was a terrible experience for my family.

And then came the questions:

Drugs? *No.*

Alcohol? *No.*

Trouble at school? *No.*

And on and on . . .

Josh's classmates and teachers were questioned, and they all said the same things: My brother was quiet and introspective. Gentle. A loner. Thoughtful. A girl he'd been paired with for a history report said he was an enigma, and a few students mentioned how rarely he spoke. One boy said he was afraid of my brother. When questioned further, he admitted that Josh had never given him reason to feel such a thing—he was simply uncomfortable with the intensity of my brother's eyes.

The summer following my brother's disappearance, I was in the drugstore and bumped into a local farm girl named Molly Ferguson. I had known a bit of the story from a conversation I'd had with Mama, but it wasn't until Molly talked with me that I got the full picture of what had really happened.

When Josh was a junior in high school, he'd asked a girl in his class to a winter dance. Her name was Gretchen Millner. According to Mama, my brother went to great lengths to make Gretchen a corsage, polishing walnuts and acorns with beeswax until they glowed like satin, then drilling each one with a tiny hole so he could wire them together. Colorful feathers from his prized collection were added, and the corsage was finished off with slender strands of white velvet ribbon he'd looped between the nuts. He backed the corsage with felt and attached a pin.

God only knows how long it must have taken him.

When the corsage was completed, he showed it to Mama. She said it was one of the most beautiful things she'd ever seen. She told me Josh had spent hours cleaning her car on the morning of the dance and had even gotten a haircut. At seven o'clock he walked down the stairs dressed in a sport coat and tie. Mama said he looked so handsome she got teary. From the porch she waved goodbye as he set off to pick up Gretchen.

Mama was stunned when he returned less than an hour later. When she and Daddy asked him what had happened, Josh told them that Gretchen had come down with the flu. He never mentioned her name again.

But Molly told me an entirely different story.

When Josh arrived at Gretchen's house, Molly and her date were already there. The four of them were planning to go to the dance together. When Josh proudly presented Gretchen with the corsage he'd made, she took one look at it and returned it to my brother's hands. She told him she couldn't wear it—that it looked silly and homemade and wasn't pretty like the roses and orchids all the other girls would be wearing. Molly said streaks of red colored my brother's cheeks. Without saying a word, Josh turned and walked out the door.

Though what Molly told me had nothing to do with my brother's disappearance, I wondered what other cruelties he'd weathered in his teenage years. Within a year's time, Josh had gone from making a beautiful corsage to crafting what lay hidden in the towel.

We had lived together, shared meals together, and run through the fields together. And we had laughed and told each other our secrets. But even so, I wondered—how well do we really ever know someone?

I took in a deep breath and sat on the edge of my brother's bed. Slowly, I unrolled the towel. What lay inside was as beautiful as it was frightening. Even to my novice eyes, there was no doubt it was finely crafted. Had my brother shown it to me when he'd made it, I would have been awed, barraging him with questions about how he'd done it and how long it had taken.

The shaft was straight and smooth, about thirty inches long. Perhaps made of beech or birch. The tip was surprisingly sharp, and though I had no way of knowing, I believed that my brother had shaped the flint with his own hands. Attached to the shaft with tightly wound lacings that were waxed to a satiny sheen, the black arrowhead had been set firmly into place. The fletching was made from rusty striped feathers, most likely those from a red-tailed hawk.

How had it come to this? We were a simple farm family—good country folks who did our chores, said grace before meals, and minded our manners. We watched out for one another and were always ready to lend a hand to a neighbor in need. I thought we were as plain and uncomplicated as cotton.

The morning breeze pushed through the open window and lifted a corner of the bedsheet, the dead moth whirled to the floor, and suddenly nothing seemed real, as if all of this were a bad dream that I'd soon blink away. When I set the arrow aside, I could feel my imagination edging toward dangerous terrain. Resting my elbows on my knees, I leaned forward and buried my face in my hands.

I was startled when someone called out, "Miss Overman . . . hello?"

"Coming," I called back. I left my brother's room, closed the door behind me, and descended the stairs. I found Gabe standing outside the kitchen door.

"Sorry to bother you, but we're ready to take a look in the workshop."

"Oh, yes. The lock. Sorry, I completely forgot." I glanced at the clock. I had been in my brother's room for more than an hour, yet it felt like only moments. After fishing the key from a drawer, I stepped outside.

Gabe fell in line with my stride, his manner of walking slow and easy. "That building enclosed in wire, what did you keep in there, chickens?"

"We had chickens when I was a little girl. But the building you're talking about was a cowshed way back in my great-granddaddy's day. Years ago my brother wired it for an injured hawk."

Gabe's eyes widened. "Really? Did he rehabilitate and release?"

"Yes. After the hawk healed and got strong enough to fly, my brother sent him back into the wild."

I took a few steps toward Daddy's workshop, but Gabe remained standing in the driveway. "What kind of hawk?"

"A red-tail," I said, turning to face him. "Actually, he was a partial albino. Other than a bit of color on one of his shoulders, he was solid white."

"I saw an albino hawk once. It was beautiful in a spooky kind of way."

I smiled. "That's probably why my brother named him Ghost. So you like birds?"

"Yes, ma'am."

"Please, call me Teddi."

"I've studied raptors my whole life. I work part-time at Shady Creek Veterinary Hospital."

"I heard that Doc Evans recently retired, is that right?"

"Yeah. He sold his practice to a guy named Matt Waters. He's a great vet. Last week I released a female Cooper's hawk that flew into a car's windshield back in March. Matt and I were worried she wouldn't heal, but she did."

"I thought you worked with your grandfather in the liquidating business."

"He needs my help now and then, and I sure can use the extra money. I only work three days a week at Shady Creek. It doesn't pay much, but it's what I love doing. Just yesterday someone brought in a beaver that got attacked by a dog. We worked on that poor guy for hours—"

"Hey, Gabe!" Mr. Tucker yelled from the barn door. "You gonna stand there chewin' the fat all day?"

Gabe looked a little embarrassed when he turned and called out, "I'm on my way, Grandpa."

"Here," I said, handing him the key. "Just lock up when you're done."

He trotted off as I went inside the house to get a flashlight.

While Gabe and his grandfather banged around in Daddy's workshop, I climbed back up the ladder to the hayloft and turned on the flashlight. Shining the beam in the dark corners and along all the cross timbers, I wanted to be sure I hadn't missed anything. I even stepped on the floorboards to see if any were loose or felt different from the others. Maybe I'd seen too many movies where secrets were hidden beneath floorboards, but I had to be certain.

There was nothing to be found.

After returning to the house, I kicked off my shoes and reclined on the porch swing. I'd been up for nearly thirty hours and could feel myself fading. With Eddie snuggled at my side, I closed my eyes. Thinking. Remembering . . .

I woke to the sound of a sturdy thud, and a moment later Mr. Tucker and Gabe walked around the side of the barn and came down the driveway toward the house. I sat up and slipped my feet into my shoes.

"Well, there's a lot here," Mr. Tucker said, glancing at his clipboard. "That old Allis-Chalmers tractor will fetch a nice price. You sure don't want to sell it?"

"I'm sure." Though I knew it was crazy for me to hang on to the tractor, I couldn't stand the thought of letting it go. It was a big part of my memories and would stay in the barn where Daddy had left it until I figured out what to do with the remaining property.

Gabe reached into the pocket of his jeans. "Before I forget, here's the key. I locked everything up."

Mr. Tucker flipped through several pages of notes and pursed his lips. "All right, we can do this two ways. Schedule an auction to be held here on the property, and whatever doesn't sell I'll haul away for an agreed price. Or I can have everything hauled away for a flat rate and sell it at my monthly auction." He pulled a handkerchief from his pocket and wiped his brow. "Having the auction here will bring you more money. But if I remember right, you didn't want to do that."

"I don't want people coming on the property."

"All right. I'll figure my price and write up the paperwork. If you agree, then I'll send my crew to come get everything."

"That sounds fine, Mr. Tucker. The boxes in the dining room go, too."

"Thank you for reminding me. I'd better have a look."

"When will you let me know what your offer is?"

"After I see what you've got inside, I can figure it up in about three-quarters of an hour."

He and Gabe followed me into the kitchen. I poured them each a glass of iced tea, then whistled for Eddie and left the house. Walking across the lawn, I took the footpath along the edge of what used to be the vegetable garden. Joe Springer had recently planted the upper fields, and tender green shoots already poked up from pleats of freshly tilled earth. While Eddie stretched out in the sun, I climbed the fence and sat on the top rail, feeling heavy with loss as I slowly surveyed Daddy's beautiful land—land I would relinquish in less than forty-eight hours.

I thought about how my ancestors worked the fields, walking behind a plow pulled by a team of dutiful horses, their necks frothy with sweat. And I tried to imagine what it must have been like when my grandfather had retired his horses to pasture and bought his first tractor. I tilted my head toward the sky and wondered if those who came before me and had loved this land were looking down, shaking their heads with sorrow for what I was about to do.

While I said a silent farewell to the fields, I saw Gabe coming down the tractor path, stirring up dust in his wake. Though I couldn't articulate what it was, there was something about him.

Something.

TWENTY-SIX

At nine o'clock on Monday morning, I walked into Kentucky Farmers Savings and Loan. The receptionist led me into a small conference room, where Joe Springer was already waiting, looking uncomfortable in a crisp white shirt that was too tight around the collar. He stood and offered me his hand, a big, meaty hand as dark and dry as old leather. His smile was genuine, but there was no missing the sadness in his deep blue eyes. Joe was as tethered to the soil as any farmer I'd ever known, and he no doubt understood that this was a devastating day for me.

"Thank you for accepting my offer, Teddi. I'm much obliged. My boys are, too. We'll take real good care of Henry's land. He was a fine man and one of the best farmers in Powell County. We all miss him."

Though only moments from becoming the new owner, the tender way Joe had referred to the land as being my father's was not lost to me. I had to work hard to manage the words. "Thank you, Mr. Springer. I know you will."

The loan officer, a stout little man named Charlie Chase, walked in and set a thick folder on the table. "All right, then," he said while closing the door, "let's have a seat. I've got the land-survey report, and everything's in order and ready to go. This won't take long."

And he was right. A half hour later, I walked out of the bank with Mr. Springer. We did so in unbearable silence. I was surprised when he gave me an awkward but well-meaning hug. I could smell the starch in his shirt, a shirt he'd probably bought for this day and would never wear again. From tear-filled eyes, I watched him stuff his big, burly body into the cab of his truck and drive away.

This was one of the worst days of my life. It was like Daddy dying all over again.

For several minutes I sat in the car with my handbag on my lap. Inside was a certified check for the sale of two hundred sixteen acres of the richest farmland in the county. The value of that land, every inch of it lovingly tended by generations of people who understood hard work and the satisfaction of a job well done, had been reduced to a piece of watermarked paper.

I drove home feeling depleted. It was an effort to hold the steering wheel. My breathing was shallow, and my head throbbed. When I entered the house, I leaned over the sink and splashed cold water on my face. "Eat something!" I scolded myself while opening the refrigerator. Deciding on a poached egg on toast and orange juice, I sat at the table and had a late breakfast while Eddie munched on a handful of treats I'd put into his bowl.

My skin felt cold and clammy, and I went upstairs to change into dry clothes. As I was buttoning my blouse, a knock sounded at the back door.

"I'll be right there," I called, zipping my jeans. I was surprised to see Gabe standing on the back porch. Two box-style trucks, one flatbed, and three pickups were parked in the driveway.

"Hi, Teddi. We're an hour early. I hope that's okay."

"No problem." I opened the door as Eddie, always the cheerful ambassador, bounded out to greet Gabe with tail wags and whimpers. I handed Gabe the key to the workshop and watched seven men enter the barn. Piece by piece they began hauling several generations of tools and equipment out to the trucks. It was more painful than I could have imagined, and with Eddie at my side I went back inside the house.

By late afternoon the barn had been emptied. From the kitchen window, I watched the two box trucks lumber down the driveway, both filled to capacity. Next came the flatbed loaded with Daddy's hay baler and plow. Joe Springer had already purchased his corn harvester and driven it away.

While the remaining men began cleaning out the workshop, I took Eddie outside to check on the progress they'd made. There was nothing left but Daddy's old tractor. I ran my fingers over one of its knobby tires and then walked to the back of the barn. Unlatching the door, I stepped into the bright sunlight and saw Gabe standing by Ghost's flight cage. The roof now sagged, and several boards along the back wall had rotted through.

Gabe turned and looked at me, dirty and shining with sweat.

"Hi, Gabe. How's it going?"

"Good, just taking a little break," he said, wiping his brow on his shirtsleeve. "Your barn is built like a fortress. And the haymow? Man, that thing's huge."

"Many a Thoroughbred crossed the finish line fueled by my Daddy's hay." I glanced over my shoulder. "This barn will be standing long after both of us are gone. But I need to get that hole in the roof taken care of."

"Yeah, I saw that, but it's not as bad as it looks. If you want, I can do the repair—it won't take long."

I threw a stick for Eddie and looked at Gabe. "You work part-time at the vet clinic, help your grandfather with his liquidation business, *and* do roofing?"

He smiled and slapped a layer of dust from his jeans. "I did roofing during the summers when I was in college. Still do it now and then."

"What did you study?"

"I'm an environmental naturalist and a vet tech. Last year I completed special training, and now I'm a certified wilderness responder, too. My girlfriend, Sally, is a vet. She's up in Minnesota taking an advanced course in avian medicine. We're getting married next spring and hope to buy a house. That's one of the reasons I take on all the odd jobs I can get."

"If you don't mind my asking, how old are you, Gabe?"

"I'll be twenty-seven in September. Why?"

"Oh, just curious."

Gabe took hold of the stick in Eddie's mouth and played tug, making low growls that delighted Eddie and got him all wound up. When Eddie let go, Gabe stepped back and sent the stick sailing into the field. We both laughed as Eddie hunkered down and blitzed after it.

"Where will you and Sally live after you're married?"

"That depends on where she gets hired. I can't imagine living anywhere else. This wilderness is part of who I am, so I hope we'll stay in this area."

"My brother loved the Gorge," I said with a sad smile.

"When my grandpa and I left here on Saturday, he told me that your brother's been missing for quite a while. Once we'd talked about it, I remembered seeing a news story on TV. I was just a kid, but I remember." Gabe looked down at the ground and loosened a stone with the toe of his boot. "I'm really sorry, Teddi."

"Me, too." Pushing my hands into the pockets of my jeans, I looked up at the mountain. "Gabe, how long have you been hiking and climbing?"

"I've hiked these parts for as long as I remember, and I started seriously climbing when I was eleven."

"I'd like to ask you something, but I want you to be absolutely honest."

He gave me his full attention. "Okay."

"In your opinion, how long could a person who's fit and well educated in wilderness survival live in the Gorge?"

Gabe pressed his lips together and looked away.

"Don't candy-coat your answer. Please, just give it to me straight."

"There would be lots of factors to consider. Nutrition, unexpected health problems, and injuries. But people have lived in the Gorge for thousands of years. Paleo-Indians thrived here."

"What if someone didn't eat meat and only ate vegetation and fish?"

"There are plenty of sources for fruits and nuts, and a good fisherman would never go hungry. So anyway, my short answer is yes, someone could live his entire life in this wilderness. But . . ."

When Gabe didn't say anything further, I stepped closer. "But what?"

The blue of his eyes deepened when he tilted his head and looked at me. "I guess the big question is, why would anyone want to?"

As silence settled around us, Gabe turned toward Ghost's empty enclosure. Reaching out, he curled his fingers through the holes in the rusted wire mesh. "Will you tell me about him?"

"Ghost or my brother?"

"Both."

My gaze traveled from the flight cage and into the cloudless sky. Taking in a breath, I answered, "Yes."

∾

On Wednesday morning I was packed and ready for my departure to Charleston. At six-thirty Gabe drove to the back of the house and parked. A few moments later, he rapped lightly on the screen door.

"C'mon in," I called from the kitchen.

The familiar squeak of the screen door sounded as he stepped inside, clean-shaven and his hair damp. Hoping for a playmate,

Eddie brought Gabe a tennis ball. I liked how Gabe scratched Eddie's ears and gave him a pat on the rump before gently tossing the ball into the living room.

"Thanks for coming by so early, Gabe. Please have a seat."

He seemed a bit nervous as he sat at the table. I smiled to myself as I poured him a cup of coffee. If I were in his shoes, I'd be nervous, too. I had called him the previous evening and asked if I could speak with him, alone and in person. I said it was important but didn't say anything more.

While we sat and talked about his work at the veterinary clinic, Gabe devoured a plate of blueberry muffins I'd just pulled from the oven. In many ways he reminded me of Josh—how comfortable he was in his skin, the way his eyes deepened with his thoughts, his voracious appetite.

"Well, I think it's time I told you why I asked you to come by." I opened my spiral notepad and slid it across the table in front of him.

Gabe looked from the notepad to me, then back to the notepad. The more he read, the more his cheeks reddened. I couldn't tell if it was from the caffeine or what I'd written. Twice he leaned back and glanced out the screen door toward Ghost's enclosure.

We talked for over an hour, discussing the what-ifs and the hows. The question of why had been answered when I'd told him the story of my brother. Well, most of the story.

I refilled Gabe's cup, and while rinsing the pot in the sink I looked out the window at the barn. *What would Daddy think of this? Would he agree with my idea? Would he understand?*

Somehow I believed he would.

I must have been standing at the sink for quite some time, because when I turned, Gabe was watching me intently.

"So anyway," I said, drying my hands and taking my seat at the table, "give it some thought and call me one way or the other." I pointed to the top of the page. "Both my work and home numbers are right here. If you call the shop and I'm not there, just leave your name and where I can reach you. Please don't say what it's about. I'd like to keep this as private as possible."

He blew steam off his coffee and studied me over the rim. "Teddi, are you sure about this? You've been through a lot, and—"

I held up my hand. "I'm sure."

When Gabe pulled out of the driveway, I packed up my car, whistled for Eddie, and left, too. I had a long drive ahead of me and wanted to reach Charleston before dark.

TWENTY-SEVEN

The following morning I was so glad to be back at work that I burst through the door two hours before opening time. After turning on the radio, I grabbed the caddy of cleaning supplies and walked to the front of the shop. When I saw the bright red Sold tag hanging from the door of the Louis XV armoire, I said out loud, "Thank you, Inez!"

While polishing the top of an antique backgammon board, I glanced out the window. Across the street a man was pushing a dolly along the sidewalk. Stacked on the dolly were two cardboard boxes, on top of which was an old blue typewriter.

I thought of the Smith-Corona that Mama had bought me for graduation, how devastated I was, how angry and ungrateful when I pulled off the wrapping paper. Now, all these years later, I saw things differently. Mama was trying to give me security. The Smith-Corona had been her symbolic gift of freedom, her own version of Daddy's red, white, and blue.

I watched the man push the dolly around the side of a building and whispered, *"I'm so sorry, Mama. I didn't see what you were trying to do . . ."*

The back door swung open, and I heard Albert come in. I left the cleaning supplies where they were and headed for the workshop. He looked up while tying his apron, "Hey, Teddi. How'd it go up in Kentucky?"

As if propelled by an unseen force, I raced forward and threw my arms around him. "I'm so glad you're in my life, Albert. Do you realize we've worked together for almost twenty years?" When I loosened my grip and stepped back, the stunned look on his face made me laugh.

"What you boilin' over about? You keep actin' crazy and we ain't gonna work together for another twenty minutes."

I wiped tears from my eyes and sniffed. "I'm just so happy— happy I have this shop, happy that you're here. Inez, too."

Albert shook his head. "Cry when you're mad, cry when you're happy, cry when you're blue. My mama used to cry when she ironed. Lord, all them tears rollin' with the steam. It was a sorry sight. Long as I live, I'll never understand you women."

"Well, if it's any consolation, I don't understand us either." I walked to my workbench and pulled tissues from a drawer. While drying my eyes, I noticed an old drop cloth draped over a piece of furniture. "What's that, Albert?"

"Don't know."

"What do you mean, 'Don't know'?"

He paid no mind to my questioning eyes and began lining up his tools for the day's work.

Stepping to the shrouded piece of furniture, I folded back the drop cloth. When I saw what lay beneath, how gorgeous and transformed it was, I whipped around and gasped. "Albert James Pickens!"

He tried to stop his lips from edging toward a smile, but I saw it just the same. "Now, don't start bawlin' again. I got work to do."

I knelt in front of the old chest and ran my fingers over the marquetry repairs. It was hard to believe this was the same beat-up chest I'd bought at the yard sale. "Whatever I owe you, it's not enough. Albert, you're amazing. How did you do this so fast?"

He flipped a dining chair upside down on his workbench and began unscrewing the seat. "Two words: Reba's sister. She came up from Alabama and plans to stay for a whole month. That woman flaps her jaws mornin' till night, starts talkin' even before I've had my breakfast. Nothin' left for me to do but come to work. Even came in over the weekend just so I could have some peace."

"I'm sorry you had to get away from home, but this chest sure reaped the benefits. These repairs are incredible."

Albert removed the chair seat and set it aside. "Don't look too close. That old chest been through a whole lot. It ain't never gonna be perfect."

I ran my fingers over the front of a drawer and whispered, "Neither am I, Albert. Neither am I."

Remembering the cleaning supplies I'd left by the front window, I went to finish what I'd started. As I was wiping down a brass coach lantern, I turned to see Inez walking around a tall chest of drawers.

"Hi, I see you sold the armoire."

"A nice couple from Boston bought it. The freight company will pick it up next Tuesday."

"Inez, you're the best."

She looked at me with the oddest expression. "Well, you won't think so after I tell you what happened on Saturday. After I sold the armoire, a woman came in and bought the silver tea service you've had since last summer."

"Inez! I didn't even notice. That's wonderful."

"Yes and no. While I was in the back wrapping it up, the doorbell started ringing like crazy. So I hurried and got the tea service into a box. When I walked out front, the shop was filled with people. You'd have thought there was a sign in the window that said we were giving things away. It was a madhouse. Everyone started asking questions and buying all at once. I sold the marble candlesticks, the pine pastry table, and that celadon jardinière you loved so much. Anyway, after everyone left, I walked around straightening things up and wiping fingerprints off the glass cases. That's when I noticed the telescope was gone. And whoever snatched it didn't even bother to take its storage case. I swear I don't know how it happened. I'm sorry, Teddi."

I turned and looked at the chest where the telescope had been. "It's not your fault, Inez. I shouldn't have placed it so close to the front door. Don't worry," I said, patting her arm.

"Well, I feel terrible about it. You pay me good money to watch the shop when you're gone. It's no consolation, but I got up early this morning and made a chocolate cream pie. It's in the kitchen."

ॐ

The day flew by as one customer after another walked in. By four o'clock I'd sold a matching pair of porcelain vases and so many pieces of sterling flatware that I nearly ran out of tissue paper. It had been a fun, haggle-free day, and though I was sill annoyed that someone had stolen the telescope, the sales had outnumbered the loss by over tenfold. At closing time I peeked into the workroom. "You ready, Albert?"

We grunted and strained and cussed beneath our breaths. It was a miracle that Albert and I managed to haul the walnut chest up the stairs of my carriage house without hurting ourselves in the process. I smiled and waved good-bye as he drove off in his truck. He'd have a nice surprise in his next paycheck. Both he and Inez were getting bonuses.

Eddie was worked up from all the commotion, his rump wiggling as he followed me into my bedroom and watched me accessorize the chest. On the left I placed the antique pewter teapot I'd wired and made into a lamp, then a framed photograph of my family, followed by a glass vase filled with early-blooming hydrangeas.

While I obsessed over the accessories, moving each item a half inch here, a little turn there, Olivia phoned. "Hey, Teddi. What are you doing?"

"Admiring the chest I bought at the yard sale. You should see what Albert did. It's unbelievable."

"Well, how about I see it tonight? I made a big salad and a loaf of sourdough bread. Want some company for dinner?"

"I'd love it. The door's unlocked. You can let yourself in."

I had just finished changing clothes when Olivia's footsteps sounded on the stairs. She walked into the kitchen with a giant bowl in her arms, on top of which was a warm loaf of bread.

"Everything smells great. Let's eat out in the garden."

While I gathered plates, silverware, and napkins and put them on a tray, Olivia went down the hall to see the walnut chest. "Sweet mother of holy restoration!" she yelled from my bedroom. "Albert's a magician."

"Isn't he?" I called out.

Olivia returned to the kitchen. "No one would ever know that chest used to be covered in cigarette burns. The finish is gorgeous."

"It must have taken him days just to repair the damaged drawers," I said, pouring two glasses of sweet tea.

We descended the stairs and went out to the garden. I set the table while Olivia served the salad. "So," she said, draping a napkin over her lap, "I have a couple things to tell you. First, I drove by a house today that just went up for sale. It's in the French Quarter. I don't know what it's like inside, but if the exterior is any indication, it has your name all over it."

I sliced a piece of bread from the loaf and rested it on the corner of my plate. "Well, God knows I've wanted my own home for a long time. But it's strange, now that I have the money, I feel odd about spending it."

Olivia furrowed her brow. "Why? My gosh, you can finally buy a house and renovate to your heart's content."

"It's not all my money, you know. Half of it belongs to Josh."

Olivia looked away and stabbed her fork into a piece of romaine.

"That bothers you?"

She propped her elbows on the table and leaned forward. "Teddi, I know you dearly loved your brother. Even though I never met him, after hearing about him for all these years I love him, too. But sometimes when you talk about Josh, it's like a part of your life stopped when he disappeared. Have you ever considered talking to . . . you know, someone like a grief therapist? I just worry that you're setting yourself up for—"

"Please stop," I said, covering my ears with both hands.

When I was certain that Olivia wasn't going to say another word, I lowered my hands. "I don't want to go on a psychological safari with a shrink. I know you think Josh is gone in the most literal sense. Everybody does. Not knowing what happened to my brother is the most awful thing I've ever been through. I *still* go through it, Olivia. Every day when I open the mailbox, I wonder if I'll find a letter. Every time the phone rings, I pray it's news about Josh, and then I'm scared to death that it is."

"That's why I—"

"Let me finish. Of *course* a part of my life stopped when he disappeared. I practically raised him. As much as it would shred me to pieces, in some ways it would be easier to know that he's passed on. Then I wouldn't be so torn up by the endless worry."

I looked into Olivia's eyes and pointed to my temple. "Up here, every bit of logic tells me he's dead. But in here," I said, lowering my hand and tapping my chest, "I have the feeling he's alive."

While Olivia chewed her lip, I waited for her to launch into a lecture on head versus heart. Lord knows I'd heard them all. From Mama to Ranger Jim and even Grammy, everyone tried to pull the last string of hope from my fingers—everyone but Daddy. For up until he died, my father would stand at the kitchen window at dusk, his gaze set on the woods as he silently drank his last cup of coffee for the night.

Olivia flopped back in the chair and raised her hands in surrender. "Mea culpa. Sometimes I think I have all the answers, but I don't. I'm sorry, Teddi. I was just so excited about you finally being able to buy a house."

"Buying a house isn't a problem. But I need to feel good about it, you know?"

She nodded, dropped the subject, and dug into her salad.

The white flag had been waved.

Olivia and I had one of those rare kinds of friendships. We could disagree and sometimes even argue. Yet after we'd both had our say, we inevitably called a truce and moved on.

"All right," she said. "So here's the other thing I wanted to tell you." She arched one eyebrow and paused for dramatic effect. "I have a date. And get this—he has a literary IQ larger than his shoe size!"

"Whoa. Give me the scoop."

"His name is Martin Armstead. He's a stockbroker from Atlanta. He bought the Churchill first edition. Outbid everyone else, sight unseen. He drove up to get the book yesterday. And guess what else. You'll die."

"What?"

"He ended up buying the Jules Verne."

"The one you've been hoping to sell for years?"

"Yes! He bought *Twenty Thousand Leagues Under the Sea.* Granted, he negotiated like a pro and wore me down on the price, but at least he bought it. And here's the best part: He knows almost as much about rare books as I do. We sat in my library and talked for over an hour. He's insanely intelligent, kept using words I'd never heard of."

I personally didn't find that to be an admirable quality, but I kept that thought to myself. Besides, when it came to men, I wasn't exactly an expert. I tried to sound interested when I asked, "What words?"

"When we talked about our families, he said he had a brother but that he was a lazy *scapegrace*." Olivia laughed. "Isn't that a great word? So after Martin left, I looked it up—it means a reckless scoundrel."

"Maybe he reads a thesaurus every night before going to bed."

"All I know is that I loved every minute I spent with him. I even loved his socks."

I nearly choked on a piece of tomato. "You loved his *socks?* Oh, man, you've got it bad."

Olivia grinned and sliced into the bread. "Really nice argyle. I don't know why, but they just seemed sexy. I think they were cashmere. I have to admit I've been having fantasies ever since he left."

"So when's your date?"

"He's coming into town for business next Friday. We'll have dinner Saturday evening. So I have a question," she said, lifting her arms and tightening the band around her ponytail. "Can you take an hour or two off work tomorrow and help me find a new dress?"

I blotted my lips with my napkin and shook my head. "I can't. I'm jammed until Monday. What about Tuesday, would that work?"

"Sure. What time?"

"Let's go first thing in the morning when the stores open. Inez won't mind watching the shop, and if you don't find something right away, you'll have several more days to look."

We chattered as we finished our salads and then moved to the two wicker chaise lounges under the oak tree. Eddie, who was happily gnawing the fuzz off a tennis ball, got up and trotted to the flower garden. Out from her hiding place beneath an azalea came his new friend. She rubbed against his legs, and they sniffed noses.

"Look at that beautiful feline," Olivia said. "Where did she come from?"

"She belongs to the people who moved in next door. Her name is Dee-Dee. Eddie adores her. She comes into the garden and waits for him. They're so cute together."

Eddie trotted toward us with Dee-Dee by his side. She was a tiny, green-eyed girl, with a pure white coat and a fluffy tail. I bent over and scooped her up in my arms.

"She's gorgeous," Olivia said, smoothing her hand over Dee-Dee's head. "Makes the cat in the Fancy Feast commercial look like a flea-bitten slut!"

I flopped back against the cushion and howled. "Olivia, the things you say! You know what I'll do when I buy a house? Go to a shelter and adopt a kitty from death row. I might even get two."

Olivia kicked off her shoes. "Why not adopt one now?"

"I can't. My lease specifically states only *one* animal."

"All the more reason to start house hunting."

"Soon," I said, scratching Dee-Dee's back.

∞

At ten o'clock the phone rang. The dishes had been washed and put away, Olivia had gone home, and I was so comfortable reading out on the porch that I had half a mind to let the answering machine get it. But on the third ring, I got up and walked into the kitchen.

"Hello."

"Teddi, it's Gabe."

I smiled and leaned my hip against the counter. "Hey, how are you?"

"Good, real good. Sally and I have had several long talks about your idea, and I talked with my parents, too." There came a long pause, and then he lowered his voice. "Teddi, you're . . . you're really serious about this? I mean one hundred percent serious and won't regret it later?"

"Yes, Gabe. I'm serious. So have you made a decision?"

I was certain I heard an emotional crack in his voice when he said, "Then the answer is yes."

"Wonderful. I'll have my attorney draw up the papers."

TWENTY-EIGHT

Inez walked past my office in a cloud of spicy perfume and called out, "Olivia's on line one."

I picked up the phone. "Hey. What's up?"

"What's up? Every hair on my head. You won't believe who arrived at my door."

"An IRS agent?"

"Worse. Much, much worse. My *mother*. She's in the kitchen right now, so if I change the subject, that means she came back upstairs. She was in Myrtle Beach for a golf tournament and decided to stop and see me on her way back to Jacksonville. She didn't even call to see if it was convenient. For the past hour, she's been complaining about how much her body aches, how life is so unfair, yadda, yadda. I'm tired of her 'Oh, woe is me song,' like she's the only one who's ever been served a shit sandwich."

Olivia spewed fire about her mother while I sat at my desk and doodled on a scratch pad.

"And I blew it but good. I mentioned I had a date and that you and I were going shopping tomorrow to look for a dress. Well, she belly-flopped right in and invited herself to go with us."

"Why did you tell her?"

"Because I'm stupid. The last time we shopped together was for my wedding dress, and look where *that* got me."

I leaned back in my chair and laughed. "Don't be so hard on her. I like your mother. I think she's funny."

"Yeah, funny as a root canal. Teddi, no matter what happens, please don't cancel out on me . . ."

❧

At ten-thirty on Tuesday morning, I flung open the door of Sylvia's Dress Shop, glad for the cold blast of air-conditioning. Though Sylvia was busy with other customers, she waved to me and said, "They're in the back."

I found Olivia's mother sitting in an overstuffed chair across from the dressing room. Her too-much-time-spent-on-the-golf-course skin was darker than I remembered, and her bleached hair was teased and lacquered into a genuine sixties French twist. But it was her jacket that gave me pause—dizzying zigzag stripes in hot pink and yellow splashed with sequins. Liberace came to mind.

As I strolled into view, Olivia's mother sang out, "Here she is!"

"Hello, Lorna. You're looking bright this morning." I bent down and kissed her rouged cheek.

"What do you think of my jacket? I found in a bargain-basement sale for eight dollars. Isn't it something?"

I winked. "Yes, it surely is."

Just then Olivia padded out of the dressing room wearing a frown and a remarkably unflattering lime green dress with a plunging neckline.

Lorna's eyes shone with approval. "You look like a movie star."

"No, Mother," Olivia said evenly. "I look like I've crammed grapefruits into a teacup. This dress belongs on a drag queen."

"Drag queen? Why do you always bring up Eric?"

"What? You're the one who mentioned his name!"

Lorna gave her an exasperated look. "You said *drag queen*. Same difference."

"Please don't ruin this day."

"I'm not. But—"

I stepped between them and opened my arms like a referee. "Hey, you two. Let's play nice."

"Olivia, if you don't like the dress, take it off. What about that one?" Lorna pointed to a lace dress on a mannequin. "It's pretty, don't you think, Teddi?"

I shook my head. "It looks like a giant doily."

Lorna raised her eyebrows, but before she could protest, I pulled a pale peach sheath dress from the rack and held it up. "What about this, Olivia?"

"That's too plain," Lorna said with a dismissive groan.

"I like it, Mother. It's classic." Olivia tossed the dress over her shoulder and disappeared behind the velvet curtain.

Lorna looked at me and sighed. "How did I raise a daughter to have no taste? That green dress was perfect."

I patted her shoulder. "Don't worry. She'll find something wonderful."

Lorna lowered her voice and motioned for me to lean close. "Why is she so obsessed with Eric? What's done is done."

"She's not obsessed," I whispered. "She's hurt. There's a big difference. And to be honest, *you* brought him up." It was time to change the subject, and fast. I stood and rested my hand on the back of the chair. "Olivia says you're heading home to Jacksonville this afternoon."

"Yes. I wish I could stay longer, but the painters are coming Thursday. I'm having my bedroom painted purple."

"I love that about you, Lorna. You're so courageous with color."

She beamed up at me, her brown eyes framed in electric blue liner. "Olivia thinks I'm garish, but color makes me happy."

The dressing-room curtain flipped open, and Olivia stepped out.

"Wow. Look at you," I said. "That color is beautiful."

The dress skimmed her body in all the right places, and there was something about the shimmer of the peach silk that brought her blue eyes to life.

Lorna dug around in her handbag and popped a mint into her mouth. "The color is pretty, but you need something more stylish. That dress makes you look like hired help."

I couldn't stop myself from reaching out and giving Lorna's arm a pinch.

Olivia stepped to the three-way mirror. "I would never have picked this dress from a hanger, but I love it," she said, turning from side to side. "Does it make my hips look big—I mean, bigger than they already are?"

"Yes," Lorna said too quickly.

"No," I said too loudly.

Ignoring her mother, Olivia looked down at her bare feet. "Teddi, what would I wear for shoes?"

"Strappy sandals with a medium heel."

Lorna's shoulders collapsed in defeat. "Well, I can see that my opinion doesn't count. If that's the one you really want, at least let me buy it for you." Reaching into her handbag, she pulled out a rhinestone-studded wallet. "How much is it?" she asked, riffling through her cash.

"Three hundred," Olivia said.

Lorna looked from Olivia to me and then back at Olivia. Snapping her wallet closed, she dropped it into her handbag. "Forget it. I'll buy the shoes."

∞

On Saturday I closed up the shop and walked home through a haze of sweltering heat. The air burned my nose, and the sky was as yellow as sulfur. After cranking down the air-conditioning, I slipped into the lightest cotton nightgown I owned and tuned the radio to a classical station. With a pad of graph paper and a box of colored pencils, I sat at the kitchen table and began sketching a layout for a chest I'd been commissioned to paint. My customer wanted it to look as though a paisley scarf were draped across the top with its fringed ends hanging over the edge. It would be the most difficult trompe l'oeil I'd ever tackled.

Eddie was sprawled out on the floor beneath the table, lulled into a deep sleep by the music. While I sketched the front of the chest to half-inch scale, the doorbell chimed. I ignored it and continued working.

It chimed again.

"Go away," I mumbled.

After two more chimes, Eddie let out a sleepy, unenthusiastic bark. I shoved back the chair, went downstairs, and squinted through the peephole.

"Wow" I said, opening the door. "How fabulous are you!"

Olivia gave me a wilted look. "Remember that old saying 'All dressed up and no place to go'? Well, that's me."

"What happened?"

She stepped inside. "Right when I was putting on my pearls, Martin called. He's sick. I guess it's the flu." Olivia looked at my nightgown. "Did I get you out of bed?"

"No, I just wanted to be cool." I latched the door and motioned to the stairs. "C'mon up."

She scratched Eddie's ears and then plunked down at the kitchen table. "And what really ticks me off is this is the best my hair has *ever* looked."

I poured her a glass of iced tea and sat down. "I'm sure he's just as disappointed as you. It must be awful being sick in a hotel. Where's he staying?"

"I didn't think to ask." Olivia turned toward the radio and

frowned. "What the hell are you listening to, Hopelessness in C Major? This music makes me want to slit my wrists."

I picked up a pencil and bopped her on the head. "It's the Adagietto from Mahler's Fifth Symphony. It's beautiful."

Olivia took a long drink of iced tea, and as she set down her glass, I saw her eyes shift to the large manila envelope sitting on the shelf directly across from the sink. The label, GANNON RAWLINGS—ATTORNEY-AT-LAW, was clearly visible.

Unashamedly nosy, or curious, as she liked to say, Olivia didn't think twice about asking, "Is that something serious?"

"As a matter of fact, it is. When I was up home in the spring, I met a young man named Gabe Tucker. He's a naturalist who's dedicated his life to animal and avian rescue. He reminded me so much of Josh that it was almost eerie. Anyway, it's a long story, but I gave him the remaining acreage of the farm, which includes the house and the barn."

Olivia looked at me as if I'd lost my mind. "You *gave* him the farm. Why?"

"Because I liked him, and I knew he'd do something positive with it. Gabe's fiancée is a veterinarian, and they're—"

"Teddi, have you lost your mind? Why would you up and give away something you could have sold?"

"I know what I'm doing and I feel real good about it, so don't beat me up." I gave her a warning look when I added, "I mean it, Olivia. I'm happy, so leave it alone. Okay?"

Though a storm of questions formed in her eyes, she didn't push for anything more. Glancing down at my drawing, she scrunched up her nose. "Do you ever not work?"

"This isn't work. It's fun."

"Well, I'll go in a few minutes so you can get back to your work, fun, or whatever it is."

"C'mon, Olivia, don't be such a cranky-pants."

"I can't help it. I'm really disappointed about tonight."

I looked at her beautiful new dress, her chestnut hair pulled up in a fashionable knot, and her perfect manicure. Gathering my pencils, I put them back into the box and closed the lid. "Don't go anywhere, and for Pete's sake don't slit your wrists. I'll be right back."

The moment I entered my bedroom, I heard Olivia change the radio station. I stripped off my nightgown and took a white eyelet sundress from the closet. With a tug and a shimmy, I smoothed it over my hips and slipped my feet into a pair of heels. After brushing my hair and pulling it into a ponytail, I put on earrings and touched up my blush. A spritz of cologne finished me off, and in less than five minutes I returned to the kitchen.

Olivia looked stunned. "What are you doing?"

"We're going out for dinner."

She pressed her lips together and squinted at me. "You're the best, do you know that?"

"Yeah, yeah," I said with a wave of my hand. "You say that to everyone when you get your way."

She laughed and rose from the chair. "Where do you want to go?"

"Fine cuisine is in order. I vote for McCrady's."

"Do you think they'll seat us without reservations? Maybe we should call."

I grabbed my handbag and car keys. "We'll flash the maître d' our best smiles and hope for the best. C'mon, I'll drive."

A tangerine sunset bled through the sky as I maneuvered through traffic. When I turned on Bay Street, I slowed while passing a grand three-story mansion. Its stucco walls were painted tropical pink, and its candlelit piazza was filled with the seersucker-and-linen crowd, no doubt all of them born-and-bred Charlestonians. I imagined the tinkling of crystal goblets, silver trays filled with artfully arranged hors d'oeuvres, and the air scented with a mélange of expensive perfumes and fine cigars. A sudden longing to be back in Kentucky washed over me—to be sitting on the warped old porch with my family, drinking lemonade from those silly Rocky and Bullwinkle glasses that Grammy collected when I was a little girl—to hear the song of my family's collective laughter move through the evening air.

Olivia broke into my moment of nostalgia when she pointed out the windshield and said, "There's one. It's probably the best we'll find."

The memory of my family faded away as I squeezed my car into the small space and cut the engine. "I hope they can seat us, I'm starved."

We hadn't walked a block, and already I was starting to perspire, and by the time we stepped inside McCrady's, the hair at my temples was wet. Though the maître d' raised an eyebrow when we declared our lack of a reservation, he ran his finger down the seating list and glanced at his watch. "Yes, I have a table. Please, right this way."

I gestured for Olivia to go first and followed behind. The aroma of sizzling shrimp filtered through the air as he led us toward the back of the restaurant. Just as we maneuvered around a waiter, Olivia stopped so abruptly that I bumped into her, nearly knocking her into a table. She caught her balance, turned, and grabbed my arm. From the look on her face, I couldn't tell if she was angry or frightened. Without saying a word, she yanked me through the restaurant and out the front door.

"Olivia, what are you doing?"

She released my arm and set off walking in the opposite direction of my car. I trotted to catch up with her. "Hey, what in the world is going on?"

Coming to a sudden stop, Olivia turned and looked at me. A

bead of sweat dripped along the side of her face. "You know what I am? A cliché—a forty-year-old fool who splurged on a silk dress, a manicure, and a pedicure, and all for nothing."

"I'm not following you. Just tell me, what happened?"

She set off walking again, her heels clicking angrily on the hot sidewalk. "Sick, my fat ass. Martin—that no-good *bastard*. He's in McCrady's with a gorgeous brunette!"

"No."

"*Yes!* And she's probably half my age."

I took hold of her wrist and forced her to slow down. "Now, wait a minute. Are you sure—do you have your contacts in?"

Stopping to face me, she flicked a tear from her cheek and nodded.

"Okay, so he's a lying sack of slime. I think it would be hilarious if we went back in there and had dinner. Hold your head high and make damn sure he sees you. Guaranteed it'll ruin his evening. He'll be destroyed."

She folded her arms across her chest and looked away. "I can't. I'm too humiliated."

"C'mon, Olivia. Don't let him do this to you. We need to go back in there, sit at our table, and watch him squirm. You'll feel great, and he'll end up—"

"Stop being Captain Positive!" Olivia pulled a tissue from her handbag and blotted her tears.

The power of her words sent me back a step. "Well then, the hell with Martin and his teenybopper date. We're all dressed up, so let's go somewhere else and have a nice dinner. You can bitch about him all you want, as long as we're sitting in an air-conditioned restaurant."

"I just want to go home. Where's your damn car?" she said, looking around. "I'm all confused."

In an attempt to prevent her from taking off in yet another direction, I stepped in front of her. "Olivia, I can understand being upset, but you don't even know this Martin guy. Why did you put so much stock into this *one* date?"

"You wouldn't understand."

"Try me."

She turned away and shook her head.

"Olivia. Please talk to me."

She blotted another tear from her cheek, her face pained and delicate in the dimming light. "I'm . . . I'm petrified that I'll never be loved again. Eric stole the best years of my life. I can't even tell you how much I loved him. Now he's happy with his California boy toy, and I'm falling apart. Every night I go to bed feeling lonely and worthless. I just read an article that said a woman over forty was more likely to die in a plane crash than get married." Olivia's voice made a little hiccup when she said, "The thought of growing old alone terrifies me."

Had she told me she was an alien from Jupiter, I wouldn't have been more surprised. Stripped of her armor of wit and biting sarcasm, Olivia had exposed a soft, vulnerable place that I never knew existed. I wondered what kind of friend I'd been. How had I missed the signs of her most painful truth?

I gently pressed my palms against her bare shoulders. "You're beautiful and smart and funny. And even though you try to hide it, you have a big heart. But you have terrible taste in men."

She took off walking at a furious pace, her purse swinging from her shoulder and banging into her hip. Though a river of sweat was dripping down my back, I sped up and slipped my arm around hers.

"I just don't meet the right men," she sputtered.

"That's not true."

"Oh, yes it is. Give me one example. One!"

This wasn't a conversation I wanted to have, but it was too late to close the door on the subject. "All right. Remember when your bathroom sink overflowed and that nice-looking plumber asked you for a date? You turned him down."

Olivia came to an abrupt halt. "Of course I did. What would we have talked about—Drano versus Liquid-Plumr? We had nothing in common, and—"

"You didn't even give him a *chance*. Well, guess what? That plumber you brushed off just published a collection of short stories. He's dating Carla Fry. Remember her? She works over at Langdon Jewelers. She told me about it when I took my watch in to get repaired."

"Well, zippity-damn-doo-dah for her!" Olivia snapped. She turned her back to me and lowered her head. "Why are you telling me this, especially after what just happened with Martin?"

I gave her a hug, which she immediately shrugged off. "I didn't tell you to hurt you, Olivia. I told you because you're my best friend. You deserve a great guy, but you're never going to find him if you don't stop being so judgmental. You're hard on people. Remember when you and I met at that estate sale? You thought I was a ninny because I couldn't get the chandelier into my car."

"Well, you *were* a ninny."

"I misjudged the size! That doesn't make me a ninny. But then we started talking, and look what happened—"

"Yeah, I hauled the chandelier back to your shop in my truck, because you were a ninny."

Exasperated, I let out a deep sigh. "Stop being so bitchy. I'm talking about the end result, and you know it. If it hadn't been for that chandelier, we never would have met and discovered we had a lot in common."

Olivia blew a sweaty strand of hair from her forehead and offered the slightest nod of agreement.

"C'mon, I'm melting. Let's get out of this heat and have dinner."

I laced my arm through hers and urged her forward. "And if we can't get a table at a nice restaurant, we can go back to my place, sit around in our underwear, and eat pizza."

While walking back to my car, Olivia stopped in front of a red Porsche. "I should smash his headlights."

"That's Martin's car? Olivia Dupree, this is exactly what I was just talking about. Forget about him, his big words, and his stupid argyle socks. The guy has no soul. He's nothing but a . . . a thesaurus-humping egomaniac."

Just when I thought she was going to start crying again, Olivia's lips twitched, and then she burst out laughing. "*Thesaurus-humping*? That was good, Teddi. You know what? You're right. He charmed me into dropping the price on the Jules Verne by asking me to dinner. I could kick myself."

"Don't worry, I'll kick you later. But for now, hold this." I thrust my purse into her hands and stepped off the curb. Scanning the street surface, I found one and then another.

"Teddi, what are you doing?"

"*Shhh*. Cough if anyone heads this way."

I knelt by the side of the Porsche and unscrewed the cap from the valve stem of the left front tire. After shoving a tiny pebble inside, I replaced the cap and listened for the *pssssst*. When I heard it, I smiled. Moving to the right rear tire, I did the same thing.

Olivia watched, her tears gone and her face beaming. "You're a *genius*," she whispered with laughter bubbling in her throat.

"Well, I probably won't be invited to the annual Mensa picnic, but I know when revenge is justified."

"Where did you learn to do that?"

I stepped to the sidewalk, took my handbag from Olivia, and triumphantly tossed it over my shoulder. "My amazing little brother . . ."

TWENTY-NINE

Summer brought an explosion of work to the shop. Several hotels were hosting conventions, and an article in the *New York Times* about Charleston's many charms had initiated a surge in tourism. I was selling antiques as fast as I acquired them, and Albert had a lengthy backlog of repairs. In August a young socialite commissioned me to paint a blanket chest to look like the game board of Candy Land for her little girl's fifth birthday. Within a week of my delivering the chest to Marilee Armstrong's home on Legare Street, everyone in her circle wanted a hand-painted piece of furniture. I was swamped with custom work and had to put people on a waiting list.

In early October, Albert and I were in the workroom. He was repairing a fracture in the side of a handsome William and Mary olivewood chest. I smiled to myself from the opposite side of the workroom doing the opposite kind of work—painting a pine desk for a ten-year-old girl—bubblegum pink with lime green drawer pulls.

The phone rang, and a minute later Inez stepped into the workroom. "Someone named Gabe is on the phone. Want me to take a message?"

"No, I'll take it."

I wiped off my hands and walked to my office, closing the door behind me.

"Hi, Gabe."

"Hey, Teddi. Sorry to bother you at work, but I wanted to give you an update. Sally and I are putting together a fund-raiser at the farm, and it would mean a lot to us if you'd come."

I sat at my desk and looked at the calendar. "Do you have a date?"

"October twenty-seventh. We think a Sunday will draw more people. But we really want you to be here, so if you need it to be a different date, we can change it."

"I wouldn't miss it for anything. What can I do to help?"

"Are you kidding? After all you've done already? Sally and I still can't believe it. She's really excited to meet you, and so are my parents."

I heard a catch in his voice when he said, "Teddi? I . . . I just want to say thanks again."

"You're welcome. See you soon. Bye, Gabe."

I circled the date on my calendar and then asked Inez if she could cover for me that weekend. She jumped at the chance to earn some overtime. While I was on the phone making my airline reservations, the bell above the front door rang and Olivia called out, "It's just me!"

After jotting down my confirmation number, I hung up the phone and stepped into the showroom. Olivia was standing by the window, holding a crystal inkwell to the light. "This is gorgeous, Teddi. Where did you get it?"

"From a dealer in France."

The inkwell sparkled as she lifted the hinged silver lid and looked at the price. "I'm crazy about it, but it's awfully expensive. Will you give me a discount?"

"If you'll do me a favor, you can have it for what I paid."

She looked at me and smiled. "Okay, it's a deal. What's the favor?"

"Gabe invited me to a fund-raiser he and Sally are having at the farm. I'm too busy to spend all that time driving up and back, so I'm flying. Would you babysit Eddie while I'm gone?"

"Absolutely," she said, wiping her fingerprints from the inkwell on the hem of her blouse. "When is it?"

"Sunday the twenty-seventh. But my flight is early on Saturday, so I'd need to drop Eddie off on Friday night."

"Bear will love having Eddie to play with." Olivia handed me the inkwell and said, "Wrap it up."

While I grabbed some tissue and a bag, she sat on the corner of Albert's workbench as if she owned the place. "Hey," she said. "What's going on?"

"Hey yourself. Looks like you been rollin' in the dirt."

She glanced down at her dirty jeans. "Actually, I have. Spent all morning digging up my side garden. I'm getting ready to plant some azaleas and thought I'd stop by and drive y'all nuts before I go to the nursery."

While Olivia, Albert, and I talked about gardening, the phone rang. I could hear Inez in her office cackling up a storm, but I couldn't make out exactly what she was saying.

A few minutes later, she appeared in the doorway, hands on her hips and her eyebrows raised. "Attention, everyone. I have an announcement. I just got a call from Kaye Farley over at Dodson's Antiques. Wait till you hear this! Saturday morning Miz Sticky-Fingers Poteet pulled a porcelain dog from a glass case and ran out the door. Mr. Dodson saw her do it and set off after her, cussin' and yellin' something awful. He caught up with her halfway down the block, and there they were, Miz Poteet holding on to that dog and Mr. Dodson trying to yank it out of her hands. I guess it was a real tug-of-war. Well, Miz Poteet refused to let go, and then she stepped backward off the curb and fell."

"Is she hurt?" I asked.

"Sprained her ankle, and her elbow was all scraped up and

bleeding. Kaye saw the whole thing happen. The rescue squad and the police came, and people were lined up on both sides of the street. I guess it was quite a hullabaloo. Kaye said the dog was smashed to bits. It was one of those expensive ones. Oh, we've had a few in the past, what's it called? They're made in England, and—"

"Staffordshire?" I said.

"Yes, that's it." Inez let out a dramatic sigh and looked at me. "Kaye said she heard that Miz Poteet's son hired someone to keep her from leaving the house. I guess this puts an end to all the designamony we've been getting. So much for that red convertible I've had my eye on."

Albert furrowed his brow. "Red convertible?"

"What's designamony?" Olivia asked.

Though we all laughed when Inez explained what designamony was and how she came up with the idea, a part of me felt sorry for Miz Poteet, so much so that I thought about her off and on for the remainder of the day.

At closing time I locked the door, gathered what I needed from the glass display cabinet, and set off to purchase a get-well card, colorful tissue, and a small gift bag. After buying everything I needed, I sat in my car to write a short message inside the card:

> Dear Mrs. Poteet,
>   I'm sorry about your unfortunate mishap. Best wishes
> for a quick and full recovery.
>
>   Sincerely,
>   Teddi Overman

After circling the streets looking for a parking space, I grew impatient and parked several blocks from Miz Poteet's home. I took my time walking and admired the architecture of Charleston's prized jewels. Though I'd seen it countless times, I slowed when I came to one of the city's most photographed homes—a colossal white-painted beauty that sat on the corner of East Battery and Atlantic. Boasting three tiers of demilune porches and filigreed from top to bottom, the house resembled an extravagant wedding cake.

Not nearly as opulent as the wedding-cake mansion, the Poteet home was a handsome Italianate that overlooked White Point Garden. The house had an original marble stairway, each of its steps showing wear and hairline fractures from the many people who'd climbed them during the past hundred years. While waiting for someone to answer the doorbell, I stepped back to admire the porch, wondering what it would be like to relax in one of the wicker rockers as a breeze rolled in from the harbor.

Though I'd never laid eyes on him before, I was certain the man who opened the door was none other than the esquire himself. On the few occasions we'd spoken over the phone regarding his mother's thefts, I always imagined him looking like a pompous toad. But that wasn't the case.

The man in the doorway was tall, with deep brown eyes and a head full of thick brown hair that was graying at the temples. Big ears aside, he might have looked handsome if he weren't wearing such a grumpy look on his face.

"Mr. Poteet?"

"Yes."

"Hello. I'm Teddi Overman. I understand that your mother took a nasty fall. I'm so sorry. I wanted to bring her a little get-well gift."

Eyeing me suspiciously, he took the shiny pink bag from my out-stretched hand. He must have thought I was playing some kind of cruel trick, because he pushed his hand through the tissue and pulled out the Limoges box. It was not the one Miz Poteet had stolen and then returned when my mother passed away, but one I'd recently purchased at a house sale—a precious little thing with a blue butterfly on its lid.

The hard edge of his jaw softened when he looked at the tiny box. "Mother is quite fond of these."

"Yes, she is."

I wondered if he had any idea how many she'd stolen from me. How many he'd paid for with designamony tacked to his bill.

"Well, I'll be on my way. Please give your mother my best. Have a nice evening, Mr. Poteet."

I was down the steps and on the sidewalk when he called out, "Miz Overman?"

I turned and looked up to face him. "Yes?"

"Thank you for being kind to my mother. And please, call me Sam."

"Feel free to call me Teddi."

I smiled and lifted my hand. He did the same.

While walking to my car I thought about how lonely he must be, living in that big old house with nobody to talk to but his wacky mother—so many rooms, so little laughter to fill them.

THIRTY

On Friday evening, October 25, I packed up Eddie's food bowls and toys and drove him to Olivia's. Bear was excited when we came through the door, and the two dogs happily raced off toward the kitchen.

Olivia and I talked for several minutes, and when I turned to leave, Eddie stopped playing with Bear and clung to me like dryer lint. I knelt and loved him up, whispering reassurances in his ear. But he wasn't buying any of it.

With an exaggerated groan, Olivia bent down and picked him up. "You're turning into a tub-a-tub." Eddie let out a pathetic whimper when I opened the front door, doing his best to squirm free of her arms. "Just go. He'll be okay once you're out of sight. I'll take good care of him, Teddi."

I gave him a kiss and scratched his ears. "I'll come get you Sunday night. That's a promise."

When Olivia turned away so he couldn't see me walk out the door, Eddie cried and cried. I left feeling guilty, and when I returned home to pack my suitcase, I missed him something awful.

❧

Thick white clouds gave way to sunshine when the plane touched down at Kentucky's Blue Grass Airport. After signing for the rental

car and hoisting my suitcase into the trunk, I was on the highway by
nine-forty. It was a brisk autumn day, and I opened the window just
enough to let the cool air blow in. The fifty-minute drive went by in
a flash, and though I'd be spending the night at Stella's house, I
drove straight to the farm.

Gabe would be waiting.

The first thing I noticed when turning in to the driveway was
what I assumed to be a large sign in the front yard. Wrapped in a
gray tarp and secured with ropes, the sign was at least six feet wide
and four feet tall. The lawn was meticulously cut and edged, and
the house had been given a fresh coat of white paint. Added to the
windows were new, slate gray shutters.

I climbed the back porch steps and was about to knock on the
door when a familiar rumble sounded. My lips parted when I
turned and saw Daddy's old Allis-Chalmers tractor chugging
around the side of the barn. Gabe waved and headed toward me,
the exhaust stack belching up pale smoke, just as I remembered.
He drove into the backyard and cut the engine. The tractor, which
clearly had been washed and waxed, shone in the sun.

"Hey, Teddi," he said, climbing down. "My buddy and I got your
tractor running."

Descending the steps, I took Gabe's outstretched hand. "My
daddy would be delighted. He loved that old dinosaur. And the
house looks wonderful."

"Thanks. We threw a painting party two weeks ago. A bunch of
our friends showed up, and we got it done in a weekend."

Clearly proud of all he'd accomplished, Gabe smiled as he
looked around. But his face grew serious when he turned his attention to me. "I'm really glad you came, Teddi. I still don't know why
you did this. I mean, I do because of what you told me about Josh,
but I . . . I just don't know what to say."

I leaned against the tractor and pointed toward the road. "A long time ago, a gentleman by the name of Jackson T. Palmer pulled up right there. He was crotchety and stubborn and had a heart bigger than Texas. He gave me an opportunity that literally changed my life. When he passed away, my dreams went up in flames. But before they burned out completely, another gentleman came into my life. His name was Preston Calhoun. He took a big gamble on me and cosigned for a hefty loan so I could have my own business. It took me years to pay it off, and some of them were pretty lean, but I never once missed a payment. When I asked Mr. Calhoun why he'd taken a chance on a farm girl who had a big dream and no money, you know what his answer was?"

Gabe shook his head.

"That one day he woke up in *a real good mood.*" I looked around the farm, willing myself not to get teary. "Anyway, I promised myself that one day I'd be in a real good mood, too. I didn't know how, when, or what it would be about. Then I met you."

Gabe's cheeks flushed, and I suspected that a plethora of emotions were hovering just beneath the surface. I tried to lighten things up when I said, "So why don't you give me that private tour you promised?"

Together we walked to the barn, and the first thing I noticed upon entering was the sweet aroma of fresh wood shavings. Lights glowed from new stainless-steel fixtures attached to the lower beams, the floor planks had been cleaned and oiled, and there wasn't a cobweb in sight. Built along the left wall were eight large cages, each with a thick bed of wood shavings.

Gabe was all puffed up with pride as he explained the kinds of animals each cage could hold and how he and a friend had made them so strong that nothing could break out or in. Inside one of the cages, a small raccoon stood on its haunches and seemed delighted to see us.

"This is Ella," Gabe said, kneeling by the cage. "She got snared in an illegal trap, but she did well with surgery. Her leg is almost healed. She's gentle and really smart."

I knelt beside him and pressed my palm to the cage. "Hi, Ella. You're a pretty girl." I looked at Gabe and smiled. "What a sweet face. She's adorable."

"Yeah, I'm pretty much in love with her."

Beyond the cages was a newly constructed wall where more than a dozen framed permits, diplomas, and certificates hung. Beyond that wall was a pair of stainless-steel stationary tubs, a refrigerator, and all sorts of cupboards. The ladder to the hayloft was gone, and in its place was a brand-new staircase. I ran my hand over the varnished rail and looked into the dark opening of the loft. "What did you do up there, Gabe?"

"Nothing yet. But Sally and I plan to use the front part for an office."

Walking deeper into the barn, Gabe opened a door to another newly constructed interior room. Three windows had been cut into the side of the barn, each one covered by wire mesh. On the opposite wall were seven cages, one with a tenant.

I stepped forward and grinned. "A barred owl. Oh, I just love them. I've never seen one this close. He looks like a curious old man."

"That's Oscar. He's a really loud eight-hooter."

"Eight-hooter?"

"Yeah, he throws out eight hoots, and it sounds like he's saying, 'Who looks at you . . . Who looks at you.'"

I laughed. "I hope I get to hear him."

"Believe me, with all the commotion we're expecting tomorrow, he'll probably hoot up a storm. A car hit him over on I-64, but he's all healed up. In fact, Oscar will be the star of the fund-raiser. We'll do a release, and I'm hoping our guests will see how important our work is and dig deep into their pockets."

Gabe turned and went to the back of the barn. "And this is something I think you'll really like." He slid the latch on the door and moved aside. "Go ahead, Teddi. Open it."

Flashing him a curious look, I pushed open the door and stepped into the sunlight. Before me was my great-grandfather's cowshed, or at least what used to be. The entire structure had been rebuilt, reroofed, and enclosed in brand-new wire.

When I moved closer and saw what was inside, I covered my face with my hands. Though I knew that Gabe surely had the best of intentions, I wasn't prepared.

Not for this.

I tried to find my ballast—fighting, fighting incredibly hard to hold myself together. My face felt hot, my breath leaving me in little puffs.

It's all right. This is now. Stay in the present moment. Breathe . . .

"Teddi, are you okay?"

I lowered my hands, my arms falling heavily at my sides.

He was perched on a tree branch, regal and unafraid. When our eyes met, he never so much as fluttered a wing, as if to make such a movement were cowardly and beneath him.

Gabe spoke softly. "Teddi, this is Noah."

He was such a stunning specimen of his species that he almost didn't seem real. Unlike Ghost, this red-tailed hawk was suited in full regalia: cinnamon-colored streaks across his pale chest, dark brown bars at his shoulders, the tip of his rusty-red tail accented by a black band.

"He's gorgeous. How did he end up here?"

"A farmer found him lying in a puddle after a big rainstorm. He was soaked to the bone and disoriented. I think the wind probably tossed him into the side of the farmer's house. We took a full set of X-rays, and he didn't have any broken bones, but he got beat up pretty bad. Most likely he had a lot of internal bruising. He was lethargic for almost a week, and I had to puree chicken and hand-feed him out of a tube."

As I stepped closer, Noah watched intently. "Is he all right now?"

"Yes. He's almost ready for release."

"When?"

"Soon," Gabe said, smiling at Noah. "Well, I'd better get going. I'm working from noon to seven at the clinic. But feel free to stay as long as you want."

Together we walked toward the house, and I watched Gabe climb into his truck. "See you tomorrow, Teddi," he said, cranking the engine. I smiled and waved good-bye as he drove away.

And there I stood, with my feet on the land that no longer belonged to my family. I could hardly wrap my mind around the finality of it, and yet, in the oddest way, I felt a deep sense of peace. Opening the trunk of the car, I removed hiking boots from my suitcase, sat on the porch steps, and pulled them on. With an extra sweater tied around my waist and a bottle of water in my hand, I set off for my journey into the woods.

The trail, once worn smooth by my brother's passage, was covered in dense underbrush, but memory guided my footsteps. The deeper I went, the more it hurt—each step pressing against my family's most devastating wound. Now and then I stopped to catch my breath and give a strong pat to the trees, many of which I'd known since childhood.

Climbing higher and higher, I moved through the shadows until I reached a sunlit clearing. It was the place where Josh and I often sat when we were children. I lowered myself to the ground, wrapped my arms around my knees, and listened to the sounds of nature's orchestra: the twitter of a wren, a squirrel foraging for food beneath the fallen leaves, the distant thunder of a waterfall. Closing my eyes, I imagined my brother sitting next to me, his hair a mess and the cuffs of his jeans dirty and frayed. Though I knew it was nothing more than imagination toying with memory, for a brief moment I smelled him—that unmistakable scent of woodland boy—a sweat-dampened shirt, ripe with the aromas of rich earth and river. I smiled and breathed deeply, willing it to stay for just for a minute longer, but the scent of my brother evaporated into the wind, just as he'd done all those years ago.

I drank the last of my water and shook out the bottle until the inside was dry. From the pocket of my jeans, I removed the letter I'd written the previous evening. Slowly, I unfolded the single handwritten page and read:

> *My dearest brother Josh,*
>
>   *It's taken me a long time to accept, but I know you're not coming back to run the farm. Daddy's gone, but I suspect you already know that. Mama passed away last year. Without you here to handle things, I didn't have any choice. I sold the fields to Joe Springer. The house, barn, and remaining land I've donated. I won't bore you with the details, but I worked everything out so the Overman farm will always be a wildlife refuge.*
>
>   *Every day I wait for the phone to ring. Every night I pray for you.*
>
>   *Love,*
>   *Teddi*

I rolled up the letter, pushed it into the water bottle, and screwed on the cap. Stepping to the large cluster of rocks, I jammed the bottle into a fissure and then turned toward the path. While making my way into the shadows, I heard the unmistakable *KEEERRRRRRRRRR* of a hawk diving down the mountain.

THIRTY-ONE

After retracing my steps back to the farm, I took one last look around. Already I could feel a pulling-away, a letting-go. Pressing my hand against the side of the barn, I closed my eyes for a moment and then headed to Stella's house.

The minute I rolled in to her driveway and parked, she opened the front door and called out, "Thank heavens you're here—I was startin' to get worried!"

"I stopped at the farm, and time got away from me. I'm sorry."

She came around the front of the car and pressed her palms to my cheeks. "You're here now, that's all that matters. C'mon inside, honey. Are you hungry?"

"I'm famished."

I sat at the kitchen table and chatted with Stella while she fixed me a chicken-salad sandwich and poured a glass of iced tea. Being here was like spiraling back to my childhood—the maple kitchen set, the oilcloth patterned with bright red apples, the toaster hidden beneath a yellow quilted cover edged in faded blue rickrack.

She set a plate in front of me and grinned. "There you go. I put in lots of sweet pickle and celery, just how you like it."

I took a bite and moaned. "Nobody makes chicken salad like you do."

Before I finished the sandwich, Stella slid a giant slab of chocolate cake in front of me. "So tomorrow's the big day," she said, taking a seat across the table. "I've seen flyers in the grocery and the dry cleaners. Loretta even has one in her beauty-shop window."

I dabbed the corners of my mouth with a napkin. "Gabe's an exceptional young man. What he and Sally have committed to do is huge. I pray it works out."

"I'm sure it will," Stella said with a nod. "Rita over at the bakery said they'll give educational classes on wildlife. Is that right?"

"Yes. That was the only stipulation I made when I offered Gabe the property."

I cut into the cake and took a bite. I swear my taste buds stood right up and sang. The frosting was so rich that after two more bites I put down my fork and leaned back in the chair, waiting for the enamel to melt from my teeth. "Oh, my gosh, this cake. I've never tasted anything so wonderful."

Stella's eyes lit up. "I suspect the extra sugar and two cups of creamed butter have something to do with it."

"*Two* cups of butter! I hope I live long enough to finish it." After taking one more bite, I raised my hands in surrender.

Stella reached across the table and scooped the last piece into her mouth. While pressing the tines of her fork into the remaining crumbs, she asked, "So who's takin' care of your little dog?"

"He's staying with Olivia. And let me tell you, he was none too happy. You should have heard him cry when I left. I felt so awful I cried, too."

"Aww, he's your baby," Stella said with a wink.

After we stood at the sink and did the dishes together, Stella refilled our glasses with iced tea. "Come sit with me in the living room. I'm making sachets for the church bazaar and thought maybe you'd help."

I followed her to the floral-slipcovered sofa, where an open cardboard box sat beneath the coffee table. Stella slid it out, lifted a plastic bag from the box, and held the opening toward me. "Smell this."

"I leaned over and took a whiff. "Ummm. I love lavender."

She removed a handful of brightly colored fabric squares from the box and set them on her lap. "Last week I sewed up these little bags. I scoop a cup of lavender inside and tie a ribbon around the top. They make nice gifts. If the lavender goes as far as I hope, I'll make eighty sachets."

I took a sip of iced tea and set it on the table. "Wow, that's a lot."

We settled in and began filling the sachets. Stella decided that I tied the ribbons better than she did, so we worked in assembly-line fashion, Stella filling and me tying.

"Was it hard on you, cleaning out the house and all?" she asked.

"Very hard. Not so much physically, though that wasn't easy, but it was emotionally draining. And you know what upset me the most? I never found Daddy's Bronze Star."

"You mean his war medal? Your mother gave it to his friend, Max Walker."

"What! When did she do that?"

"Well, when Max and Claudette got your letter about your daddy's passing, they felt awful. Drove up here as soon as they could. Of course it was too late to attend the funeral service, but they wanted to come and pay their respects. When they arrived, your mother called and invited me to come down to the farm. You'd just left to go back to Charleston earlier that morning. They were real sorry they'd missed you."

"I remember Mama telling me they'd driven up, but she never mentioned giving Max the medal."

"It wasn't but a few days after they'd gone that she felt like maybe she'd made a mistake—that she should have given it to you."

I looked away. *Damn it, Mama. How could you?*

"Honey, are you upset?"

"Yes!" I said, louder than I intended. "I can't believe she'd do that without asking me. I would have loved to have Daddy's Bronze Star. Well, there's nothing I can do about it now. At least I know it's not lost."

We sat for a few minutes, quietly making sachets as I calmed down. While tightening a ribbon, I asked, "Do you know why Mama decided to visit me? It seemed odd, because I'd been begging her to come for years but she always said no."

A sad smile crept to Stella's lips as she reached out and smoothed her hand down my ponytail. "Your mother wanted to see your shop and spend time talking with you. And she wanted to apologize."

"Apologize?"

Stella scooped lavender into a bag and handed it to me. "She'd been doing a lot of thinking. We all do when we get to be this age, believe me. Last summer when you and your little dog left to drive back to Charleston, your mother called me in tears and asked if she could come over. We sat right here where you and I are now and had a long talk. She felt real bad about some things—said it was time to stop holding a grudge and start being a mother."

I snipped off a length of ribbon and set down the scissors. "She really said that?"

"Yes, she did. I'm heartbroken that Franny never had the chance to visit you."

"So am I. I even ironed her sheets because I knew how much she loved it."

Stella leaned back against the cushion and sighed. "You know, the older I get, the more I think life's a lot like those card games we used to play. We never know what we're gonna be dealt. Seemed no matter what your mother did or didn't do, she always ended up with a bad hand."

"What do you mean?"

Stella took a slow drink of iced tea and rested the glass on her knee. I watched the condensation from the glass drip onto her apron.

"First she lost her pa, then she lost all hopes of being a nurse. When she fell head over heels for your daddy, it seemed like she'd finally found some happiness. But when he came home from the war, something was wrong with his mind."

I tied a bow and set the sachet between us. "That's what Grammy said, but I thought she was exaggerating."

"Oh, no, it's true. That man was skinny as a fence post, and he'd all but stopped talking. Franny said days would go by without him sayin' a single word. She got so worried that she packed him up and drove him to the VA hospital. But the pills they gave him didn't help much. Some days he wouldn't even leave the house . . ."

I sat, speechless, while Stella described how Mama worked the fields when Daddy was at his lowest. How she tossed bale after bale of hay until the twine cut through her gloves and into her fingers, how she sat with Daddy at night and tried to get him to open up and talk.

"Finally he got a little better. That's when he took to working long hours, and then he built that workshop on the side of the barn and started takin' in repairs. But he wasn't the man your mother married."

"I don't know what you mean. Daddy was the most wonderful man I've ever known."

"Henry *was* wonderful. But the man your mother fell in love with was fun and talkative, always joking, telling stories, and surprising her with little gifts. Before the war he used to take her dancin' on Friday nights, and every Sunday they'd go for a long drive and stop at her favorite restaurant for dinner."

I thought about what Stella had just said and had to admit that never once did I remember my parents going out to dinner or to a movie together. I had always assumed they just liked staying home.

"Sometimes I was a little jealous," Stella said, pulling more bags from the box and plopping them between us. "My George was a good husband, but he wasn't romantic like that, at least not after we married. Anyway, the man you knew as your father didn't have much to say, and he didn't want to go anywhere or do anything. It was hard on your mother, especially when she was young. But over the years she eventually got used to it and made her peace."

"But she was always so . . . so negative. It seemed like nothing ever made her happy."

"Teddi, I know I'm a simple country woman, but that doesn't stop me from thinkin' real deep about things. When I boil everything down, this is what I believe with all my heart. Her father promised her a nursing education, and when he died, she was devastated. In one fell swoop, she lost her father *and* her dream. Then, when she met Henry, she thought she had a chance for a new life. She loved your father very much. When he went off to war, she was a nervous wreck—wrote him letters all the time, waited for the mail every day, hoping there'd be a letter from him and bein' crushed when there wasn't."

Stella sank deeper into the cushion, her eyes softening. "Every time your mother had some spare change, she'd put it in a jar. She told me she was saving for something special to wear when Henry finally came home. Oh, how she scrimped. There were times she didn't even have any butter in the house. When the war was finally over and Henry was on his way home, she was beside herself with joy. So she and I drove up to Lexington to do some shopping.

"We found a little shop that had the prettiest dresses I'd ever seen. While we were looking through the racks and talking, your mother glanced toward the back of the shop. I'll never forget the look on her face—you'd have thought she was seeing a miracle take place. Next thing I knew, she was talking to the salesgirl about a nightgown. But your mother didn't have anywhere near enough money to buy it. When the owner of the store heard that your daddy was comin' home from the war, she walked from behind the counter, slipped the nightgown off the mannequin, and told your mother she could have it for whatever she could pay."

And there it was. The mystery of the nightgown had been revealed as gently as the autumn breeze moving through the open window. The truth had come to me without fanfare, right there on Stella's sofa.

"It was pale pink silk with lace, wasn't it?"

"Yes. How in the world do you know that?"

"Mama saved it. In fact, it was still folded in the box and tucked away in her dresser. I'm positive she never wore it."

"It doesn't surprise me. Henry was in bad shape for a long time. Knowing Franny, I'll bet she put the nightgown away and never looked at it again."

I closed my eyes for a moment and thought about how hurt and alone she must have felt. *Poor Mama.*

Stella had painted a picture of my mother I'd never considered. I imagined her as a happy young woman, bright and full of hope. I could see her riffling through the mail, looking for a letter from Daddy, and I could envision her in that dress shop, her green eyes shining, her red hair swinging free as she admired the nightgown. What had it felt like to be that excited and in love? And what was it like to have so many years of disappointments chip away at her spirit?

"I took Mama's nightgown home with me last fall when I cleaned out the house. But here's what I don't understand. She got upset when I saved things that belonged to Josh. She said the past was the past and best forgotten, or something to that effect. So why would she have saved that nightgown?"

The lines in Stella's face deepened. "I don't know, honey. Maybe she couldn't let go of that one memory. That girl never had anything work out. I swear, it was like she was trying to run with water cupped in her hands."

I flopped back against the cushion, suddenly tired and nearly intoxicated by the thick scent of lavender. I was also feeling the weight of guilt. I couldn't even look at Stella when I said, "And then she tried to help me by making arrangements at that secretarial school and buying me a typewriter. And I thanked her by up and running away in the middle of the night. I hurt her terribly, didn't I?"

"Yes, Teddi, you did. Now, I'm not passing judgment—I'm only trying to tell you her side of things." Stella fell quiet for a few moments and slowly rubbed her fingertips along a piece of ribbon. "When your brother disappeared, it about killed her."

"But she was so angry. I can't count how many times she said it was all my fault."

"That's the only way she could deal with it. It was her anger that kept her from coming apart at the seams. She knew it wasn't your fault. That's one of the reasons she wanted to spend time with you—to try and make amends."

Stella wiped away a tear. "I never dreamed she wouldn't get out of that hospital. Franny was a wonderful friend to me for over sixty years. I loved her more than I do my own sister. Not a day goes by that I don't reach for the phone to give her a call. I miss her so much."

I took hold of Stella's hand and we sat quietly for several minutes. "So when did Daddy get himself straightened out?"

"Oh, goodness, it wasn't until your mother was pregnant with you that he really made a turnaround."

"It took *that* long? They were married for twelve years before I was born."

"Yes, that long. You were a big surprise. The doctor said she couldn't have children. When Franny told Henry she was expecting, he was so happy that he hardly knew what to do with himself. For the first time since he'd come home from the war, Franny saw a glimmer of the man she'd married. Oh, my word, he made such a fuss when you were born that your mother was a little hurt and—"

"Hurt?"

Stella fiddled with the hem of her apron, wadding up one corner and then smoothing it out, only to wad it up again. "She said it felt like a slap in the face, as if being a father was more important than being a husband."

"But Daddy came around and she got him back, so what difference would it make how it happened?"

Stella slowly shook her head. "No, Teddi. She never got her husband back. That man was gone, just as sure as if he'd come back in a pine box."

I let out a heavy sigh and massaged my temples.

"Oh, Teddi. I'm sorry your mother wasn't able to visit you in Charleston so she could explain these things herself. She was so excited about the trip."

"Really?"

"Yes. She really was. Once she made up her mind to go, that's all she talked about. So whenever you're feelin' blue and thinking about your mother, just remember that she loved you, Teddi. Now, I know she sometimes had a hard time showin' it, but she did."

Lifting a sachet to my nose, I closed my eyes and inhaled the lavender. "I loved her, too."

ᄋᄀᄋ

After dinner Stella and I sat at the kitchen table and played gin rummy. When it began to grow dark, I excused myself and went into the bedroom. It felt good to get out of my jeans and change into the soft warmth of flannel pajamas. While pulling on a pair of clean socks, I glanced into my open suitcase and whispered, "You ready?"

I walked into the living room where Stella was sitting on one end of the sofa engrossed in her cross-stitch. Lowering myself onto the other end, I gently placed my mother's urn on the cushion between us.

"I brought Mama back. I've had her in Charleston for a lot longer than she was planning to stay. I had the feeling that she wanted to come home and be with her best girlfriend."

Stella's eyes filled with tears. Reaching out, she rested her hand over the urn and sat like that for the longest time. I wondered what she was thinking.

I put my hand on top of hers and smiled. "I think it's time we set Mama free."

Drawing a handkerchief from her apron pocket, Stella wiped her eyes. "Franny was fond of my rose garden. Should we scatter her there?"

"I think she'd like that."

Stella set her cross-stitch aside and pushed herself up from the sofa. "I'll be right back."

But she didn't come right back, and just as I was about to see if she was all right, she walked out wearing a heavy sweater and carrying a folded paper in her hand. I slipped into my shoes, pulled my jacket over my pajamas, and together we walked outside. We said nothing while making our way toward the rose garden at the back of the property.

As I held Mama's urn in my arms, Stella read from the piece of paper. "'I've said good-bye, away I'll fly. I'm on my way back home...'"

When Stella finished, I could hardly see through my tears to open the urn's lid.

Taking turns, we dipped our hands inside and let the cool evening breeze sweep the ashes from our palms. After the last dusting of Mama had swirled from sight, Stella took hold of my hand. We said nothing as we walked back to the house, but I smiled to myself as I glanced over my shoulder and wondered where Mama would be off to first.

THIRTY-TWO

I woke to the aroma of bacon sizzling in the griddle, and when I padded into the kitchen, Stella looked up from the stove. "Good morning, honey. Breakfast is almost ready." While she scrambled eggs, I buttered the toast, and then we sat at the table in our robes, reading the morning paper and talking while the sun spread its warmth across the new day.

At nine forty-five I was showered, dressed, and ready to go. While I double-checked the departure time on my airline ticket, Stella walked out of her bedroom. "I wish you could stay longer," she said, picking fuzz from the cuff of her sweater.

"If I weren't swamped with work, I would. But I'll be back."

"Promise?"

I gave her a hug. "Yes, I promise."

From a hook by the door, she removed her keys, and we set off for the farm in separate cars.

When I rounded the bend and the farm came into view, I could hardly believe my eyes. Parked along both sides of the driveway and along the tractor path were cars and trucks, even a few motorcycles. Two teenage boys in bright red T-shirts directed me to the field at the far end of the barn. In the rearview mirror, I saw Stella following directly behind me as we bounced our way to the makeshift parking lot. We had a long walk to reach the backyard, and I took hold of her arm and guided her through the rough spots.

The barn door was wide open and flanked by bouquets of balloons that had been tied to stainless-steel milk cans. People walked in and out, chatting and drinking tea and coffee. I laughed when Oscar belted out his eight hoots: "*Who looks at you . . . Who looks at you.*"

At least two hundred people were gathered in the backyard, some talking in groups, others filling their plates from long tables draped in gingham. Trays filled with strudels and breakfast rolls covered the tabletops, and bowls of colorful fresh fruit glistened in the morning sun. Several donation boxes crafted to look like birdhouses were placed on the tables, and easels had been set up throughout the property, each one featuring an eight-by-ten photograph of an animal or bird. Beneath each photo was the animal's name—Hootie, Morris, Chucky, Ella, and so many others. Stapled to the easels were brief stories of how each one had been rescued and rehabilitated.

When Stella stopped to talk with an elderly couple, I stepped into the throng. The first person I recognized was Ranger Jim. I fought back tears when he gave me a hug and whispered into my ear, "Not a day goes by I don't think about your brother. Such a fine young man."

For the next hour, I spoke with people I hadn't seen in years—former Deputy Sheriff Jeb Davis and his wife, neighboring farmers and shopkeepers—all of them lending their support. And there was the younger crowd, too, friends of Gabe and Sally. Just as I'd finished talking with Joe Springer, Gabe grabbed me by the arm.

"Hi," I said, giving him a hug. "I was wondering where you were."

"Sally and I have been in the barn showing people the renovations. Ella's charmed everyone. I think she's the best spokesperson we could have. The donation box by her cage is already full. And Oscar's in rare form," Gabe said with a laugh. "He won't shut up. Hey, did you meet my mom and dad?"

"Yes, they're lovely. And I met Sally's parents, too."

Gabe tugged me forward. "C'mon and meet Sally."

Though over a dozen young women were in the barn, somehow I knew which one was Sally. Standing every bit of five feet ten with a head full of thick black curls, she had a strong and calm bearing. With large, capable hands resting her on hips and a tilt to her head, she watched Gabe and me approach from behind a pair of horn-rimmed glasses.

Just as Gabe introduced us, a young man rushed from the crowd, all but crushing Gabe in a bear hug. He literally carried Gabe off, laughing like a hyena. Sally laughed, too, and then she turned her attention to me. "So," she said, looking directly into my eyes, "I didn't know if you were some rich hussy trying to sugar-mama my man or if you were a saint."

Before I could speak, she stepped forward and wrapped me in her arms. "Thank God you're a saint!"

I laughed nervously, feeling a bit off kilter.

She released me and motioned toward the door. "I have something to show you."

We walked out of the barn, Sally talking about the plans she and Gabe had for the farm and describing the renovations they'd started inside the house.

"Have you set a date for your wedding?" I asked.

"Not yet, but we've decided against a formal wedding. My mother is devastated, but personally I think they're a big waste of money. I'd much rather have an X-ray machine." As we neared the road, she pointed to the field at the right of the driveway. "See those pink surveyor's markers? That's where we'll build the clinic. If everything goes as planned, we hope to break ground in a year. It'll be fantastic to run the clinic and the rehab center from a single location."

"Will you have a surgery center?"

"Yes." Sally's eyes brightened as she described her ideas and what kind of equipment she and Gabe hoped to buy. "And we'll hold educational classes in the barn. Gabe wants to formulate a summer day-camp program where he'll take kids on hikes and teach them about wildlife."

She abruptly stopped talking and looked toward the barn, then the house, and then at me. "I still can't believe that all this is happening. We don't know how to thank you, Teddi. My gosh, you showed up out of nowhere and just handed this to us, and we—"

"Hey, Sally!" Gabe called, trotting down the driveway and pointing to his wristwatch. "It's time."

"C'mon." She took hold of my arm and pulled me toward the house.

People were gathering around the shrouded sign and spilling into the edge of the field. Sally tugged me to the center of the front yard. "Stay right here," she ordered, and then left to join Gabe.

Stella pushed her way through the crowd and stood next to me. "My goodness, this is quite a turnout. I don't think I've ever seen anything like it."

After Gabe and Sally unwrapped the ropes that held the tarp in place, they stood flanking the sign. Gabe raised his hands, and when everyone grew silent, he took a moment and scanned the crowd. Then his voice boomed through the crisp air. "This is a big day for Sally and me, and we want to thank each and every one of you for joining us. None of this could have happened without the kindness and generosity of Teddi Overman. When I met Teddi this past spring, I asked if she'd tell me about her brother, Josh. Well, she did, and I've never been the same since.

"From the time he was born, Josh loved and respected nature. He was quiet, gentle, and courageous. It was no secret that he had a gift—a connection with animals and birds that defied logic and mystified the lucky few who witnessed it. His story is remarkable. It's a story I'll never forget. And to make certain this entire community never forgets, Sally and I would now like to unveil the sign."

With a dramatic flourish and a loud snap of fabric, Gabe and Sally whipped back the tarp. Applause exploded from the crowd, and from behind me I heard someone burst into tears.

The wind picked up. Crimson leaves spun in pirouettes before letting go of their branches . . . falling, falling so lightly before coming to rest in people's hair, on their shoulders, and onto the ground. Over and over I read the sign that stood before me:

MENEWA

THE JOSH OVERMAN
WILDLIFE RESCUE & REHABILITATION CENTER

All those years of pent-up emotion let loose, and I turned and wept into the softness of Stella's shoulder. It took me several minutes to catch my breath, and when I finally lifted my head, Stella dipped her hand inside the front of her dress and pulled out a tissue. I felt like a child as she held my chin and wiped away a river of mascara. She was crying, too. From over her shoulder, I saw Jeb Davis take a handkerchief from his back pocket and swipe it beneath his eyes.

Sally cupped her hands around her mouth and called out, "We have one last surprise, and believe me, y'all don't want to miss it!" While she began ushering everyone up the driveway, Stella and I fell in line.

When we reached the side of the house, Gabe trotted up and looked at Stella. "I need to steal Teddi for a few minutes."

Stella eyed the pastry table and said, "You two go on. I'll be right here."

He led me up the driveway and into the barn. "It's time for the grand finale," he said, sliding the door closed. "We'd be honored if you'd do the release."

My stomach flipped at the thrill of it. "Really? I get to send Oscar back into the wild?"

Gabe smiled and removed two pairs of brown suede gloves from a cupboard. After handing me a pair and making sure they fit, he opened the refrigerator and grabbed a plastic bag filled with strips of raw meat. I followed him to the bird room, but he didn't stop at Oscar's cage. Sliding the security latch and opening the back door, he turned toward me. "I lied to you. Oscar's not ready for release. But Noah is. He's waiting for you, Teddi. He wants to go home."

Blood thundered in my ears, and the past collided with the present as I looked into the flight cage.

Look, Teddi. That's the big guy. . . . What do you think he's doin' up there? . . . Don't worry, Teddi. Everyone's got a secret. . . . I saw it because I'm awake. . . . I named him Ghost. . . .

Right when I thought I couldn't possibly carry this out, Noah turned and looked at me, his dark eyes gleaming, his head slightly tilted. I wondered what he saw in me, what he sensed.

Out of the corner of my eye, I saw Gabe step into the flight cage and toss a piece of meat onto the ground. Noah dove from the branch to get it, and within seconds Gabe had hold of him. Noah struggled until Gabe held him upside down for a moment, then brought him upright.

"Okay, Teddi."

My heart thumped as I gave my gloves a final tug and pushed open the door.

"I'm going to pass Noah to you. Hold him firm but not tight. If he flaps his wings, don't get nervous. He'll settle."

Gabe passed Noah into my gloved hands. The bird never flinched when I threaded the fingers of my right hand around his ankles. For a brief moment he spread his talons wide, then relaxed when I lightly pressed my left hand against his breast.

"You're a natural, Teddi. That's perfect. All right, here we go."

When we stepped into the sunlight, Gabe looked toward the field. "I was going to join you for the release, but I think this should be a private moment between you and Noah. You know what to do, right?"

"Yes."

Gabe patted my arm and set off to join the onlookers while I began my journey. I walked slowly, savoring the feel of holding such a magnificent creature against my chest. I was surprised when Noah turned his head and looked up at me. I smiled and whispered, "You know what today is, Noah? My daddy would say it's your red, white, and blue."

When I reached the center of the field, I glanced at the sea of people gathered along the fence, all those eyes waiting to see Noah take flight. Tilting my head forward, I spoke softly. "Go find my brother. He's out there in your world. Somewhere. Tell him his sister misses him and loves him. Have a beautiful life, Noah. Here you go."

As I'd seen my brother do so many years ago, I swung Noah low past my right hip, and with a powerful thrust I swept my arms into the air and opened my fingers. When Noah took flight, applause and cheers let loose from the crowd.

Higher and higher he flew. As Noah reclaimed his rightful place in the sky, I wrapped my arms around myself and watched until he disappeared.

THIRTY-THREE

Was it the release of Noah, his flight symbolic in marking the end of my family's history at the farm, or was it the wildlife center's being named after my brother that left me lost for gravity? Whatever it was, I arrived in Charleston feeling, for the first time since his disappearance, that Josh was truly gone.

Weeks rolled by, and though I kept up with my work schedule, a big part of me wasn't fully present. Mistakes were made. I put the wrong hardware on drawers and forgot where I'd placed work orders. Twice I spilled cans of stain, and once I forgot to lock the front door at closing time. Then came the day when I painted an antique chair cerulean blue, only to be horrified when I realized it was the wrong chair.

I was spinning out of orbit and didn't know how to stop.

In the gray months of winter, I began to hibernate. I'd curl up in bed after supper and stay there all night, the covers pulled to my chin as I listened to the hiss of the radiator. Often I'd awaken in the wee hours and stare at my brother's photograph on my bedside table. There were times I'd dream of him, times I swore I smelled him. One bitter-cold January night, I woke to hear him whisper, *The horned owl keeps secrets.*

The fog of grief had pushed its way into my life, blurring the hope I'd held for so many years. It was time to face the truth. My brother was dead, and he probably had been for a long, long time.

In December I began rising before dawn. Throwing a warm coat over my pajamas, I'd pull on my hat and gloves and take Eddie for long walks through the sleeping streets. It became a ritual, a meditation of sorts. Some mornings I'd walk all the way to White Point Garden, others I'd head toward the mists of the French Quarter. I had no planned routes, and it didn't matter where I went. All I knew was that I had to keep going.

On the fifth of February, Eddie and I were out for our early-morning walk. It was my birthday, and it was unbearable. In my mind I could hear the collective voice of my family singing "Happy Birthday" around the kitchen table, and I could taste Mama's five-layer coconut cake. With each step I grew more disconsolate, and by the time I'd walked around Colonial Lake, I had half a mind to just go back home, crawl into bed, and stay there for the whole day.

But Eddie seemed desperate to turn on Queen Street, so I obliged. He tugged on the leash and picked up speed as if tracking a scent. After we crossed Archdale, he stopped to sniff a tree lawn. While waiting for him to make up his mind on where we were headed, I noticed a tangle of vines spilling over a limestone wall. Attached to the iron gate was a red-and-white For Sale sign. I nudged Eddie forward so I could take a closer look.

Surrounded by untended gardens that had gone wild, the Greek Revival home was a depressed old place with blistered white paint, a sagging front porch, and cracked green shutters that hung askew. Two of the upstairs windows were boarded up, as if the house had closed its eyes in shame and whispered, *Look what's become of me.*

As I stood surveying the property and wondering how it had come to such ruin, I realized that unless I pulled myself together and found a way to ground myself into my life, I could end up just as sad and empty as that old house.

I thought about how low I'd fallen since my last trip to Kentucky, how I'd slipped into a state of seclusion that had drained color from my cheeks and left smudges of blue beneath my eyes. I also thought about how I had become a liar. Whenever Olivia asked me what was wrong, I told her I was overworked, that I had been fighting a sinus infection and needed lots of rest. I told her anything I could think of to keep her from asking questions. I didn't want to talk about what it was like to face my brother's death—not with her, not with anyone.

For the remainder of my walk, I thought about my long-held belief that everyone was offered a rite of passage. Mine had occurred at the age of eighteen when I'd released the clutch of that old Ford Falcon and rolled out of my parents' driveway. But maybe we were offered a rite of passage many times throughout our lives, if only we were awake enough to see it. I arrived home knowing that I had to save myself from spiraling further, and while taking a long, hot shower I knew that it was time to make a phone call.

Later that morning I unlocked the side door to my shop and found Inez running invoices on the copy machine. I raised my voice and said, "Good morning, Inez."

She turned off the machine. "Hi, Teddi. Happy birthday. I made you a pineapple upside-down cake. It's in the kitchen, but Albert's already eaten half of it."

I laughed. "Thanks. I have a favor to ask. I know you've got a busy day, but I have an appointment at ten forty-five. I won't be gone long. Will you watch the shop for me?"

"No problem."

After opening the front door for business and cutting myself a piece of cake, I sat at my desk and made a few phone calls. When the hands of my watch read 10:25, I hoisted my handbag over my shoulder and walked out the door. I headed down Wentworth and turned on Smith, where old homes lined the streets, each with its own unique quirks and details. Some had wide, sweeping porches like the open arms of a favorite grandmother, others were tall and narrow, and a few were long neglected.

Within ten minutes I arrived at my destination, and just as I reached for the antique bell chime, the heavy wooden door swung open and a silver-haired woman gasped. "Oh! You scared me half to death."

I extended my hand. "Hi, I'm Teddi Overman. I know I'm a few minutes early."

"Judy McIntyre. Please come in. But I've got to warn you—it's a mess. The cleaning crew was supposed to be here over the weekend, but they never showed up. Anyhow, I was just on my way to get a few things from my car. Feel free to look around. I'll be back in a minute."

The sound of my heels echoed through the empty house when I walked into the living room—or parlor, as it was called back when the house was built. Sunlight seeped through the dirty window-panes and fell across the dusty hardwood floor. The high ceilings were framed by ornamental plasterwork that seemed in surprisingly good condition. Stepping to the fireplace, I ran my fingertips over the scrolled end brackets and dentil molding. Crafted of creamy white marble, the fireplace was a beautiful old thing in need of a thorough cleaning. To my right a pair of Doric columns flanked the entrance to the dining room. Sheets of cabbage-rose wallpaper hung loose from walls, revealing areas of cracked plaster and broken lath.

Retracing my steps to the foyer, I climbed the stairs to the second floor and nosed around. The largest of the three bedrooms had a fireplace and a set of tall French doors. After several tries I finally got them open and stepped onto a narrow piazza that ran the length of the house. The gray-painted floorboards were warped, and I could see signs of rot along the bottoms of several balusters.

Below me was the side garden, or at least what once had been a garden.

From downstairs I heard Judy call out, "Hello! I'm back."

Closing the French doors, I walked down the stairs.

"I'm sorry, I had to get my briefcase and some paperwork. As you can see, this house needs a lot of help. It's been in the same family since it was built in 1867. Isn't that amazing? The last owner was an eccentric spinster. The neighbors said she had that problem, I forget what they called it, but it's when a person is afraid to leave their house."

"Agoraphobia."

"Yes, that's it." Judy flicked on the foyer lights and sighed. "Poor old thing, she wouldn't leave the house, but she didn't want anyone coming inside either. So whenever something broke, she just stopped using it."

Judy pulled a folder from her briefcase and handed me an information sheet. "She passed away twelve years ago, and the house has been closed up ever since. There was a legal battle among the heirs, but now they're ready to settle the estate. The house went up for sale a few days ago. You're the first person to see it." She let out a little laugh and added, "Other than me, you might be the first person to see it in fifty years. Let me show you around."

Judy turned and walked down the hallway, sending a cloud of dust rolling across the floor. "This house has wonderful bones," she said over her shoulder. "Have you seen the kitchen?"

"Not yet."

"I won't even try to make excuses for it. Last time it was updated was back in the twenties. But it has lots of natural light, and there's a huge pantry."

We entered the kitchen, and I laughed out loud when I saw the stove. "That's a crazy kind of wonderful. My gosh, it's the size of a Volkswagen!"

"And believe it or not, two of the burners still work. Now come see the pantry . . ."

I followed Judy all through the house, and though she jabbered too much and had far too many opinions, I liked her anyway. When we returned to the foyer, I stopped and looked up the staircase. "The bedroom next to the master would be perfect to convert into a combination bath and walk-in closet. I love the high ceilings and the layout of the rooms. But this poor old house needs total rehab. From what I can tell, all the mechanics are shot."

"No question about it. I've been selling houses for twenty-nine years, and if ever I've seen a bargain, this is it. I can tell by the look on your face this isn't the right home for you, but there's a darling house over on Cannon Street that just went on the market," she said, leafing through her file. "I have the spec sheet here somewhere. It's on the small side, but—"

"I'll take her."

"Take who?"

I reached out and patted the wall. "The house."

"You want *this* house?"

"Yes. So why don't I go outside and pull the sign off the gate? I don't want anyone else setting foot inside until she's all fixed up. She's embarrassed."

Judy looked at me over the top of her glasses. "The house is *embarrassed?*"

"Yes, very embarrassed."

Judy studied me. "If you don't mind my asking, how many houses have you looked at?"

"This is the first."

"Oh, my word! Let me show you others so you can do some comparisons."

I shook my head and stepped into the living room. "Sometimes a person just knows."

⤨

After work that evening, I met Judy at her realty office. Twice she asked if I was certain, saying I reminded her of her daughter, "smart but impulsive."

I just smiled and signed the papers. Nothing she said could have persuaded me otherwise. That old house needed me just as much as I needed her. But more than that, I'd discovered something on the floor of the master bedroom's piazza that had sealed the deal.

Before going to bed that night, I opened my handbag, dug out my coin purse, and removed the tiny talisman, so tiny, in fact, that I believe anyone else would have missed it. I held it to the lamplight by its quill. The feather was downy soft and tipped in bright yellow. I smiled as I remembered the four simple words my brother had written many years ago: *The goldfinch sends happiness.*

⤨

In the end happiness is just what I got. The restoration, which took a crew of craftsmen nearly six months to complete, was more monumental than I could ever have anticipated. But it was worth the headaches and the "What was I thinking?" moments that go hand in hand with old-house renovations.

By the end of July, the interior was complete and the exterior had been taken down to the original boards and repaired. I had it painted a pale gray with white trim and black shutters. I custom-mixed the color for the front door and painted it myself—a soft goldfinch yellow.

I officially moved into my home on the first Friday in August.

After the movers had gone, I climbed the stairs and got to work in my bedroom. After hanging the draperies and steaming them to perfection, I put up all the artwork. While I was making my bed with fresh linens, the doorbell chimed. Eddie barked and ran down the stairs. I opened the door to see Olivia with a grin on her face and a wrapped gift in her arms. "Congratulations, Teddi." She looked down and added, "And to you, too, Eddie boy."

"Hi. C'mon in."

She carried the box into the kitchen and set it on the counter. "This house is amazing. What a transformation. I've got to be honest, Teddi. When you first showed it to me, I had to bite my tongue. I couldn't imagine why you'd bought such a disaster."

"Disaster to you, beauty in decay to me."

Just then Olivia noticed the stove and gasped. "What! Where in the world did you get *that*?"

"That's the old stove that came with the house. I had it totally refurbished and reenameled. They delivered it yesterday."

"Oh, my God. I can't believe it. It's the most fantastic stove I've ever seen." Olivia ran her fingertips over the glossy black finish. "It's a chunkster, but a beautiful one."

With a sigh of satisfaction, I put my hands on my hips and smiled. "Isn't it wonderful? I have fantasies of learning to bake bread."

"I'll believe it when I see it." She nodded to the box and said, "Hey, open your gift."

I untied the bow, ripped off the paper, and opened the box. Inside was a book on southern-style gardens and a caddy filled with pink garden gloves, a raffia sun hat, and a shiny set of new hand tools. There was also a bag of dog toys for Eddie.

"You're a wonderful friend. Thanks, Olivia. I hope I can be half the gardener my grandmother was."

"You're welcome. Are you sure I can't help you unpack?"

"Actually I'm enjoying the work, but I could use your help hanging a mirror."

We managed to put screws into the wall without breaking the

plaster, both of us red-faced as we strained to hang the heavy Baroque mirror in the upstairs hallway. Though I would have liked her help arranging the kitchen cabinets, I knew she had a restoration project with a tight deadline.

"All right, you need to get back to work, and so do I." I gave Olivia a hug and shooed her out the door.

With the radio playing softly in the background, I tackled one room at a time. By six forty-five my bedroom was in perfect order, as were the kitchen and pantry. Though I knew I should unpack a few more boxes, I was beat and decided to call it quits for the remainder of the evening. After taking a shower, I pulled my wet hair into a ponytail and slipped into clean jeans and a white cotton blouse. Eddie and I played fetch in the garden, and then I wandered around my home in a state of wonder, admiring its architectural details and touching every surface.

That it was mine seemed a miracle.

I stood in my bedroom doorway, feeling pleased with the buttercream moiré wallpaper, the pristine white woodwork, and the lounge chair I'd upholstered in tea-stained linen damask. My bed, a hefty four-poster that Olivia and I had hauled home from a house sale in Savannah, was layered with lace-edged bedding and a white trapunto quilt. Sitting proudly beside my bed was the old walnut chest that Albert had restored.

Everything was just as I had dreamed, except for one minor detail—the lamp on the bedside chest was too short. Though I was bone tired, I knew I'd never rest until I came up with a solution. Slipping into my shoes, I grabbed my handbag and set off for my shop.

After checking to see if Inez had made any sales in my absence and being delighted that she had, I walked to the front of the shop and began hunting for the perfect lamp, eventually deciding on one made of bronze with a pleated linen shade. While I wrapped it up, my stomach growled, and though I was eager to cook something on my ancient stove, I knew that tonight wasn't the night. So I put the lamp inside the trunk of my car and walked to Marty's Café.

The red neon sign flickered and buzzed from the window, and when I opened the door, the clang of silverware and the aroma of grilled onions filled the air. The café was crowded, and I was lucky to find a small table in the corner, luckier still that the waitress took my order right away.

It wasn't until I'd finished my bowl of chili and stood to leave that I noticed Sam Poteet sitting on the opposite side of the room. When he waved hello, I smiled. After paying my bill, I plucked a peppermint candy from the basket on the counter and left.

While walking down the sidewalk, crunching my mint and thinking about my new home, I pulled keys from my handbag. I was about to get into my car when someone called, "Teddi?"

I turned to see Sam a half block behind me and waited as he approached. When he reached me, the look on his face was pensive.

"I'm . . . I'm not very good at this."

I raised my eyebrows. "Not very good at what, Counselor?"

"At trying to talk to you."

"But you haven't said anything."

I couldn't tell if it was sincerity or mischief that sparked in his eyes when he shoved his hands into his pockets and tilted his head. "See—that's precisely my point. So I was wondering . . . would you have dinner with me sometime?"

That question caught me totally off guard. "Umm, sure. Sometime. But I just moved into a new house. Well, an *old* house, but it's new to me. I'm not quite settled, and business at the shop is—"

Realizing how ridiculous I sounded, I clamped my mouth shut. "Help me out here, Teddi. Does that mean yes?"

Lord, I was uncomfortable. But I smiled, said yes, and climbed into my car. Just as I closed the door, Sam leaned forward and peered into the window. "I'll call you."

Down the street I drove, and when I came to the intersection and rolled to a stop, I glanced in the rearview mirror. Sam was still standing on the sidewalk watching me.

THIRTY-FOUR

S am called me at the shop the following week, and we fumbled
through a conversation that resulted in scheduling a date for
Saturday evening. A *casual* dinner, he'd said, saying he'd pick me
up at seven.

When Saturday came, I was in no mood to spend the evening
with anyone, much less the son of the infamous Tula Jane Poteet.
It was an effort to shower and dress. I would have preferred to stay
home and unwind with a good book. Lord, how I despised first
dates.

I stood back and examined myself in the mirror—a simple
yellow-and-white-checked dress with a scooped neckline and a
white cardigan draped over my shoulders. Was I *too* casual? What
the heck did people who lived south of Broad deem casual dinner
attire anyway? While I was slipping into a pair of sandals, the doorbell chimed and Eddie barked. After one more look in the mirror, I
descended the stairs and opened the door.

There stood Sam in a pair of khakis and a blue shirt with the
sleeves rolled back, looking as awkward as I'm sure I did.

"Hi, Teddi. I like your house. And who's this?"

"Eddie, say hi to Sam." Though a little shy with strangers, Eddie
dutifully offered Sam his paw. Sam smiled as he shook it and then
gave Eddie a gentle pat.

"See you later, be good," I said, grabbing my handbag.

As we stepped to the sidewalk, an old woman was crossing the street at a slow, wobbly pace. I recognized her immediately and hoped she'd continue on her way, but Sam stopped and said, "Good evening, Miz Zelda."

Oh, how she smiled when she saw him. "A fine evening it is, General."

"Do the clouds have any news to share?"

Zelda looked into the sky. "Yes, yes they do. There's a surprise coming your way, and it's a big one. So keep your eyes open, General." She waited as Sam pulled a ten-dollar bill from his pocket and pressed it into her hand.

Clearly done with her reading, Zelda grinned and continued on her way, her heavy tote bag bumping against her leg with each step she took.

"You *know* her?" I whispered as we walked in the opposite direction.

"I've known Miz Zelda for most of my life. She's as much a part of Charleston's culture as the bells of St. Michael's."

"Why does she call you 'General'?"

Sam laughed and took a light hold of my arm. "Teddi, I have *no* idea."

He guided me to a car parked at the curb, a very old car. With its dull black finish, wide wheel wells, and long vertical grille, it reminded me of the cars in the movie *The Untouchables*. When he started the engine, it made a *tat-tat-tat* sound before letting out a low growl.

"Sam, I love this car. What kind is it?"

"A 1932 Ford Roadster. Since you like antiques, I thought you might like to ride in one. It doesn't look like much now, but it will when I'm done working on it. Just wait, you'll see."

Between Zelda and Sam's car, the awkwardness of those first

few minutes melted away, and we chatted about how much we both loved restoration as Sam maneuvered through the streets. In just a few minutes, he came to a stop in front of a house.

His house.

Before I could ask him what was going on, he was already out of the car and opening my door. "What are we doing, Sam?"

"Come see," he said, ushering me along the sidewalk and around the side of the house. Opening a heavy iron gate, Sam gestured for me to enter ahead of him, and when I did, I was at a loss for words.

I had just stepped into a place of magic.

The walled garden was lush and cool. Giant ferns flanked a stone walkway that led to a patio where glazed pots overflowed with flowers. Sitting beneath a pergola was a wrought-iron table that had been set for two with china, crystal, and sterling.

"I wanted to cook for you, Teddi."

"Sam, this garden is gorgeous."

"Thank you. Next to working on old cars, it's my favorite pastime."

I whipped around to look at him. "This is *your* garden? I mean, of course it's your garden, you live here—but *you* do all the work to maintain it?"

He seemed pleased by my stunned admiration. "I used to have a town house over on Beaufain, but I sold it and moved back here so I could help take care of my mother. She had let the gardens get out of hand, so one day I started digging and planting, and this is the end result," he said, stepping to an iron tea cart. "So . . . what would you like to drink, Teddi?"

"Iced tea if you have it."

"I do."

With slightly tarnished sterling tongs, he dropped ice cubes

into a glass and poured tea for me, then filled a goblet with wine for
himself.

"Will you show me around?"

"I'd be happy to."

Side by side we strolled through the garden as Sam told me
about the many species of plantings—sago palms, daphne, spider-
wort. Along the left side of the garden and nearly hidden by a row
of tea olives was a set of sandstone steps. "Where do those go?" I
asked.

"C'mon, I'll show you."

He led me up five steps to a small private oasis where slabs of
stone formed the floor. In the center was a chipped marble pedestal, on top of which sat a small brass telescope.

"This is my poor man's observatory. When I can't sleep, I come
out here and watch the stars."

I looked from Sam to the telescope.

It couldn't be.

My heart drummed as I stepped to the pedestal and slowly ran
my fingers over the telescope's cylinder, feeling for the indentation
that I remembered so well. And sure enough, it was there. Leaning
over, I tilted my head. The words J. VAN DER BILDT, FRANEKER
were inscribed on the circular backplate.

From behind me Sam said, "My mother gave it to me for my
fortieth birthday."

It would have been cruel to tell him where the telescope had
come from, so I gathered my composure and slowly straightened.
"It's a beauty. What a wonderful gift. So you're an attorney, a gardener, a car mechanic, and a stargazer. And by the looks of things
to come, you're also a cook?"

"Well, I'm certainly no master chef, which I'm about to prove,"
he said with a slight laugh.

As we walked down the steps, I glanced over my shoulder and gave the telescope one last look.

"Please have a seat," he said, gesturing to a chair. "Talk to me while I cook."

After lighting the grill and refilling my glass with iced tea, Sam opened a cooler and removed a bowl filled with prawns. "Is Teddi a nickname?"

"My given name is Theodora."

"Theodora," he said slowly, as if testing the way my name rolled off his tongue.

And there I was, watching a man prepare dinner in the most splendid garden I'd ever seen while my stolen telescope sat on a pedestal a short distance away. Everything felt so strange and un-expected that I could hardly think of anything to say. But Sam filled in the lulls with chatter about his plans for the next phase of his garden. Finally I tamed the butterflies in my belly, found my voice, and asked him questions about his work—business law—and then inquired about his fascination with old cars—something he claimed to have been born with.

Sam grilled the prawns and served them over a Caesar salad that came close to being divine. Though I tried to be discreet, I couldn't stop myself from examining the sterling flatware, which had to be pre–Civil War. When I realized that Sam was watching me, my cheeks grew warm. But he just smiled and took a sip of wine.

After we'd finished dinner, Sam stood and slowly unfolded to his full height. "Shall we get more comfortable?" he asked, guiding me toward a pair of cushioned lounges. "Would you like coffee?"

"Yes, thank you."

"And how do you take it, Miss Theodora?"

"Lots of cream and four sugars, please."

Sam gave me the oddest look. "Any woman who admits that she

takes *four* sugars in her coffee is definitely worth getting to know."
He turned and set off for the house with a slight grin on his face.

Within a few minutes, he appeared with a tray in his hands and
set it down on the table between the lounges. His eyes held a glimmer of amusement when he said, "Heavy cream and *four* sugars, as
the lady wishes."

A light breeze moved through the palmettos, and a few wispy
clouds hung low in the indigo sky. After lighting several candles,
Sam moved his lounge closer to mine and sat. "You have the slightest accent, but I can't quite place it."

"I'm originally from Kentucky."

"Really? I was born in Clarksville, Tennessee. It's just over the
border from Kentucky. Have you ever been there?"

"Yes. I drove through there years ago. But, Sam, I thought you
came from a long line of Charlestonians."

He took a sip of coffee and shook his head. "My birth mother
packed me up when I was just a baby and moved us to Charleston. She worked as a seamstress during the week, and on weekends she cooked for Tula Jane and Everett in exchange for living
quarters."

He pointed to the two-story garage at the back of the property.
"There's a small apartment up there—that's where we lived. I still
remember waking up early in the morning to the sound of Everett
starting his car. It was a 1950 Hudson—a dark green Super Six
with big whitewall tires. Who knows? Maybe that's one of the reasons I love old cars so much."

Sam paused for a moment and looked at the apartment above
the garage. "When I was six, my mother had a brain aneurysm
while she was hemming a dress. She died before she hit the floor,
or at least that's what I was told. It was Tula Jane who came and got
me at school. She took me to the park, sat me down on a bench, and
told me that God needed my mother to repair a hole in the sky.

Like most young kids, I had no concept of death, so I asked Tula when my mother would be back. She said I'd see her every night in my dreams. Anyway, it's a long story, but Tula Jane and Everett ended up adopting me. It's amazing when you think about it. They never had children and were practically old enough to be my grandparents."

The moment I asked about his biological father, Sam's face darkened. "I have no idea who he is—or was. And I'm not interested in finding out. He and my mother never married. The only thing she ever said about him was that he went away."

I stirred my coffee, and the teaspoon made a light chime when I set it on the china saucer. "Do you mind if I ask—what was your mother's name?"

"Madeline. Madeline Marshall."

"So you began your life as Sam Marshall. When the Poteets adopted you, how did you feel about taking their last name?"

Sam smiled. "That was my idea. You know how kids get things in their heads that they believe to be absolutely true? Well, I wanted to make sure Everett and Tula Jane would never leave me. I thought if I had their last name, I'd always be safe. Everett was a terrific guy. You'd have liked him, and he would have been crazy about you. He passed away when I was in law school." Sam took in a breath and let it out slowly. "So . . . this dissertation on family history brings me to Tula Jane."

Resting his elbows on his knees, Sam clasped his hands beneath his chin. "She's developed some serious problems over the past few years, not the least of which is Alzheimer's."

His eyes saddened as he glanced over his shoulder to a lighted window on the second floor of the house. "I was in denial for a long time, which I'm sure you probably figured out. But after the recent episode, I had to face the facts. I've hired round-the-clock care and will keep her here as long as I can."

I reached out and smoothed my hand over Sam's arm. "I'm so sorry."

Visibly brightening at being touched, he scooted closer. "All right, now it's your turn. Tell me about yourself, Teddi. Tell me everything."

"Okay," I said, resting back against the cushion. "I was born on a farm by Red River Gorge . . ."

And what began as an awkward dinner date with a man I had thought peculiar transitioned into a wonderful, relaxed evening of great food and conversation that lasted well past midnight, all within the walls of a magical garden. I even forgot about my stolen telescope.

Well, almost.

THIRTY-FIVE

On a Tuesday in early September, I arrived at the shop feeling lighter and happier than I had in years. Throwing on a smock, I began the day by sanding a Venetian footstool while Albert mixed wood filler to repair a chair leg that the owner's puppy had chewed.

His radio was tuned to an oldies station, and when the Four Tops began to sing one of my favorite songs, I belted out the words right along with them, "*Reach out for me!*"

Lost in a moment of joy, I shimmied around the workroom, snapping a rag against my hip, the wall, and my bench. I wiggled and jiggled and had myself a gay old time. When I looked up and saw Albert watching me, I stopped and said, "What?"

"If you don't stop singin', I'll be the one *reachin' out* to turn off this here radio. Ain't nobody ever told you?"

"Told me what?"

"That you can't sing." He shook his head and added, "And you sure can't dance neither."

I laughed. "C'mon, Albert. Lighten up."

The bell above the front door rang, and I went right back to singing as I shimmied out of the workroom. Behind me I heard Albert chuckle. Straightening my shoulders and tossing the rag aside, I went to greet whoever had come in. I was surprised to see Olivia.

"Hey, I stopped at that junk shop over on Meeting Street this morning. Look what I found." She handed me a bolt of fabric. "Something told me this was special."

I pulled off the rubber band and turned down a corner so I could examine the face of the fabric. It was the most gorgeous watermelon-and-cream silk stripe I'd ever seen. "Oh, my gosh, this is outstanding." I counted how many times the fabric had been rolled around the tube. I think there's enough to make draperies for my home office."

"So that means you want it?" Olivia said with a knowing smile.

"Absolutely. What do I owe you?"

"Twenty-five bucks," she said, admiring a silver rice spoon on the display table.

"That's a steal. C'mon back so I can pay you. Do you have time for coffee?"

Happy for the invitation, she followed me to the kitchen. I poured a cup for both of us and was about to sit down when the bell above the door sounded again. Inez called out from her office, "Stay put—I'll go. It's probably the mailman."

Not a minute later, she walked into the kitchen and sang out, "Flowers for Miss Theodora Overman!" She placed a lush bouquet on the table—white hydrangeas, pale pink roses, and fragrant purple stock, accented by seeded eucalyptus.

I didn't need to look at the card to know who'd sent them. From a narrow white ribbon tied around the vase, I removed the small envelope. Trying to look nonchalant, I slipped it into the pocket of my smock.

"These are spectacular," Olivia said, turning the vase in a slow circle. I adore hydrangeas."

Inez folded her arms across her chest. "So who sent them?"

"Yeah, Teddi, what's the card say?"

"I'm sure they're from one of my clients."

Inez arched one perfectly drawn-on eyebrow. "Baloney. I'm not leaving this kitchen till you open that envelope."

"Me neither. Where is that card, anyway?"

"She tried to be sly and put it in her pocket," Inez said.

I removed the envelope and opened it. The card simply read: "Sam."

"I told you, it's a *client*."

Inez snatched it from my fingers. "I do all the billing around here. We don't have a client named Sam." She tapped the card with her finger and narrowed her eyes. "Except for one."

When I grabbed the card away from Inez, she let out a hoot. "So it *is* Sam Poteet."

"No!" Olivia bleated. "Son of Miz Sticky-Fingers Poteet? But you said he was a toad."

"That was before I met him."

Inez asked, "How long have you been dating him?"

"Just a few weeks."

Olivia flashed me a look. "And you didn't tell me?"

"I wasn't ready to tell you. It's not a big deal."

"Of course it is. He's sending you *flowers*."

Inez leaned against the doorframe, her lips curving into a knowing smile. "You like him. I can see it in your eyes."

I lightly touched a hydrangea. "Yes. I do."

❦

I walked home from work that evening carrying Sam's flowers. They were so heavy that by the time I set them down on my front porch and unlocked the door, my shoulders ached. After I played ball with Eddie and fed him supper, I carried the flowers upstairs. Just as I set them on my bedside chest, the phone rang. I flopped onto the bed and smiled when I answered, hoping it might be Sam.

"Teddi. It's Gabe."

"Hi, I was just thinking about you and Sally this morning. How are—"

"Teddi, are you watching TV?"

"No. Why?"

"Good. Whatever you do, promise me you won't watch any news channels." Gabe let out a long breath. "I hate having to tell you this, but it's better you hear it straight from me and not from some newscaster."

"What?"

"Remember when we talked last month and I told you about the poaching going on in the Gorge? Well, it was worse than I led you to believe. A lot worse."

"What do you mean?"

There was no response.

I pressed the phone tighter to my ear. "Gabe?"

"I don't want to talk details, and believe me, you don't want to hear them. But some sick psycho was . . . was slaughtering wildlife."

My hand flew to my mouth. "Oh, no!"

"On Sunday the rangers closed off all entrances to Daniel Boone Forest and shut down access to the Gorge. About sixty of us started to hunt for whoever was responsible. Yesterday a group of climbers found . . . Well, it was so bad that CNN came out and filmed parts of the area where one of the slaughters took place. I don't think they'll show much of the footage, but they did several interviews with the rangers."

As Gabe talked, I pushed myself up from the bed and began pacing around the room.

"Early this morning four us set off for Clifty Wilderness. I guided the group—Doug, a buddy of mine who's an ace tracker, and Mike and Ben, two marksmen who volunteered in the hunt. Doug picked up some tracks that led us into a really rugged area between sheer drop-offs that had to be two hundred fifty feet. Anyway, we found the bastard."

"You did? Oh, thank God. Is he in jail?"

"No, he's—"

"What! Why isn't that son of a bitch behind bars?"

"Because he's dead."

I shook my fist in the air and cheered, "Good! Was it Mike or Ben who did him in?"

"Neither. Someone shot him, but we don't know who. Not yet anyway. It looked like he'd only been dead for a couple hours when we found him. Does the name Leland Boles sound familiar?"

"No, I don't think so."

"He was a notorious poacher from West Virginia. In one year alone, he killed eight bald eagles. Back in 1980 he was convicted of twenty-one counts of multispecies poaching. He served seven years in the West Virginia State Penitentiary. According to his ex-girlfriend, the minute he got out, he started poaching again."

"And you're sure he's the one who was slaughtering—"

"Oh, yeah. No question about it. The investigation is under way, so I can't tell you what all we found, but it was the sickest . . . Well, anyway, he was the guy all right. A handgun with a silencer was lying not far from his feet, but Boles obviously didn't have time to fire. He was shot with an arrow, and whoever did it was either one heck of a marksman or just plain lucky, because the arrow wasn't high-strength carbon or even aluminum. It was handmade."

I lowered myself to the edge of the bed. "Handmade? What did it look like, do you remember? I'm . . . I'm just curious, that's all."

"Yeah, I remember. I'll never forget it. Boles was lying on his side with the arrow sticking out of his back. And by the look frozen on his face, the bastard got a real good look at who sent him straight to hell. He was shot from the front.

"Doug's an archer and studies Native American artifacts. He

said the arrow was expertly made. The arrowhead was a Clovis point—very sharp and lethal. The fletching was made from black feathers. Probably from a crow, but I couldn't get close enough to be certain without disturbing the scene."

Squeezing my eyes closed, I leaned my forehead against the bedpost. Thank God I'd never told Gabe about the arrow I'd discovered in the barn. "Are . . . are handmade arrows rare?"

"No, I wouldn't say they're rare. I'm really sorry I had to call and tell you this, but Sally and I didn't want you seeing it on the news. All the animals were dead except for a young female bobcat that somehow managed to crawl away. Sally and Doc Waters worked on her for hours. They had to amputate her right front leg. We named her Lucky."

"I pray that poor creature lives up to her name."

"We do, too."

"Gabe, if you hear anything that you can share, anything at all, will you call me?"

"I will. 'Bye, Teddi."

I returned the phone to its cradle and looked out the window.

THIRTY-SIX

Snow. It began after supper. From the kitchen window, I watched fluffy snowflakes blanket the fields and build on the barn roof. The timer dinged, and I pulled a sheet of oatmeal cookies from the oven. While I was sliding them onto the cooling rack, Mama came up from the cellar. "Teddi, where's your brother?"

I turned, spatula in hand. "I think he's in his bedroom."

Daddy walked in and poured himself a cup of coffee. "He's in the barn, Franny."

"Doing what?"

"Setting up his sleeping bag."

Mama's eyes flared. "He is *not* sleeping in the barn. It's twenty degrees outside. He'll get sick."

Daddy glanced out the window. "I told him he could, so let it be."

"Now, why would you go and do something like that?"

"Franny, he's a *boy*. If he gets too cold, he'll come in. It's good for him to harden up."

With a scowl on her face and her lips pressed tight, Mama walked out of the kitchen.

When the cookies had cooled, I put a handful into a paper bag and filled a thermos with hot chocolate. Buttoning my coat, I tucked the cookies into one pocket and the thermos into the other.

The snowfall was so heavy that I could hardly see the glow of the light above the barn door. Other than the muffled sound of my footsteps and the dry scrape of a tree branch rubbing against the house, the landscape was hushed.

I gave the barn door a tug, opening it just enough to squeeze inside.

"Josh? Can I turn on the lights and come up?"

"No, wait a second." A moment later my brother shone a flashlight on the floor in front of my feet. "Leave the lights off. Just follow the beam to the ladder."

I stomped the snow from my boots, the thermos warm and heavy against my thigh as I climbed the ladder. When I reached the hayloft, Josh pointed the flashlight toward a shelf of hay topped with his sleeping bag. "It's nice up here."

I pulled the thermos and bag of cookies from my pockets. "Surprise."

"Wow, thanks." He took a big bite of a cookie and grinned.

We sat next to each other on the sleeping bag while Josh scarfed down another cookie. After he drank some hot chocolate, he jammed the flashlight into a bale of hay, sending a soft circle of light shining high above the rafters.

"Teddi, watch this."

A quick shadow of a bird moved through the circle of light. I smiled while my brother adjusted his fingers and made a hand shadow of a bird diving from a rafter.

"That's a hawk," he said. "They're wind masters. Did you know they dive at a hundred twenty miles per hour?"

I nudged him with my elbow. "You're making that up."

"Nope." He thumped his finger on a book resting on his pillow. "Read it right here. And peregrine falcons are even faster."

As I opened my mouth to ask a question, Josh sat upright. "*Shhhh.* Did you hear that?"

My eyes widened. "What?"

He switched off the flashlight and whispered, "Follow me."

We tiptoed to the back of the hayloft, and without making a sound my brother undid the latch and inched open the loading door. He stepped to the edge and motioned for me to come look. We were more than thirty feet aboveground, and I held tightly to the doorframe and peered out. At first I didn't see what Josh was smiling about, but as my eyes adjusted to the shadows and falling snow, I smiled, too. Below us was a bobcat.

I turned toward my brother and whispered, "What's he munching on?"

"Leftover chicken."

Josh lowered himself to a sitting position with his legs dangling out the door, and I joined him. We sat in the moonlight and watched the bobcat eat his supper. When not a morsel was left, he turned and limped into the woods.

"Poor old guy. I'm tryin' to help him along by giving him food every night. But I don't know how much longer he'll be around."

I leaned against my brother. "I love your big heart. There's a special place in heaven for you."

Josh shrugged. "I don't much care where I go when I die, as long as it's where the animals are."

We fell silent, our legs dangling free as the vapors of our breath clouded together. Minute by minute the snowfall increased until the woods became a lacy blur. Giant flakes swirled through the open door, and from the corner of my eye I watched my brother turn white in nature's benediction.

THIRTY-SEVEN

Down the hall and into my office I went, my legs rubbery as I turned on the lamp and opened the closet door. Unable to reach the uppermost shelf, I dragged my desk chair across the room and stood on the seat. Stretching my arm, I removed a cardboard mailing tube and then brought down the old shoe box.

I pulled the chair to my desk and sat. The lid of the mailing tube went *pop* when I opened it. Angling the tube, I let the arrow slide into my hand. The black arrowhead had been honed to a razor-sharp tip with serrations along each side.

I held it for a moment, feeling its weight before placing it on my desk.

It took me several minutes to gather the strength to untie the white ribbon and lift the lid off the shoe box. All the notes my brother had ever written me were folded and neatly stacked in chronological order, the one at the top being the last I'd received. Blood pounded in my ears when I drew the box close and reached inside.

The edges of the paper had yellowed and felt brittle. For the first time since 1977, I opened the note.

The feather slipped out and landed lightly on my desk. It was just as I remembered—smooth and shiny and pitch black. Holding the note in the lamplight, I leaned forward and read the words:

When shadows take flight
and the moon turns away from the stars,
the raven delivers divine law

Slowly, I ran my thumb over the five words my brother had written at the bottom of the paper—words that had forever altered so many lives:

Don't come looking for me.

I set the note down, removed a phone book from my desk drawer, and riffled through the pages until I found what I was looking for. Then I dialed the number of the nearest library.

"How late are you open this evening?" I asked the woman who answered.

"Eight o'clock," she said.

The hands on my wristwatch read 7:25. I thanked her, raced down the steps, and grabbed my keys. At 7:38 I pulled my car into the library's parking lot. My heart drummed so wildly that I could hardly think straight, but with the help of a librarian I found what I was looking for and was back home by a quarter past eight.

After pouring myself a glass of water, I climbed the stairs and returned to my desk. Opening the book, I leafed through the pages until I came to the chapter on Clovis points that read:

"*Clovis is a prehistoric Paleo-Indian culture that first appeared 11,500 radiocarbon years before the present. Archaeologists believe this age is 13,500 to 13,000 calendar years ago. The Clovis is the first point type to appear in North America and is not found elsewhere in the world . . .*"

From one page to the next I searched, holding my brother's arrow against the photos for comparison. But of the hundreds of photographs I examined, I couldn't be certain if the arrowhead in my possession was a Clovis or not. If I had to guess, I would have said it most resembled those called Copena.

There was no disputing that two feathers of the fletching were from a red-tailed hawk. The third was solid black. Whether from a raven, a crow, or a blackbird, I didn't know.

So what did all this mean?

I pinched the bridge of my nose and let out an anguished sigh. During the past hour, I'd learned more about arrowheads than I cared to know, yet I had no answer to the questions that were squeezing the air out of my lungs. A man named Leland Boles had made a decision to inflict unspeakable torture on animals. Someone else had made a decision to bring that torture to an end. As of this moment, that person was nameless.

Rising from the chair, I put everything away and turned out the light.

While hot water thundered into the tub, I lit a candle and slowly undressed. A cloud of steam rolled in to the air as I sank deep into the water. Submerged to my chin, I closed my eyes.

Let go. Just breathe out and let go . . . Heavenly Father, full of grace, please help me through this night . . .

THIRTY-EIGHT

While sitting at my workbench munching on apple slices, I leafed through an old issue of *National Geographic* and came upon an article featuring the big cats of Africa.

It was a quiet Thursday afternoon in early October. Albert was repairing a split in an Irish console table, and I was getting ready to paint a Gothic-style chair I'd come across at a garage sale—a massive old thing with wide arms and a high, solid back. I wanted to do something unexpected with it, something daring that would make a statement in my front window. After deciding on a bold cheetah print, I tore a picture of the exotic cat from the magazine and thumbtacked it to the wall above my bench. Pulling out a bin of oil paints, I was busy selecting the colors I'd use when the bell above the door rang. I heard Inez leave her office to see who it was.

Just as I picked up a tube of burnt umber, Inez stepped into the workroom. "Teddi," she said, dropping her voice to a whisper, "there's a *very* nice-looking man asking for you."

"He's not a salesman, is he? I don't have time to listen to—"

"Just go," she said impatiently. "He's tall and has gorgeous eyes, *and* he smells good."

Albert shook his head and chuckled. "Smells good?"

Removing my smock, I smoothed my hair and set off for the front of the shop.

I walked around a pine linen press and came to a halt when I saw him. Dressed in a dark blue suit with a crisp white shirt and a tasteful striped tie, he looked handsome and perhaps a bit ill at ease in an endearing, boyish way.

"Sam! What a nice surprise."

He put down the jade turtle paperweight he was admiring. "Your shop is beautiful, Teddi."

"Thank you."

I was about to invite him to take a tour when he said, "Listen, I know you're busy, and I've got to get back to the office for a meeting, but I'd like to ask you something. Would you have breakfast with me Saturday morning?"

"I'd love to, but I have to open the shop, and—"

Inez practically yelled from somewhere behind me, "I'll be here early Saturday morning!"

My cheeks grew warm as Sam peered over my shoulder in the direction of Inez's voice. "Well," I said, "then I guess the answer to your question is yes."

"Great. But I'll need to pick you up at six-fifteen."

"Where are we going so early?"

"It's a surprise."

He looked at me for a moment, as if there were more he wanted to say, and then he leaned forward and kissed my cheek.

❦

Wearing my favorite gray herringbone skirt, black tights, and a lightweight wool turtleneck, I stood at the window and watched for Sam. Yawning, I looked down at Eddie. "Where do you think he's taking me so early?"

Eddie tilted his head as if to say, *Beats me.*

At precisely six-fifteen, a pair of headlights cut through the pre-dawn mist. As Sam pulled up in front of my house, I gave Eddie's ears one last scratch and stepped out the door.

"Good morning," Sam said, walking around the side of his car.

I leaned against his chest for a moment and closed my eyes. "It feels like the middle of the night."

He gave my back a brisk, wake-up kind of rub. "Ah, but it'll be worth it."

For a moment I remained there with my face buried in his neck. He smelled of Ivory soap. Stepping back, I took in his worn jeans and canvas jacket. "I think I've overdressed."

"You look great. Better than great," Sam said, opening the door. He turned his car north, and we left the deserted streets of downtown Charleston behind.

"When are you going to tell me where we're having this mysterious breakfast?"

His lips curved into a slight smile. "If I told you, Theodora, then it wouldn't be much of a surprise."

As curious as I was, I didn't press further. Mile after mile disappeared behind us, the street lamps glowing warm in the morning vapors. From somewhere off in the distance, I heard a foghorn sound on the Cooper River. Closing my eyes, I rested my head against Sam's shoulder and listened to the hum of the tires. I might have fallen asleep if we hadn't hit a pothole that made the car shudder. I sat up and looked out the windshield. Chain-link fencing surrounded low, windowless metal buildings, and to my right I saw a lone train engine sitting on a set of tracks.

"Sam, this looks like some kind of industrial park. What are we doing here?"

"Patience," he said with a wink. Just as we drove over railroad tracks, he pointed and said, "Look at that big crane, Teddi."

It was still quite dark, and I had to squint to see what he was referring to, but there it was, looming in the fog like a huge praying mantis. Then I saw ships.

"Where are we?"

"This is the Charleston Naval Shipyard. You've never seen it?"

I shook my head. "Are we having breakfast with an admiral?"

Sam looked at me, his eyes bright with his secret. "Oh, no. Our breakfast will be much, much better." A moment later his face clouded and he slowed the car. "I can't believe I forgot to ask you this. Are you afraid of heights?"

"Well, I wouldn't want to wash windows on a skyscraper, but no, I'm not afraid of heights."

He let out a breath. "Good."

Sam turned left, and we passed a long line of eighteen-wheelers parked by the side of the road. Ahead of us was a yellow-and-white-striped barricade flanked by two construction barrels topped with flashing lights. While Sam came to a stop, a security guard got out of his car and turned on a flashlight. As he approached, Sam rolled down his window and took a piece of paper from behind the visor.

The security guard leaned down and looked in the window. "You'll have to turn around. Road's closed till—"

"I have clearance," Sam said, handing him the paper.

The guard shone his flashlight on the paper. "All right, just drive in to the lot and turn left. Park on the other side of the fence where the red barrels are." He returned the paper to Sam's waiting hand and stepped aside.

When Sam pulled around the barricade, I tried to see what this place was. Off in the distance, a serpentine shape rose from a sea of concrete, and to my right a string of red and white lights flickered a few times and then stayed on. The faint smell of caramel wafted through Sam's open window, and when he parked and we got out of the car, I heard the clang of metal on metal and then someone shouted, "Back it up! Whoa! That's enough!"

Sam lifted a small wicker basket from the trunk, took hold of my hand, and led me around a truck. In the blue-gray light, I realized that the serpentlike shape was a roller coaster.

"Is this a carnival?"

"Yes. It's a weekend charity event for the Carolina Youth Center. My law office is one of the sponsors."

"So why are were here at the crack of dawn?"

He said nothing as he hurried me around a teacup ride and up to a stoop-shouldered man who was adjusting a length of free-standing fencing. "Good morning. You must be Fred."

"Yes, sir."

"Sam Poteet. And this is my . . . my girlfriend, Teddi Overman."

The word "girlfriend" made me smile.

As the two men shook hands, Fred said, "Tested her last night and again this morning. She's all ready to go." He walked to a wooden platform, opened an electrical box, and flicked a switch. Colored lights flashed against the dark sky and outlined a big circle.

I looked from Fred to Sam, stunned. It was a Ferris wheel.

Fred unlocked a chain and stepped to the upper platform. "Hop on."

"C'mon, Teddi," Sam said, pulling me forward.

Fred held open a safety bar, and we sat on the bench seat, the wicker basket between us. With a metallic clang, Fred snapped the bar into place, gave it a tug to make certain it was secure, and said, "Off you go."

We set off backward, the gentle *whoosh* sending butterflies flapping in my stomach. As we rose high into the air, I burst out laughing. "I . . . I don't know what to say!"

Sam looked enormously pleased with himself as the Ferris

wheel made one full rotation and then another and another. Then, just as we neared the top, the wheel slowed and we came to a stop at the highest point.

"Time for breakfast," Sam said, opening the basket. Inside were napkins, a foil-wrapped package, and two thermoses. "Heavy cream and a pound of sugar for the lady." He unscrewed the cap of the first thermos, filled it with steamy coffee, and handed it to me. Incredulous at where we were, at everything, I started to laugh. And I laughed even harder when Sam opened the foil package that contained breakfast pastries and said, "You pick first."

"It's a good thing heights don't make me queasy," I said, selecting a cinnamon twist.

Sam picked a cherry turnover and bit into it with enthusiasm. "Well, if we were kids, we'd be eating cotton candy and corn dogs."

And there we sat, suspended in the air, with pastries and coffee. Everything about the morning was so unexpected that I kept giggling. "How in the world did this come about?"

"One day I read an article in the newspaper about a seven-year-old boy who was rescued from living in the streets by a youth-center employee. That story really hit me. If Everett and Tula Jane hadn't taken me in, that could have been me. So anyway, I've been a donor ever since."

"Did your law firm arrange for this carnival?"

He took a sip of coffee and shook his head. "No. A buddy of mine got this location. His dad's a retired navy captain. I came out here with him on Thursday when the carnies were starting to set up, and that's when I got the idea—"

Sam abruptly stopped talking and stretched his arm on the seat behind me. He pushed aside my ponytail and slipped his fingers along the collar of my blouse. With his eyes set on the trees, he smiled and said, "This is why I brought you here. Look, Teddi."

Though I followed his gaze, I wasn't sure if he was referring to the ships outlined against the sky, the cranes that loomed over the shipyard, or something else. I was about to ask when he slid his hand along my shoulder and gave me a gentle squeeze. "Watch. Here it comes."

The flat bluish gray of the sky began to pull apart, and above the trees there came a soft glow—pale violet and lightly feathered at first, then turning deep pink as it raced along the horizon. Within a few minutes, the pink gave way to a brilliant orange that set the clouds afire in luminous shades of gold. And then, pushing a stray cloud away from its face, the sun peeked above the treetops.

It was a glorious moment—not only for the palette of colors that nature had painted across the sky but because Sam had thought to do such a thing. Slowly he turned and looked at me, his eyes searching my face. "I thought this would be one helluva way to see our first sunrise together."

THIRTY-NINE

I stood in Olivia's kitchen and looked around. Gone were the gumball machines, the dusty hand puppets, the Felix the Cat wall clock, and the tons of glass decanters she'd collected over the years. The walls had been freshly painted the color of lemon custard, the woodwork was white, and the old pine floor had been polished to a warm glow.

But Olivia looked bewildered. "I made a mistake by painting the walls yellow. It's too *happy*, isn't it?"

"Actually, the color is really soft. Maybe you're just in shock at how different it is from those old blue walls. Once we get the artwork hung, I think you'll love it."

"I hope you're right. If I have to repaint these walls, I'll scream."

"So what made you decide to do all this?" I asked while adjusting the ladder. "I can't believe that you didn't tell me about it."

"Last Thursday morning I came downstairs to make coffee and it hit me like a slap in the face. My house looked like hell—like a crazy person lived here. Before my toast popped up, I had already started to clear things out of the kitchen. I didn't tell you about it because, well . . . I felt a little embarrassed." Olivia raised her eyebrows and looked at me. "I really let things get out of control after Eric left, didn't I?"

I gave her a wink. "Maybe a little. Well, okay—a lot."

"Why didn't you say something, Teddi?"

"It wasn't for me to judge. Our friendship isn't based on what you have in your house. I knew you were having a rough time and figured you were trying to fill up your empty heart. Instead of using food, you used gumball machines and puppets," I added with a slight laugh.

"Yeah. What man wants to sit in a kitchen and have coffee with sixty sets of glass eyes staring at him?" Olivia scanned the bare walls and chewed her lip. "Now that I've got a clean slate, I'm not sure what would look good."

"No problem," I said, selecting a small oil painting of an apple orchard. "I'll start with this. And that Chagall print would look wonderful on the wall by your table."

Olivia smiled. "I already feel better just having you here. I made egg salad, *and* since you're helping me when you could be doing something a whole lot more fun on a Sunday afternoon, I made a loaf of cracked-wheat bread, too."

"Great. Let's get these hung. I'm really hungry."

While Olivia stood at her kitchen counter and opened a package of picture hooks, I grabbed a tape measure and a pencil. We jabbered about her most recent restoration project, a first edition of *Stuart Little* that had survived a house fire but was covered in soot, and we laughed when she confessed how, just the night before, she had unashamedly gone through her neighbors' garbage when she saw they'd thrown out two boxes of books.

But when I told her about my Ferris-wheel adventure with Sam, Olivia's smile faded. She picked up a rag and began cleaning the frame of a photograph. Her voice was barely audible when she said, "That's the most romantic thing I've ever heard."

After pounding a hook into the wall, I stepped off the ladder and set the hammer on the counter. "Olivia, are you upset?"

"No," she said, avoiding my eyes as she polished the glass. "If ever I've known someone who deserves happiness—it's you. 'Upset' isn't the right word for what I'm feeling. It's incredibly childish and small of me, but I'm envious. You met a nice guy when you weren't even looking. And then there's me—Olivia 'The Pathetic Loser' Dupree."

"Stop it. You are not pathetic."

"Well," she said with a small shrug, "I'm just being honest. That's how I feel. When Eric left me, I thought I'd die. Then, when I finally accepted that he really was gay and there was no hope for us, I thought my life would open up—brand-new start and all that happy self-help bullshit. But it's like everything went retrograde and stayed that way. While I was painting the kitchen, I started thinking that maybe it's time I called a dating service. And then—"

She stopped talking and heaved a long sigh. "Honest to God, I don't know why you put up with me, Teddi. I am *so* sorry. Seems like all I do is bitch about my life. I shouldn't have hijacked the conversation about Sam with my ridiculous self-pity." She did her best to smile as she handed me the photograph. "So tell me more about him."

I set the framed photo next to the ladder and said, "Look, I was going to talk to you about this while we were having lunch, but I might as well say it now. Remember the plumber?"

"You mean the one who had his stories published?"

"Yes."

She held up her hand and avoided my eyes. "Please don't give me another lecture about how I screwed that up. I know I've made a mess of my life."

"Hey, I'm not going to give you a lecture. What I'm trying to tell you is that he's no longer dating Carla Fry. I ran into her at the grocery, and when I asked what was new, she said they broke up last month."

Olivia rolled her eyes. "Boo-hoo for Carla."

"Wow, you sure are snarky today. Anyway, I'm telling you this so you can call him. The timing is perfect."

Olivia gave me a sour look and began cleaning a painting. "Call him? No way. What would I say? Hey, sorry I blew you off when you asked me for a date, but I've spent the past year going through the Judgmental Bitch twelve-step program and now I'm—"

"Oh, for the love of Pete! Just call and make an appointment for him to look at a water problem you're having. Then you can strike up a conversation about his book."

"Forget it," she huffed, tossing the rag into the sink. "I'm not calling him. I refuse to grovel."

I planted my hands on my hips. "Excuse me? Who said anything about groveling? While he's looking at your plumbing problem, just casually bring up his short-story collection. I'll bet anything the two of you will be talking about books within minutes."

"I don't *have* a plumbing problem, and I'm not going to pretend that I do. Let it go, Teddi. It wasn't meant to be."

I don't know what got into me, but before I even thought it through, I picked up the hammer. With all my might, I smashed it against the side of Olivia's faucet. Her mouth flew open in shock when a geyser of water shot up and slapped her in the face.

Grabbing a dish towel, I tried to seal the break while Olivia screamed a string of expletives and threw open the cupboard door beneath the sink. She was still swearing a blue streak as she cranked the shutoff valve. Though it took her only a few seconds to get the valve tightened, there was water everywhere.

When I looked at Olivia sitting on the floor in a pool of water, I started laughing hysterically. "There," I said with a snort. "*Now* you have a plumbing problem!"

∽

It was just two days after I wrecked Olivia's faucet that all communication from Sam came to a halt. At first I thought it was because of his heavy work schedule, but when I hadn't heard from him by Wednesday, I started to worry. Since we'd begun dating, Sam and I had fallen into a comfortable schedule: He usually called me every day or two, we had dinner at least once during the week, and we hadn't missed spending a single Friday or Saturday night together.

When I hadn't heard from him by Thursday afternoon, I called his office, only to be told by the receptionist that he wasn't in and she didn't know when to expect him. I left no message. On Friday I sat at my desk and stared at the phone, willing Sam to call, but he didn't. And when I got home from work, I went straight to my answering machine, but there was no message from Sam.

I arrived at work on Saturday morning feeling so low I could barely force myself to talk with customers, let alone feign some semblance of interest. Every time the phone rang, I sprinted to answer it, but none of the calls were from Sam. When he hadn't phoned by the time I closed the shop, I walked home with crazy scenarios banging around in my head. Was this his way of cooling things off? Had he met someone else, or had something happened?

Eddie greeted me at the door with a tennis ball in his mouth, his tail wagging so hard it slapped against his flanks. "What do you think?" I asked when we went outside to the garden. "Is Sam done with us?" I flopped onto the chaise, and my faithful pup jumped up and lay by my side as if to say, *We have each other, so what's the big deal?*

But it *was* a big deal.

Though I tried to stay busy and not let my imagination take me on a dangerous journey, the evening dragged. By seven o'clock I was certain that Sam was out on a date with a younger woman who was far more interesting than I could ever be. When the hands of the clock reached seven forty-five, I curled up on the living-room sofa and stared out the window. My thoughts spun back to the first time I'd met Sam in person, and then, one by one, I relived each encounter we'd had over the course of our eight-week relationship. Even in hindsight I could detect nothing in his manner or his words to indicate that things were going in any direction but forward.

As the sky deepened, I remembered something I'd thought about only once or twice in the past twenty years. In light of what I was going through, it was more profound than I could have imagined.

AUTUMN 1970

A school dance was scheduled for Friday night. Excitement had been building all week, and I was aflutter with anticipation that David Tyler would ask me to be his date. In a rare moment of mother-daughter sharing, I told Mama about David, how he teased me and pulled my ponytail whenever he passed me in the hall.

I waited and waited for him to ask me to the dance, but he never did. When I arrived home from school on Friday, I ran straight to my bedroom and curled up on my bed with my annihilated ego. Mama came upstairs to see what was wrong, and when I told her what had happened, she nodded and quietly left the room.

A little while later, she knocked on my door and peered in. "I made you something." She walked in and put a chocolate milk shake on my night chest and sat down on the bed. "Teddi," she said, resting her hand on my thigh, "don't let this bring you down, or the entire weekend will be ruined."

"My weekend *is* ruined."

Mama put her hand beneath my chin and leaned close. "If you allow things like this to ruin your day, pretty soon you'll wake up and your life will be nothing but an endless string of ruined days that stretch as far back as you can remember."

She turned toward the window, her profile soft and blurred in the afternoon light. "Believe me, if you let disappointments take you too far, you'll end up getting lost. You'll never find your way out of it."

"But I hurt everywhere, Mama. How do I make it stop?"

She looked at me with a sad smile. "I don't know. Only you can figure that out. But try to remember something, Teddi: Never tie your happiness to the tail of someone else's kite."

Mama gave my legs a pat, rose from the bed, and left the room.

ଉଚ

And though that conversation took place a long time ago, tonight I felt just as hurt and confused as I did back then. I closed my eyes and remembered my mother's touch, how gentle it had been. I even remembered the apron she was wearing—a pattern of tiny violets with green piping sewn on the tops of the pockets. That was the only time we'd ever talked about the tender places in a woman's heart. I wondered what other words of wisdom she might have shared if we'd been closer, if I had reached out to her, if I had not been so independent and stubborn.

Right then I missed her so much I could hardly breathe. Knowing I was heading for a rapid spiral downward, I pushed myself up from the sofa and walked into the kitchen. "C'mon, Eddie, let's have a date, just you and me." I clipped the leash onto his collar, and we headed out the door.

While walking down Queen Street, I thought about Sam. Was he sitting in his garden with a glass of wine, talking and laughing with another woman? It took all my willpower not to head toward his house, sneak down the alley, and try to get a glimpse over the back wall. But I'd never once spied on a man, and I'd be damned if

I'd start at this stage of my life. I looked in the direction of Sam's house and said aloud, "You can take your old car, all your boyish charm, and *my* telescope—and just go jump in a lake. I am *so* glad I never slept with you, Sam Poteet!"

Those words had barely left my lips when I realized that someone had been walking close behind me. In my periphery I saw a young man cross the street, shaking his head with a smirk on his face. Most likely he thought I was one of Charleston's "colorful" characters, or worse.

At that moment I couldn't have cared less.

My ramblings were of no concern to Eddie. He happily trotted at my side and enjoyed sniffing the cool air. We turned on Franklin Street, then left on Broad, passing mansion after mansion, most of them lit up and glowing from within. I walked slowly so I could peer into the windows, sometimes getting a glimpse of a stunning antique chandelier or an heirloom sideboard that had surely been waxed to within an inch of its life.

About halfway down the block, I heard someone thundering through a Rachmaninoff piano concerto. From the open windows of a grand old Greek Revival, I could see people gathered together in a large living room. It must have been a very special party, as the women were wearing gowns and the men were decked out in black tie.

I stopped outside the elaborate iron fence, unashamedly peering into the windows and admiring the salmon-striped wallpaper while I listened to the music. I had come upon an accidental kind of happiness, and I curled my fingers around the top of the fence and enjoyed the performance. When the concerto came to an end, applause and the clinking of glasses rolled in to the cool air. I stood on the sidewalk and clapped, too.

Uninterested in the music, Eddie let out an impatient bark, and we continued our walk. By the time we turned on Legare, I was growing tired, so we headed for home. As we approached the house, I laughed when Eddie sped up and yanked on the leash. "You think there's a treat in your future? Well, you're probably right."

While opening the gate with one hand and trying to keep Eddie from bolting to the front door with the other, I caught my sweater on the latch. It took me a moment to pull it free, and when I turned, I saw someone sitting on my front steps. For a split second, I stood frozen in fear before I recognized who it was.

"Teddi," he said, his voice soft and contrite. "Am I ever glad to see you."

I didn't know what to say, and I sure didn't want to appear thrilled to see him, even though I was. I took my good old time walking toward him, and when Eddie reached the steps, Sam gave him a few ear scratches and patted his rump. Then he stood, and I gasped as the porch light illuminated the side of his face.

"What happened, Sam?"

He said nothing as he reached out and gathered me into his arms. For a long moment, he held me close, his face buried in my hair. "May I come in?" he murmured.

I unlocked the door, and Sam followed me inside. "Would you like something to drink?"

"Just water."

He sat on the sofa while I walked into the kitchen and poured a tall glass.

"Were you in a car accident?" I asked, handing him the glass as I sat by his side.

"No. On Tuesday, my secretary came and got me out of a meeting. She told me that one of Tula Jane's nurses had called and said there was an emergency and I should come home right away. I was annoyed by the interruption, but I cut the meeting short and went home. You should have seen it, Teddi. I don't think a bunch of drunks at a frat party could have done more damage—smashed dishes all over the kitchen floor, the silverware drawers overturned, two of the windows broken.

"I ran upstairs and found Tula Jane in her bedroom, crying hysterically. She accused me of stealing her jewelry, and when the nurse tried to give her a shot, Tula slapped her and started screaming. Well, once I convinced Tula that everything was all right, she calmed down enough for the nurse to give her a shot. Then I phoned her doctor and made an appointment for early Wednesday morning.

"The glass company came and replaced the broken windows, but it took me half the night to clean up the mess she'd made. The next morning while I was getting ready to take her to the doctor, the owner of the home-health-care company called. She said they wouldn't subject their employees to violence and physical danger. She terminated our contract and suggested I bring Tula Jane to a geriatric psychiatrist."

Sam took a sip of water and groaned. "It went downhill from there. I called my secretary so she could cancel my appointments, and then I went upstairs to get Tula dressed. The minute I walked into her bedroom, she started all this crazy gibberish about how I was a thief and had hidden all her money. I knew better than to argue, and I knew I'd never get her dressed, so I tried to get her into a robe. That's when all hell broke loose. She tried to bite me, and then she screamed and cried and ran out of the room."

Sam stopped talking, and I could see the anguish in his eyes. I wanted to wrap him in my arms, but I knew he had more to say.

His voice dropped low as he went on. "When she saw me coming down the hall, she climbed up on the window seat. I was scared to death she'd fall through the window, so I rushed forward to get a hold of her. She grabbed a figurine from a shelf in the niche and walloped me in the head. I never even saw it coming until it was too late."

Sam raised his hand and lightly touched the massive bruising that surrounded a line of stitches above his left eyebrow. "So anyway . . . we both ended up going to the hospital in an ambulance—me bleeding like a pig and Tula screaming and crying. After I got stitched up, I had a meeting with Tula's doctor. It took a lot of work, but he arranged for her to be transferred to a special-care facility."

"Is that where she is now?"

"Yes. She was taken there late this afternoon. I stayed with her until seven o'clock, but I doubt she knew who I was. She's pretty heavily medicated."

I lifted his hand and pressed it to my cheek. "What a terrible thing to go through."

He closed his eyes and leaned his head against the back of the sofa. "It's the beginning of the end for her, Teddi. And there's not a damn thing I can do about it. I can't stop thinking about how she and Everett jumped through hoops to adopt me."

Sam stopped talking for a moment, and his voice splintered when he said, "And now I've put her in a home where she'll die not knowing who I am, where she is, or why she's there."

I moved closer. "What can I do?"

"There's one thing," he said, resting his hand on my thigh. "But I know it's a lot to ask."

"What is it?" I said, kissing his temple.

He did not open his eyes when he said, "That you'll forgive me for leaving you in the dark. I'm really sorry, Teddi. I meant to call you a dozen times, but everything was so overwhelming that I got lost in the fray."

Slowly, I ran my fingertips over Sam's forehead. I could feel him relax and sink into the cushion with every circle I made.

"You're forgiven. But just this once."

FORTY

In the days that followed, I often thought about the irony of it all. The person who was bringing Sam heartache had unwittingly brought us together. Had his mother not made a habit of stealing from my shop, had she not twisted her ankle, and had I not delivered a get-well gift, Sam and I would never have met.

One evening while I was having supper with my grandmother, I told her the story of how Sam had come into my life. I told her everything, from the many Limoges boxes that Tula Jane had shoved into her handbag to the theft of the telescope. Grammy's eyes grew wide when I told her about the incident with the Staffordshire dog and how that had precipitated Tula Jane's spraining her ankle.

Grammy licked pudding from her spoon and looked at me thoughtfully. "My mother used to say that each day was a gift and how we chose to unwrap it would determine our happiness." Her lips spread into a smile as she added, "That was a nice thing you did, Teddi, taking that present to Sam's mother."

"Even though she'd driven me nuts for years, I felt really sorry for her, you know?"

My grandmother nodded. "I don't imagine she'll get any better."

"No," I said, taking a sip of ginger ale. "I don't imagine."

"How's your beau doin' with all this?"

"He doesn't say much, so I don't push. But I know he's having a tough time."

"I like the way you smile when you talk about him, Teddi. He sounds like a nice man."

"He is, and I'm bringing him to meet you soon, if that's okay."

Grammy's eyes lit up. "Well, that would be wonderful. Let me know ahead of time so I can get my hair done. I don't want to scare him off."

"I promise. You won't believe what we're doing this weekend. One of Sam's friends is throwing a come-as-you-were party."

"What's that?"

"Well, all I know is that Sam said they do it every year and the guests are supposed to dress up as if they were living in a different era. Sam's going as a gangster, and I'm dressing like a flapper. I found the perfect beaded white dress at a rummage sale. It weighs a ton, and the hem swings . . ."

☙❧

I had just stepped from the shower when the doorbell chimed. Throwing on a robe, I descended the stairs and peeked out the window. Sam's old car was parked on the street. He was forty-five minutes early. I smiled at his gangster outfit—black double-breasted suit, black shirt, and a white silk tie. Tilted rakishly over the eye where he had the stitches was a black fedora.

When I opened the door and he saw me in my robe, he raised his eyebrows. "Whoa, is this some kind of trick? Because if it is, it's working."

I laughed and pulled him inside. "You're early."

"Well, I guess I am. And by the looks of things, I'll make it a habit from now on." Sam took off his hat and tossed it on the sofa, then cupped my face with both hands and kissed me once, twice, and then again. He slid his fingers beneath my ears until they disappeared into my hair.

"Sam, I . . . I have to get dressed."

"Just let me tell you this one story," he whispered, kissing the side of my neck. "Once upon a time, there was this guy with goofy ears. He was kind of surly," Sam said, moving upward and kissing my temple. "And then one day his doorbell rang," he said, running his lips across my cheeks to my eyelids. "When he opened the door and saw a pretty girl standing on his porch," Sam said, untying the belt of my robe and slowly pulling it free, "something happened . . ."

Next thing I knew, it was two hours later and Sam was asleep in my bed. He was on his back with his right leg flopped outside the covers, his breathing deep and steady.

Night had fallen, and blue-tinted shadows stretched across the bedroom walls. I heard a whimper and turned to see Eddie's nose pop up over the side of the bed.

"Hi, little boy," I whispered. "C'mon up. There's room."

He wiggled, pushed off his haunches, and jumped onto the bed. I wrapped him in my arms and tucked him against my chest. Sam stirred, rolled onto his side, and drew me close, his breath warm against the nape of my neck. I closed my eyes, wanting to preserve the moment for as long as possible, like pressing a leaf between the pages of a book.

I woke to the wet tickles of Eddie licking my face and glanced at the clock—another hour had passed. Slipping out of bed, I quietly threw on a fluffy white sweater and a pair of jeans. After brushing my hair, I padded down the stairs. My robe was where Sam had left it, right by the front door, along with his suit jacket, his shirt, and his belt. His tie was hanging on the doorknob. I picked everything up and laid the bundle over the arm of the sofa.

A cool breeze blew in when I opened the back door to let Eddie

run out into the darkness. Only a few minutes later, he barked at
the door, and when I let him in, he ran so fast that he skidded on
the kitchen floor. Eddie looked around and seemed relieved that
Sam wasn't there.

"Are you jealous?" I asked, giving him a pat on the head and a
chewy treat.

He flopped down at my feet and thumped his tail.

Knowing that Sam and I wouldn't be going to the party, I rummaged through the refrigerator. I had to come up with something
for us to eat, but what? Deciding on pancakes, I walked into the
pantry to gather what I needed. As I was about to take a skillet
from a lower shelf, Sam appeared in the doorway, his hair tousled,
his cheek creased with sleep, and his shirt in his hand. He walked
toward me with a sly grin on his face.

"You're one helluva dame, Theodora," he murmured into my
hair.

I gave him a kiss on the neck and relaxed into his arms.

"So we're staying in for dinner?"

"Yes. Are pancakes all right with you?"

"I love pancakes," he said, slipping into his shirt and turning up
the cuffs. "Would you let me make them? I'm dying to cook something on that old stove."

"Sure. I'll set the table. What would you like to drink?"

"Tea," he said, giving me another kiss.

When Sam fired up a burner and a ring of blue flames shot up,
he grinned like a kid. "This old thing is so cool. Hey, I've got an
idea. Let's go grocery shopping tomorrow, and I'll cook a big Sunday dinner here."

I smiled at him over my shoulder. "I'd love it."

When the pancakes were ready, I lit a candle and dimmed the
lights. As I walked toward the table, I experienced a fleeting moment of déjà vu—the cast-iron griddle sending out its last sizzle,

the heat radiating from the stove, Sam's old car parked in front of the house. Though I had no idea why, all of it seemed so familiar and comfortable.

The flicker of candlelight illuminated our faces while Sam told me stories about a few of his most eccentric clients—from the heiress with empty eyes and a heart to match to the man who hid a fortune in gold locked inside an old freezer in his basement and how, when he was out of town, his new wife of only a few months (who hated the old monstrosity) had it hauled away, not knowing what was inside.

Swirling a forkful of pancake through a puddle of syrup, I looked at Sam. He had become my friend and my touchstone, and now he was my lover. I'd never dreamed I'd find those three attributes in one person. I took a sip of tea and wondered if he felt the same.

That thought had barely taken form in my mind when Sam swiped his napkin across his lips and said, "Sometimes it's hard to believe we spoke on the phone at least a half dozen times before we met in person." He laughed and shook his head. "I still remember the first time you called. You were so chilly."

"Was I?"

Sam's eyes brightened with amusement. "You introduced yourself as *Miss* Overman, and you hissed just a little when you said 'Miss.' Anyway, I'm sorry for what Tula Jane put you through, but I sure am glad you showed up at my door."

I finished the last bite of my pancake and studied Sam for a moment. "If you don't mind my asking, what made you follow me out of the diner? I mean—we'd met . . . what? Seven or eight months before that night?"

"Well, when you came to the house with the gift for Tula Jane, things were tough, as you might imagine." He hesitated for a moment, pushed his plate aside, and rested his elbows on the table. "Plus, I was swamped with work. So I spent several months digging myself out."

Sam reached across the table and ran his fingertips over my hand. "And then, when I saw you at the diner, I had the same feeling I had when we first met. That's when I knew it was time to free myself."

I furrowed my brow. "What does that mean?"

"I was in a relationship."

When his words sank in, I gasped. "You ended a relationship because of *me?*"

"Yes, Miss Theodora. I certainly did."

"But you didn't know anything about me. I could have been involved with someone, or . . . or what if we just didn't click?"

His face turned serious. "Everything in life is a gamble, Teddi. It was one I was willing to take."

"Well, I'm—"

The shrill ring of the phone cut into the serene atmosphere. After the second ring, Sam said, "You're not going to get that?"

"The answering machine will pick it up."

My recorded greeting was followed by a beep. After a pause there came the words, *"Teddi, it's Jeb Davis. Call me as soon as you can. Something happened in the Gorge."*

I jumped from the chair and raced to the phone, smacking my elbow against the pantry doorframe as I groped through the darkness. "Jeb, I'm here!"

While listening to what he had to say, I ran my hand along the wall, my fingers trembling as I felt for the light switch.

When I hung up, I turned to see Sam standing in the doorway. "What is it, Teddi?"

I pressed my palm to my chest and took in a breath. "That was Jeb Davis. He's the former deputy sheriff from up home. This afternoon three guys were hiking not far from Natural Bridge. They came across a boy who apparently fell down an embankment. He was airlifted to the hospital."

Sam pulled me close. "You're shaking, Teddi. Come sit." He led me into the living room and guided me to a chair. Pulling up an ottoman, he sat directly in front of me and took my hands in his. "What else did Jeb say?"

"They don't know who he is. He was unconscious and needed surgery. Apparently he has a head injury."

"Why would Jeb call you about this?"

"When they took off the boy's clothes at the hospital and looked for ID, there wasn't any. But inside his back pocket was a folded piece of paper." I took in a gulp of air, feeling as if I were heading toward a heart attack.

Sam leaned close. "And what does that piece of paper have to do with you?"

"It's *my* letter, Sam. The current sheriff allowed Jeb to read it to me. It's one of the letters I wrote to Josh a long time ago, just shortly after he disappeared. I put it inside a pickle jar and left it in a special hiding place where Josh and I went as kids." Taking in a breath, I added, "Over the years I've left my brother dozens of letters, but this is the first one that's surfaced. And—"

"I don't understand. Why would anyone call you about this?"

"Jeb's a good friend of the family. He and Daddy were close. He *had* to call me. Years ago he promised that if anything relating to my brother was ever discovered, he'd tell me right away. And another reason he called was because he didn't want me to hear about it secondhand. Slade's a small town, and news travels fast."

"All right, so he kept his promise. Now we wait."

"I'm going up there. I need to pack and leave tonight."

Sam smoothed his thumbs across the tops of my hands. "Teddi, unless they get some rock-solid information, you'll go all the way up there for nothing. When the kid regains consciousness, the authorities will talk with him."

"What if the boy found my brother? Or what if my letter wasn't in the place where I'd left it? Maybe that means—"

"Did Jeb ask you to come up?"

I closed my eyes.

"Teddi?"

"No. He said to sit tight, that he'd call and let me know what they found out."

"Then that's what you should do. I know it's—"

I pulled my hands away and stiffened. "You couldn't *possibly* have any idea what I'm feeling." I looked at Sam, my eyes stinging with tears.

He raked his fingers through his hair, rose from the ottoman, and walked to the window. Standing with his back to me, Sam spread his arms between the moldings.

"You're absolutely right. I don't know what you're feeling. But what I do know is that you're a willful woman, Theodora. And I *do* understand how even the smallest thread that links to your brother is important. But your physical presence won't alter any of the facts. Plus, the boy has a head injury. Who knows how long it might be before he's able to talk to the authorities? He probably found your letter where you left it and—"

"I need to be there the moment he wakes up."

Sam slowly shook his head and drummed his fingers on the window frame. Every bit of his body language spoke of exasperation. "If you absolutely have to go, I'll drive you," he said, turning to face me. "But you're setting yourself up for a huge disappointment. Teddi, how many times have you already had your heart broken over this?"

From across the room, we looked at each other, me chewing my lip, Sam with his hands on his hips.

I thought about all the false leads that had surfaced over the years—waiting for dental records to reveal that the human remains found wedged between two boulders were not those of my brother; the campers who came across a cave where clearly someone had been living for quite a while, only to find out it wasn't Josh. Sam and Jeb were probably right. Chances were good that the boy had found my letter where I'd left it and for whatever reason had kept it. Maybe it meant something, or maybe it meant nothing at all.

The panic I'd felt only moments ago was starting to fade. I let out a long sigh and buried my face in my hands. "You're right."

"Does that mean you've changed your mind about going to Kentucky?"

I nodded, suddenly so embarrassed I could hardly look Sam in the eyes. "What you must think of me. I'm sorry. I got a little crazy for a few minutes, didn't I?"

His shoulders relaxed, and he tilted his head. "Teddi, given the circumstances, I think you've got a right to go crazy now and then. I can't fathom what you've lived through for all these years."

Right then the taut wire that had been squeezing my chest loosened. I took a full breath, letting it out slowly. I had the sensation of being tethered to goodness, to a calm that was steady and reliable. I looked up at Sam and slowly took him in—from his mussed hair to the pink scar above his eyebrow to his wrinkled shirt that I only now noticed he'd buttoned cockeyed.

"You know what?" I said, glancing at his feet. "I'm really glad you don't wear argyle socks."

He looked at his plain black socks and wiggled his toes. "Is there a hidden meaning to that statement?"

"Yes," I said, rising from the chair and walking toward him. "And I'll tell you about it if you'll sit with me in the garden."

While Eddie bounded around the yard, happily sniffing the scents of night, Sam and I reclined side by side on the oversize chaise I'd recently bought.

"This thing is great," he said, pulling me close. "So what's the deal with the argyle socks?"

When I told him the story, including how I'd put pebbles in the valve stems of the tires, Sam laughed. "I've never met anyone like you, Teddi. You always surprise me, in good ways I might add."

The evening was beautiful and cool as we lay beneath the stars and talked, the easy kind of talk that arrives with darkness. When Eddie grew tired of checking every corner of the garden, he jumped on the chaise and flopped down by our feet.

Sam threaded his fingers through mine. "I'm glad you're in my life, Theodora. I hope you'll let me stick around."

I leaned my head against his shoulder. "I'm glad you're in my life, too. Thanks for talking me off the ledge tonight. If you hadn't been here, I'd already be on my way to Kentucky."

"It's obvious how much you loved your brother, but I just don't want you getting hurt anymore."

"I wish you could have known him, Sam. He was amazing. Animals and little children were drawn to him in ways I can't describe. He had a . . . I guess you'd call it an *energy* about him. He was very gentle."

Sam kissed my forehead. "Sometimes when you talk about your brother, I get the feeling you're not telling me the full story. And if you don't want to, that's fine. But—"

"I've not lied to you, Sam. Not ever."

"Whoa, hold on a minute. That's not what I said or even implied. It's just that I've noticed a certain reticence when you talk about Josh. There are times when you speak of him in the past tense and others when you use the present. I guess it's the lawyer in me working overtime."

I burrowed deeper into his shoulder. "After the fund-raiser for the rehabilitation center last autumn, I finally accepted that my brother was dead. It took me all winter to work through the grief. But then something came up that set my whole universe into a tilt. Now I honestly don't know if Josh is alive or not. And there's something I've wanted to tell you, but I'm scared."

Sam turned and scanned my face. "I never want you to be scared. I want you to feel safe with me. Always."

"I *do* feel safe with you. And I've told you everything about Josh, except . . . except for this one little thing."

As Sam waited for me to elaborate, I looked into the sky and gazed at the expanse of stars, wondering if my brother was watching them, too. Was he thinking about me as I was thinking of him? Was this the connection he spoke about when he had described being awake?

I could feel the rise and fall of Sam's steady breathing. Without looking at him, I whispered, "I . . . I have this arrow . . ."

Sam listened and never uttered a word, nor did the calm expression on his face change. When I'd finished talking, he didn't look at me. I wondered if I'd made a terrible mistake, but I knew sooner or later I would have to tell him the whole story.

"So," he said, resting his arm behind his head, "a demented guy got waxed by an arrow from an unknown marksman. Sounds like a victory for the gene pool if you ask me. But better I should paraphrase a quote by Clarence Darrow: '*I have never killed a man, but I have read some obituaries with great pleasure.*'"

Sam turned toward me, his face serious. "As fascinating as your story is, Theodora—and yes, it *is* fascinating—I want you to know something. None of it matters to me in the way you might think." He raised his hand toward the sky and made a circle with his thumb and forefinger. "That's right, a big fat zero. Not one bit of it has anything to do with you. Or us."

I couldn't recall when I'd felt so relieved. "I wanted to tell you about it last week when we went for that long walk, but I was worried what you'd think of me and my family. How you might judge us— especially my brother. And the worst part is that I have no idea if the arrow I found in the barn has anything to do with what happened in Clifty Wilderness. It's an awful secret to carry around, Sam."

He held me closer, and we lay in silence for several minutes. Right when I wondered if he had drifted off to sleep, he turned toward me. "Well, Theodora, I have a secret, too. I've been debating when I should tell you, but I think now is the perfect time. So listen up, okay?"

I smiled. The last person I'd heard use the words "listen up" was Mr. Palmer.

"The day I saw you standing on my front porch, something hit me. It hit me again when I saw you in the café. And then, when you asked for coffee with *four* sugars, I knew what it was. And see, it's the damnedest thing, but every time we're together, it keeps hitting me."

Sam abruptly stopped talking. I waited, and when he didn't say anything more, I gave him a nudge. "What is it?"

"Are you sure you want to know?"

"Yes."

"And no matter what it is, you won't judge me?"

"Promise."

Even in the darkness, I could see a glint in his eyes when he pressed his nose to mine. "I'm in love with you. That's right, *Miss* Theodora Grace Overman. I love you. And no mysterious arrow is going to change that fact. Not now, not ever. So keep that thought in your pretty head."

Sam tucked a loose strand of hair behind my ear, his hand lingering. "But I do have a question. Do you think, maybe sometime, you'd be real sweet and tell me that you love me, too?"

I opened my mouth, but Sam touched his fingers to my lips. "Don't answer. Not now. Surprise me."

FORTY-ONE

Following that evening something within me shifted. Not that I experienced anything so monumental as an epiphany, but the days loosened and the nights softened. Maybe that's what love does—smooths the hard edges of life, giving us a gentle place to land when we fall and lessening our bruises when we do.

When Jeb had called to give me an update, somewhere deep in that quiet center where we feel the weight of our truths, I already knew what he would tell me—the injured boy had indeed found my letter in the old pickle jar, exactly where I'd left it.

But there was a surprising twist.

Earlier that morning the boy had learned of my brother and his disappearance. And the person who'd told him about it was sweet old Norma who ran the ticket booth for the Natural Bridge Sky Lift. When the boy, a sixteen-year-old native of Kentucky named Paul Jameson, came upon my pickle jar, he was fascinated. But he couldn't open it because the lid had rusted. So he broke the jar against a rock to see what was folded inside. Paul said he was stunned when he read the letter and realized it had been written to the missing boy Norma had told him about earlier that same day. He said he knew he had a piece of Kentucky's history and thought it might be valuable one day.

When Jeb told me that although the boy had suffered multiple fractures, he was expected to make a full recovery, I breathed a sigh of relief. Paul Jameson was one of the few who took a fall in the Gorge and was lucky enough to tell the story.

Unfortunately, I wasn't as lucky.

I belonged to a club where the dues were unimaginable—a club where members lived each day not knowing what had become of a loved one. Though our circumstances varied, one thing was constant: We couldn't stop waiting for a miracle. Over the years I had experienced the convoluted kind of grief that accompanies the unknown. It was a twisting, churning process that had the power to drive even the strongest and most faithful to the brink of madness. When the pain was too much, we'd let go and try to get on with our lives, only to have the next day, month, or year bring us a slender thread of hope that more often than not broke in our hands.

Statistics were never in our favor.

It was my home and my relationship with Sam that kept me grounded in ways I hadn't before experienced. And for the first time since I'd moved to Charleston, I felt as if I'd crossed the line of initiation and become a true Charlestonian—not born and bred, but that I belonged just the same. Olivia claimed that Charleston had embraced me from the moment of my arrival, and in retrospect I realized that was true. From Mr. Palmer to Albert to Tedra Calhoun and the surprise her husband had left for me beneath his breakfast plate, Charlestonians had indeed opened their arms.

Olivia also claimed that Sam was the best thing that had ever happened to me, and though I was reluctant to give any relationship that much power, I had to agree. She and I talked about it early one Sunday morning as we browsed through a yard sale.

"Sam's good for you," Olivia said while examining a small writing desk. "It's about time you stopped working all those crazy hours and started having fun. You know, I was all set not to like him, but did that ever change when I met him. Sam's a great guy."

"He likes you, too. He thinks you're a firecracker."

She smiled as if she liked that idea. "Any news on his mother?" Olivia asked as she opened the pencil drawer.

"From the things Sam has told me, I get the feeling she's nearing the end. She's unresponsive and hasn't said a word in weeks."

"It's sad. I hope she takes her last breath sooner rather than later—for both their sakes." Olivia ran her hand over the top of the desk and looked at me. "I really like this. Do you think it would work in my bedroom?"

I stepped back and took a good look. "The scale isn't right. It would be dwarfed by your other furniture."

"Damn. I think you're right."

"So what about the plumber—how's that going?"

Olivia sounded a bit annoyed when she said, "He has a name, you know."

"Sorry. I guess he'll always be 'the plumber' to me." I set down the mercury-glass candlestick I was admiring and looked at her. "So tell me more about *Michael*."

"I like him a lot," she said, lifting a pearl-handled letter opener and squinting at the price tag. "He's coming over tonight—we're making pizza together. Do you know what he does that I love? He reads to me. Sometimes he pulls a book from my shelf and I curl up with my head on his lap and he just reads and reads. He's not like anyone I've ever dated."

"And now for the next question: Are you glad I smashed your faucet?"

From over her shoulder, Olivia looked at me, her lips curving into a lopsided smile. "Yeah. But thank God he wasn't a fireman or you'd have burned down my house."

❦

Sunday, December 6, was a brilliant, blue-skied day. Sam and I arrived at the nursing home with a bouquet of flowers, a chocolate cake, and several gifts tied with colorful ribbons. I rapped on the door and peeked in to see if Grammy was dressed. She was waiting for us and had chosen to wear a raspberry pink sweater over a yellow flannel housedress. On her head was a periwinkle blue velveteen hat with a red paper flower pinned to the brim. I set down the cake, and when I hugged her, I detected the faintest scent of baby powder.

Sam leaned down and kissed my grandmother's cheek. "Happy Birthday, Belle. You look pretty."

"I do?" She sounded so young, so delighted to receive a compliment from a man, that I got a lump in my throat.

"Yes, Belle, you certainly do. I like your sweater."

She touched the sleeve reverently. "Teddi gave it to me."

"Are you sure you don't want to go out for a drive?" I asked, fiddling with the flower on her hat. "Sam said he'd take you anywhere you'd like to go."

She thought for a moment. "Well, you know what I'd like?"

"Just name it, Belle, and it's yours," Sam said.

Grammy reached for his hand. "I'd like it if you'd push me around the block."

"Then a birthday ride you'll have."

I got her into a jacket, and then Sam grasped the handles of the wheelchair and pushed her out the door while I grabbed the afghan from the end of her bed in case she got cold.

As we headed out the front door and down the ramp, we approached Mr. Lamb sitting in a spot of sun. Though it was unseasonably warm for December, he had a stocking cap on his head and was wrapped in a blanket that looked like a dried-out cocoon. "Where you off to, Belle?" he asked in a quivery voice.

"My granddaughter and her beau are takin' me on a birthday ride."

Mr. Lamb perked up. "How young are you today?"

"Ninety-four!" Grammy proudly announced.

"Ahhh . . . you're just a kid," Mr. Lamb said with a chuckle. "I'll be ninety-nine come March. You gonna have cake?"

"Yes. My granddaughter made chocolate. I'll save you a piece," Grammy said with a wave of her arthritic hand.

Down the walk and across the driveway we went, heading for the sun-dappled sidewalk. Grammy seemed tickled by Sam's many questions about her life. With stunning detail she recounted what it was like to live off the land in the foothills of Kentucky and how by the age of fourteen she'd sold enough of her homemade jams, jellies, and bread at the side of the road to buy her mother a milking cow.

"Might seem hard to believe," my grandmother said with a laugh, "but when I was a young girl, I drove the boys crazy. My pa used to chase 'em off our land with a scythe. Oh, you shoulda seen those boys run! When I was sixteen, a young man walked onto our property with a bouquet of wildflowers in his hand. When my pa saw him comin', he did like always and grabbed his scythe. I'll never forget how he stood in front the house, turning the scythe real slow so the sun sparkled on the blade. But that young man held his head high and just kept on walkin' straight toward my pa. It was the bravest thing I'd ever seen! His name was Otto Forrester. A year later we were married, and it wasn't too long before he and my pa were thick as thieves."

Sam let out a hearty laugh while Grammy launched into another story. She was having so much fun that she kept asking if we could go farther, and by the time we arrived back at the nursing home, we had pushed her for well over an hour. My grandmother was so tired from all the talking and fresh air that she fell asleep before unwrapping her last gift. So I removed her hat and tucked a pillow behind her head, and then Sam and I quietly left the room.

I laced my arm through his as we walked down the corridor and out the door. While crossing the parking lot, we laughed about how animated and entertaining my grandmother had been.

"She's a remarkable woman," Sam said, opening the car door for me. "And a great storyteller."

He held the door, but I didn't get in. Instead I turned to face him.

The time had come.

"Sam, I haven't told you everything. I have one last secret."

His smile faltered ever so slightly. "You do?"

"Yes," I said, looking down at my shoes. "And I can't go any further in our relationship without telling you."

There was no mistaking the concern in Sam's voice when he said, "What is it, Teddi?"

Slowly, I raised my head and looked into his eyes. I was surprised how easily the words came. "I'm in love with you, Sam."

Though I wasn't certain, I thought he exhaled the slightest sigh of relief as he wrapped his arms around me and spoke into my ear. "I suspected as much, Theodora. But it's nice to hear you say it. Real nice."

We stood in the parking lot, making out like sex-crazed teenagers, and when I thought Sam might try to take things too far, he stepped back, held me at arm's length, and smiled. Just then an elderly couple came walking across the parking lot holding hands, both of them dressed in their Sunday best. I was shocked when Sam called out to them, "Guess what? She loves me!"

❧

And love Sam I did—fully and freely and without reservation. Even during those rare moments when I feared what would happen to me if we ever split up, I knew the flight into the crazy skies of love would always outweigh the uncertainty of days that didn't yet belong to me.

Sam would often show up at my house with bags full of groceries. He'd ignite my old stove and cook something divine while I sat at the kitchen table sketching designs for trompe l'oeil commissions or compiling lists of supplies Albert and I needed for the shop.

In January I was in bed watching late-night TV when a dance competition came on. I watched the couples move in ways that left me mesmerized. I lay propped up on pillows, longing to learn the tango and the cha-cha, and I fell asleep fantasizing about Sam and me dancing across my moonlit patio. The next evening I asked him if he'd consider taking dance lessons with me, and though he claimed to have no sense of rhythm, he was a good sport, so we signed up for an eight-week Latin dance course for beginners. Neither one of us was very good, but we had tons of fun, and by the end of the fifth week we could do our own version of a steamy tango that ended with Sam driving us back to my house in a fevered rush. Then we'd race up the stairs and dive into bed.

I laughed when, after dance class one evening, Sam pushed back the bedsheet and moved sweat-dampened strands of my hair across the pillow. "Teddi, maybe we should just try doing a simple polka."

"Why?"

"Because if this is what happens when we tango, what the hell will happen when we get to the *paso doble?* You'll kill me."

FORTY-TWO

My bedroom drapes swelled in the warm breeze as I stepped out to the piazza. The morning air was saturated with the fragrance of spring, the birds were in full chorus, and my azaleas were popping with deep pink blooms. I breathed deeply, feeling alive and whole and, as my brother would have said, *awake*.

Leaving the French doors open, I dressed for work while making mental notes of the plants I wanted to add to my garden. I knew it would be a fun project for Sam and me to do together. I took my time walking to the shop, stopping to admire an arbor smothered in Confederate jasmine. As I turned the corner and walked down Wentworth, I saw a man hammering a sign into his lawn. I knew I'd be late for work when I read those two magic words: YARD SALE.

"Got a lot of stuff here," the man said. "If you have any questions, just let me know. My name's Stanley."

"Thank you."

I wandered past two card tables piled high with clothing and headed for a row of furniture that sat along a hedge. First in line was a green plaid sofa that was without a doubt the ugliest thing I'd ever seen in my entire life. Next was a pine dinette set followed by a giant console stereo. Beyond a cluster of metal file cabinets sat a small bedside chest. With its French styling and tapered legs, it was almost identical to the one I'd sold to Mr. Palmer over twenty years ago.

The memory of that day made me smile, and despite its poor condition, I decided to buy the old chest. I carried it to the front yard, where Stanley was sitting on the porch steps. "There's no price tag on this piece," I said, setting the chest down on the grass. "How much are you asking?"

He thought for a moment. "Thirty-five and it's yours."

"Thirty-five and you can keep it."

Stanley eyed the chest. "I guess I'd take thirty."

"I'll pay fifteen."

He looked from me to the small tin cash box sitting next to him. "Well, I was hopin' to get more, but . . . all right."

I gave him the cash, tossed my handbag over my shoulder, and lugged the chest all the way to the shop. When I walked into the workroom and set it down with a huff, Albert stopped what he was doing and furrowed his brow. "Where'd that piece of junk come from?"

"A yard sale. It used to be in a fine home until someone threw it out. Then someone else picked it out of the garbage and didn't take care of it."

"Who told you that?"

"The chest did—told me its whole story while I carried it to work."

Albert screwed up his face. "Well, if the chest told you that story, I guarantee ain't none of it true. *That* chest," he said, pointing a screwdriver at the cracked drawer, "is a liar." And then he launched into the richest laughter I'd ever heard. I started laughing, too, and pretty soon we were both howling.

Albert was still laughing when he loosened a hinge from a cabinet door and shook his head. "Walking in here with a talkin' chest. Lord, Teddi, the things you come up with."

I smiled and went into the kitchen to make a pot of coffee. After checking out the front of the shop, I straightened a few paintings and polished a mirror. When I heard the coffeemaker stop gurgling, I walked to the kitchen and poured Albert a cup.

"Here you go," I said, offering him the mug. "Guess I'd better get busy and—"

Albert took a sip and grimaced.

"What's wrong?"

"If I drink any more of that, I'll be seein' through walls."

"Well, *some* people like my coffee."

He grumbled while I went into my office to call a delivery company. I was still on the phone when Inez came in. She hadn't yet closed the door when Albert called out, "I sure hope you're gonna make coffee, 'cause the stuff Teddi made could poison the devil!"

A few minutes later, I heard her rinsing the pot in the kitchen.

I had barely unlocked the front door when the bell began to ring and people walked in. By eleven o'clock I'd sold a nineteenth-century rocking horse, a pair of Chinese blue-and-white porcelain vases, and a French vitrine that I'd had for ages. When I brought the sales slips into Inez's office, she let out a whoop. "You're selling antiques like your pants are on fire. You keep this up and we'll *all* be driving red convertibles!"

I gave her a wink and waltzed down the hall and into my office. Though I often thought of him, and always with great fondness, for some reason Mr. Palmer had been on my mind for the past few days. I still missed him and knew I always would.

While I sat at my desk and jotted down a few notes about what I needed to replenish my stock, I leaned back in my chair and whispered, "Mr. Palmer, things here are going just fine. And I hope, wherever you are, things are fine for you, too."

Just as I stood to pull a catalog from the shelf behind my desk, the phone rang. A moment later Inez called out, "Teddi, for you on line one."

I picked up the phone.

"Hey, Teddi, it's Gabe."

"Hi. I was thinking about you and Sally last night. How's the construction going on the clinic?"

"Good. It should be up and running by June."

"I can't wait to see it, and—"

"Teddi, can you talk—I mean, privately?"

I pushed the door closed and sat at my desk. "Yes, why?"

"Early this morning I was up in the hayloft building a wall and thought I heard something. It's Sally's day off, so I figured it was her. When I called out, she didn't answer. I put down the hammer and listened, but all I heard was the animals rooting around in their cages. About an hour later, I went to check on a mourning dove we're rehabilitating. When I walked into the bird room, I swear all the hairs on my arms stood straight up. Someone had come into the barn, and whoever it was had put an eagle inside a cage. I kid you not, Teddi. A bald *eagle*."

"Do you think it was one of the rangers?"

"No. Sally was in the kitchen and would have noticed if anyone had pulled in to the driveway. Just one look and I could see that the bird had a broken wing. I ran and got Sally, and we loaded the bird into a transport cage and drove into town. Doc Waters measured its bill depth and hallux length and confirmed that the eagle is a female. She's a big girl, too. Her wingspan is eighty-two inches. X-rays showed that her humerus was broken—that's the equivalent of a human's forearm."

"Will she be all right?"

"It's too soon to tell, but I think so. She's on pain meds right now, but once she's stabilized, Sally and Doc will operate."

The silence that followed was so hollow that I thought we'd been disconnected.

"Gabe?"

"I'm here. Teddi, what I'm going to tell you will sound really strange, but I swear it's *exactly* what happened. When Sally and I got back from the vet's, I went into the barn and started looking around. Nothing was out of place. I opened the back door, and there were dirty footprints on the stone step. They weren't mine, and they weren't Sally's. Whoever came into the barn walked around the flight cage and entered through the back door. I looked around and found a few more footprints—one set was a lot bigger than the other. No question about it, they were definitely from two different people. I went back inside the bird room, and that's when I saw something."

"What?"

"A plastic container was shoved against the wall on the side of the cage where the eagle had been placed. Either it hadn't been there when I discovered the eagle or it probably was but I just didn't notice it. The container was dirty and looked old—it was about nine inches square."

I pressed my hand over my heart and nearly strangled on my own words when I asked, "What was inside?"

"I don't know. I didn't open it because—"

"Can you open it now, while we're talking?"

"No. The lid was sealed with several layers of duct tape. I mean, *really* sealed. It wasn't until I turned on the overhead lights that I saw a name written on the tape. Well, not written exactly—it was carved *into* the tape, probably with the tip of a knife. There was no mistaking the name."

Gabe paused for a moment, then lowered his voice when he said, "It was 'Teddi.'"

Every vein in my body hummed as I rose from the chair. "I'm coming to get it. I'll leave right—"

"I just sent it UPS to your shop. You'll have it tomorrow afternoon. Here's the tracking number."

I was so shaken I could hardly write the number on my desk pad. "Gabe," I said, putting down my pen and feeling dizzy, "do you . . . do you think it's from Josh?"

"All I know is that something told me to get it to you as fast as possible. I'm sorry. Maybe I should have called you before I drove to town. But I thought—"

"It's all right, Gabe. Really." I rubbed my hand across my face. "You did the right thing."

When we'd said good-bye, I stared at the tracking number, not knowing how in the name of God I'd get through the next twenty-four hours.

∾

Arriving home at six-twenty with a throbbing headache and a tight jaw, I downed three aspirin. Even my shoulders burned with tension. When the phone rang at seven-thirty, I nearly jumped out of my skin.

"Hello."

"Hey, darling. How was your day?"

"My day? Oh, my day was . . . it was fine."

Clutching the phone close to my ear, I came close to telling Sam what had happened, but I changed my mind. It was difficult to keep my voice steady throughout our conversation, and twice he asked if I was all right. Claiming to be nothing more than "just awfully tired," I left it at that. After making plans to have dinner together on Wednesday evening, we said good-bye.

Unable to eat or think straight, I curled up in bed with my arms wrapped around Eddie and watched the minutes tick by on the clock. At midnight I got up and cleaned the kitchen floor. At 12:45 I put a load of laundry into the washer and then ironed a stack of blouses. Finally growing tired at 1:40, I slipped back into bed and fell into a dreamless sleep, only to awaken at 4:30.

Memories of my brother flashed through my mind until I thought I might go mad. At five o'clock I got up and went down to the kitchen to make a cup of tea. With my robe wrapped tightly around me, I took my tea and went outside. While Eddie nosed around the flower beds, I paced from one side of the garden to the other. Then I sat on the chaise and rested my head against the pillow. It was damp with dew, but I didn't care.

As I lay wondering what the day might bring, I watched a lone crow move across the pale morning sky.

FORTY-THREE

The shop was filled with customers. Every time the bell above the door rang, my heart leaped. Throughout the day I paced, watching the front window for the UPS truck to pull to the curb.

At 3:40 a woman came in. She was a tourist from Mississippi who launched into a litany of questions about antiques. I tried to give her my full attention, but when the hands of my wristwatch moved to 3:55, I began inching toward the door with the hopes that she'd leave. At 4:05 she was still talking.

I wanted to set my hair on fire.

Finally she left, and I stood at the window and waited, so nervous that I could hardly keep my knees from buckling. When the hands of my watch moved to 4:40 and I thought I'd collapse from stress, the UPS truck roared to a stop at the curb. I charged out to the sidewalk, nearly mowing down a young couple walking their dog.

Tim, who'd driven this route for years, hopped off the truck and laughed when I all but ripped the package from his hands. "Must be important, huh, Teddi? Here, you've got to sign for it," he said, giving me a pen.

I scribbled my name and clutched the package to my chest as I watched the truck pull away.

Though closing time was six o'clock, I grabbed my handbag and asked Inez to lock up. My nerves were so taught when I left the shop that my ears grew warm. I walked at a brisk pace, dodging a group of Citadel cadets and blasting by two elderly women strolling arm in arm. When I was halfway down Archdale Street, I slowed. Maybe I was savoring the last few moments of wonder, or perhaps I was simply exhausted by the long hours of anticipation. Whatever it was, I turned onto Queen Street and entered my home enveloped in an eerie kind of calm.

I set the box on the kitchen counter, gave Eddie a hug, and let him outside. From the window I watched him run around the backyard. Every few seconds I'd look over my shoulder at the package sitting on the counter, aching to open it, yet terrified to see what was inside.

After I'd given Eddie his dinner, I stood at the counter and lightly touched the box.

The time had come.

Opening a drawer, I removed a razor-sharp paring knife. My left hand gripped the handrail as I slowly climbed the stairs with the box and knife held against my breast. I walked into my office and set everything on the desk. For several minutes I could do nothing but sit and stare at the box. Lifting my hand, I smoothed my fingers along its top and then grasped the tab. I gave it a firm pull and watched the perforated edges release. Opening the flap, I angled the box and gave it a gentle shake. A newspaper-wrapped bundle slid into my hand.

I peeled back the paper and dropped each sheet on the floor. And finally there it was, just as Gabe had described. The container was old, misshapen, and dirty. I could even see fingerprints smudged along its side. Though I couldn't be certain, I thought it was one of the containers I'd left for my brother over a dozen years ago. The lid was sealed with layer upon layer of gray duct tape.

I could barely swallow when I held the container to the lamplight and saw my name etched into the tape. I would have recognized the printing anywhere—all capital letters, the slightly angled *T*, the two *D*'s leaning against each other.

Closing my eyes, I whispered, "Oh, dear Lord."

Picking up the knife, I pierced through the tape on the underside of the lid. I held my breath and began slicing the tape from the edge. When I felt the blade hit plastic, I set down the knife and worked my fingers along the rounded lip. A faint *pop* sounded when the lid released.

I sat frozen.

This was it.

Slowly, I lifted the lid.

There was no letter, but the items inside revealed more than a poet's most thoughtful prose. I removed the first item—the old brass amusement-park token I'd given Josh just two days before he disappeared. I held it to my cheek and closed my eyes for a moment, fighting against tears. Next was a rusty striped feather from a red-tailed hawk.

Wrapped in a scrap of paper was a small river stone that resembled the shape of a heart. Worn smooth and cleansed by years of rushing water, it was a milky, off-white color with a wide pink vein running through its middle. I envisioned my brother smiling as he knelt and plucked it from the Red River.

Next I removed a piece of folded fabric, plaid flannel and so old it was tissue thin. I unfolded the fabric to see two pieces of cardboard. All four sides had been taped closed. With the paring knife, I carefully sliced through three sides of the tape and opened the cardboard like the covers of a book. Inside was the lone wing of a luna moth. It was such a gorgeous shade of green that it took my breath away. Perfectly pressed and preserved, it was as if the moth had offered its wing to my brother as a gift. I swallowed hard and remembered Josh's words: *Don't be sad. Maybe one day to a luna is like ten years to us . . .*

At the bottom of the container were two more items. I was so stunned by one of them that I surely must have stared at it for a full minute before picking it up. It was a slender braid of hair, about a quarter inch in diameter and at least six inches long. It was not my brother's coarse, curly hair. The hair in my hand was soft and fine and of a light, reddish brown color. I smoothed my fingers over the braid, my mind spinning.

I set the braid on my desk and picked up the last item, shiny and black and perfect. Lifting it by its quill, I held it to the light.

When did it happen? Had the moon and planets conferred with the stars on the day my brother arrived upon this earth? Or had an otherworldly light rewired him as he claimed?

From the corner of my desk, I picked up a framed picture of Josh when he was eight, perhaps nine years old. He was sitting on the back of the hay wagon, the left knee of his jeans sporting an iron-on patch, the sleeves of his plaid shirt rolled up to his elbows. Lord, what a beautiful child, a child whose eyes shone bright with passion for the wonders of nature, a child who trod so lightly and caused no harm to any living thing.

When had his passion ignited into his greatest fury? Not even with the clarity of hindsight could I trace my brother's trajectory from woodland boy to warrior.

I ran my fingertip along the feather's edge and knew, in that secret knowing place, that it had come from a raven. Holding my brother's photograph, I looked into his eyes. "Your spirit crossed over long before you left us, and now you're fully awake to a world that few will ever see. Is that a fair assessment? The raven delivers divine law, and you are the raven?"

Once again, I picked up the braid. And as it lay in my palm, I whispered to my brother's photograph, "My God, you're not alone. This hair is from a woman, isn't it?"

As I touched each item on my desk, I was overcome.

There was no stopping the tears. I didn't even try.

When the last of the evening light faded from the window, I returned everything into the container and closed the lid. Walking into my bedroom, I opened the door to the piazza and stepped out. The long shadows of dusk stretched across the floorboards as I lowered myself into the wicker rocking chair. With the container resting on my lap and Eddie curled up at my feet, I slowly rocked and watched the sky deepen.

We are the authors of our lives, and, through choice or circumstance, some of us leave our stories unfinished or untold. Though it's taken me a long while to get here, I've come to accept that life, like the vast woodlands that surround my childhood home, is layered with mysteries.

And what of mysteries?

We sift and search and question as we try to discover our truths and the truths of those we love, and sometimes when we least expect it, a mystery we never knew existed gets solved while all else remains unanswered.

I didn't know if, on that Thanksgiving night so long ago, my brother simply snapped or if the events of that day did nothing more than catapult him toward a destiny he had already seen charted in the constellations of his private sky.

All I knew was this: Somewhere deep within Red River Gorge, where ancient petroglyphs decorate the walls of hidden caves and treacherous terrain is guarded by a sentry of rocky cliffs, there lives a boy who believes. Exactly what he believes is unknown to me, but I suspect it's a truth more powerful than I'm capable of understanding.

I rested my hands on the container, moving my fingertips over my name carved into the tape. Through all the years of worry and waiting, I'd been right after all. My brother was alive. And he had, in his own special way, let me know that he was not alone. Leaning back, I closed my eyes and wondered why he'd waited so long to send me a message. But then I couldn't help but smile—because, of course, that would be just like him.

I suspected he was pleased to see the farm transformed into a wildlife rescue and rehabilitation center, though since he was such a private, singular soul, I don't know how he felt about his name being on the sign. But the more I pondered that question, the more I supposed he probably thought it was just fine.

While watching the moon roll over the treetops, full and luminous and tinted with blue, I thought about heaven and hell and all that resides in between. So clearly I remembered the words my brother had spoken on that snowy winter's night when he was just a boy: *I don't much care where I go when I die, as long as it's where the animals are.*

Though no doubt some might disagree, I believed examination of my brother's heart would gain him swift admittance into heaven.

As the moon lifted higher, I pushed myself up from the chair and went back inside the house. Gathering what I needed, I slipped into a long coat. Eddie sat at the front door and whimpered, but I gave him a pat and told him no, that he couldn't go. Not this time.

Locking the door behind me, I dropped my keys into my pocket, turned, and walked into the darkness.

I could smell it before I saw it, that unmistakable aroma of the harbor, fresh yet tinged with decay. Looking in every direction to make certain I was alone, I gathered the hem of my coat and climbed over the guardrail.

Down the rocky embankment I went, my footing as steady as the beating of my heart. When I got as close to the water as I could, water that moved swiftly and gleamed with a silvery skin from the moon, I stood in the quiet embrace of night. A light breeze moved through my hair as I listened to the gentle lapping of the tide against the rocks.

Slowly, I unbuttoned my coat. From a length of string tied around my chest, my brother's arrow dangled like a pendulum. Pulling it free, I smoothed my fingers over the tip, along the shaft, and across the fletching. I could barely hear my own voice when I said, "For years and years, I looked for you, Josh. I don't understand why you wouldn't let me find you. Now it's your turn. I'll be right here. Maybe, someday, you'll come looking for me."

With my right hand, I grasped the arrowhead and raised my arm. I hesitated for a moment and then swung back with all my might. Casting my arm forward, I opened my fingers and let go. The arrow set sail into the moonlight and then seemed to hover in midair. Just as it plunged into the water, I looked into the sky and whispered, "Menewa."

AVAILABLE FROM PENGUIN

Saving CeeCee Honeycutt
A New York Times *Bestseller*

Twelve-year-old CeeCee Honeycutt has always had to take care of her mother, who is trapped in her long-ago moment of glory as the 1951 Vidalia Onion Queen of Georgia. But when tragedy strikes, CeeCee's long-lost great-aunt whisks her away to Savannah, where CeeCee is catapulted into a perfumed world of prosperity and Southern eccentricity run entirely by strong, wacky women. Set in the 1960s, this timeless coming-of-age novel explores the indomitable gifts of female friendship and charts the journey of an unforgettable girl who loses one mother, but finds many others in the storybook city of Savannah.